ALL
———
IS SET
———
ANEW

JIM CHENEY

ISBN: 978-173668550-1 (Paperback)
ISBN: 978-173668551-8 (eBook)

Library of Congress Control Number: 2021906222

Any references to historical events, real people, or real places are used fictitiously. Names, characters, and places are products of the author's imagination.

Cover art by David S. Higdon
Author photo by Greg Johnson

Prufrock Communications, LLC
534 Ploughman's Bend Drive
Franklin, TN
37064

This book is dedicated to my wife Elena.
My greatest inspiration and my most loving critic.
And for my sons, Jack and Austin.
Finish what you start, boys.
Always finish what you start.

PROLOGUE

Life, death, eternity, heaven, hell, the voice in the woods, the edge of the knives, the mirrors and their reflective, telling language, and the long journey up from darkness and the short journey into darkness. Love. Hate. Enlightenment. These were the stones that marked the path of my life. I remember the view from my childhood window, looking out over the green fields, the wind moving among everything that was still, pushing it gently into motion and then letting it come to rest. The simplicity of seeing things for little more than their shapes. The dutiful purpose of the animals. My mother's hair and my father's strong voice. My sister's intent and needful stare. And the violence that came to me below the window and the seed that was sown and the agony of self-imprisonment. The kindness of people who had known little of kindness in their own lives. These things, these events that became memories, were with me until they were not. At the end, they were little more than fading photographs that were thrown asunder in my mind's attic, and despite my efforts to peer at them, trying desperately to make sense and relevance of the grainy figures frozen in time, I was unable to bring them forward in any way that offered a familiar comfort. And the man who had carried me out of the self-imprisonment, he too began to fade in the end. And perhaps that was the worst of all. His slow departure. I wish I could say that I was brave when it finally stopped, wish I could say that I accepted the turbid confluence of my desire to live and the fate that was rage, but I was not brave. I was afraid and I cowered at the harsh penetration of it all. The pain was terrible and deliberate, but the uncertainty of what would happen after was more wrenching. I wept at the injustice of it all, these emotions and events slamming together with such force that I finally gave in and let out my breath a final time. Sightless, I wandered away from everything that had been a life and found myself here, looking down as if a child again in my window, and instead of the wind, motion is created by the voices that move around me, some shrill and impolite and others consoling and tempered. I watch and I wait. Wait and watch. I am aware and it is the awareness that I embrace.

PART 1

MILL FIRE

CHAPTER 1

JOHN

He is coming into the yard, weaving through the trees along the hard dirt path, the soil black and compacted from our footsteps to and from the cabin. There are four of us living here: my brother Terrell, my mother, my father, and me. The man coming up the path is my father and my mother's husband. He is born of fire, I think. It burns in his face and is rancid on his breath. He is consumed with demons, and I watch carefully from the wood pile where I have been splitting the logs, not hiding, but not making myself known. The old man stops and steadies himself against the tree and spits on the ground. He is holding a black lunch box that he almost drops on the pine needle floor. He is moaning and singing to himself. He is alone in this world. We are the shadows that pass through and he lashes out at us with hands that are stained and scarred, with black earth beneath his nails. Always angry, fists and jaw clenched. His teeth are yellow and stained from the tobacco he chews, swallowing the brown juice, and when his eyes focus they look as if they would be hot to the touch. The door to the cabin opens and my mother steps onto the porch and observes him from a place of fear and hatred. She is waiting like the farm men wait for rain to bring relief. Terrell is behind her, back in the recess of the cabin room. I stand beside the wood pile holding the dull axe. The air is getting colder, the ground is harder, and the light seems always to be failing. When the sun comes it is far from the floor of the woods and it splinters through the branches. The old man looks into the yard from where he is leaning against the tree and his face is pale and there is a cut above his eye and we can see where the blood has run down the side of his face. He is unsteady and begins to walk, but falls. We do not go to assist him. Shadows are passive and only lurk. I look at my mother whose face is always pale. She is thin like a reed and there are knobs on her wrist and her skull is defined beneath the skin. She wears only one dress, as we wear the same tattered pants and loose shirts. These are the clothes that he uses to pull us toward him, and if it were not cold it would be safer to go without them as Adam did in the garden before the fall.

He has been to the mill for work and he has stayed there after to drink with the other men who hold no value for their lives or the lives of others. We stay home while he is away. Terrell goes to the county school, but I no longer go. I have learned to read and to write a little, but I am uncomfortable in the schoolhouse and while I am there I worry about Mother being alone in the cabin, because I am what stands between the old man and her. Once when I was walking in the woods, I came back to the cabin and he was standing on the rotting porch holding the axe that I am holding now, yelling at Mother to come outside. I came into the yard, as he is stumbling into the yard now, and he turned and looked at me, saying I should stay away, but I came up onto the porch and I could smell him from where I stood in front of the steps. He held the axe like a child, the wood handle balanced across his forearms, and I went past him into the room where Mother was standing in the corner holding herself and whimpering. I had left the door open, and when I went to Mother, he came into the open space and blocked out the light, and even though my back was to him, I could feel him there. I did not turn to look, but watched my mother's eyes, which were large and wet. I touched her shoulder, but she did not look at me. He made a whistling sound and I felt my heart tighten in my chest and then the light came back into the room and I heard him go down the steps and I went outside to see he had dropped the axe on the ground and was walking into the woods holding the bottle that he kept in his coat pocket, singing up into the canopy about a butcher boy.

He picks himself up and we are there to witness him. There are bits of leaves in his hair and the blood on his face is stained black,

4

crusting. The lunch box hangs from his hand and he swings it back and forth. Mother is not moving and I tighten my hand on the axe. There are pieces of wood lying at my feet that have not been stacked. Wind moves around the sides of the cabin like water around a rock lodged in the middle of a stream, pregnant with rushing water down from the slope below the cabin. I cannot see Terrell behind Mother but I know the expression his face holds. He is quiet in his observance and often our father ignores him as if he understands something about his countenance that keeps him away. Something sacred like the fine curves of the bottle he carries with him, its smooth texture and fragility protected. He stands, swaying in the yard and this is a moment that stretches as long as the coming winter. He looks at mother on the porch and then to me, standing almost his height, the muscles in my arms young and threatening. He senses the rage in the roughly chopped wood; the heft of the axe and the thick sound of the blade connecting with the pulpy tissue and the fibers of the fallen tree that was heaved onto its side, carelessly uprooted by the storms. He is confused and looks behind him as if he has come to the wrong place and the fluttering in his head is causing him to sway. "Supper," he says, and Mother is suddenly gone from the porch. I let my grip loosen on the handle of the axe. He comes to the front porch and sits on the bottom step. It is dark and cooling beneath the overhang and he pulls his coat around him and takes the clear bottle from the pocket and drinks deeply from it. There is a sadness in this and he is alone with it, the brown liquor working down his throat and filling his veins, his mind. It does not ease him, but sitting steadies his hands and body and I choose another log from the larger pile and place it on the splitting stump and bring the axe above my head and drop it, making the only sound save the wind, which has witnessed this with indifference, its prophecy a strained whisper.

There are no windows in the cabin and Mother can't see him sitting and drinking from the bottle. The door has closed on itself and she sets the skillet on top of a metal plate to heat the pieces of pork that spit in their own fat. She pours a can of beans in with the meat and stirs the food to warm it through. In the spring there are a few vegetables that she pulls from the garden she tends. Terrell helps her with the beans, a few stalks of corn, and branches of okra. I plough the soil under before she plants and the three of us stand in the small clearing looking into the turned dirt. It smells strongly and there are worms moving amongst the clods and bits of weeds. Birds descend from the tree branches and pluck the worms out, their sharp beaks precise and purposeful. In the winter, the garden is barren like the rest of the landscape and we make the trip into town to collect the butchered pork and cans of food that smell and taste like tin. Terrell watches Mother make the food and stares at the skillet. I sense he is remembering the time that I used it as a weapon against the old man, drunk and roaring in the tiny space, knocking the few pieces of furniture askew as he moved after Mother in a tightening circle. Terrell had been crying and begging him to stop. Mother was silent, concentrating on keeping the distance between them. When he picked up the knife from the cutting board, I stepped in the center of the room holding the skillet, warning him back from her. I shook with the weight of it, held up the hard, greased iron next to my face. He gripped the knife and looked at me and I could see him playing out the violence in his head. It was the first time he had backed away from me, but he looked at Mother as he did so, and later that night he had climbed on top of her and hissed as he forced himself in her. We had watched his shape moving from the bed we shared across the room. She had held the pain of it with muffled sounds and I had taken Terrell's hand beneath the blanket and looked into the dark corner of the cabin, biting at my cheek and praying for Mother.

I hide the axe behind the cabin and wipe my face with my shirt. He is still on the steps and I come around to the front and watch him go further into the bottle. I approach the steps and he sets the liquor down and watches me come. The demons are inside him and they watch me too. They warn him about me and they do not like that I know they are there. They prefer to be like the sounds coming from the deep woods that scream in the voice of a woman or a crying child or maybe a hunting cat. They are sound and dark and do not feel or breathe air. I come to where he sits and I begin to walk around him. My body is vibrating and my scalp is tight and itching. He wants but does not want to touch me; to pull me under his pounding fists that fall with precision and sustained strength. There is only the brief second and then I am past him and pushing open the door. Mother turns now and I see that Terrell has climbed onto our bed and is reading from one of his school books. We talk with one another without speaking, and then we hear the bottle fall over, empty, on the porch, and we hear him push off of the steps, humming to himself, and we wait until he enters. Mother stands over the food and does not look around. He is more unsteady on his feet now and holds the crooked frame of the door for his support. Terrell looks at the pages of the book, but I know that he is unable to read the words.

"Well now," he says, and the words are fur-lined on his tongue. He comes further into the room. His heavy boots are caked with the hardened clay from where the water spigot at the mill well leaks and the men go to drink and rinse their faces, the puddles shallow and filthy, tinged with red. His face is pained like something is eating away at his organs, birds on a carcass. I see Mother set down the wooden spoon that she has used to stir the pork and the beans and then she turns and places the hot skillet on the worn wooden table. She looks to me and I go and take down the four bowls on the shelf and return to the table and set them next to the food. The old man sits on one of the table benches and pulls at his boots, almost toppling over and cursing beneath his breath. The first boot comes loose and he holds it up, glancing at Terrell on the bed. He speaks his name and Terrell looks up, his eyes and lips drawn into his small, smooth face. "What's that you got there," he says. Terrell is trapped, his eyes dart, landing startled on perches around the room.

"It's one of his school books, Daddy," I say.

"Ah," the old man says, still holding the boot. "School books. And he so learnt he can't speak for hisself." I look to Terrell and hold him off with my eyes; cut them to keep him over on the far side of the table.

"Leave him," I say and he turns and points at me with the filthy boot.

"That one there. He has a mouth big enough for a man's foot. Care to try this one," he says and wags his socked foot at me. He laughs and then one of the birds picks at his liver and he winces. Mother sits down and motions for Terrell to sit beside her. I watch the old man, but he is struggling with the other boot and has lost interest in us, then stands with unsettling speed, stomping the remaining boot on the floor. I sit and help to spoon the food into the bowls. There is barely enough to cover the bottoms, but it is hot and smells strong and good. We eat, all of us watching him stare into the empty space of the cabin. We move our spoons carefully to remain quiet. He and the drunkenness are two beings now and they are fighting one another for control. There are no windows in the cabin, but the dark is moving into the woods in its slow crawl. It bears witness, just as the sunlight does, but unlike the sun it is not cleansing, but smothering in its presence, pushing at the walls, trying to make its way inside, relentless as spring water. Mother has the lanterns lit and our shapes are blurring in the dimness. He stands over the table, falling onto the pine bench recklessly so that I am moved off balance and have to grab the side of the table to keep from turning over. He spoons what is left in the skillet into his bowl and looks into it the way a man looks into a dry well or a hole in the ground. "Christ, Jesus," he says and spoons the pork and beans into his mouth, the fatty liquid clinging to his grey beard. He does not speak while he eats, and because there is so little he is done quickly. He clatters the bowl onto the table top and stares at Mother. She is sitting upright, her hands in her lap. When she sees him looking she pushes her bowl across the table to him and his hands come from out of sight to receive it quickly. Then he is pushing the spoon into his mouth greedily. I start to push my bowl to Mother but she warns me off with her eyes. *Eat*, they say. *Finish it.* The old man concludes eating and pushes back from the table. He belches and then, without turning, he vomits the food onto the floor. It is a wretched, violent thing, and we all stand and back away. He hacks and spits and then sits up, seeing us standing and watching him. Then he stands and I see that this is the moment that the restless and provoking spirits in his head have been working toward. This is their orchestral movement and the instruments' sounds are colliding against one another with the same force as the hot tension of heat in the sky before the air is ripped open in serrated gashes by extreme lightning. This is the crack that fells the ancient tree standing deep in the woods, with its knowledge of the forest and the eruption of living things from the ground, toppled and left to rot. What comes next is unholy and unforgettable. It is the point of transition for my brother and for myself, if only temporary for one and permanent for the other. It is as if the projected vomit is the overflow of the old man's tortured self and the purge propels his body into a tempest of profane wind; the recollection of sinners suspended on the cross and at the base of the crucifixion, the scene's tortured soldiers nervous with spears, and casks of sour wine, carnal and unknowing until such time that they were made aware of the vengeful dismay and judgement of a broken father. This, the old man's storm, rained down upon my mother with a strength unimaginable, and when finally Terrell and I pull him away, she is crumpled in the corner of the cabin, unconscious like discarded debris yanked clean from one place and tossed to be found in another. We force him out the door and shove him over the steps and onto the ground and go back to tend to Mother, who Terrell insists is dead, but I know has survived if for no other reason than to run from that place.

He is something primordial on his back in the yard, his limbs moving in erratic gestures and his eyes without depth, his beard an invasive clot and tangle of thick white moss and his clothes nothing more than a thin layer of outer skin, patched and torn and stiff with dried sweat and urine. Beneath there is hair and pink flesh, his sternum inverted and his ribs lean, his arms thin but strewn with bands of muscle. We can hear him beyond the door. We have helped Mother to the table and she is sitting on the bench. Terrell wipes the blood away from her eyes, her mouth. Her cheeks are blossoming with bruised skin, the coloration and distorted shapes like fungus. Any movement causes her whimper and she tries to remain perfectly still as we touch her delicately and Terrell says soothing things. I walk to the back of the cabin and find the deer rifle leaning in the corner. It has been poorly cared for and I am concerned that it will not fire when I need it to, although it fires and hits its mark for the old man when he stalks the woods for deer. I walk past them and out onto the porch and point the rifle at my father. He is laughing to himself and looks at me with pleading in his eyes as if he would like to be gut shot and left to bleed to death, his conscious mind wrestling with the demons inside his head. I aim the rifle from my shoulder and I see that the barrel is shaking unsteadily, as if it is confused by its purpose now turned on the one who has commanded it before. I pull back the hammer and there is a loud click, and suddenly the woods around us are as still as the stars that are pinpoints above. The noise seems to have called us all together and the anticipation is palpable. Then there is movement behind me and I turn to see Mother in the doorway of the cabin. She is barely able to stand and I am flush with anger at Terrell for allowing her to witness what I have come to do. We look at one another and she shakes her head, slightly. I question what I see and she shakes it again. I lower the rifle and the old man laughs again. She turns and goes back into the room of the cabin and I follow her and take the rifle back to where it rested against the wall, removing the bullets from the chamber. We help Mother into the bed she shares with the old man and then Terrell and I get into our bed and we wait.

The old man remains outside and then we hear him stumble through the doorway and into the room. He is standing, backlit by the faintness of the moon, observing us. A calm has overtaken him and I know from experience that he has moved through the drunkenness and is now subject to the fatigue that comes after. He is recalling the damage he has inflicted and he is trying to make peace with it. There is no declaration or concession, just the profile of his figure. He walks across the floor, still in only one boot, and falls next to Mother in the bed and soon the quiet is replaced by his rasping breath and physical rejuvenation. He must be at the mill in the morning or risk losing the work.

Terrell sleeps beside me, but I remain awake, playing the scene of the old man beating mother over and over in my head with the steadiness of a ticking clock. There is a sound from their bed and I turn to see mother sitting up and then pushing herself to her feet. She is in her clothes and I can see the blurred motion of her movement but I am unable to see what she is doing. Then I hear the creak of the old trunk opening and I am certain that the old man will wake, but he continues snoring. There is a movement like the sound of a large bird's wings and I realize she has taken one of the old quilts from the trunk and covered herself in it. I begin to sit up on my elbows and speak to her, but stop when I see that she is opening the door to the cabin. Her face is not clear, but I can imagine its ruined look, the split lips and swelling eyes. She is looking toward our bed and I can smell the breath of the sinister thing that is inside the old man beginning to spill into the room. It is not hot like the exhalation of an animal, but frigid like water trapped below surface ice. She stays in the doorway looking and then she is through and out and pulling the door closed. I consider waking Terrell so that we might go after her, but I remain in the bed, the coldness wrapping us in a shroud of fogged breath that will recede back into Father to resurrect his nightmarish state, which is there in repose but will soon be waking.

CHAPTER 2

TERRELL

After mother left, we remained in the cabin. I was asleep when she had gone so my recollection of the night contains only the violence of the attack and the fear that I felt, huddled in the cold bed next to my brother before falling into a deep sleep that spared the sight of her departure. Father raged the next morning, kicking at the walls of the cabin and scattering the few things that we owned onto the floor. My brother shook me awake and we lay in the bed watching him transform into fire. He was wearing his pants and nothing else and his gaunt torso was slick with sweat; his eyes a forking branch of exploded capillaries and profanity spilling through gritted teeth.

"Where's she gone to," he yelled at us. "Where's that whore run off?" We sat stone still. John's fists were clenched by his legs and the tension mounted in the small room like a slow-paced thunderhead, moving in a black cotton pattern over water.

"We was asleep," John said.

"Sleeping," the old man said and wiped his lips with the back of his hand. Then he picked up the edge of the table and slammed it back down onto the wood plank floor. The cabin shook. He continued to look at us and John swung his legs off the bed into a sitting position. He freed his legs from the blanket so it would not trip him if he had to rise. Sunlight came through the crack beneath the door and birds were waking and singing. Father paced back and forth and we waited, hoping the spell would pass and he would leave. My school books were stacked neatly on the far side of the bed and I thought about the serenity of the schoolhouse and the kind teacher who would walk quietly up and down the rows of seated children, peering over their shoulders and sometimes kneeling beside them and assisting with their numbers or sentences. Unlike the church house, the school was a true sanctuary where what you learned could be applied, offering a way out of the back woods, which swallowed people whole in an impoverished yawn. Nature's indifference was everywhere you looked, and its loud and perpetual weight was like swimming in your clothes.

"You know," the old man said, stopping and looking at the cabin wall. "She weren't of use. Give me two suckling piglets and slop food and always talking about leaving this place. Out of here, where we come from and where we belong. She'll see," he said, narrowing his eyes and running his tongue over his lips. "She'll see what waits for her out there and she'll be back. You wait and see. She will be back like a hungry bitch." Then he spat on our floor and grabbed a filthy shirt that hung on one of the pegs protruding from a post that propped up the roof in the center of the room, and went out the door without his lunch box or his jacket. He left the jacket because there was no bottle in its pocket, but he would find one at the mill and consume most of it on the walk home through the woods, drunk and forgetting that Mother had left in the night until he came in and found nothing to eat and me and John waiting for him like starving birds in an abandoned nest.

We went two weeks this way, making do. Father brought home venison one night and I cooked a stew that lasted several days, although the fat would congeal in the pan and the meat and its gravy looked like something thrown-up by a dog. It was a warm fall; the fullness of the dark winter waited patiently. There was a long stretch of days when the sun burned hot. Indian Summer, John called it, and said it was nothing but a cruel trick and that the cold would have its revenge for being delayed. I went to school and tried to keep my attention there and thought of running like Mother, but each day I made the walk home thinking of John and how if I left he would be alone with father and soon one of them would kill the other. John had crossed over after Mother left, and the only thing that kept him from disappearing was me. I felt obligated to stay with him even though I knew that the demons might also take me; that they were watching me more closely than my brother because they understood his contemplation and reasoning but could not understand mine. Mother once said that we should not try and make sense of Father's anger because it had no direction but was driven instead by the spirits in his mind and those that washed his throat as they poured from the mouth of the bottle. That same mouth was speaking to John. I came into the cabin yard one day and found him swinging the hatchet over and over into the side of a dead tree that bordered the open space. There was no purpose in his action. It was the need to strike against something innocent and silent; something that would suffer his pent-up hostility with solemnity. I did not speak to him, but looked and saw the clear bottle on the ground, dry and standing straight up like a small acolyte. The personification of these inanimate instruments—the bottle, the skillet, the axe, the cabin itself—these were the extended tools of a malevolent mind.

That same night, with the sun still red and burning in the sky, John and Father drunkenly collided. The old man had called Mother a whore and knocked the bowls to the floor, breaking two of them. He yelled for John to pick up the pieces. John went around the side of the table, still drunk, his frame wilted from swinging the axe, and picked a shard off the floor.

"Come and pick it up yourself, you mean fucker," he said. Father looked at him from where he sat and opened his mouth to expose his yellowed teeth.

"Now it comes," he said and stood, the two of them only feet apart. "Now the whore's piglet wants to cut me. Come here, boy," he said. "Come here and let me open you up with that." John went around the side of the table and Father met him half way. John swung the white bowl shard at the old man's face and sliced open his cheek, the blood bursting like a ripe berry. Father screamed in surprise and his hand went up to the wound. The blood came through his fingers and he took the hand away, looking at the red palm. John shook, holding the shard to his side, gripping it so that I thought he would puncture his own hand.

"You ought to know better than that," Father said and started forward. The shard came through the air again in a slow arc and Father blocked John's arm and they were locked together, both of them seeking balance over the other, their forms twisting in a single struggle. They grunted and fought for breath. John's foot slipped, and when he fell, he twisted his body and the old man went to the floor first. John fell on top of him and straddled Father's chest and brought his fists down over and over, the sound like beating the dust from a stretched quilt. I stood watching, stationary, my mind whirling with the blows. Mother's ruined face came into my vision and I felt my own fists clench, my jaws lock, and then my leg was going up and coming down solid on the floor of the cabin. The three of us were like something from a maniacal circus where the clowns had turned murderous. John was crying and screaming and Father was no longer moving. Mother's face moved out of focus and I saw the silver blade of the axe biting the rotted wood and I began to cry as well, screaming at John to stop. When he finally did, sitting upright astride my father's chest like a broken rider, he retrieved the shard from the floor and raised it above his head.

"No," I screamed and John dropped the shard as if my word had torn it from his hand. He stood and, without looking at me, went out the door. Father was motionless on the floor and I went to him and stood over his body, watching for movement in his chest. He was wheezing, and I remembered him on his back in the yard, laughing at the sky and Mother turning to go back in to prepare the pork and the beans and then Father on the table bench, holding the boot and speaking to John, then vomiting the mire from his belly. I went out and found John standing in the cabin yard, looking into the dark woods. When I called to him he muttered something, but did not turn around. Then he spoke again, barely above a whisper.

"Is he dead?"

"No," I said. "Maybe."

"You have to know."

"I don't, John," I said. "Did you mean to kill him?" John did not answer.

"Mean," he said. "I thought you would want..."

"John. What are we gonna do now. If he's dead, I mean."

"And if alive?" he said. I did not know, and put my hand in my pockets, looking at the ground, moving dirt with the toe of my worn shoe.

14

"Terrell. Terrell." He had turned and was looking at me, suddenly, so that I thought father might be in the doorway. I looked behind me and the fear came into my limbs and my head felt light and distant.

"Yes," I said looking at the open cabin door. But he did not care about a response. He turned back to the woods and walked into the trees. It would not occur to me until later, after the fire and the child he gave me to raise, that when I thought of John, he would always appear to me from this vantage, retreating into blackness on a trodden path of self-sacrifice and ever-emerging rage.

CHAPTER 3

THE FIRE

The night that John Hicks beat his father half to death, the old man slept where he had fallen. John and Terrell stayed out of the cabin the entire night and watched from the woods the next morning when their father came out the door and stood surveying the yard on shaking legs, holding onto one of the porch posts for support. From a distance, his face had no distinct features. It was bruised purple and large swollen masses had formed around his eyes and at his jawline. His standing and readying for work was testament alone to his endurance for pain, and the two boys watched him cautiously despite his frail state. He stepped off the porch, almost falling to his knees, but recovered, and went down the path toward the mill, which was a two mile walk through the woods. The sun had barely risen, and when he was far enough down the path, the boys came out into the yard and watched his crippled figure be absorbed into the shadows.

"We have to kill him," John said and Terrell stood looking at the space where the old man had walked. It seemed to be breathing, the curtains of foliage on either side of the wooded corridor pulsing and feeding on the spirit of their father's passage.

"What do you mean?"

"You know what I mean," John said and turned and walked back toward the cabin. Terrell followed him. John went inside and came back with a pouch of tobacco and rolled a cigarette for both of them and then took a match and lit the tip of the rolled paper and handed one to Terrell.

"He'll never forgive this," John said. "And he won't turn his back on me again. Even when he's drunk. He knows better, and besides, even if he didn't, those things in his head would wake him up."

"What things?" Terrell said, but John did not answer. Then he spoke from far away, smoking with his eyes glassed.

"If we kill him here, we'll get caught. Someone will come looking from the mill if he misses more than one shift, and with Mamma gone, they might talk to the sheriff." He was planning as he spoke, and Terrell watched him intently. "It's got to be somewhere else besides here," he said.

"What about on the way?"

"To the mill? I thought about that, but then we'd have his body and what if someone came along? No, it's got to look like he done it hisself or maybe an accident." The death of their father had been an abstract thought that both had entertained. For John, his mind drifted toward the violent end he was now contemplating. For Terrell, it had revolved around a disappearance with no explanation. His hatred of the old man was outweighed by his need for a sense of calm, to be done with the distractions of the cabin, and the innocent desire for the woods to go back to simply being a natural place, free of underlying voices and festering temptations. With their mother gone, the abstraction had undergone a metamorphosis, like something borne out of the damp slime, its form emerging and assuming an unrecognizable shape. Now it stood silently, observing them sitting and smoking on the porch, patiently awaiting the outcome of their conversation.

"You know the doors to the mill building?" John said. Terrell nodded. He had been to the mill with his father only twice, watching the workers come and go out of the single-story structure where the wood was cut and hewn, the five or six men covered in sawdust that clung to their sweaty skin, itching and catching in their hair and beards like dry snow. His father had introduced him as his boy who liked his books, and the men had laughed and left him standing alone as they went back to their stations, cussing at one another and the antiquated equipment, which was loud and ferocious and sounded dangerous like dogs fighting. Terrell had been afraid of the mill, but not as afraid as he was of his father, who, even when sober, had nothing kind or encouraging to say and looked at he and his brother as if they had been conjured to torment him.

"There are slats on both doors," John was saying. "You could take a tamp bar and set it across those slats and shut them closed so that no one could get out." Terrell could see the image that his brother was describing as if he were looking at the locked doors from a tree branch hanging out over the mill yard. He stared at their wood frames and winced when he saw the center bulge forward like something was trying to get out. The wooden frames strained under the pressure from the other side and then Terrell saw flames licking through the crack between the two doors, but the bar held. And then came the screaming.

"If we locked the doors and nailed the side windows shut, we could trap him inside. We would …"

"Start a fire," Terrell said. John looked at his brother.

"Yeah," he said. Terrell pushed the glowing end of the cigarette into the step.

"And what about the rest of them inside?" John dragged off his own cigarette and tossed it into the yard. "Sure, what about 'em," he said. "They've known what he's done. What do we owe them? Ain't one of them ever come out here to check on us, or Mamma when she was here. Think they didn't know? Think they don't go home and knock hell out of their own kids and women? Everybody's got what coming to them. You and me got what's coming to us. And if we wait around here he'll kill me one of these days. And then he'll have to kill you too cause he can't have you sitting around knowing what he done. You seen, Terrell. You know just like I do."

They waited around the cabin for the rest of the day. When the light began to recede, John gathered a hammer and nails from a wooden crate behind the cabin and placed them in a burlap sack. Then he picked up the axe and the two brothers walked out the path away from the cabin, listening for the old man's whistle or singing. They were halfway to the mill when they heard him coming toward them. They stepped off the path and waited for him to go by. He looked worse than he had that morning, his face like a strange, overripened fruit, but he was carrying a bottle and seemed not to notice the painful disfiguration. He stopped in the path close to where they hid and drank. They

18

watched him silently and waited for him to turn his head and look in their direction, sensing he was being watched. "Goddamn you," he said looking instead into the dark tree limbs overhead and raising the bottle. "I ain't never asked for your help, you son-of-a-bitch. Ain't never got on my knees for you. What for? What good? A whore and pigs to watch over. Lies is what you give. I'll send you and your son something to pray over. Wait and see. I'll send you something." He shook the bottle and stumbled forward. The boys waited until he was out of sight and then went back to the path, walking close together, not speaking. John had the sack slung over his shoulder, the axe dangling from his right hand.

It was dark when they reached the mill, but the moon had come up and cast a white light over the squat rectangular building that stood in the clearing on piers, three feet off the ground to keep the air running below the boards so the moisture would not warp them. Off to the side, next to the water pump, a cluster of tools was propped against a stacked pile of lumber. Shovels and picks, several axes, and two grey metal tamp bars. Terrell hung back, but John put his sack and axe on the ground and went to the tools, picking up one of the tamp bars and walking around the far side of the building. When he returned, he motioned for Terrell to join him.

"I put the bar on the ground back there," he said pointing. "There's no windows on that side so no one can get out that way. You go around and pile sticks and limbs underneath. Make sure they're dry. Put them on top of leaves so they go up quick." Terrell nodded, looking at the front doors, which were closed. "Go," John said, and Terrell crossed in front of the building. He could hear his brother moving in the brush. John picked up the sack, went to the other side, and stopped at the first window. He reached inside and pulled out the hammer and a handful of nails. He set one at an angle and pounded it into the sash, feeling the point bite into the wood's sill. He went down the elevation of the building, driving the nails. When he finished, he went to find Terrell and help him pile the brush. They worked without stopping, and when they had piled brush in four different locations, out of sight from the front of the building, they went up a rise and sat amongst the thicker trees. John rolled cigarettes for them and they sat smoking in the early hours before the sun would call the men back to work. Terrell studied the empty mill yard. "John," he said.

"Yeah."

"I'm not sad for what will happen to Daddy, but these other men…"

"I ain't got another idea to be rid of him. You?"

"No," he answered, and looked at the ground defensively. They were just boys and he knew it. He also knew that the plan they had started into motion would become a haunting for the rest of their lives, and he wondered how long and what form their reckoning would take.

Just after daybreak, the first of the men came into the yard, greeting one another tersely and without ceremony. They waited for their father to appear, and when the men began to work without him, they worried that he would not be coming. They were anxious in their hiding spot and were ready to leave when the old man finally came into the yard. The foreman came out to meet him, and after cursing him for being late, he walked back into the building, shaking his head. Their father stared after the man, his pinched eyes focused on the foreman's back. Then he followed. John touched Terrell's shoulder and looked at his brother. Something passed between them, and then Terrell stood and went around behind the building to retrieve the bar. The men were inside, saws screaming so that they had to yell over the noise. John went down the rise to the first pile of brush and struck a match, touching the flame to the pile of leaves, which ignited instantly. He stood and went to the next pile and then the next, and when he reached the final spot he saw Terrell standing next to the front corner of the building, holding the bar. "Now, Terrell," he said, and his brother went around to the front. He closed the heavy doors and dropped the bar into place, locking the men inside. John lit the final pile and could see the flames roiling beneath the building and climbing up the sides. The heat was intense and bright and he stepped away, watching the fire lick the side walls and settle furiously onto the roof. Inside, the men were yelling. The saws were quiet and they were scrambling across the wooden floors, the orange heat coming up for them, the flames devouring the oxygen through the cracks. One of the men started to scream and John knew that they had tried to go through the door. He ran to the front to find his brother. Terrell stood back from the fire, watching, and John grabbed him by the shoulder, and they went together back to the rise. The mill was consumed. They stopped at the top of the hill and watched as the roof trusses caved. Cottony smoke moved through the structure, and through it they could make out the murky shapes of the mill workers, frantic and passing one another in front of the clouding windows, flames trailing their forms.

"Let's go," John said and tried to pull his brother away.

"Wait," Terrell said, pulling roughly back. "I want to see." As he spoke, a figure stopped in front of one of the windows and pressed his searing head against the glass. His body was tortured with flame, but they could make out the pale smear of their father's face. He looked at them, his lips peeled back over his teeth in a sneer.

"C'mon, Terrell. We got to go."

"Wait," Terrell said. "Let him fall first." The old man placed both hands on the side of the window and leaned closer. Then he dropped.

"C'mon," John yelled, and ran. Terrell turned and followed his brother back into the woods. Overhead the smoke rose in thick columns, its scent tinged with char and suffering.

They ran from the fire and back to the cabin. As they came into the yard, they collapsed onto the ground, panting.

"Goddamn," John said, his voice high and stretched. "Goddamn Terrell, we did it. He's dead. The son-of-a-bitch is dead." Terrell lay in the dirt looking at his brother, who was holding himself and twisting back and forth, laughing now, possessed by the intensity of their actions and the dead men smoldering in the mill building, the fire having singed black the weeds and grass of the yard and possibly the close trees as well. The sheriff would be on his way to each of the men's houses, telling the women and the children that their husbands and fathers had burned alive and that someone had placed the tamp bar over the door latches and that nails had been discovered where they did not belong near the window frames. Terrell stood quickly and went to the edge of the yard and got sick. He looked back and John was sitting up staring at the front of their cabin. The nausea swirled around him and his hands were numb. He held his stomach and wretched again.

"We'll have to run," John said. "Both of us. When they find out mother is gone and it's just you and me here they'll want to send us to the state to be placed in one of them homes. I ain't going in one of the homes. I'd rather live with that cocksucker we just burned," and he began to laugh again. "Can you believe it, Terrell. He's dead!" John climbed the front steps of the cabin and went inside. Terrell could hear him breaking things and yelling at their dead father. He stood, still trying to settle himself. John emerged carrying the rifle and blankets. "C'mon," he said. "Help me get this shit out of here." He set the rifle on the porch, throwing the other things to the side, turning to go back in the house.

"I'm not going with you," Terrell said. John stopped and looked across the yard at his brother. "What do you mean you're not going with me? We have to run."

"I know, John. But not together. I can't see past this and to be with you, I feel like it will always be this way. That who you are is not…"

"What are you sayin'?" He came down from the steps and stood, hands to his sides, fists clenched without realizing it. "What are you saying, Terrell?"

"I don't know," Terrell said. "Just that I don't want to go with you. Not like this."

"You won't make it by yourself, Terrell. You need me. You needed me to get rid of him and you'll need me when there's a thousand more like him out there." He pointed his finger at the woods. "I leave you now and I won't come back for you. You'll be on your own with your goddamn books and your sniveling and your wanting Mamma back." He stopped then and thought. "She left us, Terrell. She left us when she knew what he could do and still she left and now we need to get out of here before we get caught…" He stopped a final time.

"Brother," he said, and then turned and went back in the cabin for the few things that he had. When he returned he had stuffed his belongings into a pillowcase. He stooped and took the rifle and came down the steps. "Stay here at the cabin then," he said, looking past Terrell. "When they come around asking tell them I took off and you don't know where to. Tell them you think I went south. That will give me some time to get ahead of them." He waited to see if there would be a protest or a change of heart. What he had said about Terrell on his own was true. But John also understood that he had set his life on a course and his brother would slow him down, would eventually lead to them getting caught. He could be at peace with running, and if he was being honest, he liked it. Everything that was natural to him had been under the shadow of the old man, while at the same time he was learning about himself and his motivations and desires were becoming more apparent. It was not that he wanted the old man gone for the sake of safety, but for the sake of independence.

"I can't do that, John. They'll see that I'm hiding you."

"You can and you will," he said. "We left the nail bag and the hammer there, Terrell. They'll figure it out sooner than later that someone set the fire. The old man's initials are in that hammer. I watched him carve them into the wood myself."

"But . . ."

"The hell with it, Terrell," John said and walked past him. "Good luck to you. And remember, I went south." Then he was gone down the path and Terrell was alone in the yard. The shock of the isolation began to overtake him. The sun was fully up and the sky had patches of clouds that were still and fat. Terrell tasted the acrid vomit on his tongue and in his throat and he went to find water to rinse it away.

CHAPTER 4

JOHN

I left Terrell behind because he was weak. I knew that long before the fire, but I was conflicted by emotions that I left naked in the empty yard as I walked away from the cabin, him standing alone and frightened. He could never embrace the fear like I could and that meekness in his character angered me in a way that I could not explain or push away. I wanted him to be like me, but that was not something that either one of us could control. He had come with me to the mill and had helped to start the fire and had been the one to stand on the rise and wait to see the old man's face in the window. It was like he knew and wanted to see, but I had wanted to run from that place because I believed Father was born of fire and the flames would release him from himself, but whatever allowed his soul to pass would seek another human cave. I was afraid of this and so I made us run from there, but I know now that the soul followed and found its place to settle and begin again.

Mother had been right to go. The old man survived on his resentment for her; drank it like the liquor he craved morning and night. She was a decent person and her decency plagued whatever possessed him. It was like stepping on a hard stone with your bare foot. The bruise is not visible but the pain that it creates is imbedded and awful if pressed. None of us were free from the influence, as if the well water we drank was poisoned, tainting our blood in a way that made our hearts beat strangely and in loud clangs that were sharp things in the caverns that lead into your head. I chose to respect this poisoned blood and went from that place despite the needs of my brother, turning away from it all and seeking a path in the world that was not tethered to any one man or woman. So I professed.

From the cabin I made my way east, finding work and discovering those things in life that were sometimes pleasant to touch and to control. My body grew hard and resilient and I learned to go without food when there was none and I learned to use the bottle and tobacco to quiet the rumbling pains in my stomach. The world away from the cabin was foreign and there were things that I encountered that I did not know existed, and I found that people were not inherently kind, but driven instead by self-pleasure and simplicities that exposed their vulnerabilities. I found that Negroes were like wild animals and that they could see inside you and into your thoughts and that their movements were more certain than white men and that they were fools to not recognize that they had only to rise up against their persecutors and cut them down with the same indifference as butchering a hog or goat. And women were unclean things whose bodies were like soil for male seeds; their mouths deceptive, unfaithful cisterns with a stench of stale water. Those white men who held positions of power lived in fear of losing it and this too created opportunities for me to consume and deceive.

Before they locked me up, year flowed into year, but these thoughts did not evolve, and like my body, my perceptions hardened and my tolerance for all but the simplest of pleasures dried to the muted color of bleached bones.

There was a preacher who held sway over a small congregation in Tennessee who took me in late in the fall. I chopped wood for the church as I had at the cabin and would listen to him work his sermons at night where he wrote them in an open window. I found him one afternoon near the riverbank with a small boy who I had seen come to the church with his mother and baby sister. I watched them from a stand of trees, and when the preacher unhooked the straps of the boy's overalls, I came from behind him and asked what nature of God he was teaching. I looked at the boy and told him to pull up his bib and go home. He looked at me with large eyes and something in the air smelled of rotting carcass. When the boy had gone up the path away from the river I grabbed the preacher by his thin throat and forced him off the bank and into the water and pushed his head beneath the black surface. His hat floated away from where I held him under, and when he no longer struggled, I pulled him free of the water and dragged him back to the bank where he coughed and wretched. I stood above him and said, "I want you to see, preacher," and I took a knife from my belt and cut his own belt loose and pulled his pants to his ankles. Then I took his prick in my hands and held the knife to it. "Look here," I said, holding the blade against the pale skin. "Lean up and look," I said, and he did, his face wet and his throat working with the taste of river water. "I'll take the head just like those vipers you preach," I said and he cried out and took my hand away. "You go back to that church," I said, "and you ask your God how to get free of this place, or I'll bring you back here and fill your throat full of river mud and follow it with this blade." He ran from there and I left the next day, going further into Tennessee. These are the things that I learned and saw, carrying them with me not as memory but as the evolution of a person whose past was destined to overshadow his future.

CHAPTER 5

INCIDENT AT BISHOP'S WELL

The building sat in solitude surrounded on all sides by open fields where no farms had encroached. The lot was rutted and thick with brown dirt, and the men who came and went did not linger outside the edifice, but went in quickly and drank where they would not be seen. The patrons were poor and did not frequent Bishop's in celebration of their common occupations or to share their collective hardships. They sat at the leaning tables or the bar drinking until the world beyond the clapboard siding of the building was nothing more than a blur. The owner, a man named Bishop, asked nothing of them other than to keep their tabs current and the fighting to a minimum. He went up and down the bar with a filthy rag, mopping up spilled beer and liquor. Then he would weave in and out of the tables to straighten the wooden chairs or to sweep the clods of field dirt out the open door, which he propped wide by wedging a rusted horseshoe beneath the door itself. There were small rooms behind the bar where Bishop lived with a young boy who everyone assumed was his son but may have been a nephew. No one knew for sure. Sometimes they would allow one of the field hands in to play the guitar in the corner, but this was rare because it inevitably led to an altercation with one of the patrons whose need for silence and rumination outweighed the intended solace of the music and the soft, whispered singing of the field hand who would look up from his playing every time a voice elevated.

Eli Stearns and several men from the farm he worked outside of Taylor Branch were sitting at one of the tables, a bottle between them, when John Hicks entered. They did not know him, and so each of the men watched him cross the room and go to the bar, where he ordered a drink, not turning around, while he waited on Bishop to pour the dark liquor into a squat glass and push it across the wooden bar with a flick of his fingers. Hicks drank it quickly and motioned for another, which Bishop poured before speaking.

"We don't pour on credit here. And I don't know you. You can pay for this?" Hicks drank the second shot and made an exaggerated face, holding up the glass and looking through it at the bottles placed in rows behind the bar.

"So that's a greeting in Taylor Branch, Tennessee," Hicks said. Bishop nodded and smiled at him.

"Well," he said. "Money is money whether in Taylor Branch or up to the state capital. I've learned over my years that trust is not to be given out without an understanding of the other's intent." Hicks looked at the barman and considered continuing the conversation, but pulled a bill from his pocket and set it down on the damp wood of the bar. "This will cover it, I should think," he said. Bishop leaned over the bar top and looked at the bill.

"Yeah," he said. "For now." Hicks grinned and clapped.

"Then maybe you could quit all this talking and pour another one." One of the men at the table behind Hicks coughed and he looked around to see their eyes on him. Bishop poured again and Hicks picked up the glass without looking and mocked a toast to the table of men who remained motionless. He drank the shot and grimaced. He turned and pointed at Bishop, who came back with the bottle. Hicks leaned and drank.

"I'm looking for work," he said. "You boys all smell like you work for a living. Any ideas on where I might sign-on?" A chair scratched on the floor and Hicks turned around. Stearns spoke.

"You always come in someplace strange and run your mouth like that?" Hicks looked at him. Stearns was heavyset with thick forearms

28

and a shabby beard. He wore a fedora-style hat tipped back on his head and his clothes were stained with soil and grease.

"I don't ask for no one's permission to speak, if that's what you mean." Stearns laughed and looked at the other men sitting at the table.

"Maybe that's something that you should reconsider," he said, and now the other men laughed as well. Hicks smiled at the table, his back against the bar.

"Maybe," he said. "Maybe not."

"Maybe not," Stearns repeated.

"That's right," Hicks said.

"Uh huh," Stearns said. "May be that you picked the wrong spot to drop in."

"Boys," Bishop said and they all turned to look at him. He stood stooped behind the bar, the towel tossed over his shoulder. His white hair pulled back in a ponytail and his eyes yellow and droopy. "I ain't got time for this shit today. Last thing I need is the Winchester sheriff out here asking who did what and how it all got started. You hear me?" The other men at the table nodded and went back to their glasses, but Stearns and Hicks continued to look at one another. Hicks kicked at the floor.

"Yeah boys," he said. "Listen to your daddy. He ain't got time for this shit today." Stearns stood. "Eli," the man closest to him said and tried to grab his arm. "No cause for that." But Stearns yanked his arm free and crossed the floor toward the bar. Hicks stood to his full height, put a hand inside his pocket, and pulled the knife free, unlocking the blade with his thumb. Stearns glared at it and then back at Hicks's face, mouth set in a thin grin, his eyes red, perspiration on his forehead.

"What do you aim to do with that?" Hicks flicked his wrist and shrugged.

"C'mon over and might be we'll see."

"Boys," Bishop said. "I'll call the law if I have to."

"C'mon," Hicks said, his grin widening. "C'mon over here, you soiled piece of shit. I've knocked down men meaner than you." Stearns started forward and Hicks met him, swinging the blade in an arc toward the man's head. Stearns blocked his arm and the knife came loose. The other men scratched their chairs back from the table and stood watching as Hicks and Stearns locked arms and moved around the room, knocking over furniture. Bishop went into the rear room and came back with a short piece of pipe, moving in a shuffle from behind the bar. "Uncle," a small voice called from the back. "What's that?"

"Stay," Bishop called back and the two men crashed onto the floor. Bishop began to walk toward where they were rolling atop one another, but one of the other men who had been at the table put out a hand and stopped him. "Let them go," he said. Bishop stopped and watched, the pipe by his side. Stearns outweighed Hicks by forty pounds, but he was slow. He would gain the leverage, but Hicks would slip free, and soon Stearns was losing strength, his breath labored and his efforts to push Hicks away from him weaker and weaker. "Goddamn it, let me hit him," Bishop said and the man who had stopped him the first time stepped aside. Bishop was raising the pipe above his head when the door opened.

"Bishop," the deputy, whose name was Sykes, called, taking his hat off. "You think you could poor me and Darrin a beer, we gotta be..." and he stopped just inside the door, looking down at the two men. "Darrin," he called over his shoulder. "Get in here." Then he looked at Bishop holding the pipe and the other men standing and watching. "Jesus Christ," he said and then the other deputy was behind him and they both went to pull the men off one another. The one called Sykes grabbed Hicks by the back of the shirt, and when he did, Hicks turned and swung his fist, connecting with a flat thud into the deputy's chest. "You son-of-a-bitch," Sykes said and grabbed Hicks by the hair, pulling him back toward the bar. The one named Darrin had pulled Stearns in the other direction and now the big man sat on the floor, blood on his face from where he had been bitten. Hicks continued to struggle, and Darrin watched with amusement from where he knelt on the floor. Hicks kicked and screamed, Sykes jerking his hair well off the top of his head. They twisted and writhed like they had electric current running through them, and when Hicks would not stop, Darrin left Stearns sitting on the ground, pulled his pistol, crossed the room, and used the butt to crack Hicks in the side of the head, which ceased his motion entirely. Both deputies were panting.

"What the hell, Bishop," Sykes said, leaning over with his hands on his knees, looking up at the old man. One of the men who had come in with Stearns picked up the knife from the floor and handed it to Darrin. He pointed at Hicks. "He pulled that on Eli. Meant to use it too. Ask Bishop. We was sitting and minding our own business and he started running off at the mouth." Both deputies looked to Bishop. "Yeah," the old man said. "He done that and likely would have done more if you two hadn't shown up when you did. Get him out of here and I'll bandage Eli up. Goddamn idiot that he is."

CHAPTER 6

WINCHESTER

John Hicks awoke confused. He lay on what felt like a metal shelf, and each time he turned his head to see where he was, it felt as if someone was driving a screwdriver into his eye. Sunlight came in through a small window from somewhere behind him, and the room was hot and cramped. He started to sit up and a wave of nausea made him think better of it. He closed his eyes and set his head back on the bunk. He could hear men talking somewhere to his left, and after listening to the style and the topics of their conversation, he came to the realization that he was in jail. The men down the corridor were laughing. He felt like retching, and swung his legs off the bunk and sat with his head in his hands, which smelled thickly of cigarettes. He ran them through his hair and the spots where it clotted. He pulled them away and examined them. They were clean, save for dirt, and he put one hand back in his hair and pinched his thumb and index fingers together, pulling his fingernails through one of the clots. It came back with flecks of dried blood. He cleared his throat and spat on the floor. A door banged open down the corridor and footsteps came toward his cell. A skinny white man who looked like he was wearing his father's uniform stopped and looked in at him.

"Mr. Hicks. How nice of you to wake up." His voice was bright and soaked with an east Tennessee accent, shrill in the cramped cell.

"Can we get you anything? Maybe something for your head?" Hicks nodded, not looking at the officer. "Yes sir," he said, even though the man looked to be ten years younger. "I would greatly appreciate it."

"Well," the officer said. "He does have manners, boys. You hear that?" He turned and yelled back up the corridor. "Mr. Hicks here called me 'sir.'"

"Much improved from last night, Sykes," a voice yelled back.

"I suppose it is," he said, rocking back on his heels. Then he turned and continued walking the way that he had come.

Hicks stood up and then sat back down. A few minutes later Sykes returned with a glass of water. He handed it through the bars and Hicks took it gingerly with both hands. The officer fished two aspirins out of his shirt pocket and handed them through the bars as well. Hicks took them and placed them in his mouth, letting the acrid taste coat his thick tongue before taking a long drink of the water and handing the glass back through the bars.

"Sorry about the crack on your head," he said. "Took three of us to get you in the cell and you took one too many swings. You ought to know better than that, swinging at an officer." Hicks sat back down on the bunk and nodded his head.

"Yeah," he said. "I do."

"Don't suppose you remember anything either?"

"No," Hicks said, more to himself. His mind stumbling over the rough, pitted terrain of his morning.

"Anyway," Sykes said. "You've got a few more hours in here and then we'll get you cleaned up for court." He started to leave but turned around. "You're lucky you landed in here on a Monday night. Judge is only in Winchester once a week, otherwise you'd be with us for another..." he counted on his fingers, "seven days," he said. He walked back up the corridor and somewhere down the hall a door slammed behind him. Hicks lay back on the bunk and waited for the aspirin to work. His heart banged and he knew he was terribly dehydrated. It pounded in his chest, and then suddenly he had the sensation that it had stopped altogether, and he shot upright, grabbing the side of the bunk to steady himself. The hitch subsided and he lay back down and tried to remain still, taking deep breaths of air.

They came for him a couple hours or so later. He had drifted back to sleep but woke up as soon as he heard them approaching down the hall. There were two of them, Sykes from earlier, and another man, who stared at him through the bars like he was something exotic to be observed as if he were in a zoo. Hicks guessed he was the one who had hit him. He stood up off the bunk and backed away from the cell door. They opened it with a key and came inside. The man whose name he did not know told him to turn around and face the wall. His tone was taught and edgy.

"Now, Darrin," Sykes said in a mocking voice. "He's learned his lesson I think."

"Cuff him anyway," the man named Darrin said. Hicks felt his arms pulled behind him and the cuffs go around his wrists. They led him out of the cell and turned him down the corridor until they came to a white door. They stopped and Sykes unlocked it and Darrin pushed him through the entrance. It was a small room with a showerhead and a tile floor with a grimy drain. They unlocked his handcuffs and he stood, facing away from them.

"Get undressed," Sykes said. Hicks dropped his pants and took off his shirt and turned to face the officers. "All the way," the man named Darrin said. "Don't be shy." Hicks dropped his underwear and Sykes crossed the room and picked up a bar of soap that was sitting on a shelf next to a towel. He took them both and, holding them in front of him like a gift, he motioned to Hicks.

"Shower up," he said. "Make sure to get that blood out of your hair. We don't want the judge thinking we mistreat our guests." Hicks walked over and turned on the shower. Cold water strained through the head and he stepped under the frigid spray, and then stepped out again.

"Catch," Sykes said, and tossed the bar of soap across the room. Hicks caught it and stepped under the shower and back out again, looking back at the officers.

"Sorry about that," Darrin said. "We're fresh out of hot water." Hicks stepped back under the water. His flesh prickled under the cold and he washed quickly, rubbing the bar of soap over his body and then into his hair, scrubbing vigorously. The water going down the drain was stained from the blood, and he stepped away from it, watching the muted red swirl disappear. He turned off the water and stepped back toward the two officers, shivering. Sykes tossed him the towel. Hicks dried himself off and walked back to where his clothes lay on the floor. He dressed in silence while the two officers watched.

"You got a job?" Sykes asked. Hicks shook his head.

"You got any prospects for a job?" Hicks shook his head again.

"Well," said Sykes, "there's lots of labor jobs around here. Farming and the like. I was you, I'd start thinking about what you are going to tell the judge when he asks you that question. Cause he's gonna ask, and he will not like hearing 'no' for an answer." Hicks nodded, still looking at the ground. The officer was trying to be helpful, but the shallow pity made the anger swell even more. Darrin took a pair of gray pants and a dingy looking shirt off of a side table and dropped the clothes in front of Hicks. "Put them on," he said.

"Where you from, Hicks?" He looked around the shower room, its non-descript color and peeling paint wet with moisture.

"All over," he said.

"Yeah, that right?" Sykes said. Hicks nodded, looking at Darrin. He saw traces of a familiar temper flicker in the man's stare as he buttoned his shirt, and he knew that it would not take much to set him off.

"Well," Sykes said. "I'd try and come up with a better story than 'all over' if I was you. Judge can be hard on vagrants." Hicks looked over at Darrin. He looked back. *Jump, you son of a bitch,* that look said.

"I ain't a vagrant," Hicks said. "I just move around a lot. Ain't a law against moving around, last I checked."

"Yeah, well, tell it to the judge," Sykes said. They escorted him out of the room and back to his cell.

The Winchester courtroom had a single public entry. The walls were painted beige and simple chairs were lined up in two neat rows on either side of the room with an aisle between them. On the back wall was a desk with a larger more ornate wooden chair pushed beneath it. There was an ashtray on the desk next to a small stack of file folders. To the right stood a chair by itself, placed there for the bailiff. The light in the room was dull and the air was still. Sykes brought Hicks, along with several other prisoners, into the room. The bailiff followed behind him and stood watching while Sykes sat each prisoner down individually. The men slumped in the chairs, their heads lowered on their chests.

Sykes walked back up the aisle and leaned against the wall, facing the prisoners. No one spoke and the only sound was the occasional clearing of a throat or restless shifting of the creaky chairs.

Hicks looked around and felt the familiar wash of guilt and irritation. This was not his first time in judgement and he had learned to tamp down his disdain for authority when he was not half-cocked on booze, sitting quietly in rooms not unlike this one, suffering the judicial vernacular and predatory eyes glaring down at his meager and godless existence. They wore their law cloaks as if they were nobility and Hicks knew that what they really relished was the opportunity to identify and exploit the weaknesses of their subjects. They spoke of their rulings on fairways and in wood-paneled libraries, their secretaries groping their cocks while their wives made casserole for dinner or followed their off-spring around, guiding them in the direction of their fathers. They were an ancient breed of hypocrisy and privilege and their small-town circuit made it all the worse, because there were no real rules in a Winchester courtroom or any backwater courtroom for that matter. *Who would care, after all?* Hicks thought. Fighting in a bar or killing a family on the highway, the rules were the same, and if you gave them any excuse to shut the door, they would take it, because that would be what they called justice, and there being no higher power to which a man such as Hicks could appeal, it would be rot, rot, and rot in some cramped hole that smelled of your own shit and desperation.

He heard a commotion in the small entryway of the courthouse building. The officers were welcoming the visiting judge—all smiles and *how-ya-been* greetings—and then they were asking after his family, and Hicks knew that the judge would be providing the obligatory responses, even though Hicks also knew that this judge would care only a hair more for these officers than he would care about the men he had come to sentence. The prisoners sat facing forward and the bailiff came in through a side door and waited for the judge to enter the room. When he did, the bailiff cleared his throat and asked them all to rise, and as Hicks stood, he looked over his shoulder and saw the old man turn down the aisle of chairs, making his way to the desk. He looked at no one as he came forward in a slow shuffling walk, and Hicks felt the empty space in his stomach expand.

The judge took his time sitting down, the prisoners and handful of other attendees shifting their feet waiting to reclaim their seats. When the judge finally scooted the chair beneath the desk, the bailiff went through his speech about the court now being in session. Hicks clenched his teeth and waited. They called the first case, a petty theft charge, and it was decided before it had really begun. Then came a charge of attempted arson, and then another case of theft. Each sentence stiff and handed down with a rehearsed exactitude. Then Hicks was called to stand and he took the three steps so he could be in front of the desk.

"John A. Hicks," The judge read from a single sheet of paper. He appeared more casual now that the docket had thinned and his schedule was clearing by the minute.

"Drunk and disorderly at Bishop's Well. Anything you want to say, Mr. Hicks?" The judge sat back in his chair and coughed. He looked at the bailiff and the man stood and left the room through the side door.

"No sir," Hicks said. "I was drunk and I got into a fight." The judge looked briefly at him and then back at the sheet of paper. He paused and coughed a second time. The bailiff returned carrying a glass of water. He came up the aisle this time and set it on the desk in front of the judge and then he went back to his seat. The judge took a long drink of the water and then coughed again. Hicks waited.

"And it says here that you pulled a knife. Did you pull a knife, Mr. Hicks?" Hicks looked at the judge and tried to hold his expression evenly.

"I don't remember, sir," he said. "I was drunk and I got into it with a guy who was giving me a hard time. If that's what it says, I suppose I did."

"You suppose?" the judge said.

"Yes."

"You can't recall whether or not you pulled a knife on someone, Mr. Hicks?"

"No sir."

"Is pulling a knife on someone common for you, Mr. Hicks?"

"Pardon," he said, but the judge was not waiting for his answer. He was jotting something down on a piece of paper. *Just another throw-away piece of shit,* Hicks thought. The judge raised his head to speak when he began to cough again, this time more violently, until soon he was bent over in a spasm, hacking and choking. The bailiff stood up and walked to the table to retrieve the water glass and the judge saw him from the corner of his eye and waived him away. When he finally stopped, he turned back around and apologized to the room. "So you don't remember anything…" *Cough…* "about the knife or the fight…" *Cough.* He stopped and cleared his throat.

"You know," *Cough.* "Mr. Hicks, I'm inclined…" and he froze. His face went instantly pale and his eyes fixed on the ceiling like a man noticing a crack for the first time. He grabbed his left arm fiercely just above the elbow and then his torso contorted and he flung forward as if shoved from behind, bringing his head down hard on the desktop. The bailiff was up and running toward the desk and the judge fell from the chair, knocking it over, and landed on the ground in a crumpled heap, his face twisted into a red mask of pain and surprise. Spit was forming in the corners of his contorted mouth and he was making a tortured, grunting sound. Hicks stood perfectly still and watched, his hands closed together in front of him and a slight smile forming. The officers were now coming up the aisle, Sykes in the front. They stood over the bailiff who was calling for someone to get the doctor whose practice was across the street. Sykes turned to leave and his eyes met the cold stare coming from John Hicks. He ran past the prisoners and Hicks sat back down in his chair, watching the old man writhe on the floor and the frantic bailiff and officers standing over him, all talking at once. A look of satisfaction on his face, Hicks crossed his ankles and leaned back in the chair, tilting his head to the ceiling as if the scene before him were boring and part of the natural order of things.

That afternoon, the Winchester city attorney came to visit Hicks in his cell. He was short, dressed in a neat suit, and his black hair was brushed back and glistening with whatever cream he used to keep it in place. He wore large round glasses and his shoes were newly shined. He stood in front of the jail cell and Hicks looked at him, outstretched on his bunk. He felt no need to stand to address the man's questions. He had been taken back to the courthouse and told nothing about how things would proceed after the morning's events, and he was becoming impatient. The attorney looked at Hicks with a familiar expression of disappointment and indifference.

"Mr. Hicks," the attorney said. Hicks stared at him. "Mr. Hicks, the judge who was conducting your hearing has passed. He had a massive heart attack and died before he could receive medical attention." He waited to see if Hicks would react, and when he did not, he continued. "As you know, you were never sentenced for the charge and we don't know what the judge intended to do with you. There was nothing written down. So, I'm here to make you an offer." Hicks sat up on the bunk and studied his hands. He tore at a sharp piece of fingernail with his teeth and spit the nail onto the cell floor. The attorney checked his watch and stood waiting, unimpressed with Hicks and obviously irritated to be having the conversation in the first place.

"Would you like to hear my offer?"

Hicks smiled and stood up. "That's one nice suit," he said. "Where can I get a suit like that?"

The attorney took a step back as Hicks came toward the bars.

"Go ahead with your offer," he said. "I ain't gonna bite you."

The attorney tried to stand taller and Hicks stepped in close to the bars, enjoying the uncomfortable feeling that was beginning to spread between them.

"I'm willing to drop the charges based on the circumstances of the case," he said. "The guy you were fighting was a man named Eli Stearns. He uses this cell you are in now as a second home, so the probable reality is that neither one of you was entirely innocent at Bishop's." Hicks turned away and looked out the small cell window.

"Why don't you call me John," Hicks said. "Nobody calls me Mr. Hicks except fuckers like you who have no more respect for me than you'd show a lame horse. Don't insult me with that formal shit. Just get to the point."

The attorney stepped back once more.

"My terms for your release are simple. Leave town as soon as you are out and don't come back. That is non-negotiable. You show up in town again and I'll have you arrested for vagrancy and put you in a hole for a few long months." Hicks put his hands on the bars and looked out at the small man in front of him.

"That old man kicks-off on his bench and they put you in charge, that how it goes?"

The attorney stared at Hicks between the bars. "Mr. Hicks, or John if you like, your alternative to trusting me is to sit here until we can get another judge scheduled. That could take as long as six weeks. You're choice, Mr. Hicks. One time offer."

Hicks nodded and stepped away from the bars. "All right," he said. "When do I get out—" but the attorney had already turned to leave. Hicks looked through the window in the back of the cell, thinking how strange it was that death and luck were so closely aligned.

CHAPTER 7

AN ENCOUNTER
ON THE STREET

John Hicks stepped out of the small municipal building that served as Winchester's courthouse, a free man with only one string attached, which he considered to be tenuous at best. He had not seen the attorney after their conversation in the cell, but soon thereafter Sykes had come to retrieve him and he was ushered out the front door with the clothes on his back and a warning to move along if he did not want to return for a longer stay. His head had stopped throbbing, but that did not relieve the pressure he felt behind his eyes as he tried to decide where to go. He was broke and without options. He stood on the sidewalk in front of the court building and looked up and down the deserted street. He saw the figures of two men standing in front of a filling station further up and Hicks stepped off the curb and crossed the street. The sun was in his eyes, but he could tell as he got closer and listened to the two men talking that they were Negroes. Hicks came close to them and stopped. They both turned to look at him, and then the man on the left said, "You need something, mister?" Hicks studied the two men. They worked outdoors from the look of their clothes.

"I need a job," Hicks said. "Either of you boys know where a white man can get work around here?" The men looked at him suspiciously and with an inherent caution. Hicks was taller than both.

"What sorta job you looking for, mister?" the smaller of the two asked, eyes lowered. Hicks considered the question and then smiled at the men.

"Kind that pays," he said and then gave a sharp laugh that made the men shift and look to one another.

"Got some farm work where we is," the taller man said. He was older and wearing a brimmed hat and Hicks thought he might have some authority over the other man, who had yet to meet his eye and was slightly built, childlike.

"That so," Hicks said.

"Yes sir," the man wearing the hat said.

"Where-bouts?"

"Up in Taylor Branch, sir."

"Taylor Branch?" Hicks asked.

"Yes sir. It's up the road from here. That's where we work. Down to Winchester for some parts and some feed."

"You boys walk down here?"

"No sir. We come in the farm truck. It's over there," and the man with the hat pointed across the street at a battered pick-up with wood slatted side panels and a rusted hood.

"They bringing people on up there?" Hicks asked.

"Don't know sir. I suspect."

"I don't want no field nigger job," Hicks said and smiled again at the men, looking at the boy, studying him. The casual use of the word hit them like a bath of ice water. They wanted now to retreat, Hicks could see that clearly.

"No sir," the man with the hat said, and looked at Hicks from under the brim. Hicks turned to look at him and the man again lowered his gaze. Hicks stepped closer. The heat of the day was rising. He could feel the sun on his face and it pulled the perspiration from his pores. His stomach was sour and he realized he had not eaten and that he had no money to do so. The Negroes stood their ground and waited. To them, it seemed that they were always waiting for what came next, having little say so in their own actions or sense of self. For them, men like Hicks were simply a fact of life, like flies landing on a bowl of fruit or rain coming through a hole in a tarred, storm-torn roof. Their pride was always being stripped away by men like this, and to compensate they were forced to closely control their emotions and respond in a reserved and demure tone that served to deescalate the potential for reprimand that was never far away.

Hicks nodded and stretched his arms above his head. "What say you boys give me a ride to this farm. Up in…where was it again?"

"Taylor Branch, sir," the man in the hat said and fell silent. Then Hicks spoke again, lowering his volume and looking toward the truck.

"I guess you probably know I'm not asking you." The threat hung in the air between them, bloated and consequential. "You got the parts you came in for?" They nodded together.

"And the feed?"

"Yes sir," they said together.

"Then let's get going, boys. I believe I've seen all I need to see of Winchester." He motioned for them to walk to the truck and they did as they were told. The three of them crossed the street, the farm hands in front, followed by Hicks. When they got there, the man in the hat opened the driver's side door and slid into the cab. Hicks and the smaller man walked around the front of the truck. The smaller man put his hand on the handle of the passenger door and Hicks slapped it away. It made a flat sound and the man flinched back, holding the hand against his chest.

"You expect me to ride in the back with a couple of niggers up front driving?" The look on the man's face was wounded and cowering. His eyes were both surprised and scared, but showed no hint of defiance. Hicks waited to see if there would be any protest, and when the boy simply stood and looked back at him, risking a brief glance at the driver. Hicks pushed him roughly out of the way and yanked open the door, which came-to with a shriek of worn, rusted metal. He climbed into the cab. The man with the hat kept his eyes forward and his hands on the steering wheel. They heard the smaller man climb into the bed of the truck and felt the slight increase of his weight settling behind them. The man with the hat turned the ignition key and they drove out of Winchester. The man in the bed of the truck faced the space where the vehicle had been parked and saw that they had forgotten to load one of the feed bags, which was sitting next to the curb, folded over itself. He started to slap the back of the cab but looked at his hand as he began to raise it and saw the imprint where Hicks had hit him. He lowered it back into his lap and closed his eyes against the penetrating sunlight.

The truck rumbled out of the town limits and onto the county road that led to Taylor Branch. The two men in the cab rode in silence, Hicks with his elbow on the open window and the man wearing the hat with both hands on the wheel. On either side of the road, open fields stretched out, bordered on their distant outskirts by rows of Hackberry trees whose gnarled trunks and lightning-struck crowns looked like dismembered piles of fallen marionettes. The air coming through the windows of the truck was humid, tinged with turned earth, manure, and the smell of the oily rags piled on the floorboard. Hicks saw a pack of cigarettes and a box of matches laying on the seat and he pulled one out and struck a match, shielded it with his palm. He inhaled deeply and rested his head against the back window.

"You gotta name?" Hicks said.

"Edgar," the driver said. Hicks looked out the window, exhaled through his nose. Edgar drove carefully around a turn and Hicks saw a squat building further ahead.

"What's that up there?"

"Sir?"

"That building up there ahead. What is that?"

"Bishop's," Edgar said. Hicks sat up in the seat.

"The roadhouse?" Edgar nodded. Hicks dragged again on the cigarette and threw it out the window.

"Pull in," he said. Edgar took his eyes off the road to look at Hicks.

"No sir," he said.

"What was that?" Hicks said.

"No sir. Can't do that. Mr. Dennis…"

"You pull in there boy or I'll break your fucking nose," Hicks spat. "You and that sawed-off little nigger in the back both." Edgar stiffened in his seat and then turned off the road and into the dirt lot of the road-house. The truck came to a stop and sat idling roughly. Hicks stared at the building and then turned in his seat.

"Look here," he said and Edgar did. "Might be that I got something to take care of in there," and he pointed at the building. "And when I come out this truck better be here and the two of you in it. I come out and you've gone and I'll find my own way up the road to this farm and then I'll come find both of you and when I do you'll wish you never stopped to talk in front of that filling station. You understand me?"

Edgar nodded. Hicks got out of the truck and walked quickly across the parking lot and pulled open the door and walked inside.

He came through the door of Bishop's Well almost at a trot and stopped three steps into the room to let his eyes adjust. He could remember next to nothing about the night that he was there, but he could vaguely recall the short bar and where Stearns and his buddies had sat. He narrowed his eyes to sharpen his focus and he saw a man hunched over on the furthest stool from him. There was no one behind the bar and there were no other patrons. Hicks crossed the small space of the room and came to stand directly behind the man on the stool. Hicks tapped his shoulder and the man turned quickly around, startled and angry. He looked up drunkenly; his eyes were sunken and one side of his face drooped a little. He had a blue-purple splotch of bruise covering most of his left jawline, a deep cut across his forehead and another puncture mark on his cheek. Hicks stared at him and suddenly Stearns' mind cleared.

"You remember me?" Hicks said

"Goddamn right I remember," Eli Stearns said. Hicks hit him in the mouth. He felt teeth give against his fist and the man was instantly knocked from the stool, unable to break his fall as he dropped to the floor. He landed on his shoulder and then rolled over on his back, both his hands clutching his mouth. Blood was coming through his fingers and he was screaming and gargling, muffled by his palms. Hicks stepped back and kicked the man in the ribs. Then stepped back again and kicked him in the groin. The man curled and bellowed from his bloody mouth, his hands now holding his testicles. Hicks dropped to one knee and grabbed the man's thinning hair and banged his head up and down on the floor, the sound a rhythmic *thump, thump, thump* on the wooden boards. Hicks stood and looked at his own hands, saw there was blood on them and leaned back down to wipe them clean on the front of the man's shirt. Still bent over and out of habit, he went for his knife in his back pocket, but they had taken it from him when they arrested him. He stood again and was about to leave when he returned to the man on the floor and launched a kick into his side that forced an almost inaudible moan carried out on a thick spray of bloody breath. Hicks turned again and walked across the room to leave.

He was pushing the door open when someone cried out from behind him. He let the door close and turned around to face the bar. It was a small boy, no more than eleven or twelve and he was holding a rack of glasses. He wore a pair of denim overalls and no shirt and he was struggling with the weight he was holding, bracing it against his waist with his arms outstretched. He looked at Hicks and then he looked at the man on the other side of the bar who had lost consciousness. Hicks thought that there might be a father or an uncle somewhere in the back of the building and his first concern was that the boy would drop his load and make a racket that was impossible not to hear. *And if the father did come, he would be the owner of the bar and would certainly recognize him from the night before and then, well then he'd have to take steps to make sure both of them stayed quiet.* The boy stood absolutely still looking at the ruined face of the man on the floor. Finally he looked back at Hicks who put a finger, streaked with blood, to his lips and held it there for what seemed like a long time to both of them. Then he took his hand away and waited. The boy shifted the weight of the glasses which made them rattle against one another, and Hicks inhaled a breath, but the boy held his grip. Hicks winked at the boy who remained frozen in place, then Hicks was moving quickly for the exit. He pushed open the door and the room was briefly washed in bright sunlight. He saw that the truck was still there and he jogged across the parking lot and got in the passenger side. Edgar sat looking at him.

"Drive," Hicks screamed at him. "Drive you black-hearted nigger son-of-a-bitch," he screamed and pounded the side of the passenger door.

The truck was two miles from Bishop's Well when Hicks took another cigarette from the pack on the seat. He took up the matches and as he fished one from the box, he saw the blood that remained on his fingers. He reached for the rearview mirror and turned it to face him so he could examine his face. There was a splotch of blood on his chin and his lower lip. He took one of the oily rags from the floorboard and found a clean spot on it and used his tongue to wet it, then scrubbed the blood off his face. Then he opened the cloth on his lap and laid his hand in it and wrapped it up. He put the cigarette in his mouth, and with his free hand he rubbed at the blood on his fingers. He pulled it out, examined it, and, seeing that it was clean, he tossed the rag back onto the floor of the truck and took up the box of matches again and lit the cigarette. He looked at his reflection in the rearview as he spoke to Edgar.

"Guess you're wondering what that was about," Hicks said, still examining his face in the mirror.

"Ain't none of my business," Edgar said.

"That's a good answer," Hicks said, and turned the mirror back where it had been.

"Even so," he said, looking out the passenger window, "I'm gonna tell you. I went in there to finish what I started the other night. I would have finished it before if that deputy had not wandered in when he did. Lucky for old Stearns I guess. How it happens sometimes. You boys," Hicks motioned toward the man in the bed of the truck, "know all about that I'm guessing. Well luck's a funny thing. Or maybe it's fate if you're a believer. Which I'm not." He pulled on the smoke as if to emphasize this point.

"See, I believe that there's such a thing as luck, but I think that you have more of a hand in how it treats you if you are willing to do things that other people ain't. You take a nigger's life for instance. It ain't your fault that you're burnt coal-black like that, no more than it's a Copperhead's fault for being poisonous. But if I were a nigger, I sure as hell wouldn't let people treat me the way that niggers get treated. Even if it meant getting strung up. I'd rather make my own path and cut any man down that got in my way, white or not." Edgar kept his eyes forward, moving the truck through the open land and listening for whatever came at the end of what Hicks was talking about. Hicks knew nothing about being a black man and had probably inflicted as much harm on his people as any white man before him.

"See, Edgar, nigger or not, I need you to understand that I don't suffer any man taking an interest in my business or what I do and don't do. And if he does, then that man can count on retribution, and it will be swift and it will be harsh. That I can promise."

Edgar turned and saw that Hicks was staring at him. He nodded at him and Hicks continued to stare.

"I need for you to say it," Hicks said.

"Say what, sir," Edgar said.

"I need to hear you say that you understand."

"I understand," Edgar said. "And Levi in the back, he understands too."

"That's good," Hicks said. "I'd hate for us to all get off on the wrong foot."

CHAPTER 8

RENEE

Renee Winslett sat in the upstairs room of the farm's big house, thinking about marriage. She had reached an age when her interest in the farm had almost vanished, all of the things that had attracted her attention as a younger girl like the creek and the animals and the fields with their rich smells and seemingly endless pathways had given over to boys, more specifically boys in town who worked in offices and wore nice clothes and did not smell like sweat and tractor grease all the time. She saw life beyond the farm road as an open invitation to break loose from the provincial and predictable routines that she had known her whole life. Her distraction and criticism of her comfortable home life had not yet reached the point of angering or over-concerning her mother, but she was growing restless and losing patience with being treated as a petulant child. She spent hours in her room making up elaborate stories in her head about extravagant trips to places like Europe, and evenings spent dancing with men of money, and status and sophistication. And even though her parents were people of money, status, and sophistication, she found that unsatisfying and meager. They were content and felt no need to flaunt their success, whereas Renee saw their family's societal position as a stepping stone for something vaster and infinitely more entertaining.

She had also begun feeling a tremendous need to have sex. Her older sister Katherine certainly had not had sex, probably not even dreamt of it or done the thing that was as close to it as was possible when you were by yourself on a farm in the middle of nowhere. As far as Renee could tell, Katherine had no ambition at all beyond being a model Winslett and marrying someone safe and dependable, someone her father would approve of and her mother would lavish with praise and encouragement. It all made Renee want to vomit in the hall sink. Something was aching in her. It had started slow and had grown to the point that she was constantly preoccupied with escaping, and naked-ness, and men in suits and ties, and English castles, and royal gardens and the dresses that were as beautiful as they were expensive. Her head jammed full of images that were constructed from raw, evolving emo-tions, she would be almost fully consumed with romantic visions when her mother would ask whether she had done some asinine chore or her sister would ask how her day had been or her father would speak to her in a tone that he had used since she was a child. All of it would make her want to scream until she passed out. The sincerity of the family, the incessant manners and work ethic made her feel as though she were suffocating over and over again, tossed in the river bound and swaddled in some quilt made by her mother's mother. The constant dust in the farm yard, the horse shit piles on the way to the immense and always needy garden, the way the Negroes stopped when she approached and stood with their hat in their hands, the once-a-month trips to Win-chester for a dinner or some other banal outing—all of this and a thou-sand other reasons were churning through Renee's head when the farm truck turned up the road toward the house.

The truck approached, trailing a plume of dust behind it. She could see the outlines of two men in the front seat. It rumbled toward the house and stopped. She stepped closer to her window that looked out over the yard, and she could see that the two men in the front seat were talking and that one of the men was white and he was using his hands to speak with Edgar, who she recognized from the hat and his slump-ing posture. She stood still in the window, wearing a light dress and her hair down. Edgar climbed out of the truck first and then she saw Levi come around from the back of the truck where he must have been rid-ing in the bed. Then the white man stepped out of the truck on the pas-senger side and he closed the door and stood looking around. Renee's eyes fixed on him. He was tall with tangled hair and his shoulders were broad. He stood with his legs apart and he had folded his arms in front of him. She heard the familiar smack of the screen door in its frame and then her father was crossing the yard. The new man stood still and made no motion to greet her father as he came closer, and then she saw that her father had stopped and not closed enough space between he and the stranger to shake hands. Dennis Winslett stood and Renee could tell that he was questioning the man, who was likely answering with yes and no-sirs. Occasionally the stranger nodded or shook his head. Then her father turned, with his back still to the house and Renee in the window, and he was asking Edgar and Levi questions. The man looked at Edgar and Levi as her father spoke to them; he did not move and he seemed to study them intently, his head turned but not his body. Then another of the farm hands whose name she could not remember came into the yard from the barn and he and Levi went around to the back of the truck and appeared again with pieces of equipment which they laid on the ground, then returning to the truck to finish unloading it. Edgar moved away to the barn and her father looked again at the stranger.

Renee came away from the window and went to her dressing table, examining herself by bending at the waist and peering into her reflection. She had black hair and almost black eyes. Her skin was fair and unblemished. She cupped and positioned her small breasts and felt a warm sensation spread inside of her like a fire moving through dry hay or leaves. She stood and smoothed her dress and then left the room, walking down the hallway past Katherine's door and then down the stairs to the sitting room, running her hands along the smooth banister wood as she descended.

Dennis Winslett was shaking the man's hand when she came out on the porch. She was careful not to let the screen slam behind her, but the men heard it and turned to look at her. Winslett let go of the man's hand, still looking at his daughter, then he turned and said "Okay, John. It's not for me to judge, and we need the help. But I won't have any of that on my place. First offense and you are gone. Either on your own two legs or in the back of the sheriff's car." He did not await an answer but turned instead to survey the equipment. He motioned for it to be taken to the barn and then he came back toward the porch. The stranger did not follow her father's movements, but instead stood still, staring at Renee. Winslett came up the porch steps, his boots clumping on the wood. Renee was looking over his shoulder and her father turned back to the yard, observing Hicks watching them on the porch. He took his daughter's arm and moved her toward the screen door. She smiled at him and he returned the look with a disapproving frown. She went in ahead of him and he turned a final time to the yard before following her.

Once they were inside, Hicks looked away from the porch and headed to the front entrance of the barn. Levi appeared from behind the truck and came and stood next to Edgar. The slap he had received in Winchester no longer stung but had left an indelible mark on him just the same, and as he looked at Hicks through his wide brown eyes, he spoke. "That man," he said. Edgar's fixed expression did not change, his own eyes shielded beneath the brim of the hat.

"You leave that man alone, Levi. You see him coming, you find another way to go. You hear me?" Levi nodded. Hicks was talking with one of the other white men and then, as if he had heard his name mentioned, he looked in their direction, focusing his eyes with a glare that made it feel as if it were only the three of them standing in the yard. Levi began to pull away and Edgar whispered for him to be still. Hicks smiled and then turned his attention back to the other white man and pretended to laugh at something he had said. Edgar adjusted his hat and told Levi to go around to the kitchen door in the big house and see if LoLo needed anything, never taking his eyes off Hicks. When the boy was safely on the other side of the house, Edgar turned and walked toward the fields. The crops were alive with the soft breeze and their stirring bothered him. It was as though they were breathing in or out, patiently observing, waiting for something to occur, but he could not understand what that might be. He removed his hat and wiped away the sweat from his forehead. He thought of the man Hicks striking Levi and the expression in his face went taut. He replaced the hat and went on, disappearing down the slope with the unknown eating at his stomach.

In addition to its hay production, the Winslett farm also dealt in hogs, corn, and some small tobacco fields. Dennis Winslett's father, George, had procured the land some fifty years before and had passed it down to his son, a respectable one-hundred-acre parcel that had helped to establish the family early on as respected members of the small rural community. Since taking over the operation from his father, who had dropped dead of a heart attack one August afternoon, Dennis had amassed an additional two-hundred acres, parceling the pieces together over time and pouring every ounce of energy into building an enterprise that would firmly keep the Winsletts in a place of prosperity for generations to come. Dennis and his wife were natural leaders in the community, spiritual and civic. They were keepers of decency and diligent subjects of the church, which benefited from both their financial contributions as well as their moral stewardship. And through all of this, Winslett had been careful to monitor the men who worked for him. He had turned many transients away, preferring to proactively avoid the fighting, petty theft, and drunkenness that inevitably followed those who wandered, dragging their laziness and failing self-confidence behind them like broken mules struggling with decrepit plows. On one afternoon he had found two men in a bunk together, their shirts off and a bottle of cheap liquor next to them on the floor. On another, a man had gutted one of his Negroes in a tobacco field and the man had bled to death waiting on the doctor. Winslett had knocked the attacker to the ground with a shovel and walked alongside him and the sheriff when they took him off the farm and locked him up in Winchester. He considered that type of behavior an insult to his intelligence, and of course was constantly bothered by the obvious threat that men of that nature posed to his wife and his daughters. And so his hiring of John Hicks, with his transparency of having been newly released from jail, went against every fiber of his better judgement, his cautionary nature even more ablaze when he saw the way that the man looked at Renee, and more disturbing still, the way Renee responded. Now they stood in the foyer together and Renee would not meet his eye.

"Do I have to explain to you why you need to stay away from the hands?" Winslett asked.

"I'm not a little girl anymore, daddy," she said, her hand playing with a strand of her black hair.

"No, you're not," he said. You're a young woman and I know that you think that you can manage your own affairs." She looked at him with what he hoped was gratitude for his admission, but there was something equally unsettling in the way that her eyes kept finding the screen door.

"But, Renee," he said and paused.

"I know," she said, and now she was looking fully at him, wearing a face she knew would make his warning harder to deliver.

"You don't have to tell me to be careful," she said. "You've been telling me to be careful my whole life."

"And I will continue to do so as long as I'm drawing a breath," he said. "It's my job as your father. I love you and I want the best for you and a man with no more ambition than holding hands with a shovel is not what your mother and I want for you. God forbid you should get…"

"Daddy, you can stop now. I'm not going to mess with them boys."

"Those men," he corrected, "They are men. Not boys. There's a difference." She waited as she always had with him and he knew that she could empower as much patience as she needed to get through one of his talks. He also knew that she was keenly aware of the difference between men and boys and that was what kept him awake at night; between the figures in the ledgers and the weather patterns, there would always be Renee.

"Go on," he said and waved her away. She came forward and kissed his cheek and then Renee turned and went back up the stairs. She turned at the top and headed to her room but stopped in front of Katherine's door when she heard her sister behind it singing softly to herself. Renee knocked and the singing stopped. She heard her sister cross the room and then the door opened. Katherine, slightly shorter than Renee, smiled.

"You see the new man Daddy hired?" Renee whispered.

"No," Katherine said, and she turned and walked back into her room. Renee followed.

"He's nice looking," Renee said. Katherine looked at her as she sat down on her bed. She said nothing but picked up a pillow and set it in her lap. Renee closed the door and crossed the room, then took a seat next to her sister.

"Edgar must have found him in town when he went in this morning. He came back in the truck with him. Daddy hired him on just now. He looks strong. He's tall and…"

"Daddy wouldn't like you talking like that," Katherine said. "You know he wouldn't."

"You're right," Renee said. "He already told me not to mess with *those men*. I swear I think he still believes I'm nine years old or something. I'm old enough to decide for myself who I want to be around." Katherine looked down at the pillow in her lap. She knew it was best to let Renee run on till it was out of her system. She loved her sister, but seldom understood where she came from. She found it easier to smile and nod, wait out the storm.

"How come you never talk about boys," Renee said. Katherine looked up.

"I talk about boys," she said. "I just don't talk about boys the way that you do. I'm not in some huge hurry to take off my clothes like you are."

"You aren't just a little curious?" Renee asked, not acknowledging the slight admonishment her sister had given her.

"Renee," Katherine said. "I don't feel like talking about this now."

"You act like you don't feel anything at all," Renee said. "I just wanted to talk." Katherine set the pillow aside.

"You just wanted to talk about sex," Katherine said.

"What's wrong with that?"

"You know what's wrong with that."

"I guess I don't," Renee said. "I guess poor old dumb Renee doesn't understand."

"That's not what I meant," Katherine said. "You know that's not what I meant."

"I know what you meant," Renee said. She felt the warmth she had encountered while looking into the mirror returning with a quickness that she knew would be coloring her cheeks. It was not the same feeling as before. It was not tingling, but a slow simmer. She stood up and started to leave the room. Then she turned again to face her sister, her hair coming around behind her spinning frame, falling partially over her eyes as she steadied herself.

"I know you and mother talk about me. Pretend to worry about me. Think I'm not as smart as you both are with all your society talk and dainty little family heritage." Katherine's eyes grew wider. "You heard me," Renee said. "All that prim and proper polite talk. It's a bunch of horseshit. And I'm as smart as you are. I'm as pretty as you are. And someday I'm gonna leave this farm and never come back and you can have all your Sunday afternoon glasses of lemonade and porch talk with mother and father and the Baptists and all the other *praise-Christ-Jesus* that comes along with it. I'm gonna find some man that never even heard of what it means to be a Winslett and you know what the first thing I'm gonna do is when I meet him? You want to know, Katherine? I'm gonna drop my dress and let him run his hands all over me, and when he's done with that I'm gonna climb on top of him and ride him right out of the front gate and all the way over the goddamn mountain." She was breathing heavily and her hands were clenched. Her sister sat stunned on the bed, a look on her face that was somewhere between tears and outrage. Then she collected herself and stood.

"Who says any man would want that from you, Renee? Who says there's even a man out there for you in the first place? I think about those things that you talk about. I just don't talk like some street whore in Nashville. You want to know why mother and I talk about you? Do you?" Renee was out of breath, looked as if she had been chased across the farm. "I'll tell you what we talk about. It's how all the women look at you at church or in town and steer their men in the other direction. It's how you walk out on the porch half-dressed while the hands are out by the barn, just begging one of those boys to follow you out into the field and have his way with you. And how you talk. That'd be just fine with you, right little sister? Shame mother and father and end up like a wretch. You keep talking like that and I'll keep on the way that I have and we'll see who finds a man first. And I won't have to drop my dress to make him pay attention."

"Stop it, Katherine," Renee said.

"Why," Katherine shouted back at her, advancing. "Want to take our clothes off and go talk to the new hand? Let's go, Renee. Let's go out there together and show them what Winslett girls are all about. Maybe go get drunk after and have another go in the hay barn."

"Katherine…"

"Shut up." She was almost panting, her hands clamped in front of her choking off the color. "Mother talks about you because she's worried what you will do, and I listen because I have to. But you bring this on yourself, Renee. Always having to push this and push that, flitting around like you are some star in the movies. You're just a cheap lit-tle girl from Taylor Branch, Tennessee, Renee. And when you finally make everyone mad enough, you'll get your wish. You'll…" She stopped abruptly and they looked at one another. Renee was close to tears and Katherine started to put her hand out, and then stopped.

"Renee, I'm sorry," she said. "I'm sorry."

"Go to hell," Renee said very quietly. "Go to hell for how you've made me hate all of you." She backed out of the room and went down the stairs and then the screen door slammed behind her retreat. Kath-erine stood in front of the bed, went to the window, and saw Renee run out through the yard and turn off a path that led to the creek and the hog pens. She stood in the window for what felt like a long time, and as she was finally collecting herself a man walked into the yard who she had not seen before. He was carrying a pickaxe over his shoulder and he stopped next to the truck, leaning the tool against it. He reached into the window and came out with a pack of cigarettes. He pulled one of the smokes free and then went back in the truck for the matches. He struck one and touched the tip of the cigarette, then stood leaning against the truck. The breeze had stopped and the clouds of exhaled smoke sat in the air above him and moved slowly away until they were no longer there.

CHAPTER 9

EDGAR

Most of us on the Winslett farm came from slaves. Mr. Dennis's great-grandfather brought them here and after slavery was over most of them stayed on to work. Mamma came from those people who arrived on ships, but she did not like to talk too much about it. She learned to read and write on the farm and she did like to talk about that and she taught me how to do both. She said that being able to read and write was a gift and that being able to put your thoughts on paper made you a thinking man and not some *field nigger* like that man Hicks called me and Levi. Sometimes I get feelings around people. My hands tingle and I get a bad taste in my mouth like old well water and it's like I am seeing through someone, seeing into their soul. Mamma says that she can get those feelings too and says that she passed it on to me just like the reading and the writing. I got that feeling around Hicks. Real strong. But I did not want to see inside of him. Now that I think about why, it seems like maybe he had the ability to see into people too and I was afraid that if I stared too long at him he might look back and through me and I knew from the day that I saw him coming up the street, out of that court house, that I didn't want nothing to do with him and I didn't want him inside of me. He gave off something strong and mean, like being sick with a fever.

I was thinking a lot about that feeling that I got from Hicks when Miss Mary asked me to help her with what must have been the most awful thing a mother could live through. Her husband and my boss, what happened came close to breaking him down to nothing. He's a strong and decent man, but children are our weakness, Mamma says. Only those who have embraced the devil himself can turn their back on the little ones, and so for decent people, something wicked that touches their children will lay waste to them and make them as a cripple. It was my own weakness for Levi that brought about John Hicks. I let Levi talk me into staying longer in town and had we been in the truck and on our way to Taylor Branch, we would have never crossed paths with him and what I have to tell would not be as it is.

Hicks came on as a hand and it was clear from real early that he had no desire for working hard or long on the Winslett place. He was using it for the quick money and he tried his best to do nothing. He was good at it too. He always seemed to be moving, but if you watched him for a minute or two you would see that he never really did much more than stand around and smoke and pick at people for no good reason. Mr. Winslett in those days was so busy that he didn't have time to keep everyone in line and because I knew that Hicks was not planning on being there long, I didn't say anything and tried to keep people clear of his temper, which would snap out of him like a whip. He was hate all the way through and he could disguise it when he wanted to and turn it loose when he needed it.

The sheriff came around a couple days after he was on the place and I thought about saying something to him about pulling over at Bishop's Well, but that sheriff back then didn't think much of us and I didn't know what Hicks had done in there, only that he had blood on his hands and was in an awful hurry to leave out. The sheriff came up on the porch and talked with Mr. Winslett and if it was about Bishop's they must have come to some kind of an agreement because the sheriff left and Hicks stayed and nothing more was ever said about it.

About two weeks after Hicks got there, I was working with the hogs. It was coming on dark and I was just finishing up with the last of them. I'd put everything away and was walking back toward the row houses where all the hands and their families lived. It was a nice community we had. Small but everyone got along good and we'd sit out late and the men would drink some and the women would sing along with the guitar that Levi had learned to play pretty nice. That's what I thought I was hearing as I came down the path between the corn fields. I could see the roof of one of the smaller barns over the tops of the stalks. It came in and out of view as I walked, and then I heard a woman's voice and it sounded maybe like she was singing, but the kind of singing some of the women sometimes do on Sundays in church when they are eaten-up with the spirit. I stopped and listened and then it stopped. I kept walking down the path and then I heard it start up again, only this time it sounded more like crying. Like a child crying. I turned back the other direction and ran up the path toward the big house and came around the side of the corn field and saw the barn and the trees on either side of it. I went up the rise toward it and could see that someone was on the ground beneath one of the trees. I ran harder then and came up under the shadows of the tree branches and I saw Miss Katherine there on the ground, holding herself and rocking from side to side. I stood very still. I could see the blood on her dress and I could see that her hair had leaves and twigs stuck in it. I wanted to go to her then, and I started toward her but stopped and thought how me being there at that time would be. How she might not know who had done something to her and that I might be blamed. I walked back under the shadow of the barn and then moved alongside it and I could see the light on in the big house and I knew that they would be getting food ready. I ran toward the light and then came around the side of the house where the tables are set out for dinner and then around to the back where I could go into the kitchen. I came running up the back steps and into the hot kitchen. Mamma was there at the stove and I called her name out.

"What are you doing in here, Edgar?" she said.

I told her where I had been with the hogs and then about Miss Katherine down by the barn. She looked at me with a hard face. She was sweating from the pots on the stove and the cramped kitchen and I knew she suspected me and so I told her how I had started to go to help Miss Katherine but had stopped for the same reason that she was looking at me that way. She came to me and touched my face and then went into the living part of the house. I don't know why Mr. Winslett was gone that night, but Mamma came back into the kitchen with Miss Mary and she had her husband's rifle and she told me to take her to Katherine.

I said, "Mam, I didn't touch Miss Katherine," and Miss Mary said that she knew I had not and would I please take her to her daughter right then. So we came out of the kitchen and I ran and she was behind me and Mamma was behind her trying to keep up. We got to Miss Katherine who was shaking on the ground and crying and Miss Mary handed me the gun and then she knelt down by her daughter who screamed when she touched her, but stopped when she saw that it was her mother and that she meant her no harm. Mamma and I stood back a few steps and Miss Mary was holding Katherine and she was crying so hard she started to choke and cough and then Mamma turned to me and said to go get a pail of water and some wash rags. I ran back to the house and found the pail in the kitchen cupboard and some wash towels too, and then I ran back to the tree. I remember the water sloshing out of the pail, wetting my pants as I ran, and I was afraid I would spill too much so I slowed down and I came back under the tree and Miss Marry and Miss Katherine were still on the ground and Miss Katherine was wheezing and then she would make a terrible sound like an animal that's hurt. Mamma took the pail from me and stuck the wash rag down in the water and went and knelt down beside the two women on the ground, and I remember she touched Miss Mary's shoulder and Miss Mary turned around quickly and almost knocked Mamma to the ground when she did. Then she saw it was just her and she let her put the cool rag to Miss Katherine's face. Miss Katherine tried to turn away from it, but they held her together and they were wiping her face and neck.

I stood back and looked out across the yard thinking there must be someone around the place that had seen what happened or at least heard all the commotion now, but it was quiet and coming full-dark. Then I saw something move down toward the corn field where I had been, and I stood still and watched. I thought I saw someone standing on the edge of the field, but I was afraid to call out and scare the women there under the tree. I took a step closer toward the field and I pinched my eyes to see if I could make out who was there, but I could not. The air had become cold and there was a breeze and Miss Katherine was shaking harder now. Miss Mary told Mamma to take one of Miss Katherine's arms and then she took the other and they lifted her out of the dirt and her hair hung down in her face and she was limp so that they had to struggle with her weight. I could see the blood on the front of her dress and it was filthy from the dirt and the patches of grass, and there was a rip in it too. Miss Katherine found her legs and they started back toward the house.

I waited until they passed and then I followed them back toward the light of the house and around the side where they helped her up the steps and into the kitchen. I watched them into the house and then I remembered that the rifle was still leaning against the tree where I had set it down after Miss Mary handed it to me, so I went back to get it, and when I got there it was gone. I stood under the limbs of the tree and the mouth of the barn seemed to be filled with black storm clouds and I could not hear anything moving inside and I was more scared then because I knew someone had been watching us with Miss Katherine and I knew that it was the one who had done it to her, and that he was at peace with the sin he had done. I remember the moon had come out from behind the clouds and it was a bone-colored moon and I remember looking up at it and knowing that it had seen what happened but could not say, like God's word is silent. Then Mamma came to the side of the house and told me that they needed my help with Miss Katherine and I turned around fast and walked toward my mother and I could feel the eyes on my back. I came into the kitchen and I saw there were drops of blood on the wood and that they led out to the hallway, and when I looked through the door there I saw Miss Mary holding up Miss Katherine near the stairs. She called to me and said "Edgar, please help me get her upstairs to her room," so I came slowly into the hall and I stood next to them and she said take her arm.

"Edgar, like this." So I lifted up her arm, which had no strength and fell around my neck like a thick length of rope, and we lifted her between us and began to walk up the stairs that creaked under our weight. We came down the upstairs hall and went to her door and I could see further down the hallway and the other room was empty and dark and I felt my hands start to tingle and so I looked away because something was coming from that dark room, but I could not stop myself from looking again and when my eyes went down the hall I could see Hicks standing there holding the rifle and then he was gone like a breeze had blown him away and I shook my head to clear it. Then Miss Mary said, "Edgar, help me get her to the bed," and I did, setting her down softly and then Miss Mary helped to lay her down and I stood and backed away from the bed and then Mamma was in the room too and she looked at me and meant for me to go and I went out and down to the kitchen. After some time Miss Mary came down and she came in the room and then went out again and came back with a bottle and she crossed to the cupboard where I had found the pail and she took out glasses and came across the room and sat down and I stood up but she told me to sit again and I did and then she poured some of the liquor into the glasses and pushed one across the table to me.

"Edgar," she said, "what did you see?" I told her about the hogs and hearing Miss Katherine from where I was on the path between the fields and that I had found her under the tree near the small barn and had come straight to the house. She drank from her glass, then filled it again. I left my glass on the table. I knew that the sheriff would probably be called to the place and I did not want to have liquor in my mouth. Then I remembered that the rifle had been taken and I told Miss Mary that I had gone back to get it after Miss Katherine had been brought back to the house and that I had leaned it against the tree near the tables and when I came back it was gone. Miss Mary looked at me then and she put the glass back on the table and we sat like that for a bit and then she told me to go and lock the front door and make sure that all the windows were locked too and I got up from the table and did as she asked and came back to the kitchen and she was standing looking out the back kitchen door into the yard. I told her that the doors and windows were locked and she nodded. Then she told me to go back into the hallway and get the pistol that was in the closet there, sitting on the top shelf, and to make sure that the pistol was loaded and to bring it back to her in the kitchen. I went into the hall and pulled open the closet door. It was filled with coats and I stepped into the closet and reached up on the top shelf and found the pistol where she said it would be and I pulled it down and broke it open and saw that there were six bullets in the cylinder, and I locked the gun back and carried it into the kitchen and I asked Miss Mary if she would feel better if I held the gun for her and she looked at me and said that she would take it. Then we heard Mamma calling from upstairs and also heard Miss Katherine screaming and Miss Mary went out of the kitchen quickly and I heard her going up the stairs and I looked again at the glass of whiskey on the table in front of where I had been sitting and I thought how it would be good to drink it and calm myself, but I did not drink it.

CHAPTER 10

JOHN AND RENEE

John Hicks stood in the shadow of the corn stalks watching the boy Edgar who seemed to be looking at him. If he called out Hicks would have to deal with all of them. His hand rested on the handle of a knife he had tucked into his belt. The boy peered in his direction and he almost came out from where he was hiding, but he backed away when they started to take the girl to the house. Hicks's shirt was covered in his own sweat and he had a long scratch on his neck from struggling with the girl. He waited until they were behind the house and then he ran to the tree and took the rifle, then ran back to the shadow of the cornfield and down the row that led to the small houses where the hands stayed. There was no one in the yard when he came into the clearing. He waited a few more minutes to make sure no one was outside and then he came across the yard in a trot and up the steps to his door and stopped. It was cracked, but there was no light in the room. He pushed the door open and looked inside but could not make out anything. He stepped in and waited, letting his eyes adjust the dark. He crossed the small space and put the rifle on the bed. He bent down and pulled an old duffle bag, which a previous tenant had left behind, from beneath the frame and threw that on the bed as well. He went to a small dresser where he had kept the few belongings he had acquired while he had been at the farm. Then someone spoke behind him.

"I know what you did," the voice said. Hicks turned around quickly and saw the shape of someone standing in the dark corner of the room. He tensed.

"Who's there?" he said.

"I'm not going to say anything." Hicks stood still and realized that the voice belonged to a girl.

"Who are you?" he asked.

"Renee," the woman said.

"The sister?" Hicks asked.

"Yes," she said, and stepped closer. Hicks touched the handle of the knife and tried to make out the girl's face. The assault on the other sister had been on his mind for weeks, ever since he had seen her sitting on the porch reading a book. It was not so much the way she looked, but her scent of unobtainability that pricked at his mind, an ever-present lust to make others submit to his will. He had waited and watched her from a distance, both literal and mental, to learn her movements around the farm, to spot a weakness and an opening. The longer that he delayed, the more violent the notion became until it reached a point that he thought he might physically explode. When he saw Winslett leave with his suitcases, his wife and daughters saying their goodbyes beside the car, he acted. He caught the girl from behind, coming around the side of the house and had used the knife to keep her quiet. He had driven her away from the house, down the slope, and had immediately violated her with a barely controlled savagery. She had tried to resist initially and he had spoken to her in a rasping voice that threatened something even worse. When he finished, he stood over her, panting, and watched as she crawled away from the spot back toward the house. He retreated to the cover of the corn field after she had collapsed beneath the tree, and he wondered now why he had not run then and realized that the lust wanted more, wanted to witness the pain of the aftermath, which had been almost as satisfying as the vulgar act itself. But now, with his hand on the knife once again and the girl's cornered stare speaking to him from inside his room, he thought about whether or not he had made a mistake.

"What do you want?" he said. She moved toward him and Hicks almost pulled the knife where she could see it. Her eyes were wild and shifting and she held a suitcase in front of her.

"I want to go with you," she said. Hicks looked at her. His mind choked like a sputtering engine. He left the knife in his belt and could feel its blade pressing against his bare waist. Her declaration made him pause and want to laugh.

"You don't know me and I sure as hell don't know you," he said and returned his attention to the bed.

"I don't see how that matters," she said, "seeing what you've done." Hicks spun around and took several quick steps toward the girl. She shrunk down but did not retreat.

"You don't know nothing about anything I've done," he said.

"I want to leave here," she said. "I know that much."

Hicks turned again to the bed. "I ain't nobody's meal ticket."

"I ain't looking for a meal ticket," she said. The word *ain't* sounded so unnatural coming from her that Hicks again wanted to laugh.

"Look here," he said. "What's your name again?"

"Renee," she said.

"Renee. I don't know what kind of fucked-up game you're playing, but I'm not the kind of man that you want to test." She did not say anything in response and he began to wonder if she was simple.

"I need, no I want, to get away from here," she said.

Hicks laughed. "And go where?"

"Doesn't matter," Renee said and stepped closer. She was slight, but pretty and Hicks wet his lips and considered. The fact that she had come to him after what she must have seen him do made him curious and also suspicious. They stood looking at one another, neither sure how to proceed. *I'll test her,* he thought and moved closer. He was much taller and she had to look up at him. He reached out his hand and firmly grabbed her right breast. She sucked in her breath and closed her eyes.

"Something wrong with you, Renee?"

She did not answer.

"Might it be that you want the same as your sister got?"

Her eyes remained closed.

"I won't fight it if that's what you mean." He pulled his hand back, suddenly unsure of her motivation and now thinking about his escape. She opened her eyes and looked up into his face.

"I want to leave," she said. "I don't care where you are going, just take me with you. Out of here."

"And if I say no?"

She closed her eyes again and seemed to consider the question thoughtfully. Then she opened them again and smiled. "You won't say no," she said.

"Is that so." She nodded and continued to smile and he realized that she meant to leave with him whether he accepted it or not. He would have to hurt her, maybe kill her to be clean of it, and that seemed more than he could handle. And what had she said? *I won't fight it, if that's what you mean...* Hicks laughed, but now it was tainted with a nervousness that both of them heard. She put the suitcase down and reached out with both hands and found his crotch between them. She worked him through the denim.

"We can wait around for my mother to call the sheriff to come for you, or we can leave together and I can show you the quickest way off the farm." Her hands were moving faster and now it was Hicks that closed his eyes.

"Okay," he whispered and she stopped as soon as the words were out. He looked down into her upturned face. "Goddamn," he said. "What kind of ..."

"Stop," she said. "We need to go."

They came out on the front porch and Hicks pulled the door closed behind him. She stood waiting next to him. She carried her suitcase, which was covered in a pattern of Texas Blue Bonnets. He had the duffle's strap over his left shoulder and he carried the hunting rifle in his right hand. They stepped off the porch and went back up the row that led to the big house. Then they turned left off that path and followed another that went deeper into the corn and led to the fence line that bordered the Winslett property. Neither one spoke. When they got to the fence, they tossed their bags over it and he helped Renee climb the slats. When she was on the other side, he handed her the rifle without thinking about it and then climbed the fence. When he dropped to the other side, Renee was holding the gun and looking at him. He stood still and then she handed him the rifle and began walking to the road. He slung the duffle over his shoulder and started after her.

They walked in single file off the side of the road, following it toward Winchester. The sun was coming into the sky by the time they got to the town limits. They cut into the woods with a pre-dawn fog seeping through the trees, and stopped near a creek that was loud with running water and set their bags down and slept for an hour or so, and then she was pushing his shoulder to wake him up. He went to the creek and splashed water into his face while she waited behind him on the bank. When he was done, they went back to the road and followed it into Winchester. She waited beyond the tree line for him while he went into town to find a vehicle. He found an unattended truck on one of the side streets with the keys in the ignition. He started the engine and thought about leaving her there but decided against it and went back to where she was waiting. She climbed into the cab and he put the truck in gear and they headed east into the sunrise. Beams of shrewd light came through the windshield as they made their way toward the mountain and then they were climbing the grade, neither one speaking. The old truck slowed against the incline and then they crested the top and it sprang back to life. The top of the mountain was clear of the fog and a radiant blue colored the sky. Nothing on either side of the road indicated habitation. The wind coming through the open windows of the truck smelled clean and was slightly cold. Renee folded her arms in front of her chest while Hicks smoked and drove. They started down the other side of the mountain and then they were in the valley.

"Where are we going?" she asked.

"East," Hicks said.

Renee looked out the window and thought about her mother. She would know that she was gone, but she would not be thinking much about that. She would be thinking about Katherine and what she was going to tell her husband. But once Mary had taken care of that, she would put the pieces together: Hicks had left and so had Renee. She thought about the fights she had picked with her mother, begging for more freedom. The shrill, hateful screaming that had poured out of her. The accusations that Katherine was her favorite. That Katherine got all the attention.

Katherine. Katherine. Katherine!

Renee looked at the man driving beside her. He would never be what she had dreamed of. He would never be a wealthy man with distinction and status. But he was a man that did not ask for permission to do what he wanted. He had taken Katherine because he wanted to. Maybe she didn't deserve what happened, but then again, maybe she did. Maybe now she would not be so high and mighty and flit around like the princess everyone thought her to be. Maybe now people would talk about Renee instead of her being an afterthought, or just the little sister. Maybe now they would see that she was her own person and that she had ambitions beyond *goddamn* Taylor Branch and all its this and that. *East* was fine for now. *East* was at least far away and a new start. Going east, with this man, would mean that her mother would never forgive her. And wasn't that what she had really wanted, to make an enemy of her mother? Hadn't she given up seeking praise and validation a long time ago? Of course she had. And now that she had gone, under circumstances that she could never have imagined, she could will herself to accept the decisions that she had made and the opportunities that she had taken advantage of when they presented themselves. Hate, she knew, could be stronger than guilt. Guilt was something she had enabled in herself most of her life, recognizing that Katherine would always be more elegant and favored. Guilt is what she had swallowed by the gallon since she was a little girl, choking it down like a spoonful of red syrupy cough medicine and gagging on the wretched aftertaste that coated her tongue in a medicinal reminder that she had not risen to the expectation of Mary Winslett. Mary who walked on water and paraded her Latin and French around the kitchen like a show pony. Mary who was kind to niggers and spoke of them as if they were indeed actual equals. Mary whose goodnight kiss with Katherine always produced laughter and giggles, but whose goodnight kiss with Renee was perfunctory and almost cold. Mary, whose unwavering commitment to societal propriety often made Renee wonder whether she had been conceived through a sexual act or delivered in a buggy by the preacher. Renee sat looking at the road rolling out before them. Hicks had turned on the radio and was singing along to it. She looked across at him again and imagined looking up at him on top of her, thrusting all of her past from her mind with his animalistic bad breeding. She smiled and reached across the seat to take his free hand.

CHAPTER 11

KATHERINE

Katherine Winslett was in her bed, looking at the ceiling. Her body was numb and her thoughts gathered in charcoal-colored waves above her bed. Everything was frozen in an obscenely foreign state. She had been thrown from a horse when she was younger and it had broken her arm and bruised several of her ribs. She had been bedridden for a few days, stuck inside as she listened to the voices outside of her window, working and playing in the sunlight. This felt like that, but there was also a pressure of emptiness like being inside of a lightless cave, feeling along the damp walls with her fingertips, hearing only the random drip of water, the beating of her speeding heart, and the inhalation and exhalation of her harsh breathing that was forced by the absence of the sun and the impending threat of what she could not see. All she seemed able to project was a single event over and over, as if she had opened a picture book with each page containing only one evolution of an image, and that image changed and progressed as the book advanced until she reached the end and saw a completed depiction of her body beneath the tree.

She was alone in the room, although her mother and LoLo had been in and out throughout the night and into the morning. The last several times she heard someone coming down the hall, she had closed her eyes and tried to slow her breathing, pretending to be asleep. She had done that because the idea of talking with her mother about the images she was replaying in her head terrified her. She was certain that what had happened had not been her fault, but there was a voice somewhere inside of her that kept calling that into question. This voice was part of the obscene unfamiliarity because it was biting and angry and accusatory. This voice was profane and insistent and each time the imaginary book was reopened it would speak to her in short, saliva-filled bursts that worked their way out of a mouth framed with yellow, cracked teeth:

What have you done, Katherine...?
What have you done, Katherine...?
What will your mother say about this...?
What will your father say about this...?
What will your savior say about this...?
What will the devil say...?

She clenched her fists beneath the covers when a sharp pain seized her. She locked her jaws and fought off the urge to call out. The wash-cloth they had placed on her head was warm and heavy. She was dressed in a simple white gown that they had helped her into after they had cleaned her. Her mother had given LoLo the bundle of soiled clothes and instructed her to burn them.

She felt an urge to fold into herself, to make herself as small as she possibly could and to stay that way, squeezing her legs against her chest and tucking her head into her knees, squeezing harder and harder until she was a solid knot of flesh and bone. A knot that would not be undone by the ferocious arms that had grabbed her from behind, clamped a hand over her mouth, and dragged her out of the porch light and back into the shadow where they had forced her to twist and convulse and ultimately fall completely still. And the knife that had been wavering so close to her features and her vision that she could see its scratched history in the metal. Staring up from the ground, the sky had seemed so vast and unconcerned with her as though it were almost complicit in hiding the attack. And when it was over and he was pushing off her and moving away, her eyes did not follow his retreat but

71

instead remained fixed on the black canvas above her that then felt like a judgement she desperately wanted to understand and for which she wanted to atone.

"Katherine?" Her mother was standing in the door to her room. She stood straight and was holding a mug in her hand. The shades to the room had been drawn, but morning light was coming through them weakly, making the scene all the more surreal and uncomprehending knowing that the business of the farm had commenced outside and that her sense of normalcy would never again be the same, no matter how many times the sun rose. Her mother came across the room and sat on the bed beside her and motioned for her to sit up. She did, and Mary handed her the mug, which she now smelled was tea. She realized that her throat was painfully dry and she took the mug and sipped, wincing slightly at its heat. She handed it back to her mother who set it on the nightstand next to her bed.

"Mother," she said, and reached her hand out and Mary took it gently and kissed it and then set it in her lap.

"Katherine," Mary said. "I have called for Dr. Charles."

She looked up at her mother with panic.

Her mother squeezed her hand firmly. "I have called for Dr. Charles," she said again. "He will be here soon. We have to see how badly you may have been hurt." Katherine began to cry softly. Her mother sat quietly and waited.

"I feel so ashamed," Katherine said. "I don't understand. I don't know what I did. I don't know why..." Mary reached out and gently took Katherine's chin in her hands and looked at her with what she hoped would convey strength.

"You did nothing wrong," she said and held her daughter's gaze. "You did nothing and you must understand that. You must understand that what happened was as senseless and evil an act as there is, and that sometimes terrible, unspeakable things happen to people who neither deserve them, nor will ever understand why they were made to endure them." Katherine had assumed a look that indicated she comprehended but had no faith in the vague reasoning.

"I have spoken to LoLo and Edgar," Mary said. "They have been told not to speak about this to anyone. Your father will be home the day after tomorrow. I have not decided how to handle that, but I will.

For now," she picked up Katherine's hand and placed it against her own chest, "we need to make sure that you are not seriously injured and Dr. Charles will take care of that. Do you understand?" Katherine nodded.

"Okay," Mary said and leaned over to kiss Katherine on her forehead.

"Drink the tea," she said as she stood up, "and then get some rest."

"Mother," Katherine said, sitting up slightly. Mary stopped and turned around to face her.

"Yes."

"I'm sorry."

"No," Mary said and almost crossed the room, back to the bed, but she stopped and stiffened in the doorway, torn between her anger and her own need to apologize. "You have nothing to be sorry for."

She was turning to leave when Katherine spoke again, this time hesitantly. "Where's Renee?"

Mary looked cautiously at Katherine and tried to keep her voice even. "Sleep now," she said. "We'll talk after Dr. Charles has seen you."

She went out and down the hall and into the quiet kitchen where she sat estranged from the familiar items and smells that clung there.

CHAPTER 12

MARY

D ennis Winslett did not return home as expected. Instead, he called from across the state and told his wife that the governor had recruited him to serve on a regional agricultural commission based out of the state capital. Mary tried to keep her voice measured and calm as he gave direction on who was to be in charge of the farm operations, leaving instructions on what needed to be packed and delivered to him in terms of clothing and other essentials. Mary said that she understood and that she was proud of her husband and that she would have his things packed up and delivered immediately. In their many years of marriage, she had kept very little from her husband. He was a considerate man and very rarely lost his temper with her. But she realized that what had happened with Katherine and Renee's disappearance would be his undoing. She knew this in her heart, and while she realized that she would be unable to keep these things from him forever, she could control it for the time being.

Dr. Charles had been to the house the previous day and tended to Katherine. He had not been more than a minute into examining the girl when he sat back on the footstool he had placed beside the bed and taken off his glasses and looked at Mary with disbelief and horror. He said nothing, reading Mary's knowing expression, and went back to examining the girl with as much delicacy as his old shaking hands could manage. Despite the protests he raised with her standing outside of the bedroom door, Mary would not let him call the sheriff and made him swear that he would not contact her husband. As he left, Mary watched his car head down the long farm road and out through the front gate. She considered her decision over and over in her head, flipping it up and down like an hourglass, letting the sand run through until one side was empty, then turning it back over and going through the exercise again. Time, she believed, would likely get them through this, as it did most things. Having grown up on a neighboring farm and being privy to dinner table conversations with her severe, but kind parents, she understood that all living things moved in overlapping cycles, and that to allow the tailwinds they threw off to sway your mind and your assertiveness in any one direction was to have learned nothing of the repetitive lessons that the passage of years and generations taught.

That afternoon Mary found Edgar at the hog pens and she told him that she wanted to speak with him after supper. She spent the rest of the day packing suitcases for her husband and tidying things around the house. LoLo moved about the rooms silently and Mary worried that her decision was poorly chosen each time the woman's eyes met hers. It was not a critical exchange of glance, but the way that LoLo diverted her eyes too quickly gave Mary a sinking sensation that made her want to ask her what she would do if the decision was hers. Mary's upbringing had been as pragmatic as it was cultured, so she looked to facts when challenged. They had let a man like Hicks onto the place. Logic told her that he had raped Katherine, although she could not prove it. Her daughter Renee had left with him, although she could not prove that either. Katherine was alive, and while traumatized, Mary believed that she could guide her back to health. If it got out that Katherine had been raped by a man that Renee had run off with, the impact to the family and its reputation would be devastating. And when she imagined her husband's reaction to any of this, she felt as helpless as someone looking out over an arid field, begging the merciless, baking sky for relief. *Katherine will recover,* she told herself. *She has enough of me in her that she'll find her way through.*

Renee, she thought. The decision there was even more complicated than the first. She stood in the foyer of the house and looked up the stairs to where the girls' rooms were. Renee had tested them from the day she was born. It was as if her mind was a furnace that constantly threatened explosion. As a young girl she could not be content and she could not be disciplined with any lasting result. She hated school. She hated the church. She hated the farm. Her mind as of late was hyperbolic and oversexed in ways that Mary could not understand, nor did she want to. *Still*, she thought, placing a hand on the bannister, *still she is my daughter*, and her disappearance was not something that she could hide or explain for any true length of time. Her husband's appointment to the commission would keep him away and preoccupied, and she could write to him rather than call and explain that Renee had left with one of the hands and that Mary had no idea where they had gone. And when he called in a rage, she would tell him that if he really considered things, they knew something like this might happen and after a while, Renee would tire of poverty and the realization that her fantasies were just that. She would come home beaten and lost and they could begin rebuilding her then. This explanation, she knew, would be very weak against her husband's impatience and intensity, both of which could have Hicks found and likely dead within the week. Perhaps it would come to that, she thought, but considering that Dr. Charles now knew and so did LoLo and Edgar, and if Hicks ended up dead—wherever the two of them were—there would certainly be an investigation and that investigation could end up at her front door. Despite all of his influence, which reached as high as the governor's office, there was always the possibility that Dennis could be charged with murder, Katherine raped or not. And just then, looking up into the half-light of the stairwell, she was not ready to lose her husband to Renee's betrayal.

That evening, Katherine took dinner in her room. She was able to be up and around but was unsure of herself on the stairs and Mary had told her that staying in bed was fine for now. LoLo put a meal of meat loaf, green beans, and mashed potatoes on a tray and took it up to Katherine's bedside. Mary sat at the kitchen table and ate. She turned when LoLo came back in the kitchen, and Mary gestured for her to sit. LoLo poured herself a glass of water and came and sat down. Her kind face made Mary want to weep. It was full of emotion and a sensible wisdom that was written in the lines around her eyes, which were a rich brown and deeply haunted in contrast to the soft nature of her other features. Mary set her fork down.

"LoLo," she said. LoLo looked at her.

"LoLo, I'm going to ask Edgar to take Levi and try to find where Renee went." LoLo looked back at Mary, touched her water glass.

"She went with that man Hicks," she said.

"Yes," Mary said.

"That man," LoLo said. "That man will kill them boys. Renee couldn't stop him if she had a mind to."

"I know," Mary said. "I don't want them to try and bring anyone back. I just want to know where they are." She started to pick up her fork and set it back down again.

"I just want to know where they are," she said and reached across the table for LoLo's hand. The black woman took it and held it.

"Miss Renee," LoLo said. "She don't want to be found. Not now anyhow."

"I know."

"Why you want to send Edgar then?"

"Because I have to know where she is. I'm her mother."

"And Edgar is my child," LoLo said.

"Yes."

"I'll go find her," LoLo said quietly. Mary looked at their clasped hands on the table, and took a deep breath, almost as if she had expected this offer to come.

"I can't ask you to do that," she said.

"You ain't asked me to do anything, Miss Mary."

"I meant I would never ask you to do that."

LoLo nodded her head. "No," LoLo said. "I can't let Edgar and that boy Levi go after that man. They find him and he'll butcher them like hogs. He's been touched by something dark. I seen it in his eyes and the way they studied things like a bird would do, watching a field. You can't send them boys out there after him, Miss Mary." She dropped her eyes, recognizing how overtly defiant she was being. Mary looked at her and then lightly shook her hand.

"Miss Mary," LoLo said, still looking down.

"Yes."

"We got to wait anyhow."

"What do you mean?"

"Miss Katherine," LoLo said. "Wait to see…"

"What?" Mary interrupted. "Wait to see what, LoLo?" she asked in a louder voice. LoLo looked up at the woman whom she had known most of her life. Her posture sunk in the chair.

"What then," Mary said again and then she stopped, looking across the table at LoLo who waited patiently for her to draw the conclusion on her own. Mary withdrew her hand quickly and placed a fist to her mouth.

"My God," she breathed.

CHAPTER 13

EDGAR

I went up to the big house to see Miss Mary like she had asked, but she sent me away at the door and I walked back to our house and sat in the front room and read from one of the books that we kept in an old trunk on the floor by the stove. My mother came in. She looked tired and her hands played with her apron strings. She sat down in the little brown chair across from where I sat and asked me if I knew where Hicks had come from. I told her that I didn't know. She asked me to think hard and I told her the first time that I saw the man we were in front of the filling station in Winchester. She asked who he had worked with while he was on the farm and I told her nobody really. She looked at me again and then she asked me to see if I could find out anything from any of the other people working there on the farm. I told her I would and then she went into her room where her bed was and I laid awake a long time thinking about that night.

I could see Miss Katherine on the ground and I could feel those eyes looking at me from down near the corn stalks and I got up from my bed and went to look out the window. I saw a few of the men outside across the way. They had a fire going in a barrel and I heard Levi picking at his guitar and some of the men were clapping and laughing and I saw that they were passing a bottle around. I put on some pants and a shirt and walked out onto our small porch. The house where Hicks had been was still empty and I knew that no one was in it but I felt something grip me when I looked into the black windows and at the chair next to the door where he sometimes sat and smoked, not saying anything to people who passed, but always looking in that way he had. I stepped off our porch and walked over to where the men were sitting and I sat down on one of the steps and listened to them talking about different things. I waited till they got quiet and then I asked if anyone knew where that man Hicks had gone too. They all looked at me and one of them asked what I wanted with Hicks. I told them I just wanted to know and then all of them said they did not know where he had come from, but they were glad he was gone. I nodded and Levi started to pick at the strings, never looking at me, asking these questions, and then he stopped and thumped the guitar and put it down. Then a man named Joshua who was sitting off toward the far side of the porch said that Hicks told him that he had been in Alabama before he came here. I asked him how he knew that and he said that he and Hicks were working together just before he left and they had gotten into a fight and Hicks told him that niggers in Alabama would never talk back to a white man the way that he did. And Joshua asked Hicks how he knew anything about Alabama, and Hicks told him that he'd come up from outside of Tyre and that niggers there still knew their place.

I sat a while longer and then went back across to our house. I tried to open the door quietly, but it creaked and I heard Mamma stir in the back and she called out to see if it was me and I said it was. Then she wanted to know if I'd been out there drinking with them and that I knew better than that. I asked if I could come into her room and she told me yes so I stepped into her doorway and I saw that she had been asleep because she had to squint her eyes from the light coming in from behind me. I told her that I might know where that man Hicks had gone and she sat up in the bed and part of her was in the dark and she asked me how I knew. And I told her about what Joshua had said about *Alabama* and asked her why she wanted to know about Hicks and was she planning on going where he was. She sat there being quiet and I could hear the men getting louder in the yard outside. Then she looked up at me and it was hard to see her face, but I knew from her voice that it was set in that way I knew from being a child in her house. She told me that likely she would have to go away for a while and that I would need to stay behind in Taylor Branch. I asked her why and she told me that I did not need to worry about that. Then she lay down and I went back to my bed and turned off the light in the house and that feeling that I had when I looked at the porch where Hicks used to sit started to crawl over me from beneath the sheets and it was cold and creeped up the inside of my legs and then over my private parts and then it was crawling over my chest and around my neck and I closed my mouth to keep it from crawling inside of me. I did not blink and held my breath till I thought that my lungs would rip open and when I finally let it out, the thing washed over my face and then it lay atop me like I had pulled the thin white sheet over my head and I wanted to call for Mamma, but I did not because I wanted to hold the fear of Hicks myself and not poison her with it the way he had poisoned Miss Katherine and would go on poisoning anything he could until he had laid it all to waste in his path.

CHAPTER 14

MARY

Mary made several trips to the state capital to visit her husband. She lied about the girls' welfare, making up stories about why he had missed them on the phone. Once or twice he had spoken directly with Katherine, but the conversations were brief and of little substance. He wanted mainly to speak with Mary and the farm superintendent about the crops, their potential yields, and the weather. Mary would stand out of sight while the farm superintendent walked Mr. Winslett through the farm operations. She did not believe that anything family-related would come up in their conversation, but she wanted to be prepared in the event that it did. The deception bothered her on many levels. She and Dennis did not harbor secrets. There were of course aspects of the business and finances that he kept to himself, but his motivations and planning were things that he shared willingly with his wife, always valuing her opinion and honest perspective. As for the raising of their children, that was a shared responsibility, and while he was somewhat lost when it came to intuition with young women, he was not willing to be absent in their nurturing and education. Hiding Renee's behavior and actions felt like a fundamental disloyalty that when discovered would not only destroy his relationship with his daughter but threaten to harm the confidence and trust that sustained their marriage. And so, while standing outside the office, listening to the superintendent's recitation of mundane facts and figures, Mary Winslett found herself holding her breath.

After three months and several short trips back to the farm which Mary could easily plan for, Dennis called to say that he would need more time with the commission before returning home, and that the Governor had asked if he would stay on to help him push some additional agricultural agenda items through the legislature, one of which was a delegation to South America to discuss commodity exchanges between the United States and their neighbors to the south. He offered to come home, but Mary told him that she would be fine, and that she might take the girls and LoLo to the retreat cottage they had on the mountain and spend some time there now that summer had arrived. When she hung up the phone, she called LoLo into the kitchen and told her that it was time. They spent the afternoon packing the car and then had an early supper in the kitchen together as they had been doing ever since the night they had discussed LoLo leaving to track down Hicks. The next morning they rose early and, making sure that they had everything they needed, they brought Katherine down from her room and settled her in the back of the car with pillows and quilts from the upstairs hall closet. Mary spoke briefly with the superintendent and then got in behind the wheel and the three of them drove out of the farm and onto the road that led to Winchester and then on to the mountain.

Edgar watched them leave. His face was heavy and sweating. Behind him was the big house and the outdoor tables where they took their meals in good weather. He looked small in comparison to the landscape. He saw his mother's head in the passenger seat and Miss Mary's head driving the car, neither one moving or turning to face the other. A breeze came up through the fields and it was cool on his face and he spoke quietly to himself, praying for their safe keeping. He stood that way until the car was gone and then one of the other men called to him and he turned and walked back toward the barn, whose large opening seemed to swallow everything that entered it.

Mary and LoLo drove up the mountain road, tree-lined and dense to the point of being abstract, like a glob of thick green paint being spread over a dark brown canvas. LoLo looked out the window while

Mary drove. Katherine slept in the back. They came to the top of the mountain road and Mary steered the car down a battered two-lane to the little vacation community called Stoney Mount where her family had owned a house for many years. The cottages, mostly Tudor and craftsmen architecture with the occasional colonial bulwarked by wide, gleaming white wrap-around porches, lined a small maze of simple streets. Tree canopies cast large shadows over all that stood or moved beneath. They arrived at their cottage, an unassuming single story with white siding, and a large front porch that offered a cool shelter from the sun in the hottest parts of the day. The yard was dense with trees and the wispy mountain grass, intertwined with tall wild onion shoots, was littered with rotting leaves that needed to be raked and burned. The foundation of the house was raised on piers and the open, dark space between the porch and the ground was covered by lattice work to keep animals out. The two women helped Katherine inside and settled her in an ornate guest bedroom on the front side that was decorated as if it were never meant to be used by anyone or anything other than a child's doll. The bed that they placed her in had a brass frame that needed a polish. The dust ruffle was an ancient lace pattern that had suffered dry rot, and LoLo noticed it right away and called it to Mary's attention. They went back outside and took the suitcases from the trunk and brought them into the house, thumping their weight against the porch steps as they climbed. Then Mary left to go to the small market to stock the pantry and to call her husband to let him know that they had arrived, leaving LoLo to begin cleaning the house for their stay.

LoLo moved the broom across the floor, feeling its worn, smooth handle in her calloused hands. She had been to the house many times in her life, and each time she entered, its history and heritage rose up as she approached and the large front porch seemed to open like the lower jaw of something vicious and hungry, and she would climb the steps with a determined reticence that had served her well ever since she was a child. Its smell and the way that natural light fell into the room played on her senses, and at times she believed that she could see the shadows of previous inhabitants moving through the low-ceilinged spaces, their loud and authoritative voices booming and laughing, reckless and one low-ball sip away from lashing out at a quiet Negro carrying a tray of drinks or possibly carrying in a load of firewood. She swept and listened for Katherine, who was sleeping in the other room.

Mary returned and LoLo walked outside to help her bring the groceries into the house. The two women worked side by side in the kitchen, opening and closing cabinets and the pantry door. LoLo hummed to herself quietly and Mary smiled, appreciating the simple, but strong character of the woman and her understated perseverance. She closed one of the doors and turned.

"LoLo?"

"Yes mam," LoLo said, not looking at Mary. Mary paused and it lasted long enough that LoLo stopped what she was doing and looked across the kitchen.

"What is it, Miss Mary?"

"I just wanted," she was trying not to cry, "I just wanted to say 'thank you' is all." She turned away quickly and wiped at her eyes. LoLo came across the kitchen floor and stood next to her. She reached out and touched her shoulder and gently spun Mary around to face her. Mary's tears began to appear and LoLo took her head in her hands and held it the way one might pick up an expensive piece of china.

"Miss Mary," she said, "there's no need to thank me. I love that girl like she was my own. I helped raise her. Ain't nothing we could have done. Ain't no way we could have known about him." Mary roughly pushed the heel of her hands into her eyes and let out a rush of air.

"I know that," she said. "I know that, but it does not really help, does it? All this lying and sneaking around. And Renee gone. Gone with that man who raped her sister. And Dennis. God, poor Dennis. He knows nothing about this and here we are thinking we are going to take care of this ourselves and I don't really even know where to start. Suppose we do find them, LoLo. Suppose we do. What then?" LoLo looked at Mary with sympathy and a slight hint of admonishment.

"What do we do?" she said. "Miss Mary, we do what we planned back in Taylor Branch. We make him take back what he left here."

"And Renee," Mary said. "What about Renee?"

"Don't know," LoLo said. "She has always been one to leave, I suspect. She knows what she's done is wrong and against God, but she made up her mind and I don't think it's for you or me to say whether or not she has to come back. She can't see what it is that she's done…

maybe she don't need to come back." Mary looked at her, the pain of it all coming over her face in red color and lines that cut across her forehead.

"Oh, goddamn this," Mary said. "How could I have been so stupid? How could I let this get so far out of my control? How did I not see what should have been right in front of my face!" She stepped away from LoLo and started toward the door that led out of the kitchen and onto the porch, when Katherine called out in the back room. She stopped and then they heard the girl retching. Mary turned and walked quickly out of the kitchen toward the bedroom. LoLo went to the sink and picked up a clean wash rag and reached to a shelf above and took down a bowl and filled it with warm water.

That summer on the mountain was very hot, and despite the evening breezes that came through the open windows the nights were thick with humidity. Flies buzzed through the rooms, fat and black, and LoLo often sat next to Katherine's bed and fanned them away. The girl's morning sickness would often drag into the mid-afternoon and her cheerful nature had been replaced by an indifference that showed no sign of abating. Sometimes Mary would force her out onto the porch to be in the daylight, and she would abide for an hour and would then stand up quietly and retreat back into the dark rooms of the house, leaving Mary and LoLo without saying a word. The two women would sit and look out over the porch railing into the small little street, patterned with shadows and pine needles and small grey rocks that the neighborhood boys were fond of scooping up and throwing at trees, aiming at their trunks, scooping and pitching the stones again and again until a mother or neighboring parent told them to stop and they would drop what they had in their hands onto the road and they would be moving again, their little boy arms flapping and whirring as they pretended to be fighter jets, comic book heroes, race cars or anything else that was driving their vivid imaginations. Mary and LoLo would watch the children and let their minds drift back to days when Katherine and Renee had been among the small marauding bands roaming the mountaintop, cobbling together made-up games to fill a summer day. And when they were older, they would gather at the pool and they would interact in a way that seemed cool and aloof on the surface, but was really a thin sheen of wanton awareness that was coming up inside all of them, their first experiences with sexual indigestion.

But that had been manageable and, if objectively considered, natural, and it never gave way to the grave-cold grip of something so hideous as assault or the soulless greed of rape, which unto itself must have awakened and presented its rationale as natural and necessary to its perpetrator, but was in reality an act with no sustained satisfaction, but only a need to inflict pain and exploit vulnerability for no other reason than the shaming and humiliation of the innocent. Mary and LoLo knew what Katherine could not and should not have been made to know—that the burden of her victimhood, the circumstances under which she found herself bruised and bleeding on the ground in the farmyard with twigs in her hair and the taste of soil in her mouth, were not enough truth to warrant the accusation against a white man who had left in the same automobile as her sister. That accusation would only collapse under the counterweight which would ultimately suffocate and defile them with the permanence of spilled wine on white linen.

Over the course of the summer, Mary made several trips back to Taylor Branch. On one trip in mid-July she learned that her husband had come through for a night and she held her breath while Edgar told her that he had considered sneaking up to the mountain house to surprise them, but had decided against it at the last minute. He had gone back to the commission the next day. He left behind a note that Edgar said was sitting on the dining room table. Mary went into the house alone, feeling the sweat running beneath her blouse. She found the note where Edgar said it would be. She read it with fear rising in her throat.

Mary,
I miss you and the girls terribly. The commission has kept me
extremely busy, but I do believe that it will pay off in the lon-
g-term. I wanted to come up to the mountain house to be with
you, Katherine, and Renee, but I have to leave tomorrow. We are
going to South America with a commodities delegation to see if we
can improve economic conditions for our regional agriculture. I'm
not completely sold on the idea, but I am working with some fine
people and I think the experience will be a good one. I will see you

when I return. We should be gone for about six weeks, then I'm back to Washington to produce a report and then I will be home with all of you. Thank you for doing such a good job with the place. I will write to you and the girls.

Love,
Dennis

Mary put the note down and cried from both relief and the honesty of the letter. It was the first time since arriving at Stoney Mount that she had permitted herself to openly weep. She loved her husband and realized how strongly she missed him and the reassurance that he provided simply by being in the same room. She would tell him everything in time, she promised herself. Mary checked on a number of things around the farm and spoke with Edgar about LoLo and Katherine, telling him that things were fine and that they hoped to be back as soon as possible. Edgar asked about Hicks and Mary reached out and took his hand. "I won't let anything happen to your mother, Edgar," she said. Edgar had tried to offer a look of confidence, but knowing it was impossible, he gave Mary a quick nod and went away in the other direction, shoulders slumped and head hanging.

She packed some items in the car: Katherine's bedside radio, some clothes from her closet, a typewriter, and several bottles of pills from her own medicine cabinet. She was getting ready to make the trip back when she stopped and returned to the house. She went into her husband's study and found the key to the gun safe in one of the open shelves of the roll top desk. She unlocked the safe and removed a shotgun and a box of shells. She locked the safe back, took a blanket from the back of one of the wingback chairs to drape over the gun, and then she returned to the car and left. When she arrived back at the cottage, there was a strange automobile in the small brick-paved driveway. Mary's pulse ticked-up. She pulled the car off the side of the road, and as she was getting out, she saw LoLo come out the front door followed by a tall man in a tan suit. He was carrying a bag with him and he stopped on the first step down and spoke to LoLo, who was still almost a full head shorter than he was. The man motioned at the window to Katherine's room and LoLo nodded her head to indicate that she understood. Mary climbed quickly back in her open door and eased it shut, ducking below the steering column. The man came down the steps and climbed into his car. Mary heard the engine start. A minute later she eased her head up to make sure the car had moved completely out of sight. She opened her door and came up the walk to the house. LoLo was still on the front porch, her arms folded in front of her chest, looking down the street in the direction that the man had gone.

"LoLo," Mary called coming toward the house. "Who was that?" LoLo looked down at Mary and her face was both surprised and pained. Mary came up the steps and stood where the man in the tan suit had been standing.

"It's Katherine, Miss Mary. She got real sick while you were gone. I thought I could take care of her, but she couldn't stop getting sick and she got so pale and couldn't stand at all."

"Who was here, LoLo? Who was that man on the porch?"

"Doctor, Miss Mary," LoLo said, looking sheepishly at the ground. She pointed at the neighboring house. "Woman over there who cooks for the Turners, she let me use their phone to call for him."

"A doctor?" Mary said, trying to remember the Turners.

"Yes mam," LoLo said. "I went next door and used their phone. They had the name of a doctor up here on the mountain. That woman said I could use their phone if we needed some help. He came here about an hour ago. He says Miss Katherine, she's gonna have the baby soon."

Mary climbed the steps and went into the house. LoLo remained on the porch. Inside the rooms were bathed in rambling shadows that moved across the wooden floors and over the furniture in dark, shapeless forms. Mary stood in the small entry hall and listened, expecting to hear her oldest daughter's audible suffering in the front bedroom. She thought again about the weight that she had taken upon herself and the pressure that she was putting on LoLo and Edgar, and the precarious nature of the truth leaking out and making determined strides back to her husband. She felt faint and steadied herself on a bulky hutch that had been placed inside the front doorway many years before, its wood grain patterned with age and an almost pliable texture from decades of unconditioned air. Something hollow and nauseating blossomed low in her stomach and she had to stand and wait until it passed. When it did, she walked with purpose into the main room and turned to stand outside the door of the bedroom. Katherine lay in the bed, her knees tucked against her growing stomach and her head bent to meet them, a posture she recognized from when the girl was little and sick with a stomach virus, or the time that she had suffered mononucleosis and had been bedridden for six weeks during her fifth-grade school year. Her hair piled in front of her face like a dam of debris, thick curls twisted and matted in a careless fashion that would have otherwise horrified her.

Mary felt the water welling in her eyes and she fought back the urge to scream in protest, but let the tears come until her cheeks were wet. Katherine did not move and took no notice and Mary wondered if she was asleep or simply racked with shame and the mounting depression. *Even the strength I imposed will never let her move beyond this,* Mary thought. *My insistence for composure might as well have crippled her. I have sown ruin into her and never realized what I was doing. Never realized what I was demanding. And now I have not lost one daughter, but two.* LoLo came in and stood behind Mary. The two women whose relationship was based on a mutual need and trust in one another, looking over the child that they had both cared for since she was an infant sitting on one of the front room rugs in the farmhouse, toppling over and laughing in her good-natured and careless way. LoLo touched Mary's shoulder and let her hand rest there. She reached up and placed her hand atop LoLo's and then turned and spoke over her shoulder.

"I will go back to Taylor Branch and get Edgar to come and watch her while we are gone," she said. "We'll leave instructions on what to do if she turns for the worse again." LoLo nodded and stepped back away from the bedroom door.

"The doctor," Mary said, "What did he say, specifically?"

"That she was real sick, Miss Mary. That he thought the sooner the baby was delivered , the better Miss Katherine would be. He asked about Mr. Dennis and I told him he was away and that we were…"

"He knew Dennis?" Mary asked.

"No mam," LoLo said. "He asked if her parents were here in Stoney Mount and I told him that you were here with me and that her father was away on business."

Mary nodded

"All right," she said. "That's fine. I'll go and get Edgar. You stay here with Katherine and tomorrow morning we'll go find…" she tapered off and looked back through the open bedroom door at her daughter. "We'll go find Renee and that man."

"Hicks," LoLo said.

"Hicks," Mary said, and walked past LoLo and went to her bedroom to gather her thoughts and courage.

It was late when Mary returned with Edgar. The young man came into the house with the shotgun cradled in his arms. Mary followed him, her expression showing the fatigue and anxiety of all that she had undertaken and had yet to undertake. LoLo met them in the front room and placed a finger to her lips to let them know that Katherine was sleeping. She took the gun from Edgar and placed it on the dining table and then she hugged him. His face was taut and his eyes moved around the room, trying to take everything in and process it. LoLo stepped back from Edgar then reached out and took his shoulders and looked up into his face. She smiled warmly and he smiled back at her, the smile uncharacteristic from his usual wide grin, which was more trusting. Mary observed them and allowed herself a brief moment of emotional warmth. They had been a part of her family in a way that had always been a source of peace, their presence an affirmation of a mutual, selfless respect and admiration for one another. LoLo had made a bed for Edgar on one of the sofas in the living room. She took him to it and he sat down and she sat down next to him and they spoke to one another in hushed tones. Mary said goodnight and went into one of the back bedrooms. LoLo kissed her son on the top of his head and went in to check on Katherine one last time before going to bed herself. She had built a pallet in the girl's room when she had gotten sick the last time so that she could be near her if she woke in the night. Mary had insisted on staying in the room, but LoLo had firmly pushed back, telling her that she needed her strength and rest. With all four in bed, a stillness fell over the house. Mary, LoLo, and Edgar lay awake in their beds, looking up into the darkness of the ceiling and feeling the clock in the front room, not hearing its normally calming and soothing rhythm but now its ominous, methodic countdown toward a finality for which none of them felt adequately prepared. Each eventually drifted into sleep only to confront their respective dreams that moved through their unconscious minds with an unsettling, almost kaleidoscope perspective that blurred menacing shapes from the corner of rooms and pushed forth, in stark colorations, indistinguishable figures that moved with menace and a persistence that lacked mercy and dismissed with comic curiosity the pleas that seeped from their sleeping lips and twitching bodies.

Mary woke the next morning to the smell of breakfast. She got out of bed, dressed, and came into the front room to find LoLo feeding Edgar bacon and eggs. The young man sat by himself at the table and LoLo was talking to him about caring for Katherine. Mary stopped outside the doorway of her bedroom and listened.

"We ain't gonna be gone long, you hear?"

"Yes mam."

"All you have to do is keep an eye on her, make sure her fever don't get too high. If she needs to get sick, you help her. And clean up after. There are some books in her room and some out here in the main room. You could read to her if she likes. If she feels up to it, take her out on the front porch and let her get some air. I know you're scared, Edgar, but this ain't nothing you never seen before. You know Miss Katherine and she knows you. Just ask her what she needs and she'll tell you. Me and Miss Mary will be back as soon as we find out where they are, and when we do, we'll come back and then we can all go home again." She paused. "You're a good son, Edgar."

"Indeed you are," Mary said, coming into the kitchen, touching Edgar's shoulder as she went past. "And I'll never forget what you are doing for me and for Katherine."

"Want a plate, Miss Mary?" LoLo said, her back to them.

"Yes, LoLo," she said, sitting down next to Edgar. "That would be nice." LoLo spooned some eggs onto a plate and placed two strips of bacon alongside. She brought the meal to the table and set it down and Mary reached out and grabbed her wrist, reaching with the other hand to take Edgar's. She bowed her head and closed her eyes, speaking silently to God and asking for his strength. She held them that way for a full minute then she released and LoLo smiled down at the two of them sitting at the table. Then Mary began to eat, steam coming off the eggs as she moved them around with her fork. Edgar continued looking at his mother, who nodded at him to finish his breakfast.

When they were through, Edgar took the dishes to the sink and began to clean up. LoLo had packed some sandwiches for the day, and a Thermos of coffee. She put everything into a basket that was in the pantry and took it to the car. As she came back in the house, she saw Mary at the table loading the shotgun, her hands expertly placing the cartridges into the loading port. LoLo stood still until Mary looked up.

"In case," Mary said, and laid the gun back on the table, checking the safety. Edgar came in from outside where he had wandered trying to shake off nervous energy. He came back into the kitchen and was about to say something when he too noticed the shotgun. He looked at his mother.

"Edgar," LoLo said. "You know what you need to do while we're gone, right?"

"Yes mam," he said.

"Most likely we ain't ever gonna need that gun."

"Yes mam," he said, his voice tight and low.

"Okay," Mary said and stood up. She picked the shotgun off the table and covered it with the blanket that she had placed in the chair beside her. She wrapped the gun and walked across the room to where Edgar stood. She stopped in front of him.

"We'll be back tonight," she said, and went out. LoLo turned and went to her son, touched the top of his head, and went out the door and down the steps to the car, which Mary had started, sitting upright with both hands on the wheel.

The car meandered out of Stoney Mount and turned onto the mountain road that led east into the long valley. From there they would turn south toward Tyre. They rode with the windows partially down, the warm air filling the car, almost making them drowsy. As they crossed over the state line, LoLo let out a breath of air and Mary looked across the seat at her.

"Alabama," LoLo said and Mary nodded, understanding without explanation. The land was familiar to both of them, but it had a desolation about it despite the trees and sloping topography. The stillness of the empty fields and the windless branches almost suggested a slow decay had settled in. They rode for several miles without speaking, taking in the landscape with preoccupied glances out the window and through the windshield which was a harsh yellow as they advanced into the rising sun.

"You remember that man that used to work on the farm named Kitch?" LoLo said above the highway sound.

"I think so," Mary said, her eyes fixed on the road. She was pushing the car harder than her husband would have allowed. LoLo paused and looked out the window.

"He came down this way after he left working on the farm," LoLo said. "He was always in a bottle, Kitch. That's why he was sent off the farm. He fought too. Pulled a razor on some boy in the yard one afternoon, liked to have cut that man to ribbons if they hadn't pulled him off. Had eyes like hot iron. Just trouble and meanness like young men can be when they don't have no one to look up to. Anger boiling out of them like a covered pot of water. I heard he came down here looking for work after he left Taylor Branch. Went to Winchester first but he couldn't find anything there. I suspect people knew about him before he got there. He left and came down here and found a job on another farm. He went into a store one day and I hear that he got to smarting off with the owner's son about something or other. Whole group of white men sitting there in the store when he done it. I can see him in there talking big and not knowing his place, see it just like I can see you sitting there now. Never would back down, that man." LoLo told the story as if re-living it, her head turned to look out the window, contemplative in her recounting.

"They came and got him one night, Miss Mary. Came to where he was staying and dragged him out in the front yard and hanged him right there. Time it got back to Taylor Branch, men in the yard says they left him hanging in that tree for two days before the sheriff came and cut him down. Buried him behind the house where he was staying."

Mary drove in silence.

"That was Edgar's father, Miss Mary." Mary's face clouded over and she stretched her fingers and regripped the wheel. The air in the car grew hotter and something chemical filled her nostrils.

"I had no idea," Mary said. "My God."

"Yes mam," LoLo said, the vision of the man swinging from the tree limb swarming over them both. "Weren't no God involved in that, though," she said. "Kitch, see he knew one day he would step over a line that they would never let him come back 'cross. He knew and he never did care. See, I think maybe he needed to go out like that. What's that word…peculiar. That's it. Only way to pin a name on it. Ain't a case of want or don't want, case of need and have to and supposed to. Kitch. I can see him in the yard, bigger than life. His head was up near the top of a horse's head. Had shoulders like a bull's and hands that could break bricks. All that strength and he never was gonna beat any white man. Never was gonna prove nothing to nobody. Me and Kitch, we had messed around a couple of times and when he left, I was pretty far along with Edgar." Her voice softened, speaking of her son. Mary watched the road, embarrassed that she had given no thought to the fact that LoLo's child had no father, even though it had been obvious that there was no husband. She wondered now why she had never bothered to ask, and she was ashamed, considering the depth of loyalty that LoLo had shown for their family.

"Why are you telling me this?" Mary asked, trying to keep her voice even. LoLo worked her hands in her lap and then turned and looked across the seat.

"Cause I know that you can't understand why Miss Renee run off with someone like this man Hicks," she said. "Why someone you know and love could do something like this even though they know that it's wrong and hurtful to everyone that ever cared about them. And cause sometimes, men like Kitch and Hicks have to go back to where they came from—before they can stop hurting. Taken back to where they are supposed to be."

"And where is that, LoLo? Where is it that they are supposed to be."

"Hell, I guess."

Mary suddenly felt acutely callow. The sheltered nature of her upbringing and the innocence that had guided her early years came rushing back at her along with the intense, full understanding of the recent events and their potential and real consequences. She pushed aside a strong impulse to pull the car over and get out so that she might walk into one of the vacant fields and wander for as long as it took to get her head straight, the ploughed rows and broken stalks crunching beneath her shoes and the sky growing broader in a hazed-over blue that made you wonder if what you had now was all you ever would. She thought of the plaintive conversations with God as a small child, kneeling on the floor of her bedroom, arms propped on the soft bedspread, knees beneath her cotton nightgown feeling the bite of the hard floor, speaking rehearsed prayers that contained a list of people to be blessed and the arbitrary, sweet addition that she would often throw into the end of the recitation, always derived from an incident that day or from a previous encounter at school or a sick animal that was more companion than pet.

"And Renee," Mary said, her breath raspy and choked.

"Miss Renee? What you mean?"

"Is she ruined too?" LoLo looked through the windshield.

"Can't say," she answered. "But she has been touched by it and it may be hard for her to let it go now that she crossed."

"You did," Mary said with a sharp note in her voice.

"Yes and maybe no," LoLo said. "I had Edgar. He was something good came of it all."

"And if you'd gone with Kitch. If you had followed like Renee?"

LoLo looked back out the passenger window and did not answer. She was realizing the similarities in her story about Kitch and the events that were taking place now, a realization that a child was at the center of both things: one which had been loved and cared for by a community of people who were inclined to share hardships and a second child who they would abandon willingly to a man who knew nor understood anything about compassion and whose own life had likewise been predetermined and robbed of any kindness. LoLo did not know if Mary had made this same connection yet. Probably she had. But over the past months, they had silently agreed that any discussion that sought depth on this circumstance was best left unsaid.

CHAPTER 15

TYRE

They drove into the Tyre city limits and both women sat up straighter in their seats. The outskirts of the town looked windblown and the buildings were all the same dull brown brick, two stories in small clusters around a vacant town square. Their car crept along like a lost vessel entering a deserted port. They navigated around the square, a monument adorning its center with a Confederate soldier atop a rearing horse, sword drawn in a posture that could be perceived as either a call to retreat or charge. Three-quarters around the square they saw an old man standing watching the car. He leaned heavily on a cane, dressed in baggy khaki pants and a sleeveless t-shirt. His posture was stooped and he had turned his head sideways to observe the automobile, a weathered face that bore sunken, yellowish eyes burrowed in a ruddy, whiskered mask that had sprouted scraggly brows and thinning streaks of hair. LoLo looked at the man and he turned his head to meet her gaze. As they passed, he smiled, showing mostly gums, and raised his cane to point at the car.

The road out of the square gave way to a row of little box homes with front porches in need of paint, and steps, railings, and roofs that needed mending and replacement. The lawns were mostly patches of dirt and the trees had bulging root systems that rose out of the ground like the humped back of a large fish just breaking the surface of the water and then diving down again, into the depths of the packed clay and chert. Mary held onto the wheel with both hands and kept the car at a low speed. They passed the homes and entered into an open stretch of road flanked by vacant lots with an occasional abandoned building whose eyes were smeared windows. Litter had blown up against the sides of the structures, catching in a fractured stack of pallets or settling behind an empty metal drum. Less than a mile from the square, they came to a cross street. On the corner was a gas station and market that appeared to be open. Mary turned the car into the parking lot and let the engine idle before saying anything.

"I'm going to go in and see if I can find out if Hicks has come back here with Renee."

"I'll come with you," LoLo said.

"No," Mary said opening the car door. "You stay here and lock the car behind me." She got out and walked to the front door and went inside. The store smelled and looked as Mary had imagined. Like the streetscape of Tyre, its shelves were mostly vacant. The heat from the outside sat in the closed space like stagnant pools of oily rainwater. A small bell had sounded when she had opened the door and Mary stood just inside waiting for an attendant to come out. One of the coolers in the back was buzzing loudly. Smoke from a recent cigarette clung in the air and Mary looked at the ceiling and could see the stains from the nicotine and tar and what looked like fire damage that had never been properly repaired. A thin man came from out of a back room and up behind the counter and looked at Mary a long moment before speaking. He was well over six feet tall with arms that hung comically from his narrow shoulders. His face was sunburned and appeared almost hot to the touch.

"Mam," he said. Mary took several steps toward the counter.

"My name is Mary Winslett," she said. "I'm looking for my daughter and a man named John Hicks." The clerk said nothing while he reached for a pack of cigarettes Mary could not see and brought one to his lips in a swift motion. He reached into his pocket and produced a lighter, clinked open the latch, spun the wheel, and lit the tobacco. He drew in deeply and then exhaled a large cloud into the space between himself and Mary.

"Hicks, you say?"

"Yes," Mary said. "John Hicks. He would probably be with a younger girl. A pretty younger girl. Her name is Renee." She coughed slightly at the smoke gathering around her face.

"Yah," the man said. "I know Hicks," he said. "Don't know nothing about a pretty girl with him though."

Mary started.

"What you want with a man like Hicks?" the store attendant asked. Mary thought about the question.

"I don't want anything to do with Mr. Hicks," she said. "I'm actually looking for my daughter. She left with him from our home and I'd like to know that she's okay." The man pulled on the cigarette and grunted. The bell went off behind Mary and she turned to see a small boy come through the door in a ragged pair of jeans and no shirt

"I catch you stealing in here again boy and I'll whip you myself," the attendant said.

The boy turned around and gave the clerk a raw and feral look. "I ain't stole nothing from you," he said.

"That so," the clerk said. "Well make sure it stays that way, you hear." The boy walked to the back of the store without looking at Mary. She watched him move down a row and then out of sight. She turned back to the counter. The clerk stubbed out the cigarette and looked at Mary.

"Hicks was in here," he said. "Been a couple days. Bought some bread and eggs and some gas. I ain't seen him since then."

"Do you know where he is staying?" Mary asked.

"Said he was staying in a place out Pell Road."

"Where is Pell Road?"

"Just up the way from here."

"How do you know it was John Hicks?"

The attendant let out a phlegmy cough.

"Everybody 'round here knows John Hicks," he said.

"Are they out there now?"

"Couldn't say. Not sure I care to know, to tell you the truth."

"Why is that?" Mary said. She felt self-conscious questioning the man. The way she sometimes felt out of place when reprimanding a farm hand back in Taylor Branch. The small boy re-appeared with a bottle of soda. He walked past Mary and set the drink on the countertop. The attendant set his mouth like the cigarette was still there and reached out his hand. The boy placed a couple coins on the countertop and took the bottle and went out the door. The clerk picked up the change and turned back to Mary.

"Hicks's family been around these parts since I was smaller than that little stealing bastard just walked out the door. Had a brother too, but I can't remember what they called him. He moved on a while back. Hicks boys was always into something," he said. "My God. There was this one time when my brother was with them out where the tracks come into Tyre. They had this old rifle and they shot this stray coming up the fall alongside the tracks. One of them, I don't know which, gutted the dog and they hung it from one of the signals crossings so you'd see it coming into town. My brother never did see much of them after that." He laughed, although it was not good humored. It was a nervous laugh and it personified his fidgety movements behind the counter. Mary was growing impatient and the rotting smell of the building was making her anxious.

"Why are you telling…I don't see what…"

"Cause I don't want to be the one to send you up there without you knowing who you're going to see. That stray story don't begin to tell all. They never could prove it was the Hicks, but a while back, there was a fire in one of the sawmill buildings outside of town near the river. There were ten or so men inside when the building caught. It being a saw mill in the middle of summer, they probably would not have expected anything other than a stray cigarette or some other fool thing, but because all of those men burned in the fire, they thought that was kind of suspicious that at least one of them did not get out. They looked around the building after they pulled the bodies and the first thing that they found was a tamp bar laying on the ground in front of a set of doors leading into the main cutting room where all of them men had been working. That got them to looking further and when they went around the outside side of the building they saw where the windows had been nailed shut from the outside. My uncle's cousin died in that fire," he said looking down one of the store's empty aisles with the sad, empty shelves. "So did John Hicks's father." He turned his glance away from the aisle and looked at Mary with what she thought might be pity. Or possibly fear. "If your daughter is with John Hicks, pardon my

100

saying so, mam, then she is with him, and if I were you, I would let it
rest at that. I'd climb back in my car and drive back to where I came."

"I can't do that," Mary said. The clerk examined his fingernails and
put one finger in his mouth and used his teeth to clip a cuticle. He
shrugged in a way that indicated that he had done his duty and was
also disappointed that the conversation was over. Mary imagined that
the interaction with the boy was what passed for discourse in the store.

"Like I said. He's up on Pell Road." Mary turned to leave.

"You got a man could go with you?" he called after her. Mary
stopped and turned around. "Thank you for your help," she said and
pushed through the door, the bell tinkling as she went. LoLo reached
across the seat and unlocked the car to let Mary back in. They turned
out of the gas station lot and drove further away from town until they
found the sign indicating Pell Road. They turned and found themselves
on a narrow one-lane lined on each side by deep ditches. They drove for
less than a mile before the road turned to dirt, and soon they were in a
corridor of pine trees and the car was bouncing over the rutted surface.
They came around a sharp bend and saw a small house sitting above
them on the side of a hill. The house was a filthy white and looked no
bigger than one of the farm shacks used to cure and smoke pork after
slaughter. Mary stopped the car and waited to see if anyone would
come out. When no one did, she reached into the back and found the
shotgun under its blanket. She had to move the sandwich basket to
get the stock free. She pulled the gun into the front seat and let it rest
across her lap, the barrel just touching LoLo's thigh in the seat next to
her. She looked at LoLo and nodded. Then she pressed down hard on
the car's horn.

Hicks picked his head off the kitchen table. An empty, smeared jar
sat next to a half-empty bottle of bourbon. His head throbbed and he
was slick with sweat. He looked around the room, confused. After the
horn sounded again, he stood up and looked out the window and saw
a woman, nicely dressed, standing below the house, holding something
across her arms under a blanket. A Negro woman stood on the other
side of the car. Both of them were looking at the front door. Hicks
stepped away from the window and walked into the back room. Renee
was asleep on her stomach, lying crossways on the unmade bed. She
had her shirt off and a skimpy pair of underwear was pulled down

low over her hips. Hicks turned and walked back into the front of the house. He went to a kitchen drawer and found his gun. He checked the cylinder and tucked it into the small of his back and walked outside. The sunlight caused spots to float in his field of vision. The strong taste of the bourbon was sour in his mouth and the headache was now accompanied by a rotting sensation in his guts. His frame was shaky and uncooperative and there was a dull pain in his chest that seemed to come in a ten-count wave. He stepped onto the porch and looked down the slope at the two women.

"John Hicks," the white woman said.

"That's him, Miss Mary," the Negro said.

"What the hell is all this? Who the hell are you?"

"Is my daughter in there with you, John?" Mary said. Hicks gave his head a couple of quick hard shakes to clear it.

"Your daughter?"

"Renee," Mary said. "Renee Winslett." Hicks placed a hand over his eyes to cut the glare and the reality clubbed him. He spat a thick glob of spit and mucus and stepped back toward the front door and then came back to the railing and leaned against a rotting column that held the slanting roof, looking down at the two women as if they had just dropped out of the sky.

"I'll be goddamned," Hicks said. "Miss Mary of Taylor Branch and that nigger Edgar's Mamma, here to see me all the way in Tyre. Looking for a lost sheep no less." Hicks dropped his head back and ran a hand through his hair. He looked into the sun and closed his eyes.

"Don't guess you ladies want to come up to the house and have a drink?"

"Is Renee here, John?"

Hicks swung his head in all directions in a taunting animation.

"Not here," he said. "Not here, but close I suspect. You might want to let her get some more clothes on before she comes out to be social." Hicks grinned at Mary and then turned to LoLo.

"What you studying, nigger?" he said, his voice carrying a low rumble, his eyes in slits, alert. "I got enough of your glaring back on that fucking farm of yours."

"John," Mary said evenly. "John, we want to see Renee, please."

"Please? You want to see Renee, pleeeeeease." He made a flitting motion with his hands over the porch boards, which groaned and creaked under his weight.

"Let us see Miss Renee," LoLo said, and it surprised all of them that she had spoken. Hicks came off the porch and down the hill toward them, loping and touching something behind his back and then bringing his arm in front of him, clasping his hands together into one large fist which he swung back and forth in front of LoLo.

"You ought to watch that mouth of yours, you old black bitch," he said, stopping a few feet from where the two women stood on either side of the car. The muscles in his neck and shoulders tensed and Mary placed her had under the blanket and found the trigger guard on the shotgun.

"I ain't afraid of you," LoLo said.

"Aw see, that's a mistake," Hicks said. "Out here in the middle of nowhere…"

"I want to see my daughter, John," Mary said. "I'm not here to take her back. I just want to see her." Hicks looked at Mary with a bemused expression. "Who says she'd want to go anywhere with you even if you did aim to take her back." They observed him quietly, watching him work things out. Then he pointed at them.

"What's under that blanket?"

Mary pulled the blanket off of the shotgun and let it fall to the ground. It piled on top of her feet and she held the gun tightly in front of her, never taking her eyes of Hicks. Now he turned to fully face Mary.

"What do you plan on doing with that?" he asked.

"Nothing that I don't have to," she said. "That gun in your pants. Take it out and lay it on the ground." Hicks started to smile and Mary raised the shotgun to her shoulder.

"Please," she said. "All we want is to see Renee." Hicks looked at the woman holding the gun on him and could find nothing in her eyes that indicated fear or apprehension. He stepped away from the car and put one hand in the air and carefully put the other behind his back. He brought the hand back, holding the handle of the gun, its short barrel pointed at the ground. He bent and laid it in the dirt.

"Okay," he said. "Okay." He stepped backwards up the hill and back to the porch, his hands in the air in an animated posture, a grin spreading as he went. When he reached the first step, he turned and went into the house, no longer looking at the two women in the yard who had not moved from their original positions. They heard loud talking in the house, Hicks yelling at Renee to get up and she protesting. Five minutes went by and then Hicks reemerged on the porch. Renee came out behind him, wrapped in the bed sheet. Her hair was loose and hung in her face. She came around Hicks and looked at Mary and LoLo.

"What are you doing here?" she said. Mary and LoLo took the girl in, each trying to reconcile her disheveled appearance with the child they had nurtured, fed, bathed, dressed, kissed. Renee stepped off the porch and into the yard, pulling the sheet tighter around her body. Its thin threads allowed them to see the outline of her breasts and ribs.

"What are you doing here?"

"We come to let you know that Miss Katherine is gonna have a baby," LoLo said. "It's his," she said, waving an arm at Hicks. Renee said nothing. She pushed a strand of hair out of her face and looked from LoLo to her mother.

"Renee," Mary said. "Katherine is very sick. The pregnancy has made her very sick." Renee spared a glance over her shoulder at Hicks, who was again leaning against the porch railing.

"The rape," Mary said and stopped, letting the word sink in. "The rape damaged her insides. The baby has to come early."

"Don't see what that has to do with her," Hicks said and nodded his chin at Renee who could not see him. "And who you accusing of rape anyway. Nobody here raped anybody."

Mary said, turning to face Hicks. "You know as well as I do what you've done. Everything that you've destroyed. Don't treat us like we are fools, John. Even you should be able to keep from doing that while I speak with my daughter." Hicks looked at the ground and swallowed, then spat over the railing again. Renee remained motionless. She looked down at the pistol lying in the dirt between she and her mother.

"What do you want me to do about it?" she said. Mary looked at her daughter and felt something cold close like a fist in her chest. The sun overhead was almost white. The pine trees that surrounded the small plot where the house stood were extremely tall and they looked diseased and malnourished in their straightness and blotchy brown bark. Spindly branches with small tufts of needles grew at the tops and Mary imagined that they would look frightening in the dark. Her daughter's adoption of Hicks's perverse and vacant sense of decency cleaved her mind like an axe through aged wood. Renee's whorish appearance, standing half-naked in the soiled yard of a monster who would no doubt turn on her when he lost interest, the weight of the shotgun in her hand and the sunlight's glint of the silver pistol between them, the immense bravery of LoLo standing with her...*Oh God help me through this,* she thought. She looked at Renee.

"You are going to take the baby," she said, gripping the shotgun and looking at Hicks whose head shot up. "You're going to take the baby and what you do with it is your own business, but you will take it and you will make a home for it somewhere."

"The fuck you say," Hicks spat, but Mary cut him short.

"I'm speaking now," she said. "You are going to take it or I will do everything in my power to see you in prison for raping my daughter," she said, staring fiercely at Renee. "Maybe you two have not spent enough time together, but Renee should know well enough that if I set my mind to something, it will come to pass. And if my husband were to find out, prison will be an option you will wish you still had. Because he will hunt you to the end of this godforsaken state and no matter what hole you climb in, he'll dig you up and when he's done with you he'll put you back in the same hole and cover you over and no one will ever know that your sick soul ever existed."

Renee looked at her mother for a long time but showed no emotion. LoLo watched the girl and inside she was breaking apart. She was thinking of Edgar and how sweet he was. How he trusted her with everything and believed her in a way that was so painfully innocent and full of mercy and forgiveness. She looked at Mary and wanted to go to her but did not. Could not.

Renee turned in the yard and walked to the house. The sheet dragged behind her. She climbed the porch steps and stopped briefly to speak into Hicks' ear. He bent to hear her and nodded. She went past him and through the open door, and like an apparition she disappeared from their sight.

"When?" Hicks said.

"Soon," LoLo said. She knew that Miss Mary was close to collapsing and would make her ride home instead of driving. She would make her a late dinner and they would sit on the porch and be quiet together.

Hicks turned and walked into the house and closed the door, leaving them alone in the empty yard. Mary looked down at his gun in the dirt in front of them. *Everything had moved so quickly,* she thought. Everything had moved quickly as if something beyond all of them was playing itself out, like they were all characters in a tragedy or maybe even a comedy, she thought, because the absurdity of it all, the evil, her own deceptions, the creation of a child, the loss of a daughter and the ruin of another—was that not almost laughable in its complexity? No, she thought, looking at LoLo and indicating that it was time to go, not resisting when she insisted on driving.

They drove out Pell Road and back past the sad row of homes and back through the square and then out of town. And when Tyre was behind them, LoLo pulled the car over and they ate their sandwiches by the side of the highway, not saying much to one another. The day was getting late and they drove back to the mountain with its afternoon hues of purple and pink and red painting the horizon in front of them and as they climbed the slope heading west, the colors were bleeding together. Behind them, night was dropping its veil.

CHAPTER 16

LOLO

The arrival of the baby was painfully prolonged. She suffered much of the time and despite everything that LoLo and Mary tried to do to comfort her, it seemed that nothing would let her be at peace. Mary had arranged for a doctor and a nurse to attend the birth. It was to take place in the house on Stoney Mount, and despite the warnings the doctor communicated, Mary insisted that they could collectively deliver the baby and save Katherine in the process. She had come too far, she reasoned, to bring the pregnancy and the rape out into the open, and while gambling with her firstborn daughter's life was beginning to make her physically ill, she persevered.

Mary had a phone installed in the house at the doctor's insistence, explaining that should Katherine go into labor, they would not have the luxury of time. Her contractions set in before the sun came up on a Tuesday morning, and Mary left LoLo in the room with Katherine, washing her sweating face with a clean white cloth, while Mary made the phone call. The doctor arrived with a small woman who he said had been his nurse for more than twenty years. The woman had a tight face and a large round body, but she moved with a level of competence and assertiveness that Mary found comforting despite all that was unknown before them. The delivery could only be described as violent, the child forcing its way into the room. The doctor went about his work with diligence, speaking in bursts at the nurse, who responded without hesitation. Mary and LoLo had been forced out of the way and they stood in the doorway together, watching the young girl writhe on the bed, terrible pitched screaming coming from her throat. The doctor and the nurse paid very little attention to their patient, focusing entirely on getting the baby out as quickly as possible. What seemed like hours was actually less than forty-five minutes, a hard, intense calamity of shrieks and blood and finally the yowling infant that the doctor pulled from Katherine and handed to the nurse with no emotion or any sign of relief. The nurse toweled the child off and carried him to Mary and LoLo. Mary looked down at the open mouth of the infant, which was exploding with ear-splitting cries that cycled like a siren. LoLo reached out and took the baby from the nurse and took him into the other room. The nurse returned to the doctor's side and assisted with sewing Katherine back together. Both the doctor and the nurse's arms were slick with blood up to their elbows. Katherine had released her grip on the side of the mattress and lay still, a look of shock deep-set in her eyes. The nurse ordered Mary to retrieve clean water. She left the doorway and went to the kitchen sink and ran lukewarm water into a large bowl and brought it back to the nurse who got off her knees and came around the side of the bed to accept it. Mary came into the room and sat next to Katherine on the bed. She swept her daughter's hair from her forehead and spoke in low, soothing tones. When she looked down the length of the bed, she saw that the doctor and the nurse were speaking to one another in short whispers. Mary went back to stroking Katherine's hair. Her fingers wanted to tangle in the sweaty curls and she was careful not to pull them free with any force.

The doctor stood and gave the nurse directions on finishing. He motioned for Mary to meet him outside. She stood and led them both out. She walked through the front entry and onto the porch. The doctor came out behind her, toweling off his arms. He pulled a pack of cigarettes from his shirt pocket and offered one to Mary, who took it. The doctor lit their cigarettes and looked out past the porch at the quiet neighborhood street. Mary smoked in silence beside him. He explained that Katherine had endured a lot. That she was lucky that the birth had not seriously jeopardized her health, possibly even killed her. He explained that she needed to stay in bed for at least a week and drink as much water as she could stand. He took a bottle of pills from his pocket and gave them to Mary, along with instructions not to allow her too many in any one given day. He smoked through his cigarette and crushed it out in an ash tray sitting on a wicker end table. Then he immediately lit another. The nurse joined them on the porch, but she walked past, moving on short legs down the steps and out onto the sidewalk. She found her own pack of cigarettes and lit one before walking back to the doctor's car, which was parked on the curb. She leaned against the car looking in the opposite direction of the Winslett house. The doctor asked about the circumstances of the birth and if Mary needed help finding a place for the child. Mary stubbed out her own cigarette and thanked him for his discretion. Mary stayed on the porch until the doctor and nurse had driven away. Then she went inside to check on Katherine and the baby.

The next morning, Mary went back to Taylor Branch to get Edgar, whom LoLo had taken back to the farm after locating Hicks and Renee in Tyre. She called her husband before she left and they had a long conversation about all of the exciting things that he was doing in Washington. She was animated in speaking with him, but careful not to set off any alarms by overdoing it. She told him that they would be returning home from the mountain in a week or so and that they were all very excited to see him. She hung up the phone and she and Edgar climbed into the car to make the final trip to Stoney Mount. When they arrived, Mary sent LoLo and Edgar to the market store. LoLo handed her the baby and went to hug her son. They left and Mary went back to her bedroom with the boy. Katherine was sleeping. She had taken one of the pills and they were helping her to rest. Mary set the baby on her bed and looked down at it. After its initial rage at being born, he had not made a sound since. Even when he was laid down to sleep, LoLo or Mary would look over the edge of the make-shift crib and find the baby staring up into the ceiling, not blinking and silent. She looked down at the child on the bed and then she picked up a pillow without thinking about it. She held the pillow in front of her and considered placing it over his face. *It would be simple and over*, she thought. It would be over. It would be over. It would be...she looked down at the baby. His eyes were a slate color and his tiny frame was compact. He'll be small, she thought. Like a runt. Then she realized that she was holding the pillow and she dropped it as if it were hot to the touch. It landed soundlessly and the baby was not disturbed, nor did it break its stare. Mary felt something washing over her, and she folded her arms in front of her chest. *No,* she thought. *No, I won't do that.*

Three days after the birth, LoLo and Edgar drove the baby to Tyre. Mary had tried to go, but LoLo said that Katherine needed her and that she and Edgar could handle things. They left in the morning and pulled onto Pell Road just after noon. Hicks came out on the porch when he heard the car. He stood looking down at them as LoLo retrieved the baby from the back seat, wrapped in a blanket. She walked up to the porch and stood below the steps looking up at Hicks, who came down the steps and took the child from her and turned and went back to the door. LoLo returned to the car and told Edgar to get in and start it. As they backed out of the drive, she saw Hicks standing on the porch looking into the baby's face. She told Edgar to stop the car, waiting to see if Renee would join him on the porch. She did not come, and eventually, Hicks opened the door and went inside. LoLo and Edgar did not stop for lunch on their return trip. They arrived back at the cottage before dinner. The house was quiet, but Katherine was sitting up in bed, sipping a cup of tea. LoLo helped Mary tidy the house and Edgar packed the car. They had dinner together that night, Katherine eating some chicken and fried corn from a plate she balanced in her lap, sitting up in the bed. The next day, they locked the house and drove back to Taylor Branch, the four passengers as quiet as if making their return from a funeral.

CHAPTER 17

EDGAR

We came back from the mountain. Me and Miss Mary, Mamma, and Miss Katherine. It seemed like a long, long drive. Nobody said much of nothing and I kept my mouth closed cause I never felt good about saying anything at all when everyone else was keeping quiet. We came up into the farmyard and it was dark and I supposed that was good cause no one could keep things to themselves on the farm 'cept for me and Mamma and we was different cause Miss Mary had been so kind to us and we knew how to respect that. Miss Katherine was in the front seat with her mother and Mamma was in the back with me and I remember that when we came up to the house, Mamma reached over and took my hand and pulled it into her lap and I looked over at her.

She did not look back at me but kept staring straight ahead and I knew what she was thinking and she was passing that over to me through touch, which we could do with each other sometimes. She was thinking how things had changed in a lot of new and troubled ways and we were still Negroes and the Winsletts were white people and that we would have to be careful from now on because Mr. Winslett did not know what all had happened and he being a smart man was likely to figure things out for hisself and when he did there might be questions for me and Mamma and she wanted me to be ready for that if it came.

Wanted to be ready to be put off the farm. It felt like watching storm clouds bunch-up getting ready to break apart overhead. I remember that she looked old and tired. Her eyes were sunk into her face and the lines that were there from all of the laughing and smiling that she seemed out of place and somehow ugly. I was disturbed by the ugliness; it was like returning to a favorite pond and finding it dry and barren, the fish with their flaked, scaled bodies flapping beneath the white heat of the sun, unprotected by the water and rotting with no way to explain it. I looked the other way and tried to keep my thoughts in one line. They were jumping around inside my head like the cattle spooked by something howling in the woods. I tried to keep what I knew in place. That straight line so if I was pushed against the wall I would be able to give the right answers because I understood that Mamma's and my part in this would not be forgiven easily, we would be looked at through a painful pair of eyes that were hot and flickering with the shame of betrayal. Miss Mary would be there for us, but Mr. Winslett would not see things the same way. He would see things in anger and when white men thought with anger in their hearts they no longer looked at the world through kindness or consideration, but with the need for punishment and the belief that their place and time was more important than others. And punishment was a word that meant someone had to swing from a rope even if things on the farm had changed from long ago. Even if things were supposed to be different and fair now. I tried to pass that thought away, but it hung over Mamma and me in the back seat, like those bunched-up storm clouds ready to break apart.

We all got out except for Miss Katherine. Miss Mary came around the front and opened her door and helped her out. She moved like a cripple and seemed to look around the farmyard like she had never been there before, her head moving back and forth in a slow way. There was a light on in the house and I wondered who had turned that on for us and then something seized me inside, down around my guts and it felt like the sudden strength of my mother's hand on my arm when I was a child and I looked around the yard and saw that there was another car parked up near the barn, and as Miss Mary helped Miss Katherine to her feet, another light came on at the porch and a man came out the door and he looked to be wearing suit pants without the jacket and he had on a broad tie that swung with his opening of the door and I looked across to Mamma who was already looking at me in a way that I knew meant for me to be still.

The man on the porch said nothing and I did not see his head move in any direction. Miss Mary spoke to him and then he turned to look at her and Miss Katherine, but he did not move to help them, he just stood in the half-light of the house and watched them make their way across the yard like two old people you sometimes see helping each other up the sidewalk, familiar with each other's movements and pace, making their way forward without paying attention to the people and things moving all around them. Then the man spoke and came down the porch steps quickly like I had seen him do so many times before when he was mad about something going on in the yard, like a fight or some new hand mishandling a chore. He came to Miss Mary and Miss Katherine and he took Miss Katherine by the shoulders and was yelling at her to tell him what was wrong and I could only see the back of Miss Katherine's head and I knew that she could not tell him what was wrong and then Miss Mary was yelling at Mr. Winslett, telling him to leave her be, but he shook her a couple more times and I saw her head rocking back and forth like a child's doll and then Miss Mary stepped in front of Miss Katherine and spoke his name in a loud yell and told him to go into the house. He stopped shaking Miss Katherine and let her go and then he turned to go back to the house but he stopped short of the porch steps and turned around and spoke to Mamma who still had her hands on the top of the car door, and she was about to speak, but Miss Mary turned around and looked at Mamma and told her to take me and go home. Mamma stayed there for a minute and then she looked over the top of the car at me and said for me to take the bags in the house and then I was to come straight home. Mr. Winslett stood like one of those statues on the square in town and he turned his head to look at me like that stone soldier had come alive, but his face was blacked out and I could not see his eyes and I was scared to disobey Mamma, but more scared to walk past him and do what she asked me to do. Then Miss Mary spoke to me directly and told me to get the bags out and take them into the front room and that would be all they needed tonight. I went around the back of the car and got the bags and Mamma came around the back of the car too and she helped me pull them out and I picked two of them up and started toward the porch, wishing that I could have taken them all at the same time, but I couldn't do that and I knew that Mamma could not carry them, so I went past Mr. Winslett with my eyes looking down at my feet and I come close to him and I wondered if he would put his hands on me and stop me, but he let me go past and I went up the porch steps and into the front room and set the bags next to the stairs, and then I came out again and went to the back of the car and got the other bags and made my way back past Mr. Winslett and into the house again and set the other bags next to the first two bags I had come in with before and then I went back onto the porch and went down next to Mamma who reached out and took my hand and we started walking away together toward our house below the black fields.

Then Miss Katherine said wait and we stopped just before we started down the path between the fields and she pulled away from Miss Mary and came down toward where we were and her steps were slow and almost like she was walking across creek stones and we waited for her and as she came closer to us she waved her arms toward herself and we walked to her and then she fell against us, hugging our necks like little children and I remember my body stiffening because I had never been touched like that by a white woman and the smell of her filled my nose and her hair brushed my face and when she let us go I saw that she was crying and then I looked over at Mamma and saw that she was crying too. Then Miss Mary and Mr. Winslett were calling for her to come inside and she gave us a look and then turned and went back up the rise and I remember wanting to pick her up like one of the bags and help her to the stairs, but Mamma took my hand again and we went away from the light of the porch and the people standing near the tree and the tables where the hands went and had their dinner meal and soon we were walking in the row between the fields, saying nothing and hearing the rattle of the dry husks and the things that came alive at night. We came into the clearing and saw that the men were out on the porch and Levi was playing his guitar, but no one was singing along with it. He was plucking at the strings and they made a mean sound and the men were passing the bottle quietly back and forth.

I thought we were going back to our place but Mamma touched my shoulder and I stopped and she walked away from me and went to the porch in a slow shuffle that was old and full of years and I watched her come close to the porch and speak to one of the men in a voice that I could not hear and then I saw him reach out for the jug that was being held by one of the men a couple of chairs away from him and then the jug was passed down to the man that she spoke to and he took a drink and then handed the bottle to Mamma, who hooked a finger into the glass ring and tilted it with a bend in her elbow and brought the mouth of it to her lips and took a long drink and never coughed like I would have coughed and then she took it away from her lips and gave out a breath and then she bent her elbow again and she took another drink and this time she coughed and handed the bottle back to the man and turned around to look back at me and all the while Levi was plucking at the guitar and I could see that the moon was covered over in cloud and something seemed to settle over the whole place, and Mamma came halfway back to me and I walked forward and met her and took her arm and we went down the row to our house, which was dark and empty and I could smell the liquor on her breath as we walked along and when we got to the small porch of our place she looked up at the sky, still holding my arm and she whispered something that I could not hear except for the name of my father which she had mentioned only once before. Then she stepped up the two small steps to the porch and let herself inside. I was afraid again like I was with Mr. Winslett and I followed her in and helped her into bed and then I came back on the porch and thought about going up to where they were sitting and listening to Levi play the guitar but stopped before I left the porch and listened hard to the plucking that was broken up with the quiet of the night, the lonely men and the rooms in the mountain cabin sliding in and out of focus, and then I found the seat of Mamma's rocking chair.

I sat down heavily with the weight of everything closing in on top of me and I sat still, looking out across the fields. I could feel the rough threads of a hanging rope biting into the soft flesh of my neck and the need to make things right and the apologies that would come spilling out like rain water through a hole in a bucket only to be kicked aside before being drained. Behind me, in the house, I knew that the steady breathing and snoring of Mamma was already happening and I wanted to laugh at her drinking the whiskey after all the times she had warned me off it, but now it was not funny and I looked across at the front porch to the other houses and my eyes went down the line counting and they stopped at the house where Hicks had been. It was dark and no one moved inside it, but I could call up the outline of him sitting on the porch, smoking like he did and watching people coming and going and puffing out thick clouds of yellowish smoke and I thought I could almost smell the stink of it. I gripped the arms of Mamma's chair tighter and stared across at that empty porch and thought about Hicks and what I knew he had done in Bishop's place, knew the look on his face when he made us pull over the truck. I knew I should have left him there then and taken my chances with what he would have done. Then I thought about Miss Katherine under the tree by the house, screaming in a raw voice that was full of pain and fear, crying out and the dirt all over her and her hair that I had smelled for the first time that night was tangled and unclean.

Something moved between two of the houses and I sat upright in the chair and waited until the dog came into sight under one of the other house's lights, sniffing and pawing at the ground. Then it went back between the houses and came into the light again and I saw that it had something in its mouth that was drooping between its jaws. I sat back and could see Hicks in the cab of the truck, talking and smoking the cigarettes I had gave him and I was ashamed that he had spoken to me and to Levi like he had. I heard the sound of Hicks slapping Levi's hand when he tried to get in the front of the truck. *You expect me to ride in the back with a couple of niggers up front driving,* he had said. He spit them words at us like he'd tasted something bad on his tongue. But mostly I thought of Katherine and how I had been the one to bring that man here and how the devil knew what he was doing when he put me and Levi out on the street that day and let Hicks come and find us so he could do what the devil wanted and put that evil into Miss Katherine. I cried some sitting in the chair, soft and to myself and when I was done I stood up without looking across the way at the house where Hicks had been, and went inside and heard Mamma making her sleeping noises and I went into my room and took off my clothes and lay down to sleep.

In my dream, I was standing outside on the porch of a store that I did not know. There was a large window looking into the store and a bench like in church that went underneath the window and I was a small child and I climbed up onto the bench and through the window

I could see a strong Negro man standing in front of the counter and a skinny white boy behind the counter and the skinny white boy was yelling at the Negro man and the Negro man was yelling back and talking about how he just wanted something but I could not work it out and then some of the white men sitting at the tables stood up and came around behind the Negro man and I could see that he was taller than all of them because the top of his head stood up above the white men's hats and then the white men parted back and the Negro man walked toward the door of the store and he came through it and went down the steps fast and heavy so that one of the step boards creaked under his weight and then the white men were out on the porch after him and one called out *mind yourself nigger* and then they were talking together and I knew it was about the Negro man because their words were like the thorns that grew in mean tangled clumps along the creek bed that would catch on your clothes and rip at your arms and I knew that the child was me.

Then the dream changed and I was a man and I was standing just beneath the trees that circled a small clearing in the woods. The air was very thick and smelled of molding leaves and mud and pine needles. In the clearing was a large tree that seemed to almost block out the light from the sun and beneath the tree the white men from the store were standing and in the center of their circle was Kitch and he was bleeding all over and they were pushing him between them and asking if he *felt like running his nigger mouth now* and then one of the men who had his back to me took hold of Kitch and pushed him toward the base of the tree and turned him around so he was facing the men and then he reached and pulled down the rope and the hanging knot and he put it over Kitch's head and Kitch was looking across the clearing at me where I was standing just inside the trees and his eyes were clouded over and his mouth was sagging and he no longer looked as big as I had seen him in the store and they were taunting him and laughing and then the man who had placed the hanging knot around his neck took the other end of the rope where it had been thrown over the branch of the tree and was swinging freely, and he tossed it over his shoulder and walked with it that way with his head down. Then he handed the rope to one of the other men and then several of them took hold of the rope in a line back toward the tree and started to pull and walk away from the trunk and there was small second when Kitch looked at me and he gave a bloody smile and then his face went blank and his eyes pushed out and he was clawing at his neck and then I heard my name and I looked and the man who had placed the knot was looking back at me where I was standing beneath the trees and his face was Hicks and I stepped back and he turned full to consider me and he smiled and drew his finger across his throat and then he turned around to watch Kitch swinging in the air, his legs flapping like clothes on a laundry line and his hands scrabbling at the noose around his neck and he yelled so loudly I thought my ears would burst from it and then I woke up to Mamma shaking me and telling me *that I was dreaming. Just dreaming.*

I lay in the bed listening to Mamma in the kitchen. She was making food and humming one of her church songs softly and I got up and put on some clothes and came into the room that was warm from the wood stove and sat down and watched her working and I did not say anything and was seeing Kitch in the dream swinging from the tree and I could hear the men laughing and making calls like vultures fighting over a dead animal and I closed my eyes and tried to push it out and listen to Mamma's humming.

Then someone knocked on the door and it was one of the white hands and he asked for me and Mamma to come up to the house. Mamma looked at the man and told him that we would be along shortly and she finished what she was doing and came over to the table where I was sitting and she looked down at me and put her hand on my shoulder and smiled and told me to come on and that everything was going to be all right. We walked up to the house. It was raining and I could tell that the weather was getting ready to change because the rain was cold. We came up on the porch and Mamma knocked at the front door instead of going inside and I thought that it was strange for us to come up on the front porch instead of going around the back to the kitchen where Mamma let herself in without knocking and then Miss Mary opened the door and she and Mamma looked at each other and then Miss Mary stepped back and told us to come into the front room where Mr. Winslett was sitting in a chair by himself. He stood up when Mamma and me came in the room and he pointed to a sofa and told us to sit down. Miss Mary came in behind us and sat down in a chair that was across from where her husband had been sitting.

"I'm not putting you off the farm," he said. "Mary told me that you were only doing what she asked, so I can't blame you for doing what you were told. But I want to know what you saw and what you know about this man. Mary will not tell me where he and Renee have gone and that is probably for the best because I would certainly find him and kill him myself without thinking twice about it. But I want to know what you saw."

He turned and looked at me and I looked at the floor and Mamma reached over and took my hand and I was again ashamed and did not want to tell all of it because it was a terrible thing and the devil had touched me and if I talked about what I saw he would be able to touch all of us. Miss Mary said that she did not see how the story needed to be told again and then Mr. Winslett stood up quickly and looked at her and she was quiet.

Mr. Winslett walked over to me and I felt Mamma tighten her grip on my hand and he said to tell it and so I did, from when me and Levi were in Winchester and Hicks came up and wanted to find work and then about Bishop's and what I thought he had done there and then how he had been on the farm and how I wanted to tell that I knew he was bad but was afraid to and then about finding Miss Katherine and how I went back after she was in the house and saw that the gun was missing and how I was sorry for all of it. Mr. Winslett stood in front of me the whole time and did not move except to make his face change when he was hearing about me finding Miss Katherine. When I was done he walked back to the chair and sat down and Miss Mary stood up then and went to Mr. Winslett and kneeled down in front of his chair and took up his hands in hers and she was crying and Mamma reached up and touched my face and we all sat in the room together and the house was very quiet and cold and the rain was falling outside and muddying up the yard and I could see through one of the windows that a wind had stirred up because the fields were swaying. Mr. Winslett was not crying but was looking at me across the room, and the white men from the dream came back into my head and I was sacred again and I wondered if Miss Katherine was upstairs and if she was scared too and if the devil would leave her alone now that he'd taken what he wanted.

CHAPTER 18

DENNIS

Dennis Winslett sat looking at his wife, shocked and enraged. They were in the kitchen and she was pacing back and forth with a glass of whiskey in her hand. His glass sat untouched in front of him on the table, the bottle open with the cap beside it. Mary talked as fast as her mouth could form the words. She was frantic and unraveled and Dennis Winslett wondered if everything that he was hearing was actually a dream and if all of the travel and places that he had been over the past months had caused some kind of exhaustion or collapsing of his mind. They had sent LoLo and Edgar home and they had taken Katherine up to her bedroom and Mary had helped her get undressed and Dennis was trying to put all the pieces together that he had learned since being home but could not make sense of any of it and did not know what was fact and what was conjecture. He could see clearly that his daughter was in bad shape and he could see clearly that his other daughter was not there and finally, and most importantly, he could see that Mary had been overseeing something that was almost impossible to believe.

She had gotten Katherine into the bed and she turned to go out and he had to step aside to let her through the doorway and he had followed her down the hallway to the stairs and she had gone down the stairs with such speed that it almost looked as if she had lost her balance and trying to keep up with her falling center of gravity. She had

120

come into the front room, past the suitcases standing neatly in a row and went into the kitchen and found the bottle and yanked a glass from the cupboard and poured three fingers of the whiskey into the glass and gulped at it by the time he was fully in the room behind her. Then she had started talking and he sat down after retrieving his own glass and pouring the whiskey that now sat in front of him, catching the light in amber bursts.

"Mary," he said, controlling the tone of his voice, attempting to slow her down. "Mary." She stopped midway across the room and looked at him.

"Sit down," he said. "Come sit down." She came to the table and sat down and took another drink of the whiskey and coughed, almost spitting it up.

"Mary, I can't..." She raised her hand to him and regained her composure. She put the glass down on the table softly and pulled her hair away from her face.

"Katherine was raped, Dennis." He started to speak and she raised her hand again, this time to quiet him and to let her get her thoughts out.

"Katherine was raped and you were gone. There was no real proof who did it. Edgar found Katherine, but it had already happened. I called the doctor after we got her settled. I made him swear not to tell anyone about it."

"But why," Dennis interrupted, standing. "What reason could you possibly have for not letting the authorities know that a man working on this farm raped our daughter not fifteen goddamn feet from the front porch! Are you out of your goddamn mind, Mary?" She was still but following him closely with her eyes. "And none of this even compares to the fact that you didn't bother to tell me. Maybe I can be made to understand not calling the sheriff, given the insanity of the circumstances, but to not even tell me, Mary? Her father!" He was yelling and pacing the kitchen, coming back to the table to stop in front of her chair, peering down, his face a deep red and his eyes straining in their dampened sockets.

"Because," she said. "Because Renee went away with the man who did it, Dennis. She left with him that same night. Her sister raped in the yard in front of the house and she left with the animal that did it.

That's why, Dennis. You don't think that for all of this time that I didn't want to tell you? You don't think the agony of it almost tore me in half? You think that I did what I did because I wanted to go it alone or to hurt you? I gave birth to a daughter—my own flesh and blood—and she left in the middle of the night with a man who violated her sister and I was horrified to have played some kind of role in that despicable behavior. And I was scared that you would never be able to restrain your anger. Not for either of them. And I guess I felt guilty in helping her achieve what she always wanted: to escape this place and all of the things that we did that we believed were good but she somehow outwardly loathed." She grew still and then repeated herself: "That's why." He stepped away from her and she lowered her head. He reached to touch her face.

"No," she said and pulled her head back. "No. You were gone and I had to make decisions and I planned to tell you when you got back, but then you were gone even longer and when we found out," she choked out a sob, voice hitching, "and when we found out that she was pregnant and you were going to be gone even longer..."

"I would have come..."

"I know," she said. "Don't you think I know that? But I couldn't tell you because I knew what you would do and I was afraid of what might happen if you did it and Renee...oh goddamn her, Dennis. I think I was trying to still protect Renee, because she is still..." She drank from the glass. "She's still our daughter and I wanted to protect her, Dennis. Despite everything that she had done, I still wanted to protect her." Dennis sat back down and reached for his own glass, drew his hand back. All his life and all of his accomplishments and the commendations and the looks from his peers that came from places of genuine admiration and here, now, he could not think beyond picking a glass off the table and bringing it to his mouth to drink from it.

"Katherine," he said. "Is Katherine..."

"She's better," Mary said. "It was a long time getting her here. I could never have done it without LoLo and Edgar. Never. LoLo was by me the whole time and I knew that she was afraid that you did not know, but she never protested. Not once, and I will be grateful to them both until the day that I die. And when they come in the morning you will not throw them off this place. They did what they were asked and never said a word otherwise. Your daughter is upstairs in her bed tonight because those two people acted selflessly and with compassion."

"I have no intention of reprimanding either of them," he said, "although it bothers me that you felt that you could trust them more than you could trust me."

"It's not that," Mary said. "It was not a matter of trusting them more than you, Dennis. They could detach from it and it was hard enough for me to do that, let alone the both of us. We would have gone mad and God only knows what else might have come of it. We have lost one daughter and would have lost two if it were not for LoLo and Edgar."

"So now," Dennis said.

"Now we get Katherine back on her feet and help her cope with it the best that we can. I'm exhausted and I need you to step in and be her father and try the best you can to focus on her healing and not what she has been through. I have taken that on for both of us and now I need you to please help us move forward. Renee is gone and I doubt she'll be back anytime soon. I thought I knew her better than I did. I thought all of her talk about getting off the farm was the fantasy of a silly girl, and at times even thought there might have been some of that rebellion in me as I was maturing, but now...now I know that I was wrong to look at things with such arrogance. Thinking you know someone, even when you have created that person, is a false presumption. There are things that we can't understand. I know that now. I have seen that clearly and I am making my peace with it and I need for you to do the same. I will never hide anything from you again. It almost tore me apart the times that I was with you. It was suffocating, Dennis, and I need you to believe that because Katherine needs your help. But so do I because this has been awful in so many unspeakable ways and we have lived in fear for so long that we don't know how to be any other way and I want to change that. I want so badly for this all to change."

Dennis Winslett stood and went to his wife. She was right; she was exhausted and her slumping form made it evident. He knelt next to her chair and took her into his arms and pulled her weight against him, which she now willingly gave. The questions still in his head were buzzing like a hive and he took in the scent of her and tried to still the frenzy through that familiar and comforting smell that had made him whole for many years.

"It's okay, Mary," he said. She began to cry in deep, gasping breaths. He held her tighter, felt her body go limp, felt the last of her determination drain out in hot drops of water that were soaking through his shirt.

"There," he said. "There now. The worst of it has passed, Mary."

CHAPTER 19

RENEE

Renee woke in the early morning. Hicks was snoring next to her. She jolted upright, sweating and breathing heavily from a nightmare that had been so real that she had to gingerly touch objects close to the bed to make sure that she was no longer inside the dream. There had been a house, or a cabin, sitting deep in the woods and it was cast in a late dusk light that bathed everything in a burnt-bronze color. She had come through the thick trees and seen a wood pile with the axe stuck into the splitting stump. She had touched the blade of the axe and it had been cold and then she pressed her thumb against it and had split the soft skin. When the blood appeared, she heard a sound and looked to see a young man standing in the doorway. He was wearing an animal skin, the animal's head and eyes covering the man's own scalp and the skin of the body draping over his shoulders. His waist and legs were bare. His eyes were a dull yellow and he stood looking at her from the doorway, his head tilting to the right and left as if trying to understand what she was. She stood still for a moment and then began to back up, thumping into the wood pile and using her hands to find her way around the side of it, never taking her eyes off of what was in the doorway. He brought up a large knife in front of his face and then raised it above his head, grinning. He stepped into the yard and Renee began to run, stumbling over a loose log and then she was crashing through the underbrush trying to regain her balance. The man from the cabin was trotting after her and had begun to make howling noises that were impossibly high-pitched and pained. She was running as fast as she could but it felt as if her legs were restricted as if running through heavy sand. She was moving up and down a trodden path, her shadow long behind her. The branches scratched at her clothes as she ran and now the howling and shrieking was running alongside her in every direction and as if a pack was hunting her. She was losing speed and the noises were coming closer and then rolling out away from her, almost mocking her frantic escape, taking their time before they came out on the path behind her and pulled her down. Beneath the knife. She burst through a clearing and found herself standing beside a lake and she turned to look back at the woods. The sounds were still there, but they were more distant and she was gasping for breath and wheezing in and out and her eyes were stinging and her nose was running. The dusk had given way to full dark, but a heavy moon was floating in the black sky and she looked back to the trees and saw the man at their edge and she screamed for the first time. He came forward, crouching and growling and spitting and Renee backed into the lake. The water was lapping at the bank and she felt its coldness on her ankles and then on her calf muscles and then it was beneath the dress she was wearing and the fabric floated to the murky surface. The man was on the bank jumping up and then falling back into a crouch. He gnashed out fragments of words in low growls and he plunged the knife through the air and shrieked at Renee, who was up to her chest in the water, the white dress billowing around her. She was shivering and pleading with the man to stop but he would not and only became more angry the more she spoke and then she felt something bump into her legs and she looked down through the fabric of the dress and the thing was rising up to the surface beneath the white and floating fabric and she yanked it back and Hicks's face bobbed from the water, blanched, with his thin lips pulled back in a snarl of red gums and chipped teeth and he was beginning to speak her name when she came awake.

She climbed out of the bed on shaking legs and went to the kitchen for a drink of water. She was shivering as she walked over the dirty floor. She filled a glass and drank it greedily, spilling the water out the sides of her mouth and feeling it run down her cheeks, her neck, and down her front. She sat on a crippled-looking chair at the cluttered table and looked back at the bed where Hicks was sleeping. She tried to find the anger and determination that had allowed her to leave Taylor Branch in the first place and when she could not find it inside of her, she uncorked the half-empty bourbon bottle, its glass smeared with handprints, and poured it down her throat. Then she stood and went to the far side of the room where they had piled blankets for a bed. She came even to where the baby slept and looked down at its upturned face, which held a blank stare as if it were disappointed in her.

"I'm not your mother," she said. "And your mother would not have you. So here you are. With us." The child continued to look at Renee. Behind her, there was a hitch in Hicks's snoring and the child suddenly turned its head and then turned it back again to stare up at her. "You don't understand," she said, tasting the liquor in her mouth. "None of you ever will understand. And you'll be a bastard and never know any different, but at least you'll ..." She stopped and placed a hand to her mouth and felt a knot uncoil in her stomach. She could not complete the sentence because her own future's imbalance was clear in the blank expression of the child. She started to reach down and pick up the baby but stopped herself. It squirmed and then tilted its head to one side and spit up, the thick mucus substance sliding down its tiny chin in a bubbly cascade. Renee wondered when he had last eaten. "Sleep," she said and went back to the bed and sat down next to Hicks. Grey light came through the covered window and Renee realized that soon it would rain and that the three of them would be closed in together and that John would have no patience for a baby and maybe not even her under that circumstance. *I won't tie my fate to his,* she thought and looked over at the pile of blankets. *Even if it comes to being alone, I won't tie myself down again. Not after running.* She leaned back and lay down on the sunken mattress. She looked at the stained ceiling and fell asleep listening to the first sounds of rain on the battered roof.

When she woke the rain was falling heavily and she saw that she was alone in the room. There were loud bursts of thunder and the rain on the roof was intimidating, heavy drops pounding angrily. She swung her legs over the side of the bed and pulled the thin tan sheet around her shoulders, stood and went to the pile of blankets. The baby was there, asleep. She wondered how it was not disturbed by the storm. She crossed the room and saw the note on the table, a stub of pencil resting beside the white paper. She stopped anticipating what had been written there. Hicks had gone. Had woken before her and slipped out the front and away for good. He had abandoned her as she had begun to suspect he might, but now there was the child to consider and she wondered if she could do the same as Hicks. Walk out and leave it behind. Call the police and tell them where they could find it. They would find a home for it and she would not wait around to answer any questions. She could make her way out of town, just as she had slipped off the farm, and disappear. *Or you could go home,* a voice in her head said very softly, realizing it would call attention to the other thoughts of potential betrayal circling for her attention. *If you went now, they would take you back. Daddy would take you back. You know he would.* Mother and Katherine would not want him to, but he would take her anyway because she was his little girl and eventually things might go back to normal. She went to the table and picked up the note and read.

Terrell. This is your brother John. I know we have not spoken in a long time, but I wanted to tell you that I need your help. I'm hoping that you get this letter. I used the address from the card and the picture that you sent me at Christmastime. I kept the picture and keep it with me. It reminds me of the old days before the Mill. I got a baby and I need you to help me raise it. I'm not in a good way with this and I don't know anyone else who I can turn to. You know how to read and write better than me and you have your education and you got free like I did and maybe if you can do this for a little while I can come back and get him when things are more quiet. He don't seem to need much. I'm gonna come your way day after tomorrow. Probably take me a couple days to get there. I'm sorry Terrell. You know I ain't got no place else to turn. I never named the baby. I thought you might like to do that. Maybe name him after one of the people in them books you was always reading.

Your brother John

She was putting the note back on the table when she heard Hicks come on to the front porch outside. There was the sound of his boots and then a large thump and Renee realized he had gone to get wood for the stove that was cold in the corner. She smiled to herself and then at John when he came through the front door, dripping, his long hair covering his face and his clothes saturated and looking too large for his frame.

"I thought you might have left me," she said. He shook off the water and pulled the hair back out of his face. Droplets of rain caught in his beard and his eyes were red and pinched.

"Left you?" he said. "Christ, Renee. I'd have let it quit raining if I was gonna run out on you." He took off his jacket and hung it on a peg in the wall. Then he crossed to where she stood and reached past her for the bottle that was still on the table. Water from his bare arm dripped onto the note.

"I saw what you wrote," she said. "You have a brother?" Hicks took a drink from the bottle and looked at her for the first time since coming out of the storm.

"I do," he said and took another drink.

"I didn't know you had a brother," and she laughed.

"Yea, well, I do. What's funny about that?"

"Nothing," she said. "There's just a lot that I don't know about you, I guess." He nodded, took another sip from the bottle and placed it back on the table. Without the stopper.

"You don't want it, do you?" She looked at the bottle and he shook his head and pointed at the blankets where the baby was asleep.

"No," she said. "I don't, but I don't think that your brother will either." She pulled the sheet tighter around her body.

"That don't matter," Hicks said. "He'll take him. He's like that. Soft hearted."

"He's like what?" she asked.

"Who?"

"Your brother. You said he was soft hearted, but is he like you?" Hicks looked at her, annoyed at the question.

"No," he said. "He ain't like me at all. About as much like me as you're like your sister."

"Why do you say that? You don't know anything about me or Katherine."

129

"I know that you don't fuck the same," Hicks said and laughed as he pulled the bottle off the table. He had dripped all over the warped wood floor and Renee looked around the room trying not to meet his eyes. She had tried to put the rape out of her mind, but now she could picture Hicks on top of Katherine as he had been on top of her, violently thrusting himself inside, his eyes closed and his black, vine-like hair dangling, glimpses of his strained face coming in and out of view, the smell of his sweat thick and threatening. He had hurt her the first few times and had not stopped even when she cried out and tried to push his penetration back. Something had come over him. Something animalistic and ravaging like he was trying to escape from a nightmare where he had been bound and left in the dark. At first the experience had been exciting, but it had quickly turned and she had shut her eyes against it, wanting to please him but also wanting him to stop. She hoped it would conform to her daydreams of what the act was supposed to be like, but his approach lacked all tenderness and the passion was savage, borne from urges that were beyond his control and the same voice that had suggested returning home before she read the letter was silent now, but she could feel its judgement and appalled reaction to her failed sense of decency and remorse. She was about to speak when the baby woke and began to cry.

"Tend to that," Hicks said. "I gotta get this fire started." He turned and went out the door and Renee stood, wrapped in the sheet, listening to the infant protest beneath the pounding of the rain.

Hicks left her that night to find another vehicle. After he was gone, she sat in one of the straight-backed chairs, holding the child, who was rigid in her lap. Everything about the baby was unnatural and Renee found that she was afraid to disturb its silence. The small amount of crying it had done since LoLo and Edgar had left it with them was now more of a comfort than an annoyance. At least that was to be expected. Its indifference and stare made her nervous. When she was a little girl she had been in the farm yard when her father shot a coyote. The animal had been lurking around the chicken houses and her father had taken it by surprise, bringing it down with a single rifle shot. Renee had come out onto the porch in the low light of the afternoon and seen the coyote on its side, blood on its dusty fur, its body moving up and down in shallow gasps and then going still. Her father told her to go back in the house, but she had disobeyed him and watched as he crossed the yard to drag the animal back to the rubbish piles behind the barns at the edge of the woods. He had come within a few feet when the coyote lurched and growled at him with blood in its throat. Her father had jumped back, startled, and shot the animal again. The bullet at that range jolted the body. Renee had carried that memory with her, and sitting in the room with the child now, the anxiety that she had felt on the porch that day when the animal had surprised her father was the same, as if the still form of the infant in her lap might at any time turn and bite. They sat that way for more than an hour when the baby shifted and began to pull at Renee's breast beneath her shirt. It did not look at her and did not make noise, but moved its tiny hands across her front, scratching against the cotton. Then it tilted into her, its weight pushing against her body, and rubbed its face into the fabric, its mouth working. Renee watched its face and then roughly pulled it back from her and stood. It screamed in frustration and began to kick. Renee held it away from her and walked across the room and dropped the baby into the blankets. It continued to scream until Hicks returned. When he came inside the baby's voice was horse and raw and the two of them stood looking over it. "Tomorrow," he said. Renee turned away and walked outside. She could hear the child through the walls and Hicks telling it to shut up, his voice tired and his agitation mounting. She went into the yard and waited until there were no sounds coming from the house. The storm that had blown through had dropped the temperature and she shivered looking back at the dark porch. *Maybe he smothered it,* she thought and the idea warmed her despite the cruelty of the thought. She went back inside. Hicks was asleep on the bed, the baby next to him, sitting up, watching her. "I'm not your goddamned mother," she said, its eyes fixed. The child reached out one of its small arms and seemed to point at Renee. She went to the table and sat. She picked up the pencil and found a scrap piece of butcher paper tucked beneath a torn wicker basket. She leaned over and began to write down instructions for Terrell. He would need them, and the exercise of writing the words down in her clean handwriting calmed her.

When John returned, they never spoke of the baby again. He pulled into the yard in the stolen truck and walked past her where she stood, not coincidentally there to greet him because something inside her had told her to come outside and wait. He climbed out of the truck and came up the slope and on past her, not speaking, but stinking of alcohol and cigarettes. The truck's engine ticked and its tires were bald and for the second time in the last few days the dead coyote came into Renee's mind and she thought about how predictable men were in their need to bring finality to the situations around them. Hicks had gone around the side of the house and when he returned he was carrying a rusted gas can. He set the can down in front of the truck and climbed back in, cranked the engine and put shift into neutral, not bothering to close the door. The truck rolled off the slope, gaining momentum as it went. Gravel crunched beneath the tires and then the truck was rolling into the adjacent field, somehow passing through a gap in the row of Hackberry trees that lined the road up to the house. Overhead a breeze stirred the tops of the pine trees. Hicks got out of the truck and stood beside it.

"Bring that can down here, Renee," he said. She did as she was told. He took it from her and then walked around the truck, pouring gas over the hood, onto the doors and side panels and then tossing the whole can into the bed. He took a lighter from his pocket and touched off the gas and immediately the truck body was engulfed. Renee watched without asking and did not move until he came back up the slope and took her arm, guiding him away from the waves of heat.

"Get clear, you idiot," he said and she allowed him to walk her backward toward the house. Something about the fire had a numbing effect and she thought she would be content to watch it burn for a long time. Then the flames found the tank and it exploded and she felt the hot wind on her exposed skin and she looked away to see John grimacing.

"It's done," he said. "Go inside and get your things. We'll take the other truck."

"Where are we going?" she heard herself ask him.

"Hell if I know," he said. "But we can't stay here. Go on. I'll be in behind you." She walked away from him and went into the house and found several pieces of clothing to pack. They would need most of what they had in the house if they were going to set up anywhere else, but she knew that John would not have the patience to load everything. She knew that patience was something that John had very little of. When they left, the truck was still smoldering at the edge of the field and Renee thought about asking if maybe they should put it out in case it caused a larger fire, but kept the thought to herself. John knew how fire spread.

They left Tyre and moved from small town to small town around the rural South. Hicks took jobs where he could find them and Renee did the same, cleaning houses or working on light industrial factory floors. The dreams that she had entertained from her bedroom window faded, replaced by their constant state of impoverishment and Hicks's degenerative nature. It was like watching a tree rot from the inside out, or a flourishing bush whose roots were over-saturated, the buried rot yellowing the leaves, only the putrid, trapped water was alcohol and the yellowing was in the whites of his eyes. Nothing felt whole and the sins that she knew she had committed washed over her with each waking moment. There were moments when she thought of leaving him, returning to Taylor Branch and begging forgiveness, but her stubbornness was aligned with his disdain for the world around him and the people who ran it and that kept her from crawling back. She suggested going to live with Terrell and instead of hitting her, which he had started to do not long after they left Tyre, he sulked in the corner of the small room they were renting and drank until he passed out sitting upright in a chair. She recognized the blank mood of the child in John's expression. There was a deadness that forced her to remain very still and she realized that going to Terrell and the baby would be a mistake because what the two of them had done was unforgiveable and just like any apology she might cobble together and offer her father and mother, the acceptance would be temporary and tainted. She and John nursed a common ailment and despite the lack of anything substantive in their being together, they were bound forward by their heedless and selfish natures, and for that, Renee knew they were damned. Their existence had no dimension except for the rudimentary principles of survival and animal need, and even those fundamentals like nourishment were clouded over with drink and insensitive behavior. She had taken what Dennis and Mary had given her and thrown it onto the same farm rubbish pile where dead things were taken to decompose, their blackening flesh returning to the earth and their skeletons stark white against the soiled ground. And Katherine, raped and discarded, crawled her thoughts on all fours, mouth gaping and ringed with dirt and dried blood, her clean night gown torn and hanging in loose sheets from her thin shoulders. She would lay awake and see her sister struggling beneath an invisible attacker, her screams hideous and unrelenting so that she had to push her hands over her ears, tears forming in her eyes not from guilt but from the pressure the images caused in her skull, like they would burst it open so that John would find her lifeless in the cold light of the morning.

They were living somewhere in North Georgia when she became pregnant with her daughter. Renee considered it a miracle that she had not had a child before then. Hicks gave no thought to precautions. After she had missed her period for two months, she told him. He was drunk and had come after her in the back of the house where they were living. He had fallen over a wheel barrow and laid on his back, spitting profanity at her while she stood looking down at him. She had gone into the small town and seen a doctor and when she returned home she expected him to be gone. She came into the house as quietly as possible and found Hicks sitting on the bed. She started to leave, but he stopped her. He was sober, but sick, and he had been crying. He told her that he loved her and that the baby would change him; that he would be better and they could find a way to make things work out. He told her that he wanted to have a family and that he wanted to be better than his father had been to him and to Terrell and that she could be a mother who did not run out and abandon her kids. They talked then and when they were through, they had made plans to return to Winchester and find work. John had made the suggestion and Renee had protested, but the more she thought about being closer to home, the more appealing the idea became. She would not be accepted, but she would also be difficult to ignore.

CHAPTER 20

TERRELL

My mother had left behind the Bible that she used to read from when it was quiet. Sometimes she would sit John and me down with the leather-bound book in her lap, picking through various passages the same way she used to take vegetables from the vines in the small garden behind the cabin. John would grow impatient, but I used to enjoy hearing her recite the language, sitting in a chair out on the porch and articulating the words fluently and with a hint of energy in her voice that was very rare. John would eventually wander off into the trees and I would watch him moving around with Mother's biblical narrative to accompany his steps. The words and his motions were incongruent and it made me wonder how he and I could come from the same place and be so different. It was not until both of them were gone—had abandoned me—that I began to question God's intent, and sitting in that same chair, staring out at the darkening woods, I felt alone like I never had before. At first the isolation made me fearful and reticent, but I came to appreciate the peace that living in solitude provided and I made plans to stay in that place and begin anew. I worked on the cabin itself, cleaning and making repairs, and the activity was comforting in its simple productivity and soon I trained myself not to look at the path leading to and from the cabin yard as I had in those first few days, expecting John or Mother to come back for me. But of course they did not and I never expected to see either of them again.

One evening I left the cabin and went through the woods to the mill site. As I approached I could smell the remnants and the stench made me want to turn around and go back, but I forced myself to go on, and as the ruins came into view, I fought with conflicting feelings of my new liberation and the murders I had committed with my brother. Sin had entered the world through contempt and rejection and one brother set to wander while the other's blood ran into the soil and displeased God. But God had forced the hand of one and set him on a course just as John was now wandering and I was left behind, my nose full of the ember smoke and my guilt for remaining upon the land instead of staining it with my own blood was confusing. The fire had erased the mill and those inside it from the earth and I stood on the rise above the yard and cried for the blameless faces of the men who would not be seeing their wives and children again having been sacrificed for the trespasses of a single black soul who had been born of the same fire that consumed his end.

It had taken the sheriff several days to figure out who had died in the fire. I was on the roof of the cabin when he came into the yard with two deputies. They did not see me above them and I crawled to the pitch of the roof and looked down at them as they spoke to one another.

"No one here," a deputy I did not recognize said.

"Yeah," the sheriff said. "But looks like someone is living here. That step looks like it has been mended. You can see the sawdust where they cut it." The deputy went over and stood on the step.

"Well they ain't here now," the other deputy said and the sheriff looked at him. He was a tall man, broad shouldered, and had been the sheriff for as long as I was alive.

"I'm here," I said. All three men looked up and I slid down the roof and made my way over to the ladder which was leaning on the side where I had climbed up. They watched me and waited until I was down to speak. I came around to the front of the house and stood in front of them.

"Which one are you?" The sheriff asked.

"Terrell," I said.

"Your mother around, Terrell?" The deputies stood on either side of the sheriff and watched me closely, their hands on their belts.

"No sir," I said. "She left a while back."

"Where'd she go?" the deputy on the right asked, and the sheriff turned on him. "I will do the talking here, if you don't mind." The deputy nodded and took a step back.

"Well," the sheriff said. "You heard him. Where's she gone to?" I shook my head.

"She left. We don't know where she went and have not heard from her since."

"We?" the sheriff asked.

"John and me. John is my brother."

"Yeah," the sheriff said. "We know who John is. Where's he?"

"Gone," I said. "Went south. I don't know where."

"Yeah. And when was that." I shook my head again.

"Been a while," I said.

"Uh huh," the sheriff said and looked up at the roof. "You know about the fire then?"

"Yes sir," I said.

"You know that your daddy burned up in it?"

"I figured," I said. "He ain't been home since it happened. Heard a bunch of men were killed in it."

"Yeah," the sheriff said. "A bunch is right. Someone set the fire while they were inside. Locked the doors and windows so they would not be able to get out. About the most wicked thing I've seen in all my years as sheriff in this county." I did not speak, just looked at the three of them.

"You wouldn't know anything about that would you?" This time it was the other deputy and the sheriff did not look at him like he had the other. I shook my head. "No sir," I said. "I been here."

"What about your brother John — think he knows anything about the fire?" I had to force myself to keep my head up. I could feel John's eyes on me from deep in the woods; could feel the breath of his anger. "No," I said.

"Why's that?"

"Why's what?" I said.

"If he's been gone, how do you know he wasn't involved in it?"

"Cause he went south," I said. "Mill's the other direction." The sheriff gave me a warning look. "You being smart with me?" he said.

"No sir," I said. "I just don't think John had anything to do with it." The sheriff turned to the deputy who had asked about my mother. "Let me see that hammer," he said and held out his hand. The deputy reached behind him and pulled a hammer loose from where it had been tucked into his belt and handed it to the sheriff. The sheriff looked at the handle and then at me.

"You know this?" he said, holding it up. I shrugged. The sheriff turned the handle around and pointed to the initials.

"These are your daddy's initials?" I squinted at the carved letters.

"I guess," I said. "Not sure."

"Yeah well, they are," he said and handed the hammer back to the deputy. "And there was a pile of nails next to it." He paused for a long second.

"Where's your brother, Terrell?" The lines from Genesis came to me and I almost asked him if I was to be his keeper but I stayed quiet. They asked a few more questions and then they left. They went out of the yard in a single file and none of them looked back. It was hard to say what they knew and what they did not. The other men killed in the fire would have relatives who would want to know what happened. Not every man who died in that burning mill was a bad person, just like my mother was not a bad person, but God never seemed to give much thought to who he tested, and for those of us who were made to endure his judgement, sympathy was not an emotion that we felt all that much. The pain and suffering were part of the natural course of things, like a late spring flood or a drought that drank the life out of living things until they were nothing more than dead stalks.

I was asleep a few days after the sheriff had come to the cabin. The weather had turned cold and the stove had cooled while I slept. I was stoking it and adding wood when someone outside called my name. I stood and listened and when I heard someone call it again I went to the door and opened it so I could see outside. There was a group of men standing in the yard holding torches and there was one man out front. When he saw the door open he stepped closer and told me to come out.

I opened the door wider and went onto the porch and looked at their shapes flickering in the shifting light.

"Terrell," he said. I did not speak "Terrell," he said again and I went down the steps so that I was even with them.

"What do you want?" I said.

"Where's your brother?" the man said. I told them I did not know and another one of the men came closer.

"Where's your goddamn brother?" he said. "We know he set that fire at the mill. You tell us…"

"Hush," the first man said. "Terrell, we know about your daddy and we know that your momma left you boys here. We just want to know where John went. That's all."

"Enough of this shit," another man said. "If he ain't talking then drag him out here and we'll get it from him the other way." I felt the coldness of the air on my skin and watched the flames play on their faces.

"John's gone," I said. "I already told the sheriff."

"We know what you told the sheriff and that don't change any-thing. Move aside unless you want to get hurt yourself." I looked at the man, his face shadowy, and thought he might have been one of the deputies but I could not be sure.

"Boys," the first man said. "We agreed…"

"You agreed," the man standing next to him said, looking at me. "We didn't agree to nothing except that we were gonna find out where he's gone to." I started to turn to go back in the cabin when someone grabbed me from behind and pulled me down into the dirt. When I looked up, two of them were standing over me and the others were walking toward the door with their torches. They went inside and I could see them passing back and forth in the room because the door was open, and then they came back out and the last one stopped and touched his torch to the doorframe and the dry wood caught quickly. The two men standing above me stepped away to watch the front of the cabin burn and the man who had called my name started up the steps, but several of the men grabbed him and pulled him back. He tried to pull away but they held him. They stood in the yard. The cabin was red and orange with the flames and they moved back from the heat. I laid in the dirt, feeling the waves pulse through the cold air. They let the man go who had protested and he came to where I was and reached a hand down to help me up, but I ignored it and soon he followed the others back down the path into the woods.

I left the next morning before the sheriff came. There was nothing left to take and I walked for a couple days without shoes or a coat until I reached the next town over and found some work at a livery stable. The owner gave me some clothes and I worked alongside his sons cleaning out stalls. When he found out that I could read and write he asked me to help with the ledgers, which I did until the late fall when I heard men in town talking about the mill fire and I decided to move further away. It went like that for several years, going from place to place, doing different kinds of work.

The library received late edition newspapers from towns around the Southeast, and I was stacking them one afternoon when a story from an Alabama paper caught my eye. The headline read "Local Man Arrested for Assault, Victim Recovering in Hospital." I read the headline over and over and something began to itch in the back of my mind. As I scanned the rest of the story, I knew before my eyes found the name in print that it was about John. He had beaten a man half to death standing out in front of a bar, over some petty argument involving a girl. A witness was quoted saying that if several men had not intervened it would have surely been homicide. *I don't know what set him off exactly*, the witness had said, *but I do know that I have never seen anyone act that crazy.* The details about the arrest gave John's address and I made a note of it and put the newspaper at the bottom of the stack. I imagined that the fight had been one of dozens since he left home and my secret hope that John had found some way of curbing the rage inside him had been a childish wish.

Then, not long before John brought the child to me, I met a man looking for someone to work some stills that he had built way back in the timber. We were sitting on bar stools late in the evening and he struck up the conversation. Talking with strangers was not something that I felt inclined to do, but he seemed to know a lot about things I did not, and the longer we talked, the more interested I became. He told me that aside from keeping the stills in good working order and making sure that the liquor got to where it needed to go, the rest of the time was free for me to spend how I chose to. When I told him I was working at the library he laughed, and when my face clouded a bit he was quick to reassure me that his laughter was more from relief than disappointment.

"How do you mean?" I asked. He drank from his glass.

"You work somewhere like that then I'm assuming you spend your time reading and don't care how quiet things are around you. Am I right?" I nodded and he tipped his glass at me. "Also don't hurt that you've got some education. I've had plenty of strong backs help me over the years, but if you can't read or write, you've got limitations that just makes my job harder. I don't want my job to be harder. I want someone to manage things so I'm freed-up. This here," he pointed at the bottles on the wall behind the bar, "will eventually put me out of business. But there's plenty of rural folks out there who need a more customized product and that's what I provide. You know anything about the liquor business?" I shook my head.

"I know what liquor does to folks," I said. He looked skeptical.

"Sound like you might have some baggage there. Maybe this isn't for you." Again I shook my head and drank the rest of my glass. "I like the sound of the job. I don't care who you sell it to and what it does or doesn't do for them. That's none of my business."

We met the next day and drove his old truck up into the hills and soon we were a long way from anyone or anything. We turned off onto a narrow dirt road and went back into the deep woods and came to a small cabin that was a lot like the one I had left years before.

"It's not much," he said. "But nobody knows it's here and nobody is gonna bother you. You can read all the books you want as long as you keep these stills operating. I got a couple of boys up here watching things for me now. They can help out if you want them. They seem to be okay, I guess. Not very bright, but they can do what they are told. They live out here somewhere." He stopped the truck and looked around. "I'd like to move all this closer to home but I'm not sure how I'd go about that now. Maybe you can figure something out." He climbed out of the truck and I followed him. We walked around the house and then he gave me a key. "Nothing inside to show you," he said. "We can get some supplies for you in town."

I nodded and then we followed a path away from the back of the house and moved through dense trees until we came to a clearing where the first still was set up. There was a skinny man sitting on a stump watching us.

"What's your name again?" the still owner said.

"Who you got there with you," the skinny man said, ignoring the question.

"Don't you worry about that. How's this thing running?"

"Tolerable," the skinny man said, not bothering to get up.

"Who's this here with you?" he asked again.

"He's gonna be running things for me up here."

"That so," the man said and now he stood up. "You gonna pay him like you do me?"

"I told you not to worry about that." The skinny man walked closer to us, studying me.

"I'm Terrell," I said and stuck out my hand. The man looked at me once more and then turned back to the still.

"We're going on up," my new boss said. The skinny man did not answer and we went past him to the next grove, about a mile and a half further up a slope, where a larger still stood. This time it was a black boy who approached us. He had been hidden in the trees, and when he came closer, he did not speak. "This here is Earnest or something like that. He don't speak. Least not to me. I hired his daddy and he brought this boy out here and then left him. I was gonna cut them loose but the boy does better than that no-count back there on the stump." He looked at the boy and smiled. "Dontcha, son?" he said and the boy smiled, but his eyes were flat and I thought that maybe he was touched, either through being orphaned or something slipping in his mind. He also looked like he had been burned on one side of his face. The skin was raw and a hot pink color against his otherwise black flesh. "You think you can show Terrell how to run this still?" The boy nodded and grinned broadly. I could tell that he craved the interaction; had spent so much time in the woods that the conversation was almost like a reward.

"Where do you live?" I said. He looked at me and tilted his head, the burned side of his face in the sunlight. He pointed to where the woods encroached on the clearing.

"In there?" I said. He nodded and ran in that direction. I followed and went after him when he ducked into the shadow of the trees. The woods were thick and it was impossible to walk a straight line. The boy was ten or fifteen feet ahead of me and I watched him weave his way through, expertly. When I caught up with him, he had stopped in a smaller clearing with a pine needle and dirt floor. He had fashioned a shelter out of limbs. Beneath it were ratty blankets, a rusted-out lantern and some empty cans of food. There were also some animal skeletons discarded off to the side and I saw that he had a rifle leaning against one of the larger limbs.

"You live in here?" I said. He did not respond and began picking up random objects and showing them to me. The still owner had stayed behind and I was glad of that because the squalor the child was living in was shameful and I was not sure that I would have been able to hold back a reprimand. But his situation was not far from the one that I had fled myself and my empathy was overshadowed by my understanding that the boy probably did not dwell on his accommodations, but rather recognized them as part of his life's pattern and likely knew nothing different.

"What about your mother. Or your father?" He stopped moving around and came to me and took my hand and placed it on the burned spot on his face and moved my palm up and down.

"A fire?" I said. He nodded.

"They were burnt-up in a fire?" He nodded again.

"Does he know." I motioned with my head back toward the still, "what happened to them?" He dropped my hand and fished in his pocket for something. I watched him intently. Then he produced a small pocketknife and opened the blade up and pointed it toward the deeper woods.

"Out there," he said, his words slow and mechanical.

"What's out there?" I said.

"Sooounds," he said then made a strained howling noise in his throat.

"Wolves?" He shook his head violently back and forth.

"What then?"

"Caaant say. Comes in at night."

"What comes…" but the boy moved away from me, still holding the knife. He ran out of the sad camp and back toward the clearing where the still was set up. I followed after, walking carefully between the trunks, glimpses of the daylight passing through the interior. When

143

I emerged the boy was not there, and the man from New Orleans looked at me and nodded that we should go. I thought of stopping him and asking about the child's living like he was, but simply went after him instead and walked at a distance as we went back down the slope and through the first clearing where the skinny man was fixing something with the still rig. When we got back to the cabin, we talked about money and how the liquor was to be handled. He showed me around the place and then we returned to his truck and rode back to town without speaking. When we arrived he got out and leaned through the window.

"I forgot to ask if you could drive," he said.

"I can drive," I said.

"Keep this truck then," he said. "And take this," he handed me a small key. "It's a PO Box key. Post office is just around the corner from the pharmacy. I put my address in the box already so you can write me if you need to but mostly we're gonna communicate by phone. There's no phone at the cabin, of course, but you can come down and use the one at the pharmacy. I have an arrangement with the owner. He won't give you any problems. You call if you need something. Otherwise, make your deliveries and your money will be behind the counter with the pharmacist. His name is Dale, but there's not much reason for the two of you to talk. Just leave the bottles back where they make the deliveries and Dale will take care of it from there. You understand?" I nodded.

"Okay," he said. He started to pull his head out of the window and stopped. "I had a boy about your age doing this job for me not too long ago. He took it in his mind that cutting me out of the deal might be a lucrative path and he took it. Might have worked out for him if he'd kept his mouth shut about how smart he was. He's up there in the woods with you now, 'cept the hands on his watch ain't ticking if you get what I mean. You'll want to remember that in case you get any ideas of your own." He never took his eye off me while he was speaking and I looked across the seat at him and thought for the first time in a while about my father and the penetrating look he would give me or John just before he hit one of us.

"I'm not taking this job to get rich," I said. "Money never meant a whole lot to me. Just what I need to survive."

"That's good," he said. "Survival is a good goal to have." Then he pushed back off the truck and left me sitting there listening to the throb of the engine turning over and over. Before I returned to the cabin I went into the pharmacy just to get familiar with it. I nodded at the pharmacist, who looked like he was expecting me, and I thought about speaking to him but decided to wait on my next trip in. I asked the girl at the register where to find the post office and I bought a card before I left. It was a simple little winter scene on the front and when I opened it I laughed seeing *Merry Christmas* scrawled in big looping letters. I wrote my name and the PO address inside the card and then addressed it to the street that I had read about in the paper and mailed it. Then I went back to begin a solitary life, save for the ghosts that I knew would follow me no matter how far I went.

The first and only letter I received from my brother John was about the child. He explained that it was his and that it was not his. He told me he was bringing him for me to raise; that he had a wife and circumstances that would not allow for the baby. He said that despite all this, he could not see abandoning our blood to a stranger. I did not respond as I knew John was not asking me, but telling me, and that he would leave the baby with me whether I took care of it or not. It's his nature, I guess. And my own nature was thoughtful despite what they say about our family. Way I see it, family is family despite the suffering and circumstances; you can't pick them and they can't pick you. A child, I remember thinking. A child to raise. *Let them come*, I told myself, setting the letter in an old box I kept beneath the bed. Let them come.

It was raining and cold when John came up the road to the cabin that day. I had replied to his letter with directions on how to get to the cabin. His truck tires were bald and the Ford slid all over the place trying to climb up the hill. I was on the porch, sitting in a chair I had set out there ever since receiving the letter. I was waiting for him. He got out of the truck and stood by it, looking at me and me looking at him. I think a lot of things came at us all at once because neither one of us spoke for a few minutes. Then I stood up and walked down the steps and hugged him and he pounded my back like he used to when we were young. The rain was starting to taper off, but the fog and cold had moved in. I told him to come in the cabin and he started to follow me and then stopped and went back for the baby. He opened the passenger door on the truck and brought out a basket. I could not see inside it. Then he reached back in the truck and pulled out a large canvas bag and tossed it on the hood of the truck and told me to take it inside. He kicked the driver's door closed with his foot and we went in together. I had straightened the cabin. Swept the floors out and had made a little crib with some old boards I found back behind the cabin under a pile of wet leaves. I'd made it up with some blankets. John pulled things out of the canvas bag I had taken from him and brought in and started setting them on the table. He had some notes written down on a piece of paper and I looked at them and could see that they were written in a woman's hand. The letters had soft round loops and slanted slightly to the right. I read through the list and told John what it said, cause I figured that he had not taken the time to read it himself. He nodded and then we both looked down at the baby in the basket. He was quiet and stared back at us with a flat expression; not curious or expectant, just stilled and somehow knowing. The last thing that John pulled out of the bag was a large bottle of whiskey and I went to get some mugs from the little pantry I kept. When he brought out the bottle, I was tempted to tell him what I was doing up there in the middle of the woods, but decided against it, knowing he would be attracted to it and would try and insert himself somehow and a cautious voice told me that to raise the child with John involved would be to hobble the baby before he ever had a chance to make something of himself.

I stoked up the fire and he and I talked for a long while about how the baby came to be, and his wife Renee. I listened most of the time and let him talk, sipping my mug and watching him go back to the bottle to refill his. He drank like our father had, taking the brown liquid down his throat in gulps, and I could see that John had become my father and that the drinking had overtaken him and it had conflicted him like Jacob and his struggle with God, and I knew that his hatred of the world around him was growing stronger every day. I saw the transformation come over him once he crossed a threshold in the bottle, and his speech swerved around the room in a dizzying way that gave you the same uncomfortable feeling that you get watching a heavy wind rock a large tree back and forth. All that time the baby never made a sound, and despite being scared about being alone with the child, I wanted John to leave because he was uncovering thoughts and anger that I felt like I had tried very hard to plough under. All that he displayed—his roaring and pacing—those emotions and vicious tones were as much a part of me as they were a part of him. But my isolation had kept me from their reawakening. He stayed through the night, growing drunker and drunker and at one point wandering out of the cabin and into the yard. I let him stay out there and when I heard the rain start back again I went out and found him sitting against a tree, crying uncontrollably. I knelt beside him and put my arm around his shoulder and he leaned into my chest and sobbed. He was trying to speak but it was not clear and then the rain came harder and I stood him up and we walked together back to the cabin porch and up the steps. Inside the baby had started to cry as well, its wails ripping through the cabin like someone had set the makeshift crib on fire. John left the next morning, telling me he would return to check on us, but I knew that it was a weak lie. He walked away from the cabin with me standing and holding the baby on the porch. The rain had set in for a while the best that I could tell from looking at the sky through the tops of the trees, which were dropping their leaves in the turning autumn air. John stopped before getting in the truck and looked at the ground with his hand on the door handle. He did not look back at me, and after a moment, he climbed in and that was the last time that I ever saw him. I went back inside and the room was still like before they had arrived, although I could sense the other life inside there with me. I looked at the note that John had brought, still sitting out, and I picked it up again and noticed a line at the bottom that I had not seen before. "I have been calling the boy Aaron," it said, and the handwriting here was different than the rest of what had been put down, hurried, like it had been scribbled in at the last moment, perhaps to conceal it from John, who had not mentioned a Christian name, or maybe because there had been a fundamental recoil from identifying a child who up until that time had been nothing more than a breathing object, and to name the boy would have been an admission of its humanity. Still, something had moved the hand that wrote it, and the decency of that was somewhat settling.

After a few days with the boy, I took him into the town and found a woman willing to come and help with raising him. It did not take much convincing. She was almost a child herself and had been working in one of the bars where the factory men went after their shifts. I went inside the small barroom and watched her move about unnoticed, attending the vacant tables, running a wet cloth over the marred tops littered with cigarette ash and spilled beer. I waited until the place closed down, the boy in the basket beside me on the floor. His eyes were open and he stared up into the smoky rafters of the ceiling. Her name was Sophia and she had a soft, open face. The kind that was enduring and patient and created for the care of children. She listened without questions and I could tell that the idea of the cabin and the woods appealed to her and I wondered if she had already raised a brother or sister in the shadow of a neglecting father who had been saddled with children without the benefits and pleasures of female comfort. She agreed to the proposition and we left and went to collect her things, leaving for the cabin in the early morning hours.

As I expected, Sophia was content with the solitude of the woods and cared nothing about the stills or my role in tending them. We spoke quietly with one another and I taught her to read and write better than she had learned before, and after some time, I began to share a bed with her and we started to live as man and wife in the most primal sense of that union. In this new role, Sophia tried to be nurturing with the baby. Despite her young appearance, she cared for the child with a maturity I anticipated she would. There was a vulnerability that she sought to overcome. I saw the faintest qualities of my mother in her finer instincts, and in some instances, I detected a genuine warmth, despite the child not being her own. I watched much of this from afar, choosing to observe them when they thought that they were alone. I would find myself standing in the doorway, the boy being bathed in the sink, or in her lap in the chair, Sophia singing into his upturned face, which was always placid but severe. I would go into town to purchase what we needed, and though I offered, she seemed reluctant to take the boy away from the cabin and the confines of the woods that surrounded us. She was guarded in that way, even as Aaron grew and became more willful, teetering across the cabin floor, determined and angry when he fell. She followed his movements with her eyes the way that you watched an animal that you had surprised.

Sometimes we would walk together in the woods, and when I tried to carry Aaron, Sophia would intervene and either pick the boy up herself or insist in her quiet tone that he did not need the help. This I never disputed because by then I could sense the shadow of my brother in Aaron's face. I'm certain that Sophia felt this too, but could not put John's name to it. And should she have been able to see John emerging, she would not have known that the seeded elements of the boy's nature were beyond that of his father and were planted deeper in the origins of my father, whose eyes were like that of the Aaron's, blank and roving. There were times that I tried to convince myself that my preoccupation with our family's intemperate past were unfounded and I would attempt to distract my thinking with small, necessary tasks. Other times I was inwardly fearful of Aaron. I could feel his eyes piercing the dark room when Sophia and I were in the bed and I know that she felt it as well, for she would turn her face to the side and look back across the black, empty expanse as if she had been caught doing something unclean and would suffer judgement as a result.

But for the most part, those years with Sophia were without judgement. Aaron continued to grow and seemed to be healthy and soon was interested in walking through the woods with me, listening to things that I knew to tell him. Occasionally he would ask questions or comment on something he had observed, but usually he would stand a distance from me and simply watch me going about my work. He learned to hunt and cut wood, and he took to reading quickly and with what seemed like very real interest. I would come upon him sometimes sitting by himself and reciting a passage and I admit that I took pride in that and was able to hope that perhaps he would become a person who would not follow in the footsteps of my father, my brother, or even myself. But these were thoughts that I kept to myself, because in reality, I began to see the darker clouds of his being beginning to cluster and storm over. He became cold with Sophia and treated her with jealousy and indignation, as if her presence was insulting to him. He would stare at her when we were in the cabin and would be purposefully loud and jarring with his movements. She spoke to me and I was dismissive but could see that something truly frightened her about the boy. Then on a spring morning while I was splitting wood in the front of the cabin, Sophia stumbled through the front door and fell down the steps. I went to her and saw the handprints around her throat. She was gasping and crying and I held her head in my lap and tried to soothe her.

Aaron stepped into the door of the cabin and looked at us on the ground in front of him. I stared back at him and saw that there was blood on his face and I lifted Sophia's hand and saw that there was blood on her nails and some on her fingers. I kept my eyes on him standing in the doorway and he held my gaze and then he gently closed the door. I took Sophia back to town that afternoon and gave her what little money I had. She took it without a word and walked toward a boarding house. I remember sitting in the truck and watching her walk stiffly up the sidewalk. It was a nice spring day, the smells of rebirth and shaken-off hibernation thick in the air. She walked up the main street and then went around the corner and out of sight. I returned to the woods and to Aaron.

When I pulled up to the cabin, he was sitting on the edge of the porch. I got out of the truck and came to where he was sitting and I stood in front of him and looked down at the top of his head. I could see the long scratch on his face where the nails had dug in. The dried blood ran in a crusting pattern across one cheek. He was holding a hunting knife that I had given him and was whittling a stick. He did not look at me and I knew that it was not out of shame for what he had done, but because he wanted to maintain our balance. I went past him into the cabin and sat down at the table and had a drink of whiskey and sometime later he came in and sat down across from me but said nothing. I rose and got some alcohol and a strip of rag and dropped them in front of him on the table and told him to clean his face. He did so without a word and when he was done, I took the rag and threw it in the wood stove to be burned . We spent the rest of the day in silence and that night when we were eating, he finally spoke and asked if we could read from one of the books and I told him that we could. I went across the room to the shelf holding the books and then I turned and asked why he had attacked Sophia. He spun in his chair to face me. "The dark," he said, and then I asked him to explain what he meant, and he turned and pointed out the window. "The voice in the dark," he said.

PART 2

BILL EDWARDS AND THE AND THE WINSLETT FARM

CHAPTER 21

BILL EDWARDS FALLS

Bill Edwards first saw Katherine Winslett in Taylor Branch's only hardware store. Her father, although Edwards did not recognize he was her father at the time, was talking to the store clerk when Edwards walked in and saw a naturally beautiful young woman standing in the carpentry aisle, casually looking over hammers, boxes of nails, work gloves, and aprons. She was humming softly to herself. He stopped to admire her and she gave him a glance that he later re-lived on an almost daily basis. Her hair was down and she wore a simple dress that just covered her knees. Her slender body, with slightly muscled arms laced behind her back and her hands clasped, was a stark contrast to the harsh and sterile tools, belts, nails, and screws. Her eyes were both curious and warm. He fell hard, there and then. He muttered a greeting and the two of them stood several feet apart, the aisle too narrow to pass shoulder to shoulder. He awkwardly made his way past her and stood looking at the shelves with contrived purpose, having forgotten why he came into the store in the first place. He could hear Katherine's father questioning the clerk about parts and their respective costs, speaking in sharp, clipped sentences that were reminiscent of Edwards's all male interactions in the service. His eyes seemed to have a mind of their own as he stood in the aisle with the girl, poorly hiding glances at her figure and trying to soak in every detail they could, from her slight, but well-postured shoulders to the streamlined curves of her hips. And then, as suddenly as he had been struck, her father called her name and with her own furtive glance, she was gone up the aisle and out the door whose opening and closing was announced by a tarnished brass bell hanging from the tin-plated ceiling of the store. Regaining his composure, Edwards selected the roofing hammer he needed for repair work on his parents' house and made his way to the checkout counter.

"That it?" the clerk asked when he came up to the counter carrying the hammer at his side.

"Who was that?" he asked and the clerk looked at the young man and smiled.

"Not what you were expecting in the tool aisle?"

"No sir," Edwards said. "Who is she?"

"That's Denny Winslett's daughter," the clerk said. "Believe her name is Katherine. She's a peach for sure. Hear that she has a sister, but supposedly that one there is the showstopper. You want this in a bag or are you gonna get straight to work?" the clerk asked, holding up the hammer. Edwards was looking out the window trying to see the girl, but she had disappeared from sight.

"Straight to work," he said absently

"Okay then," the clerk said setting the hammer on the counter with a clunk. "Winsletts are good people. Have a big spread out past the lumber mill. Farm's been out there since I was a boy. Sweet girl. Turns a lot of heads, I guess. Can't say how long Katherine has been out there on the farm, but from the looks of you, I think your ages might measure even." Edwards was not looking at the clerk. He was still looking out the storefront window. He picked up the hammer and went out, the bell marking his departure.

He drove back to Winchester in a daze, the mountain looming in the distance. Spring was coming and the hibernation of winter was giving way to buds and grass and the need for repairs and upkeep after the long winter. He pulled into town and turned into his parents' driveway, which was just off the main road. His father met him when he got out of his truck and they worked on repairing the roof that whole afternoon, the sun warming their backs and the air full of smells that made him think of tanned legs, and necklines, and other things yet to be revealed. He stayed in that state for what seemed like months but was really only days. He helped around the house and did some odd jobs for other people in town and then one night his father came home from work and they were sitting at the table, the three of them eating pork chops and apples with brown sugar, and some corn bread his mother had doctored with lard and bacon, and his father said that he had run into Denny Winslett at the bank and that Denny had asked if he, Bill, was back in town, and he'd told him that he was, and then Denny asked if Bill might be interested in helping out on the farm outside Taylor Branch and Bill's dad had told him that he would ask.

Bill sat looking at his plate of food, thinking about the offer. His father, who was quiet by nature, said nothing to influence him, and his mother, who normally would have peppered him with questions, only finished her food, and asked if either of the men wanted coffee or a piece of pie. Bill and his father accepted and when his mother was in the kitchen preparing the dessert, Bill looked at his father for a moment. He was getting older but that had not changed his sense of pride.

"You don't need me around here, Dad?" His father, who had been scratching dirt from beneath his nail, looked up.

"What for?" he said.

"I don't know," Bill said. "The roof, other repairs…"

"Stop," his father said. "I'd rather you get on with a man like Dennis Winslett than stick around here looking for something to do. Your mother and I have managed up until now and I don't see why that should change." Bill began to explain his intent, but his father stopped him again.

"Bill," he said in a voice that had been familiar since he was a child. It was a voice that was both kind and assertive. While his father had not been a talker, he had always chosen his words carefully and spoke them with a confidence that Bill found comforting. It was a voice that you carried with you into the world, and one that you could turn to in private for reassurance.

"All right," Bill said, but his father had gone back to his nails. "It's just that I've been away, you know. Down with Uncle Pete and I thought maybe you might need the help. I learned a lot down there,

Dad. I just wanted you to know that I can help out around here if you need it."

"Ah," his father said and Bill looked up to see his mother coming through the door from the kitchen holding a plate and cup of coffee. "Now this is just delightful," his father said, reaching out his hand to take the plate and the cup. His mother smiled at Bill as she handed them over. His father put them on the table and looked at the piece of pie admiringly. "Who knows, Bill. You might even find a wife out there in the working world, and if she's as sweet as your mother here, you'll have done all right by me." Bill's mother laughed and went back to the kitchen. "You're a mess, James Edwards," she said over her shoulder.

"Don't I know it," Bill's father said, and took up his fork to eat, holding the hot coffee in his left hand as he did.

CHAPTER 22

ON THE FARM

The morning after his father mentioned the job at the farm, Bill woke early and drove his truck back through Taylor Branch, arriving at the Winslett place just before the sun came up. He could see several men coming and going from the barn entrance, their features hard to determine in the sparse light. Thick smears of bug splatter covered his windshield and he sat behind the wheel of the truck, unsure of whether to approach the farmhouse or wait to be seen. After a few minutes going unnoticed, he opened the door of the truck and stood thinking that there would likely be dogs around the place. He ducked back in the cab and pressed lightly on the horn with the side of his hand. The honk brought all of their heads up, tilting to the side to make out the silhouetted vehicle and figure half in and half out of the driver's side of the truck. One of them set something to the side and began walking down the slope of the hill toward Bill. He came around the open door of the truck to meet the man halfway. Lights were on inside the house and as the two men neared one another in the farmyard, he heard the whine of a screen door opening and thought that it would likely be Dennis Winslett, coming outside to see why a horn was going off in his driveway at quarter-to-six in the morning.

"Help you," the man said, stopping several feet in front of Bill. He was young and thin as a reed, a physique that suited a high school basketball center. Bill moved toward the man, his hand outstretched, but he dropped it when he realized they were going to speak first from a distance.

"I'm Bill Edwards," he said. "My father James talked with Mr. Winslett yesterday in Winchester. He mentioned that he needed hands out here and I'm here to speak with him about a job." The tall man stood quietly regarding Bill. Behind him, another tall man was coming down the porch steps, then coming across the yard in long strides. He did not appear to be in a hurry. Bill turned his attention back to the first man, who was looking at him the way you examine a picture hanging crooked on the wall. Bill waited.

The man from the house came up behind the first man and stopped. Then he spoke. "Hey there, Bill" he said. "Did not expect to see you this soon, but we're glad you're here. You find us okay?"

Bill looked surprised at being recognized. "Yes, Mr. Winslett. No problems. This is quite the place."

"Well, it's home and more work to keep it up every year. How long you been back in Tennessee?"

"Few weeks, I suppose," Bill said. Winslett nodded.

"Father says you were down in Georgia somewhere, working with an uncle?"

"Yes sir," Bill said. "Athens." He thought of how much slower time had moved since arriving back home. The lack of things to do and the monotony of living with his parents had started to take a toll on him, and while he was grateful for them, he was also very restless. Now he felt exposed standing in front of these men whose lives had a daily purpose.

"All right," Winslett said. "We're glad that you are here." The other man standing in front of Winslett did not seem so sure about that, but he remained quiet. Bill began to relax, anticipating the prospect of laboring under the sun. *Let him size me up,* Bill thought of the man who looked at him like a crooked picture. *I'll hold my own soon enough.*

Winslett spoke again, pointing at the man in front of him. "This is Steve," he said. "He's not much on conversation or manners, as you have probably already figured out. That right, Steve?" Steve stepped out of Winslett's line of sight and adjusted his stance, placing his hands on his hips, now shaking his head in response. Winslett clicked his tongue and Bill thought it indicated a tired disappointment, as if this one-sided conversation with Steve were nothing new. "Yeah, well," Winslett said and Bill stepped forward and extended his hand.

"It's nice of you to have me here, Mr. Winslett. I really do appreciate the opportunity." Winslett shook Bill's hand, looking him in the eye. "Sure Bill. Steve here," he motioned with his head, "is our foreman. Been with me a long time now. He keeps this place running when I'm gone and while I'm here for that matter. He'll keep you busy." Bill nodded at Steve, who continued to assess him. The morning sun was coming into the yard gently, warming the air in a muted yellow light. Winslett clicked his tongue again and Steve walked in the other direction, back toward the barn. Bill watched him go then turned again to Winslett.

"Steve's wary of newcomers," Winslett said. "We run a rather large operation here and as you might imagine, men come and go all the time. Some good and others not so good. Steve worked with all of them. He'll warm up to you after a while. He's got his reasons for being cautious." Bill nodded his understanding. Winslett stood surveying the fields below the house and the barn.

"Anyway," he finally said, "come up to the house, Bill. I'd like you to meet my wife. I believe she and your mother are friends as well. Then we can talk about how you might be able to help out around here."

"Yes, sir," Bill said. The two men walked up the slope together and onto the porch of the house. They came through the foyer and then into the kitchen. It smelled deeply of fried food, grease, and coffee. Lights burned in the space and a pudgy black woman worked at the stove, frying pork, her back to the men. She was humming softly and she only turned around when Winslett picked up a mug that was sitting on a table in the middle of the room. The long wooden table appeared to be as old as the farm itself. The thick wood top was stained and gouged from years of use. There were dark black rings where hot iron pots had been set down, and chips along the edges that had been sanded to a dull shine to keep people from getting splinters. The benches that flanked both sides of the table were uneven with indentations and it looked as if a couple of the legs of the table itself had been replaced. This was the kitchen of a rural life, overseen by capable women and overrun by men breaking from laborious jobs plagued with broken parts, uncooperative or sick animals, and always the threat of financial trouble. And yet, even through the worst of times, the iron pans sizzled and spat their grease and roiled with oily gravy, the ovens like hulking furnaces, churning out sheets of biscuits and skillets of cornbread that were pulled from the heat, their contents placed on platters that fed generations, cared for and washed clean morning, noon, and night, because the food and the process of cooking that food upheld a common and proud determination to be productive and self-reliant. Bill Edwards was comfortable in this space, pungent with its ritual.

The cooking woman turned to look at them, a fork in her hand, her round torso wrapped in a blotched apron, breasts lumped on her pear frame.

"You want some coffee?" she asked.

"Yes we do, LoLo," Winslett said. "This is Bill Edwards. He is going to come work for us. Drove over this morning from Winchester. Bill, this is Loretta, but our girls have been calling her LoLo since they were children." Winslett exchanged a look with LoLo and she smiled, but Bill sensed something more in her eyes, something hidden beneath the surface that had emerged with experience and acquired knowledge that spoke to her instincts and ability to make quick and accurate assessments of men who had come and gone from her kitchen over the years.

"Nice to meet you," she said warmly. "You want something to eat, or just the coffee?" Winslett looked at Bill, who spoke back to the cook.

"Coffee would be fine, Ms. Loretta," Bill said, and she smiled again and picked up the coffee pot from one of the stove eyes and reached for a cup hanging on a peg next to the sink. She filled it and then placed it on the table, fragrant steam curling up.

"There's honey in that jar there," she pointed. "You help yourself." Bill nodded and took the cup. LoLo walked around the side of the table and filled Winslett's cup for him and then went back to the stove and moved the pork around in the pan.

"Let's go talk on the porch, Bill. We'll wait for Mary out there."

The sun was now fully stretching over the land, like LoLo's honey spilled across a warped tabletop, the fields, barns, and distant tree lines warming in both appearance and temperature. The two men sat in chairs on the porch, which stood off the ground and was broad, spanning the front of the house and disappearing around both sides. The boards were weathered and painted a dull blue color, scuffed in places with sections that had been mended over the years. Its roof and railing framed a picture of the farm, now alive with activity and noise. While they sat in the rocking chairs, Winslett observed the hands with detachment while Bill admired the operation, which was regimented and orderly in its disciplined function. Winslett looked at ease in the rocker. His long legs stretched out before him, the coffee cup held in his lap with both hands. His body was still, but Bill could see that his mind was very much at work, turning over and examining both large and small issues of concern and opportunity. Bill wondered where he might fit in the man's consideration.

"I've always admired your father," Winslett began. "He and I have known one another since long before you were born. I tried several times to get him to come to work for me, but I don't think he cared very much for farming. I told him there was plenty of carpentry to do around the place, but he always politely told me no. Some days I think I envy him." He laughed. Bill thought of his father. As far back as he could remember, the man had put in long days and often pressed on late into the night. He rarely complained, and when he did, it was after Bill had gone to bed in his small room off their kitchen. Some nights he could hear his parents talking through the thin walls of the house. Most of the time it was about money, and where they were going to come up with it to take care of one thing or another. His mother mostly listened, and when she did speak she was often consoling and support- ive, and as Bill grew older and began to establish his own work ethic, he realized that his father's perseverance was upheld, in large part, by the foundation of his marriage, which was unwavering and constant, always outlasting storms or periods of financial drought.

"Saw you in the hardware store the other day," Winslett said.

"Yes, sir," he said, The image of the girl standing in the narrow aisle rising up in Bill's mind.

"Tim Jennings gets my orders right about a third of the time. The man means well, but my Lord he is careless." Bill laughed. He had heard his father express the same sentiment about the hardware store owner.

"But there are not a lot of options, I guess."

"I'm sorry I did not speak," Bill said.

"Nonsense. How would you have known?" Bill guessed he was right.

"Anyway," Winslett said, "James, your father, is a good man, and once I recognized you I thought maybe the son might like farming more than the old man did." He smiled at Bill and sipped his coffee.

"But enough of that," Winslett said, seeming bored with himself. "All of this aside is my windy way of bringing something up before you get started. Any thoughts on what that might be?"

"Yes sir, I guess I might have an idea." Something in Winslett's face changed, and similar to the exchange that he had with the cook in the kitchen, Bill knew the look was not directed at him, but also applied to him in a way that was about to become clear.

"I don't like to start out working relationships in the contrary—this subject or any subject for that matter," Winslett said. "But, I have found that it's easier to address things up front rather than addressing them at the stage of consequence. So I will get to it."

"The girl that you saw in the hardware store is my daughter, Katherine. She gets her looks and her smarts from her mother. All of that will be evident when you meet Mary. To say that I am a lucky man is grossly understated, and to describe me as protective is exponentially more understated. I have been told by both of them, on numerous occasions, that my antiquated position is both tiresome and largely unnecessary. Be that as it may, my perspective on this matter remains unchanged. I'm first and foremost Katherine's father, and you know what that means and potentially entails. But I am also a man, Bill. No longer a young man, of course, but a man just the same. And if farming teaches you one thing, it's that putting your head up your own ass is the fastest way to lose everything you've got." He shifted in his chair, turning to face Bill. "All this is to say that I welcome your help, but I'd like your comings and goings here to be focused on farming the earth and not on cultivating a relationship with my daughter. If that sounds rehearsed it's because it is, and you will be glad to know that the lecture is close to its conclusion. I am sure Katherine will be a temptation whether she means to or not, and for that I have some responsibility, as does her mother. But I'm telling you straight now. We understand one another?"

Bill nodded. "Yes sir," he said. "We understand one another."

"Good," Winslett said. He turned back to face the front of the porch.

"Dennis," a voice called, footsteps immediately behind it. "Is someone out there with you?"

"Yes," Winslett said. "Come out here, Mary, and meet James Edwards's son, Bill."

Mary Winslett came through the screen door and both men stood. She walked across the porch and touched her husband's shoulder before extending her hand to Bill.

"Bill Edwards," she said, smiling and smelling faintly of perfume. "How are your parents?"

"Good, Mrs. Winslett," Bill said. "My mother said to be sure and tell you hello."

"You do the same for me," she said.

"Bill's going to start working for us, Mary," Winslett said and then paused. "Well, I guess I should say that I am going to offer Bill a job and he can decide if he wants to take it or not." The two of them turned to Bill and he looked startled.

"Oh, yes sir," he said. "I would very much like to start working here."

"Well that's settled," Mary said. "Welcome." She smiled and Winslett's earlier comment about his daughter's looks being closely tied to her mother was proven true; Bill had to force himself to look away. Mary Winslett excused herself and went back into the house, letting the screen door bang closed behind her. The two men sat in silence on the porch, finishing the last of their cooling coffee. Then Winslett rose from the rocker and the two of them went down the stairs and into the yard to find the foreman.

CHAPTER 23

BILL AND KATHERINE

B
ill Edwards went to work on the Winslett farm the same morning that he'd had coffee with Dennis and met his wife Mary. True to his straightforward nature, Winslett had indicated that there was no time like the present to start work, and Edwards had walked off the porch and been more formally introduced to the men milling around the barn, preparing for the day's labor. Now a hired hand, they had softened ever-so-slightly and welcomed him into the fold. Half an hour later he was pulling bales of hay off of an old flatbed truck and stacking them floor to ceiling in the cavernous barn that seemed more like a bucolic cathedral. Birds flew in and out of the open doors, perching and chirping from the rafters as the men came and went, the weight of the semi-wet bales gradually slowing their progress as the sun came into the sky and burned with the heat of an uncovered single bulb left on for too long, suspended and angry yellow. The air inside the barn was thick and dusty, and despite their labored breathing, the men took breaks to smoke in the yard and wipe the sweat from their faces and arms with oily strips of cloth they kept tucked in their back pockets. The monotony of the work was peaceful and straightforward. What it lacked in intellectual requirement was subsidized by the back and forth banter between the hands as they passed one another on their way to and from the truck, the rapport a balance between good-natured sarcasm and physical prowess. Edwards could see the

tractors moving back and forth through the fields in the distance, could hear their clunky rumble and farting exhaust.

Around lunchtime, Mary Winslett came out on the porch and yelled to one of the men exiting the barn, and he in turn whistled and everyone dropped what they were doing and walked in a group toward the house and then around to the side where two picnic tables, pushed end-to-end, were stationed beneath an enormous bur oak. On the tables were plates of food, laid out on platters with three large pitchers containing tea and lemonade. The men placed themselves and Mary came out carrying a basket of cornbread, sliding between the gap in the bench seats and setting it in the center of the table, steam seeping out from beneath the towel thrown over the top to keep in the oven's heat. Edwards picked up his fork to begin and one of the men touched his arm and motioned to Mary, who stood on the other side of the table from Edwards, her posture straight, head bowed and eyes closed. Edwards quickly put his fork back on the table and dropped his own head.

"Lord, please watch over these men to see that they remain safe from harm as they provide this good work that feeds our bodies and nourishes our souls. We ask this in your only son Jesus' name. Amen." They closed the prayer in unison and began to eat, utensils clanking against the dishes, their arms moving mechanically, pushing the food into their mouths, washing it down with long gulps from their Mason jars. Bill smiled at the simplicity of the meal and the gratitude in which the men consumed the food. Mary stood among them as if overseeing a Thanksgiving feast, asking how everything tasted and if they needed anything. Winslett had not exaggerated his wife's beauty. She was tall, unusual for women of her generation it seemed, and she moved with a fluidity that spoke to her sophistication and depth. Edwards thought of his own mother, whose appearance was nothing like Mary Winslett's, and whose demeanor was even less so. He thought that Mary Winslett shared in her husband's success and sense of purpose, where his own mother's role was one of support, and her personality veiled in a shyness that Bill imagined had been her way since childhood. He could picture his mother, dressed in plain clothes as a little girl, engaged in solitary play with a doll, or maybe a housecat, the two of them content to let the day pass without fuss or drama. Mary Winslett, while very much a hostess in the traditional sense, seemed keenly aware of her surroundings and accountable in a way that he was accustomed to seeing only in men. It was as though she had encountered more of the world's true identity and it had made an impression on her that invoked an assertiveness both steady and alert. They ate and talked and when the meal was through, they smoked and stacked the dishes for LoLo, who came out of the house in a rambling gait, humming quietly to herself as she came across the yard. Edwards watched the cook and wondered how long she had been on the farm, carrying out a multitude of chores that likely included cooking, cleaning, and watching children. She carried herself and spoke with Mary in a formal but relaxed posture and seemed pleased that the plates were empty and mopped. And the men spoke to her kindly and without demand or condescension, and Edwards appreciated the scene even more and was pleased with himself for taking the initiative to secure a job, feeling more accomplished than he had even the day before when, looking out over the late afternoon, he had begun to question his path. Above them, the oak's leaves rippled in a warm breeze coming from below the slope, and the light splintered over the tables and the air smelled like salted meat and hay. They left the table, thanking Mary and LoLo, and went back to the barn and resumed stacking the hay until late afternoon when they placed the last of the bales inside and latched the large doors. They milled about in the yard a while longer and then they wandered down toward the fields and turned up a path that led to a neat row of houses that had been constructed for farm hands. Edwards seemed to be one of the few who lived off the farm.

He carried on this routine for a couple of weeks, laboring at different tasks, helping with broken pieces of equipment, mending fences, and clearing out debris from the creek that ran through the property. He was working on a broken tractor clutch one afternoon with another man named Edgar, when his hand slipped and skidded across a pedal, opening up the skin in a deep gash that sprung fresh blood instantly, cutting paths down his tan and dirty arm in streaks.

"God Almighty, Bill," Edgar said and stepped back. Edwards lifted his arm and examined his hand where the sharp metal edge had cut deeply into the meat of his palm. He suddenly felt the heat of the sun more intently, and he sat down hard on his ass.

"Let me get something to stop that," Edgar said and was turning to go for water and towel when a woman spoke.

"Stop what," she said. The two men turned and Katherine Winslett was standing a few feet behind the tractor.

"Bill cut his hand pretty good, Ms. Katherine," Edgar said. "I'm gonna run up to the house and get some soap and a towel."

"All right," she said. "I guess you better." Bill sat looking at her, his elbow propped on his knee, his hand leaking blood. Edgar excused himself and went around the girl and started toward the house.

"You okay?" she asked and came to where Edwards was sitting.

"I am," he said. "Hurts a little, but I guess it looks worse than it actually is." She stepped closer. She was wearing a simple white dress and her hair was pulled back. Her complexion was dark and her eyes were a rich brown. She reached for his arm, and he tried to pull it back, but she caught it by the wrist and pulled it to her. She watched to see what he would do next, and she smiled and turned the arm over to look at the underside of the hand.

"It's gonna need a stitch," she said and let him have it back.

"Maybe," he said. "Probably nothing."

"Either way, you need to wash it. It can get infected." Bill nodded.

"Yes mam. Edgar went to…"

"You're Bill," she said interrupting him, looking closely at his sun-burned face.

"Yes mam," he said and started to push himself up to stand, but she motioned him back down.

"I'm Katherine Winslett."

"Yes mam," he said, easing himself back down with his good hand. "I know that. Careful of your dress," he said. "You have some blood there," and he pointed to a spot on her hand where his blood had smeared.

"Oh," she said. "Thank you." She knelt and dragged the side of her hand through the grass and then examined it to see if she had removed the blood. Satisfied, she looked again at Edwards.

"What did you do to it?" she said.

"Do to what?"

"Your hand," she said.

"Oh. Raked it across that pedal there." She walked to the tractor and looked at the pedal. Small spots of blood were drying on the flat medal. The tools they had been using sat next to it, hot to the touch in the sun. She picked one up, examined it, and set it back down quickly.

"Ouch," she said and shook her hand with exaggeration.

"You're from over in Winchester, Daddy says."

"I am," Edwards said, and stood up. She did not stop him this time.

"You like it over there?"

"I suppose," he said. "Never really known anything else save the time I spent with my uncle down in Georgia."

"Georgia," she said musingly. "And what were you doing with your uncle in Georgia?"

"Working," he said.

"Huh. Well what do you think about working here?"

Edwards shrugged and grinned, looked at his hand. The bleeding had slowed. He kicked at the ground with his boot, afraid to meet her eyes.

"Nice," he said. "I like it very much. It's beautiful."

"I suppose it is," Katherine said. She walked around the side of the tractor and momentarily out of view. She reemerged and something about the way she was walking and looking around the open spaces made him wonder if maybe she was not completely sincere in her perspective of the farm. It appeared that she had forgotten he was standing there observing her.

"It's beautiful and it has many lovely things to offer. But I want to leave someday." She looked at Bill after she said this and came back around the tractor to stand in front of him.

"You know. Your father…"

"Told you to leave me alone," she finished for him. "He tells all the new boys that."

"Well yeah," he said. "I guess I can understand that." A strand of her black hair had worked itself loose and hung in a ringlet, slightly bouncing off her cheek when she cocked her head to look at him, an expression of surprise and curiosity showing itself in her eyes and in her slight smile. She had a smallish mouth that reacted to what she was thinking.

"Is that so," she said. "And does that mean that I'm breaking a rule here by speaking with you?" Bill continued working the ground with his foot.

"I don't know," he said. "I'm just telling you what he said."

"And what exactly did he say?"

"Edgar's gonna be back. I don't know that we need…"

"Edgar's probably forgotten why he went to the house in the first place," she said, setting her stance.

"He told me that you were his daughter and that I was here to help with farm work and that was it." She smiled and looked up at the sky.

"It wasn't my rule," he said quickly, feeling as though he had offended her. She kept her head turned upward, chin sharply lined and jutting out, and then she brought her face back down even with his. For the first time, he *really* saw her and was struck by the effect of her presence. Something. No, everything about her was remarkably distinct and without pretense. She radiated an effortless grace and whatever was passing between them was, at the same time, slightly sad, and Edwards knew that he wanted to know more, wanted her in the most visceral sense, but he also felt a compelling need to protect her and maybe drive out some of the melancholy that was barely concealed behind her smile and replace it with a lightness that he felt she deserved, felt she had always deserved. The mounting feeling was profound and thoroughly confusing to the point that standing in front of her made him so painfully self-aware and foolish that he wanted to laugh.

"I see," she said absently and then nodded, biting her lip as she did so. "Daddy thinks he is protecting me from myself," she said. "As if I'm still a little girl playing along the creek, ignorant of snakes or slippery rocks. He means well," she said, turning away, "I suppose there have been times when I needed his protection. But I don't think anything bad will come from me helping someone—boy or not—to mend a cut." She turned back and started to walk away and Edwards followed at a distance.

"I didn't mean anything by it, Katherine. I was just trying to be respectful." She looked hard at him.

"Respectful of me or my father?"

"Both, I guess," he said, but he was not entirely sure which was correct.

"We've met before, Bill Edwards," she said. "In the hardware store in Taylor Branch."

"I know," he said too quickly. "I remember."

"Do you?" she said and resumed walking. This time he did not follow.

"Take care of that hand," she said over her shoulder, "and let mother know if it needs a stitch. She can do it herself. Would not be the first time someone got sewn up around here." Then she was gone, and soon thereafter Edgar returned with a towel and metal bucket with soap and water in it.

"I spilled some on the way down," he said.

"That's alright, Edgar. This will do." He took the towel and dunked it into the bucket and then cleaned his hand and arm, the soap stinging slightly. When he was done, he wrung out the towel, dumped the water and soap out of the bucket, and then dropped the towel back in. The two of them went back to the tractor and the broken clutch. Bill tried to focus, but could see nothing but Katherine's face. Even the sound and scent of the man working next to him could not distract his thoughts, and the heat of the day and the thick smell of grease and gasoline coming from the tractor made him dizzy and unsteady on his feet. He knew he was not reading too much into the brief conversation. There had been something there. An attraction of unnamed origin, like something magnetized and pulling at him. He imagined how her skin might feel beneath his calloused hands, running one finger along the contour of her neck. It was intoxicating, and before he realized he was going to, he spoke out loud.

"She's something else," he said, but Edgar did not look up.

"She is," he said and gave a small grunt pulling on the wrench.

"Think Mr. Winslett means what he says about staying away?"

"Yes," Edgar said. "I think he means exactly what he says."

"Maybe," Edwards said.

"Maybe?" Edgar said, and Edwards turned around to see the man no longer looking at the tractor clutch but staring at Edwards with a stern look on his face.

"Hey, Edgar…" Edwards started.

"Look here," Edgar said. He passed a hand over his hairless head. "There's things that you don't know about when it comes to that girl and Mr. Winslett ain't the only person on this farm that keeps an eye out for her."

"Edgar, I didn't mean anything by it. I was just…"

"I know what you 'was just,' but I'm telling you that you need to keep your thoughts to yourself when it comes to Miss Katherine." Edwards took a step back. The conversation was making him uncomfortable and his hand was starting to throb. He kept his eyes level with Edgar's face and offered a slight smile, touching the injured hand. "Understood," he said and after a second, Edgar smiled back. "All right," he said. "All right."

They went back to the tractor and before the sun was setting over the western fields they had it running smoothly again and Edgar seemed in good spirits and to have forgotten the sharp conversation about Katherine. Edwards climbed on the back of the machine as Edgar steered it out of the field and back toward the barn. The fumes from the exhaust were thick and before they reached the front yard in front of the big house he had to hop off and move away from it to breathe fresh air. He walked slowly up the slope, taking in the massive scope and production of Winslett's place. It was impressive beyond anything that he had ever seen. It moved toward the horizon in all directions and the significance of this tamped down the image of the girl that had rattled his nerves as if he were standing atop a tall ladder whose footing suddenly shifted. *Still*, a voice hiding somewhere in the back of his head whispered, quietly, but loud enough to get his attention. *Still…*

CHAPTER 24

KATHERINE

Still. There are times when I come awake at night and I am under the tree and he is breathing heavily and forcefully over top of me and I can't get the scream out of my throat because he has covered my mouth with his filthy hand and I can smell the scent of his flesh and it makes me sick to my stomach and then he is penetrating me in such an unholy way and I'm trying to scream, but can't and then I am trying to move my mind away and I can't because what is happening is consuming both of us and its desire is ravenous and I want only for it to stop and finally it does and I am crawling away, ashamed and spent of energy and then I am back in my room and thinking of Renee and mother and LoLo and the child that is not there. Still these things come to me in nightmare and my waking trepidation for all that is unknown and unfamiliar to me. But this man coming up the way now, moving along behind the tractor and looking around the farm with the same wonder that even now I cherish when I see it in the majestic light of the evening sun, this man has an openness that I can trust. Something in his face suggests kindness and understanding and patience. Patience that I know any man will need if he is to be with me. The idea that I can look through this window and see both promise and the sinister past that lives beneath that tree brings me some comfort that perhaps these two dimensions can co-exist inside my mind and that perhaps a marriage built on honesty and genuine love can somehow collapse the

172

dimension in the tree's shadow and send it back to its hellish beginning. I am no longer a child and have not been since I was forced to bring one into the world, so I am not being simple when I think of banishing the dark things that plague my thoughts, but still. Bill Edwards. Mrs. Katherine Edwards. I can foresee that union and more importantly, I believe that Bill can foresee that union as well. I will take my time. I will not assume that I am capable of all that would entail, but I will move things forward and I will work on my father who has suffered even more than me, I think. He takes on the full responsibility of the innocent and he has lost a daughter just as I have lost a sister. But being the victim, I can't feel or absorb the guilt that he has created. He is drunk with it, while I am chastened by it and we move around one another like two people keeping the same secret and wanting desperately to share it, but afraid of its magnitude. Mother. Mother is more powerful than both father and me. She is a giant in her strength. But I think she wants me to seek out a man such as Bill Edwards. Wants me to be a whole person again. And she takes on both the guilt and the shame with such grace. She thinks of Renee differently than father and I do. She hates her, I believe. Hatred coming from a ruptured spring of deep sadness and confusion. I don't believe that any of us will ever understand what has happened to Renee. I know only that I must put her aside and move beyond the view from this window. He walks with such purpose, this Bill Edwards. I will pursue him. I will let him pursue me. I am deserving of this.

CHAPTER 25

RETURNING HOME

Edwards climbed in his truck, sunburned and spent from the day's work. He had to make the drive back to his parents' house in Winchester. He had not made enough on the Winslett farm to put anything down on a house of his own and apartments were non-existent in Taylor Branch. Everything save the Winslett farm seemed to be non-existent in Taylor Branch. And larger than the farm itself was Katherine Winslett, moving away from him in her white dress as he stood gawking and holding his cut hand. After putting a couple of miles between himself and the farm, he had all but forgotten the gravity of his conversation with Edgar and the unfiltered warning about Katherine. Edgar had been serious about it. So much so that Edwards had thought he might put his hands on him and he felt uncertain as to what his reaction would have been should it have come to that. But it didn't and they had left things neutral between them. *Still. Still.* Wasn't Katherine an adult? And wasn't he an adult as well? How could she not be free to make her own decisions? He could not imagine what might have occurred in her past that would make her so fragile that even a conversation with a boy—*no, a man*—would be off limits. He was an only child and no one watched over him like that. *You're a boy,* he thought. *It's different and you know it. Still.*

He could not get her out of his head. The easiness about her was overwhelming and sophisticated in an inexplicable way that was far

174

removed from the pretty and one-dimensional girls he had known. Hers went deeper and much broader than her looks. He had already conceded that he was swimming out of his depth, and yet that was not a deterrent as it might have been in his past. He could tell by the way that she articulated the things that she wanted to say, how she phrased words carefully and with purpose, that she was educated. And not in a strictly academic sense, but on a level that at times was intimidating. But he knew that he could keep up, even if he had to fill some of the holes with bad jokes and self-deprecation, he could keep up. *You'll lose your job*, he thought. Maybe. But maybe not. If he was smart about it. If he was cunning and transparent in both his intentions and subsequent actions. But Winslett was clear. Clear as can be. And Edgar? Edgar was clear not of his own making, but from Winslett. Everyone had been warned, and what made him special? What made him the exception to the paternal rule? Edwards could not answer that, only knew, felt, that he had to try. To at least make the effort, and if it cost him his job, it would be worth that. Something about Katherine Winslett said that she was worth losing a job over. He could always get another job.

This is crazy, Billy. You don't even know this girl, had one real conversation with her and that was over a busted hand, a busted hand and some idle flirting with the boss' daughter. She probably does that with all you boys, likes to watch you fumble over yourselves. No, he thought. *There have not been any other boys. She's feeling you out because she's as unfamiliar with all of this as you are and this is the dance that you have to go through to find out what is real and what is not. And whether she is looking for you to lead or follow, you have to make up your own mind whether or not you want to take the chance now that the invitation has been extended. There's a sweet innocence about her, but at the same time, there is something raw as well, something that she is hiding beyond a lack of experience or an over-sheltered existence. Something that she has buried, buried deep down for fear of being discovered. But isn't that the same for everyone*, he thought. *Don't we all tuck something away even when we are prepared to share ourselves with a stranger? Maybe*, he thought, steering the truck through a tight turn, a small patch of light from the approaching town coming into view across the valley floor. *Maybe you ought not think so much.*

It was getting dark and the road ahead was empty. He was watching for deer and was starting to feel silly having this back and forth conversation with himself. Then it occurred to him that it was not Dennis Winslett who was the key to getting closer to Katherine. Dennis had an inherent, solitary perspective on the subject. Mary Winslett was Katherine's mother and thereby the contributor to her daughter's appeal. It was Mary he needed to approach. He would have to be careful how he did it, careful not to upset the marital order of things, so to speak. But if he could get to Mary by being polite and genuine, she would respect that. Hadn't she married her own husband for those exact same traits and characteristics? And when he was able to build up some credibility with the mother, he'd get her to go to Mr. Winslett on his behalf. Not to ask if he would give his permission for Bill to approach Katherine, but to ask if he would be willing to speak with Bill *about* approaching Katherine. *That's chicken shit, Edwards.* "No," he said out loud, yanking the ash tray out of the dash. He pulled a cigarette from his shirt pocket and stuck it into his mouth. Then he found the lighter in his jeans, and keeping his eyes on the road, he spun the lighter's wheel and touched the flame to the tip of the Lucky. He cracked the window and smoked contentedly, thinking about Mary Winslett. He composed his advance, speaking the lines out loud, trying different inflections and facial expressions as he pushed the Ford through the darkness, following the headlights that illuminated the twisting road in front of him.

He spent the next four weeks working harder than he ever had before. He made sure to steer clear of Katherine, but also ensuring that she saw him as often as possible. He would offer a small smile and she would return it, and more than once, he caught her looking back over her shoulder as she walked in the opposite direction. The labor was two-sided. First in the fields and around the barns, and secondly at the daytime meal, helping with the service and clearing plates even though he was not expected to. The men razzed him, asking if he was looking to get a date with LoLo, and he took it willingly and in stride. Edgar watched him from afar and when Edwards noticed that he was being observed he would look up and Edgar would give him a wink or a marginal smile that seemed to suggest that he may have done some thinking of his own on the subject of Miss Katherine, and while he was never going to disobey a direct order from Winslett, he was content to let this play out as long as the more intimate boundaries were observed and upheld.

It was late in the afternoon when Edwards came up the hill and saw Mary by herself in the garden. She was tending the herbs and small patches of vegetables, and she neatly clipped and trimmed the way he imagined an artist might go about touching up a painting. Her posture was poised and straight even when she squatted to clip a low vine or scratch a weed loose from the dirt. He paused, wondering if interrupting her would be counterproductive to his plan. He stood, blinking in the sunlight, turning the phrases over in his mind to get them right. He began to walk toward the garden gate when she spoke, her back still to him.

"Mr. Edwards," she said, and snipped a piece of squash free and dropped it into a wicker basket that was sitting on the garden path beside her. She turned holding the pair of pruning clippers and regarded him with authentic predilection.

"Mrs. Winslett," he said. "May I talk with you for a second?" She tossed the clippers into the basket with the vegetables and pulled off the gloves she had been wearing. She stepped toward him and smiled warmly.

"Is it about Katherine?"

He swallowed hard. "I—" he stammered. "Well…"

"Go ahead, Bill," Mary said and gave a slight laugh that made him forget his opening line.

"Yes," he said. "See, I was going to…" Mary looked at him with a mixture of bemusement and sympathy, and then took up the conversation before he could continue.

"Let's see," she said, picking something off of her blouse. "Tell me if I'm getting close."

Bill stood impatiently on the other side of the garden gate. Despite being late afternoon, he could feel the fresh trickles of sweat on his back.

"You've taken an interest in my daughter…" she said and looked into the sun. Squinting, continued. "My daughter Katherine." Because she was not addressing him directly, he grew more nervous, and was beginning to think he had made a mistake. Then abruptly she looked away from the sun and back at him.

"You have taken an interest in my daughter and you want me to help you clear it with my husband so that you might act on your feelings. Have I got that right?" He was not surprised by her accurate assessment. He realized that he had known all along that to conceal his desire was futile when it came to Mary Winslett. The knowledge that Katherine was of an age where the prospect of being with a man was imminent was likely on Mary's mind more so than anyone else's, including her daughter and any would-be suitor. Bill tried to appear calm.

"Come inside the gate," Mary said. He did and walked up the path slowly, stopping a few feet from where she stood next to the basket. Her posture was easier now and he attempted to relax his stance, but his nerves were making him rigid.

"Bill," she said, placing her hands on her hips in a mocking, playful gesture. "Were you listening to our conversation at the supper table?"

His reaction answered for him.

"You see, I ask because this very same topic came up just last night while we were eating. Funny how things work, don't you think? Only, the conversation last night was not about you speaking with Katherine, rather, it was Katherine seeking permission to speak with you."

"What did he say?" It came out sounding as anxious as he felt. Mary laughed loudly and came closer still. She reached out and touched his hand. *She is a beautiful woman*, he thought. Everything about her was grace and style and there was strength in her eyes that was both unsettling and comforting at the same time. Maybe that was what he was being drawn to in Katherine. He could not be entirely sure, but the radiance in those eyes was indisputable and they pinned him in place.

"Why don't you go and ask him yourself? I believe he is in his study. LoLo will show you where it is."

He looked at her and for the second time she smiled warmly.

"Go," she said.

He turned to leave, trying very hard not to run.

"Bill," she said.

He looked back.

"I don't recommend that you ask for my husband's permission."

"How's that?" he said.

"I have sown some of this ground for both of you," she said. "Tell him what you want, Bill. He will understand and respect that more than you asking for his permission. That may sound backwards, but it's what will resonate with him. Trust me."

"Yes mam," he said.

"Dennis is in his study. Ask LoLo to show you where it is." He lingered. "Go, Bill," she said and he turned and went out of the garden and jogged to the house as Mary went back to her basket for the clippers.

CHAPTER 26

BILL ADVANCES

Bill did as he was directed, and the conversation with Dennis Winslett was short and to the point. He was out of the study in less than five minutes and Dennis sat in his chair behind the large desk that had been in his family for multiple generations, feeling a seeping relief that brought him to silent tears. It was impossible for him to say if he had handled the rape of his daughter appropriately, and as a result, he had retreated into his own head, relegating the worst of the images to unhealthy dreams that tossed him like a wooden canoe trapped amidst the rapids. And even in his waking hours, the doubt preoccupied his thinking, and for a man of his constitution and motivations, this unsettled sense of self was as debilitating as the plague. He and Mary had suffered long enough. Katherine had emerged on the far side of the tragedy. Renee had drowned in the flood. He and his wife could either come to terms with it or they could perpetually tread the current until they were so numb and cold that the touch of one another's skin would feel aberrant and wholly without pleasure or grace. This prospect of losing Mary was crippling, so when Edwards had come into the study, he had been moved in a way that he had not been in a very long time. It was an honest request, with feelings as natural as the elements that nourished the farm, and he had welcomed the return of that familiar warmth by going easy on Bill Edwards. So easy in fact that he had to over-punctuate the end of the conversation for fear that the tears now rimming his eyes would emerge in another man's company.

Bill found Katherine walking by the creek, and he stopped to watch her pick her way along the bank. Her dress brushed the tops of the weeds and tall grass and her feet trampled a small path that led away from where Bill stood. He could hear water moving in the bed below and she was preoccupied with the sound and the patterns that the water made moving over the smooth rocks, methodically and without pause, seeking its lowest point. The fields were brilliant in the sunlight and he could not imagine a more fitting setting for this moment in his life that overshadowed all others in such a way that he may have come into the world only just then. He began to call her when she turned and looked back at him with a gentle and knowing face that made him aware that she too was rediscovering her own life and needed only an affirming look from him that a rebirth was possible.

He went to her and she stayed still, waiting and watching him, seeming not to know what to do with her hands. He came within a foot of her and stopped. It was silent except for the stream and then they both began to speak at the same time and they laughed together, and Bill thought that he should explain that he had spoken to her father, but studying her eyes, he was certain that she already knew. Either she knew, or she did not care. They talked for several hours, gliding from subject to subject, each one more fascinating and animated than the last and they would have gone on that way until the sun retired, but Bill realized that he had completely forgotten his work and he said goodbye and turned to go, but then turned back to Katherine and kissed her without actually touching her body and she returned the kiss and then he was gone, running toward the barns.

The days and weeks and months and years that followed were full and rich. Their relationship, which had emerged from awkward encounters, smoothed out and became uncommonly sincere and sustained; an affair that was fundamentally sound and rooted properly so that it could grow over time, in steady, seasonal bursts of new color and height. Six months after they coupled they were engaged, and six months after that

181

they were married on the farm on a spring morning with forsythia and dogwoods in full color, red buds stark against the light blue sky. Their parents, certain of the union, made easy conversation and the farm hands who had been invited were dressed in their best Sunday clothes, men women and children, both black and white, stood off to the side as Bill and Katherine committed their vows in front of the pastor who oversaw the Taylor Branch Baptist Church. They had decided to have the ceremony outside rather than in the church, Katherine citing the beauty of the farm in the spring weather and the simplicity of the fields and the natural sounds that enveloped them as they stood facing one another, oblivious to the respectful congregants and deeply in love with one another and the concept of an eternal life together.

After they were married, Bill stayed on at the farm and they lived together in one of the cabins that was vacant. They lived as the farm hands lived, with responsibilities they assumed but were not required to perform. That winter, Bill took a job as a deputy with the Winchester Sheriff's department despite the inheritance that he would certainly have received from Dennis Winslett after he was too old to assume operational duties. Bill was a proud man, and growing more proud as he got older. He had spoken to Dennis about the decision with the same reverence he had spoken with him about courting Katherine and despite Dennis's protest and desire to see the farm pass to a son-in-law he liked very much, he ultimately gave a heartfelt consent out of respect for Bill's desire to make his own way. "But the farm," Mary had said over dinner. "There will be someone to run things when the time comes," Dennis said. "And Katherine will not be cut out of anything. It would not be right to force that decision. Farming is not something that you can do effectively if your heart is not in it. Bill works hard, but he's not cut from that cloth." Mary had moved some vegetables around on her plate as Dennis spoke. She was thinking of Renee, her husband knew, and he was eager to change the topic before the discussion arose again. Renee was now a dry creek bed, and her absence and disappearance was as stark as a summer drought. Dennis knew from experience that talking about conditions out of your control was a sure way to end up with a nagging madness that could drive you into a despair that you might never shake.

Bill and Katherine purchased their home with a loan from the Winchester Community Bank and Trust. Dennis co-signed the note and helped them move Katherine's things out of the house himself, with Mary and her daughter packing her clothes and their wedding linens, the china that had been Katherine's grandmother's, books and other odds and end that had crowded the small cabin on the farm property. Mary struggled with her emotions helping Katherine leave, but smiled while she folded and wrapped the cups, saucers and plates in newspaper for the drive over to Winchester. She was closing and locking a trunk when the image of the doll house that the girls had played with came into her mind. It had been a beautiful doll house, hand crafted and ornamented to look like the farmhouse, the level of detail and craftsmanship immaculate and tender in its intricate construction. It was now in the attic collecting dust, and she reminded herself to have it brought down so that she could clean it up. Someday Katherine might want it for her own child.

"Miss Mary?" Mary turned to see LoLo standing in the doorway.

"Oh, LoLo," she said and turned around to face her. "Our Katherine's leaving home," and she felt tears in her eyes.

"Yes," LoLo said. "She and Mr. Bill are outside waiting. You coming?"

"In a second," Mary said.

"Miss Mary, you okay?"

"No," Mary said. "Yes. I don't know." LoLo came further into the room.

"Edgar came to say goodbye," she said. "He's waiting out there as well."

"That's kind of him," Mary said.

"We been through a lot, but this is a happy time, Miss Mary. Time to put the other behind us and get on with things." Mary nodded.

"I know," she said. "I'm just having trouble. That's all"

"We've all had that trouble," LoLo said. "Ever since we come back we've all had that kind of trouble. Bad visions. I have them too."

"I just wonder if she's okay," Mary said. "Renee, I mean." LoLo did not respond.

"What do you think, LoLo? Is Renee okay out there?" She waved her hand at the open door.

"Could be," LoLo said, looking around the empty room. "Could be that she's on her own now. Hard to say with that man. She's strong and maybe she found her way out."

"I want Katherine to be happy," Mary said. "I want her to stay but I also want her to forget this place and the horrible thing that happened here. She never talks about it and sometimes I wonder if maybe it bothers me more than it bothers her. I know that sounds selfish and awful, but I can't seem to get—"

"Ain't no forgetting what happened here," LoLo said. "Can't nobody forget something like that. Not by theyselves. But Katherine found a good man and Mr. Bill can take care of her now and you don't have to worry about it all by yourself. He can help you, but you gotta let him do that. That's why leaving is the right thing for them to do. Everything comes to an end. God tells us that. We have to trust in him."

"I don't have a lot of faith in God anymore, LoLo. Not like I did before."

"No, I suspect not," LoLo said. "But he sees how you are hurting and he has faith in you. Stronger than anything else. He wants Miss Katherine to be happy and he wants us to be happy too. No matter how things end up. He knows." Mary nodded and walked toward the open door.

"Then let's go see her off," she said and she walked passed LoLo and out into the yard. LoLo stayed in the empty room and smelled the familiar scent of the cabins. Nothing in that air seemed to ever change, no matter how much you cleaned or let the breeze blow through the front door and out the back. She turned and followed Mary outside where Bill and Katherine were talking with Edgar and Dennis.

"They are ready, Mary," Dennis said and clapped Bill on the shoulder. He pulled a folded envelope out of his pants pocket and handed it to Bill.

"No protest out of you on this," he said. "It's just a little something to help you get started. Mary and I want you to have it." Bill took the envelope but did not open it. The weight of it told him the significance of the gift.

"We're not going far, Daddy," Katherine said and gave her father a hug. "And stop crying, Momma," she said, looking at Mary. "We'll come back on Sundays for LoLo's dinner and when we get set-up you will all come over to Winchester and eat with the Edwards in our new house." Mary smiled and let out a laugh. Katherine went to Edgar and

LoLo who were quietly waiting. As she embraced the old cook, she whispered "I will never forget what you and Edgar did for me. Not as long as I live. I love you." LoLo smiled over the girl's shoulder, looking at Bill. *You take care of her for me*, her eyes said.

"Bye, Miss Katherine," Edgar said.

"Goodbye, Edgar," she said and hugged him as well. Bill came over and hugged LoLo and shook Edgar's hand. Then he turned and went to get in the truck. In the distance the farm house stood in the sunlight, the top of the tree outside Katherine's bedroom window barely visible, the wind's breath rustling the leaves in recitation.

PART 3

REST AREA

CHAPTER 27

———

SARAH

T he Caprice's transmission was slipping as Sarah Hicks pushed it up the grade. She had asked numerous times for it to be serviced and now, coming off a long shift, the very real possibility of the Chevy breaking down along the mountain road in the early morning hours made her grip the wheel tightly. "C'mon," she said. "Just get to the top and it's all downhill from there. Please. Just a little further. Just a little…" It slipped again as if to mock her and she let off the gas, hoping to appease the straining engine. She needed to pee. Squatting in a roadside ditch was not optimal. "You'd like that, wouldn't you," she said to the Caprice, which only groaned in response. She should call the station, but quickly decided against it. If being the first and only female deputy in the department's history had taught her anything, it was that showing vulnerability with something like an automobile only reinforced the preconceived notion that females had no business in law enforcement. The car hitched again and she held her breath and came around the last bend on the mountain road. She could now see the crest in her headlights. "Please, baby," she said.

Sarah had spent the night patrolling the county roads that criss-crossed the top of the mountain and down into the valley, falling in behind pick-ups she thought might be weaving, and looking for vehicles parked off the road where poachers would have taken their rifles and beer coolers into the thick woods to hunt. The job was more like babysitting adult men, she often told people, but it gave her time to think about her situation, futile and draining as that ultimately was. She had taken the job after a series of employment false starts that included cleaning houses, working as a cashier at the dollar store, and then back to cleaning houses. The mindless work ate away at her ambition like a slow, calculated cancer, and when the opportunity arose to join the sheriff's department she jumped at it, starting first behind the desk and eventually being trained to patrol the state highways and backroads. That was three years ago and she had long since buried the notion of "getting out" as the girls from her high school had planned, loitering on the school grounds, smoking cigarettes and listening to pop music through tinny car speakers that rattled with bass in their housings. As best she could tell, the number of girls who actually left town was small and dreamy like the motion pictures or the glamorous starlets lounging on the pages of check-out-counter tabloids dog eared and dated and splayed on the cheap coffee table at Jenny's Nails and Hair where big talk and rumors were thick as the hairspray and drugstore candles scented with an ocean breeze none of them had ever actually felt on their skin.

The Caprice made the top of the last hill. The sky looked as if a large sheet of parchment paper tented the earth with the dawning light. A messy rain began to fall, and the drizzle speckled the Caprice's windshield. Sarah turned on the wipers and the rain mixed with the bug carcasses in a clotty, yellow smear. She pushed harder on the accelerator now that the road leveled out. A road sign indicated the rest area was a mile ahead. Her bladder bulged and she thought again about the men in the station and what they might think if they knew she wet her uniform. "Jesus," she whispered over the big roar of the Caprice's engine. Both directions of the highway were empty when she pulled off the exit leading to the rest area. A strange light cast down from the lamp poles and over the parking lot. The fog made the light strange, like orbs with no physical attachment to the ground. Sarah slowed the car as she came closer to the building. There was no light inside. Maybe the fog was even thicker than she realized, shuttering the glow from the greeting area, which was always well-lit, day and night. She could make out the shapes of other vehicles in spaces in front of the building, and given their presence she dismissed the dark interior of the building. "Maybe they lost power," she said and steered the Caprice's big front end into a space. The lower half of her body felt almost numb and she again worried about making it to the toilet, and then smirked thinking about having to relieve herself in one of the dank stalls.

She killed the ignition and the Caprice's lights went off and now she was in the stillness of the fog, looking out through her window as if peering through the portal of a submarine. She put her hand on the lever to open the door of the car when she saw the bodies. There were two of them, lying perpendicular to the sloping handicap ramp, their backs to the parking lot. Nothing moved outside of the building. Sarah sat in the Caprice, her fingers on the door handle, eyes narrowed, breath held tight. They looked like rolled-up rugs, rain falling on them and soaking through their clothes. At the top of the ramp was a bank of payphones, and seeing them, uniform blue, the handsets neatly hung in place, silver cords looped and still, Sarah let her breath out and touched the window with her fingertips. The rain ran down the glass in streaks and her breath misted on the surface. Without looking away, she reached for the radio, brought it to her mouth, clicked the button on the side, and spoke just above a whisper.

"Ethan, this is Sarah." Static noise followed and she tried again. "Ethan, this is Sarah. Do you copy? Ethan, I need you to pick up." More static, then…

"Yeah Sarah. This is Ethan. You checking out?"

"Ethan," she said and stopped short. What she was about to relay was as foreign to both of them as a San Francisco streetcar.

"Ethan, I have two bodies at that I-24 rest area on the mountain. They are outside the building. They are not moving. I repeat, they are not moving."

"Sarah," Ethan said, his tone even but higher than normal.

"Lights are off in the building. Several cars in the parking lot, but no one else."

"Jesus, Sarah. Is the attendant…"

"George," she broke in. "His name is George and no, I don't see anyone outside and can't see any movement in the building." *George,* she thought. *George drinking coffee and waving to people coming through the door. George speaking in his thick accent, making conversation with strangers, greeting anyone and everyone who wondered in off the road. George kneeling down to speak to children. George who would have jumped off the eastern bluff of the mountain before he would let two people lie in the rain and fog outside of his rest area.*

"What should I do?" she said aloud. *Oh God, what should I do?*

"Sarah?"

"I'm here."

"Sarah, Bill, I mean the Sheriff is not here. He's over to Taylor Branch. It's just me. I don't know what…I mean—" Sarah continued to look at the bodies, and when something moved beside the head of one, she had to question whether she had seen it or not.

"Sarah…"

"Hush," she hissed into the radio. "Hold on." And whatever it was showed itself again. It was small and was skittering between the bodies, just glimpses of it. She thought of Sheriff Edwards and what he would do, what he would expect her to do.

"Ethan."

"Okay," he said.

"I have to check on them. I need to see if they are alive. What if they are alive, Ethan?"

"Sarah, wait," he said, his voice now clearly panicked. Sarah took a deep breath.

"Listen to me, Ethan, we have to deal with this. I'm getting out to check on them. I'll take the shotgun. I need you to get Herc and get up here as fast as you can."

"But no one's here, Sarah. Sheriff Edwards is…"

Her mind seized on something. "Where's Flip?" she said.

"Hunting," Ethan said. "He's off today and tomorrow. Should I call…"

"Okay," she said. "Get Herc and get up here as fast as you can." He tried to cut back in but she put the radio handset away and reached in the back seat for the shotgun that she had never put in the rack during the shift. *How many times have I been talked to about that?* she thought.

She looked around the parking lot again and counted the bulk of four cars. The fog obscured the license plates. She turned in her seat and looked toward the back of the parking lot for trucks and did not see any. She looked back at the bodies and saw the flash of movement again; this time whatever was there rocked one of the heads to the side. She checked to see that the shotgun in her lap was loaded and the safety was pushed to the firing position. She was closing the door of the Caprice when she heard the radio crackle her name again.

CHAPTER 28

ETHAN

Ethan stood up from behind the desk and turned slowly in a circle, running his hands through his thick hair and breathing heavily through his nose. His experience with dead people started and stopped with the passing of his grandfather, who had an open casket in what they called the Room of Eternal Peace at Cortner's Funeral Parlor in Winchester. He had been a little kid then but remembered the smell of the room, the dry heat from the wall radiators and the dull winter sky that he could make out through the flowery curtains of the window. His grandfather had died of lung cancer and he spent the last several years of his life in a back bedroom of the house where he had lived his whole life, coughing up blood and soiling his sheets. He had died an angry, broken man and the burnt-out corpse he left behind was as close to death as Ethan had ever wanted to stand.

He had been with the sheriff's department less than a year, and beyond processing drunks, speeders, and men who hit their wives, he had been lulled into believing that police work was as dangerous as using the old black Swingline stapler that sat on the shelf next to the coffee maker. Now, looking at the sad tan walls, low popcorn ceilings of the tiny sheriff's office and the booking desk that was littered with outdated magazines and ash trays, he was trying hard to process the idea of two bodies at a rest area in their rural jurisdiction. He put his hands on the metal-top desk and tried to think quickly and clearly.

Get Herc and call an ambulance, he thought. *And then get to Sarah.* She was his senior in the office, but not by much. *And she's a girl,* he thought. *What if whoever killed those people is still up there.* He picked up the phone and called the 911 dispatcher and filled her in on what he knew as quickly as he could. They could get everything in motion so he could get to Sarah. The operator had wanted to drag it out, but Ethan forced her off the line and took his gun belt from his desk drawer and strapped it on as he walked to the back of the office to get Herc. He went past the row of cells that could accommodate three prisoners at a time, then through a back door to a small outbuilding. Puddles had formed in the grassless courtyard and he kept to the poured sidewalk to keep from tracking mud indoors. He pulled a set of keys from his pants pocket and unlocked the outbuilding door and was met with the thick kennel smell. He stepped into the room at the same time the big German Shepherd came into his pen that had a half-door opening to an outside run.

'Good boy, Herc," he said and the dog sat obediently watching him. Ethan found the dog's harness hanging on a wall hook and took it down. The dog stood and began to pant, watching Ethan. It whined when he took too long with the harness, scratching at the concrete floor in anticipation, sensing the man's nervousness as he fumbled with the buckles and the leash latch. Ethan opened the enclosure and the dog moved out quickly and sat obediently.

"Good boy," Ethan said again. "Good boy." He led the dog out of the room and into the courtyard. They walked through the rain to Ethan's patrol car and he let the dog into the back seat.

You, Ethan. He stopped next to his door. The dog whined and paced in the back seat, studying him through the window. He had been at home with his grandfather one afternoon while his parents were at church. He had been watching TV when he heard the old man call from the back of the house. He'd risen from the floor and walked through the kitchen and stopped at the closed bedroom door. The old man was coughing and hacking and he was close to turning around and pretending he had not heard his name called when his grandfather spoke again.

Open the door, boy. Ethan had reached out and pushed the door open enough to see in. His grandfather was bent over, sitting up in the bed. Ethan stepped into the room and the old man looked up with his gaunt, whiskered face. There was blood around his mouth and on his chin. He reached for something in his lap and held out a shirt stained with blood and vomit.

Take this, he said.

Ethan opened his car door and climbed in, the vision of his grandfather filling his head like noxious gas. He cranked the engine and the dog quieted. He swung the car onto the side street and then turned left on the main road that dissected the town of Winchester and went on to the looming mountain now crowned in fog.

Sarah stood next to the Caprice, her thoughts turning in rapid circles, her limbs buzzing with an almost nauseating pulse and her eyes fixed on the dead people grotesquely blocking the ramp. It was as if her mind and body had broken apart like a frayed circuit and then, suddenly, an image of her mother came to her, hazy, but recognizable and strangely reassuring.

Sarah's mother had come very close to dying giving birth to her daughter. The labor and the delivery had been excruciating, and her mother had endured it by herself, with a slick sheet of perspiration and stabs of pain that made her scream until her throat was nothing but a dry husk. Sarah's father had left the day before the delivery and no one knew where he was or where to get in touch with him after a neighbor helped her mother limp into the hospital, bleeding and bent over with contractions. *You might say that you were his parting gift,* her mother would sneer and would then look away in what Sarah imagined was some hard mixture of shame, disgust, and regret. When her father left for good, Sarah's mother Renee gave up on the man she married at far too young an age and for all the wrong and regretful reasons. She held a real and sincere appreciation that he recognized who and what he was and had the fundamental decency to leave before he killed her or maimed their children. His temper and his general distaste for the world around him manifested in their kitchen or bedroom or in the supermarket parking lot, precise and without warning, but always consequential.

For the first several months after he was gone the house had settled into a cloudy rumination of *what-comes-next*, and her mother found herself clawing her way out of a hole she had never believed could be so deep. Her husband's mood swings were predictable only in their unpredictability; it was not ever a question of *if*, but *when*, and having lived through that, her mother's fight over flight instinct was very sharp; the stinking mess that had become her life was nothing short of astonishing and it would be years before she rediscovered a semblance of her former self. She had been able to spare her children the worst of him and for that she was grateful, but he haunted all of them in various shapes and forms, sometimes in the off-handed look of a stranger who bore a facial resemblance, sometimes in dreams where he chased them with the predatory grace of a large cat. Sometimes he settled over them while they ate their dinner of mac and cheese and boiled hotdogs. He was there and he was not.

Sarah moved slowly away from the Caprice and toward the bodies on the ramp.

What's moving them, she thought, looking intently at the still forms.

The rain was steady and cold as she stepped onto the sidewalk that ran parallel with the building and the parking lot. Moving to the left side of the ramp, she could see that it was an older couple lying one in front of the other, dressed in similar outfits and identical windbreakers. The woman was higher up the ramp from the man, and from this new vantage Sarah still could not determine what had occurred. She turned to look at the building entrance, the shotgun stock pressed firmly against her shoulder. Rain dropped from her hair and ran behind her uniform collar, chilling her through. She moved further up the grass slope alongside the ramp, planting her feet carefully and deliberately, and now she could see what had moved the bodies. A small dog huddled between the two of them, shivering in spasms and watching Sarah with large round eyes. She could see blood now, in rusty contrast to the cement. It had poured down the front of the woman's white shirt and the dam of her body had caused the blood and rainwater to pool slightly in front of her. The woman's face was unnaturally white and Sarah could make out the wound in her neck. The dog stood and turned in circles. She ignored it and came further down the ramp to look at the man. *It's her husband,* Sarah thought, seeing the shrunken figure lying in its odd posture, the left arm splayed out behind him. *She had gone up the ramp first and he was following her when they were attacked,* she thought and the simple endearment seized her. The blood pattern was similar on the man's shirt front, and his expression was one of both shock and resignation.

Sarah turned back to the woman and the dog. It rested its head on the woman's hip, ears pinned back and now it was making a weak whining sound. She spun around, gun raised, to see if someone was behind her, and when she saw nothing but her vehicle hulking in the fog, she turned back to look at the building.

Think, Sarah. Wait for Ethan? No, there could be people alive inside. What if people are alive in there? What if someone is alive in there? I have to see, she thought, and looked at the dark windows and doors of the entrance. *Why are there no lights? Why are there no lights?* She checked again and saw that the lamp posts in the parking lot were burning. The shotgun felt heavy in her hand and her clothes were soaked through. She looked back to the bodies and the cowering dog and something about their appearance, the fact that in life they would have posed no threat to anyone made her believe that whomever had been responsible for this would not have left anyone alive. Even with her limited experience, she knew that the horror she was witnessing had been merciless and unprovoked; something unspeakable had found its way up the mountain and descended on this little place with an intent that she felt certain was beyond control. *Evil,* she thought. This is what evil looks like and it does not stop here. She moved back up the ramp.

Everything appeared normal as she stepped closer to the front door. She checked behind her a second time, looked at her watch to see how much longer Ethan might be, then had to push the thought of waiting for him away. With her left hand she tried the door, which gave easily. She braced it open with her front foot so she could use both hands to hold the shotgun out in front of her. The lobby area, with its racks of brochures and maps, and a semi-circular information desk, was empty. The room smelled of piss and moisture and was silent except for the rain falling on the roof. She looked to her right and saw the opening to the attendant's office. The small desk where George usually sat was empty, but there was an overturned chair and little gooseneck lamp on the floor. *He got up in a hurry,* she thought. *He got up in a hurry and his foot tangled in the cord and he knocked the chair over trying to get up.* There was something pooled outside the office door. Sarah unclipped a small flashlight from her belt and pointed the beam at what she knew would be congealing blood before the flashlight could reveal it.

If anyone is alive in here it's the person who slit those old people's throats. And now I am in here with him. Her pulse ticked up and her bladder throbbed, heartbeat quickened. To the left was a set of double doors that opened to the back side of the building, where simple shelters were connected by a sidewalk system. Something bulky was left on one of the concrete tables that she could not make out. Beyond was more slope leading back to thick woods that framed the rear of the property, shapes of more picnic tables and trash cans dotting the landscape. She turned the flashlight on the entrance to the restrooms. There was a common vestibule, left for the men's and right for the women's. What looked like blood mixed with mud was all over the vestibule floor, and as she trained the light up the back wall, she could see more splatters and smears. *Jesus, God,* and she thought of the cars in the parking lot. *They are all in there. They will all be in there. You have got to get out of here. You are not trained for this. No one is trained for this. You have got to...*

She started forward again and before she lost her nerve, she stepped into the vestibule and in one quick motion, swung the gun and her body around the corner and stiffened her stance, scanning the light around the men's room. The tiled walls were a dull, gritty white, their grout chipped and missing, and there were several urinals on the right side, with sinks, soap dispensers, and mirrors on the left and a row of stalls opposite the sinks. The room reeked of waste and something else Sarah could not identify. She took three more steps into the room and saw that the stall doors were all closed. She backed against the wall and felt for the light switches, not taking her eyes from the stall doors, holding the shotgun on them as her hand searched frantically for the switches. She found them and flipped them up. They made loud clicking sounds in the tiled room and then a murky yellow light flickered overhead, accompanied by a low hum. She looked toward the sink area and saw that there were crumpled paper towels in a pile next to the middle sink, a slow drip coming from the faucet, the bulbs of water making an almost inaudible noise in the basin.

Sarah turned back to the stalls and went down the row to the one furthest from the entrance. She squatted down and peered beneath the door; she could see work boots and jeans. Sarah stood quickly and backed up. She outstretched her leg and toed the door with the tip of her own shoe. It made a soft squeak on its hinge and came only partially open. She held her breath and moved forward, using the barrel of the shotgun to force the door all the way open. A young Hispanic man was sitting upright on the toilet, his back against the wall. His throat had been cut and he stared back at Sarah in the yellowish glow of the overhead lights with his mouth open above the wound as if cut off in the middle of his final protest. His shirt had been removed and was lying in a bunched-up heap on the floor next to him. It was saturated with blood. Above his head the shirt had been used to write "YOUR SAHDOW AT MORNING" in washed, strand-like letters where it had dripped and then slicked to the white surface. In the weak light it appeared to ooze from within the tiled wall. Sarah stepped back from the stall, almost losing her balance. The door remained open and the dead man looked at her almost accusingly. She moved to the middle stall, pushed open the door, which made no sound, and found a deer's head sitting on the toilet seat. The grotesque absurdity of the image caused her to choke back a startled, disgusted laugh. The head balanced precariously on the seat of the toilet as if it had grown from the still water below, and the stench that was caught in the tight stall clawed at the inside of her nose and crept into her slightly parted lips. Its neck was like the edges of a fraying blanket and pieces of the flesh hung over the dirty seat in clotted strips. In blood above what was left of the animal was written: "THE THIRD WHO WALKS BESIDE YOU." The deer's neck showed a jagged edge indicating it had been cut away roughly and carelessly from the body. She backed away, the animal's eyes a flat black glass, and this time she slipped on blood that had pooled below the bleeding neck and went onto her backside, almost dropping the shotgun. She kicked away from the open stalls and her shoes slipped in the mess. She let out a choked sob and was finally able to get to her feet. She stood, disbelieving, in shock and horrified beyond rational thought. She pushed open the third stall door in a numb movement and found the attendant, George, straddling the toilet in a similar fashion to the Hispanic man. He was middle-aged and fleshy. His shirt was unbuttoned halfway down his chest and the blood and gore was caked on his torso and in the white hairs there. Above George's head, in splotchy blood letters was "O LORD THOU PLUCKEST."

Dear God, Sarah thought.

Dear God.

Dear God.

Dear God, please…

She backed out of the third stall and then stopped. George's eyes had been removed from his head, leaving behind raw-looking holes. Sarah wanted to shriek. She stepped away and bumped into one of the sinks. Her hands shook the shotgun to vibration. Her breathing was labored and now all three doors were open, each with its scrawled message and a corpse. She thought she was going to throw up and she turned violently around to the sinks, gulping in air, the shotgun pointed at the floor. *There is no one here but the dead,* her mind screeched, looking at the knotted towels on the floor below the sinks. *This was meant to be witnessed. Undisturbed. There is no one alive here but me. So much blood. So much…* Her stomach heaved. She bent over at the waist. The paper towels on the floor contained blood and grime. Red smears along the sides of the sinks and splattered above the faucets. *He washed his hands. He or they washed their hands after the bodies were inside the stalls.* A hot, acrid sensation rose in her throat and her bladder started to let go. "No," she screamed, enraged. The hot urine ran down her thighs and she wanted to weep and throw the gun. George's eyeless face looked on and she turned to the small half window set high in the building's outside wall. It had a rusted lever handle and the window had been cracked partially open, probably by George when he came in to clean the restroom at some point in the night. There was a weathered broom and dustpan in the corner and a wash bucket turned upside down, probably used as a step stool for opening and closing the window. Rain was still falling steadily. It struck fat and hard on the leaves of the trees grouped in clusters around the grounds. The fog had settled in the window frame, blocking out the light, sealing-off the damp and odorous space.

You have to check the women's room. She made her way shakily past the stalls and stark white urinals, her own piss warm in the cheap fabric of her pants.

She came into the small space between the restrooms and surveyed the far wall of the main lobby. Nothing there. Through the front glass doors, she could see the dog sniffing around in the wet grass and fog to the right of the handicap ramp. No sign of Ethan. She stood still, not sure now if she could make herself enter the women's room. The silence of the building and all that she had seen felt like she was pinned under an enormous weight and her lungs clamored for breath. It occurred to her then that all of this might have been a dream, some horrible dream gone on far too long and any moment now she would wake in her old bedroom in her mother's house and stumble down the hall where she could use the bathroom instead of soaking her uniform.

You have to check the women's room. She went in. The set-up was opposite of the men's, stalls on the left and sinks on the right. She found the light switch and filled the room with the same eerie cascade of yellow, the hum and drone above her in the fixtures. She looked at the long mirror above the sink and saw another message scrawled there in glistening blood.

"THOSE WERE PEARLS THAT WERE HIS EYES. LOOK!"

What the hell does that mean? she thought. *What sick shit is this?* The word *look* was faint. *He ran out of blood,* she thought. *Where is he getting it from?* She looked around and could not find the source. Sarah moved deeper into the room and opened the first two stall doors, where she found nothing but the toilets and metal boxes holding toilet paper. She backed out and held her breath before opening the third stall. Sitting on top of the toilet was a large hunting knife with a serrated edge on the top of the blade, sticky with blood. She stared at the knife and then turned back to the message scrawled on the mirror.

He wants me to find something there, she thought. *It's not they. It's he. And he wants me to find something there.* She crossed to the sinks and looked in the bowl closest to the wall. Folded neatly in the bottom was a red bandana. She rested the shotgun against the sink and then pulled her hand into her shirt sleeve and pinched the fabric between her thumb and finger and lifted the cloth. Sitting side by side were two eyes, cleanly plucked from George's face. She dropped the cloth and, picking up the shotgun, backed away. The rain was hammering the roof and the smell of the building seemed to rise up in a wave of revulsion and disbelief. She banged the shotgun on the tiled wall backing out and its sound bounced around the room like shouts in a cave. She held her hand to her mouth, the burning came up through her throat again. She backed into the main lobby and thudded into the information desk. Outside a car door slammed and then Herc's loud, deep bark and then Ethan shaking her shoulder. She was looking from him to the entry of the restrooms and then she was sliding jerkily to the floor, the thick rubber soles of her black shoes leaving marks on the tile, the gun belt scratching the faux wood finish of the half-circle desk. Ethan bent in front of her, holding both shoulders now and she could see that he was speaking, but she was not hearing what he said. The whir of the congested HVAC was somewhere above her, the smell of the rain on Ethan's shirt and his deodorant. There was water in his hair and he was speaking, speaking louder and louder and she could see that he was very afraid, and then a blur behind him, moving somewhat low to ground, with purpose and agility and she realized that it was Herc and he was sniffing madly at the floor and the carnage in the two rooms filled his nostrils, pulsing steady and perfunctory, the way she'd seen him track the scent of an animal when they took him back behind his enclosure and let him roam the woods when nothing much was going on at the station. Then she knew that the dog had gone into one of the restrooms even though she could not see past Ethan. Herc was barking with frenzy and panic and the innate animal sense of time and space out of order, and then Ethan rose and turned to go to the dog's whining and yelping, and she thought again of her mother and a strand of fake pearls she had been given when she was just a girl. She kept it in a ceramic dish on her dresser, and she turned her head and she heard Ethan, heard him now as if far away or locked in a steel drum, and he was yelling at the dog to *stay*, the fierce realization overcoming both man and canine, and then she was retching and the bile was slick and thick on the shotgun's stock. She could smell the urine in her pants. She wiped her mouth with her shirt and slowly stood as Ethan came back into the room, his terror a white, taut mask on his face. He had gotten a leash on the dog somehow and Herc was pulling against the restraint to return to the restroom, and Ethan yanked hard and pulled them both further into the lobby.

She steadied herself against the information desk and checked her shotgun. She wiped the vomit from the stock onto her pant-leg and looked at Ethan, the dizzy, weak feeling gradually beginning to ease. "There are two dead in the men's room," she said. "The two outside. The weapon, I think it's the weapon, is in the last toilet stall in the women's. He, they, killed a deer and put the head in one of the stalls. There are messages in blood. There are. Ethan?"

Ethan was holding the leash tightly in his hand, his service revolver in the other. He had forgotten his shotgun in the car, rushing to get inside. The dog perched on its haunches behind him, whining and looking at the restroom entrance. He was looking out the rear double glass doors and she followed his stare and she could see the remaining carcass of the deer had been left on one of the stone tables near a trash can. A stream of blood ran from the table to the doors. She looked through the doors before going into the restrooms but had not made out the carcass in the low light of the building and the fog outside. Sarah held her shotgun in front of her and looked at Ethan.

"Walk Herc toward the rear doors," she said. "I'll open them and let him out." Sarah started toward the back of the building and she could hear Ethan struggling with the weight and determination of the shepherd. There was another small vestibule between the interior doors and exterior doors, and she moved around the side of the information desk and to the left so she could see into one of the corners of the dead space between the exit doors. She came even with the first set and, seeing nothing, she swung around and pointed her shotgun at the other corner which was also empty. There was pooled blood on the floor where they, he, must have carried the deer's head into the small space, pausing long enough to shift the weight of the animal so the interior doors could be opened. Sarah banged the metal push bar and stepped over the blood, looking back at Ethan briefly to make sure that he saw and to keep the dog as best he could from disturbing anything. Then they were both outside and the rain blew across their faces and she could see where the animal's blood washed across the sidewalk in irregular patterns and rivulets.

A chest-high cyclone fence ran along the back of the rest area's property. Herc cleared the distance from the building to this fence in the time that it took the two young deputies to reach the second picnic table. They ran into the weather with the hard rain stinging their faces, making them grimace and want to shield their eyes. Herc abruptly stopped short of the fence and dropped his head, moving along the base in a controlled rhythm. Back and forth, back and forth, all the while making progress toward the end of the see-through barrier that fell off into the tree line and ended at the edge of a ravine. He smelled something watching him from back in the trees. Something that belonged there but did not belong there. Not in a natural way of belonging. It was an intrusive smell, like the smell he got around the men who were locked in the cages in the place where he lived. That smell was a mixture of fear and confused anger because it was also sadness and guilt and stupidity. This smell was also like that, but it was also very calm. It was the smell of observance and judgement, and he was scared of its strength and its cunning. It was a smell of dominance: raw and carnivorous. A smell that he gave off but was careful to control around the people who cared for him. The smell—*this human*—was unable to control the rawness, the animal part that Herc knew was bad to show. He came back up the hill and stopped short. He turned perpendicular to the fence and asked his eyes and his nose to work together, and then it was there. The smell. The human. The uncontrolled thing, standing deep in the woods, half-hidden and all hidden if the humans who were now coming tried to see it. *Him.* Herc knew this and so he did not bark. He sat and merely looked because his instincts were cowering and uncertain. And the thing that saw him, the human that saw him was admiring him and he knew just as he knew the strength of his jaws, that this admiration was born from a primal connectivity.

Sarah saw the dog had locked onto something. It had stopped its pacing and was now sitting unnaturally still, and had she been able to remove the fence, Herc would have taken off into the woods straight toward whatever was out there looking back at them, but because there was a fence and because the fog was playing through the trees like wet smoke, and because the rain was hammering, she could not see and was not sure she was prepared to see what was out there in the woods, patiently watching and waiting.

"Sarah," Ethan yelled over the rain, pointing at the dog. Sarah nodded but said nothing. She moved back up the fence, up the slight incline but found nothing. They could follow it until it stopped, but she decided against it. They would be chasing blindly into thick woods and the ferocity of what she had witnessed inside the building had shaken her badly. She no longer trusted her physical strength. Someone had piled the dead leaves along the bottom of the fence, rotting and thick. Ethan shielded his eyes from the rain, peering into the trees and scanning the underbrush. The dog remained still, save the current that was demanding chase, coursing through his blood, head and muscles. Behind them they heard the sirens approaching on the interstate, getting close.

"Stay here," she yelled to Ethan. He held his gun by his side and watched her start back down the slope, turning as she left to look back into the woods. "I'm going back to the building." He nodded and she turned and jogged back, steering around the right side of the building, glancing at the deer carcass on the picnic table as she ran. She rounded the corner and saw the ambulance coming fast up the exit ramp, its lights whirling and the sirens going full tilt. She realized that she was still holding the shotgun and she lowered it to her side, slowing down to a fast walk as she came alongside the handicap ramp where the older couple was lying. She looked around for the little dog and saw that it was under the overhang at the front entrance. She went to her car, secured the shotgun and then went to retrieve the dog. She came up the slope calling gently to it, but the dog backed further under the shelter of the building, placing itself in the corner. She came up the slope and stood in front of the dog. She bent down and stretched her hand out for the animal to smell, and then in a quick motion the dog came to her and was scrambling to get into her arms. She scooped it up and walked back to the car with the dog nuzzling her. The ambulance had stopped in the middle of the parking lot. The EMTs had killed their siren and were getting out wearing rain jackets. They ran to where Sarah stood alongside her Caprice, holding the frightened animal.

CHAPTER 29

NORTON

After getting off the phone with Ethan, the county 911 dispatcher had notified the small EMT unit in Winchester and had then called Brent Norton, the county's coroner. Norton had just sat down at his desk with a cup of coffee when his phone rang. He picked it up on the second ring and listened intently while the dispatcher told him about the likelihood of a double homicide at the rest area on top of the mountain. Norton took short notes on the back of an envelope, thanked the dispatcher and hung up. He then called the sheriff's office and got a woman named Rhonda on the phone, who knew next to nothing about what was going on and seemed perturbed that she had arrived to an empty office. Norton filled the woman in the best that he could.

"Where's the sheriff?" he asked.

"He's out today," Rhonda said. "Took his wife over to Taylor Branch to look at a new vehicle. She's ill, you know."

"No," Norton said. "I did not know that."

"Yeah," she said. "Something in her mind, and…"

"Okay, Rhonda," Norton said. "Here's what I need you to do." He went on to give her instructions about calling the state police and the sheriff over in the neighboring county where he also served as a back-up coroner's unit. When he was done he asked her to repeat it back. "Make sure you find Edwards too," he said, and before she could answer, he hung up and went out to his car to make the drive to the crime scene. As he drove, he considered how woefully inadequate everything in Franklin County was. He understood the financial pressures and the lack of expertise, but he also understood that crimes like murder were not exactly discriminatory, and the highways could as easily bring criminals to your door on the farm as they could bring them to the inner cities. He pushed the county vehicle hard up the slope and arrived just after the ambulance. He found the two EMTs standing bewildered in front of two bodies on a handicap ramp. A very young-looking female deputy was talking to them and holding a small dog. Norton put the car in park and crossed the lot in long strides.

The deputy looked beyond repair. The vacancy in her eyes was disturbing and he kept glancing around to see if there was anyone else from the sheriff's department on the scene. It had rained like hell all morning and he was thankful that it had finally stopped. He started to speak but went back to his car instead and opened the trunk and found a roll of yellow tape. Recognizing that the state cops and the deputies from over in Marion County would probably not arrive for at least fifteen more minutes, he went back to the small group and pulled one of the EMTs aside.

"I want you to help tape off the scene," he said, handing the man the roll.

"I'm not a cop," the EMT said.

"I know that," Norton said. "But we're kind of short on them right now so I need you and your partner to fill in. I've got a guy in my office that should be here pretty soon and he'll help you out. Then we're gonna have to wait until we can get someone with some better forensic resources here before we move these bodies around. Start down at the east-bound exit. Nobody comes in or out for now." He paused then looked at the EMT. "What did she have to say?" The EMT appeared sheepish.

"She says there are these two bodies out here and that there are two more inside," and then he let out a long breath, rubbed his hands together, "and there's a deer head and carcass too." Norton looked at him. "Yeah," the EMT said and not seeming to know what to do with his unsettled hands, he stuck them into his pockets.

"What do you mean, head and carcass?"

"You'll have to ask her," he said. He called to his partner and the two of them went to start taping things off. Norton looked at the deputy and tried to soften the way that he felt. She looked beyond fragile. He approached her, hand outstretched.

"Deputy, I'm the county coroner," he said. My name is Brent Norton." She took his hand and attempted a smile. "I'm Sarah," she said. "I mean, Deputy Hicks."

"Anyone else up here with you from the sheriff's office, Deputy Hicks?"

"Yes sir," she said. She was holding the dog as a needed distraction. "Ethan's in the back with Herc. Our K-9." Norton nodded. "Okay," he said. "You want to tell me what happened here?"

"There are these two here, and there are two more bodies inside," she began. "One is George, the attendant who works here, and I don't know who the other one is, must have just been passing through. All of them had their throats cut." She said this last gruesome detail with no emotion.

Norton stayed quiet.

"I only know that their throats were cut. There's blood everywhere inside and the bodies are in the stalls."

He looked across the lot and saw another deputy coming from around the side of the building with a German shepherd.

"And out here?"

"I don't know," Sarah said. "I pulled in from my shift early this morning and found them like this. This dog," she held the animal up, "was with them. I think they were probably his owners." Norton nodded and scanned for the EMTs.

"Mr. Norton?"

"You can call me Brent."

"You know if anyone got in touch with Sheriff Edwards? I'd really like for him to be here."

"We're working on that," Norton said. Sarah nodded and turned to look at Ethan and Herc coming toward them. Ethan waved and Norton thought again how incompetent all of this was. It was almost comical. Behind them the coroner's van pulled into the parking lot and Norton excused himself and went to meet it. A tall skinny man was in the driver's seat and he got out when he saw Norton coming and met him as he came down the parking lot. The two of them went to the rear of the van and the skinny man opened the double doors in the back, blocking their upper bodies from view. Sarah could see their heads moving through one of the van door's windows but could not hear what they were discussing. Sarah watched them move and tried to manage the ferocious thoughts in her head. The dog shivered in her arms and she held it tightly. Her eyes were drawn to the old people on the ramp and she wanted to yell out loud at the images moving through her mind. Time past and time present were merging into one and she was suddenly conscious of wetting herself and she wondered if the men could smell it or if the rain had washed the scent out. She looked at the Caprice with its slipping transmission and she recalled how not long before she had been consumed with worry about breaking down on the road and having to squat in a ditch.

"Sorry," he said, when she looked at him, startled. "You mind coming with me for just a minute? You can bring your friend," he said, motioning at the dog. They began to walk in the opposite direction of the rest area building, veering away from the van and toward his blue sedan. She noticed that he was checking his stride to stay even with her, and only when they got closer to the car did he speed up and open the passenger door for her and indicate for her to sit. She stood a second, looking at him.

"His eyes," Sarah said.

"What was that?"

"His eyes," Sarah said. "He took out his eyes and wrapped them in a bandana."

"Whose eyes?"

"George. They—*he*—took George's eyes and said they were pearls."

Norton looked at the young deputy a for a long minute, but she did not seem to notice.

"Let's have a seat here, Deputy Hicks," Norton said. "You think that Ethan can handle things for a few minutes while we talk?" Sarah looked around for Ethan and saw him walking Herc under the trees away from the building. She looked back at Norton and nodded.

"We've called the state police and we have also called the sheriff in Marion County and Lee from my office is going to start getting things ready for their arrival." He pointed toward the van where Lee was assembling items in the back. "In the meantime, let's get you dried off and warmed up." He motioned for her to sit again and she went past him and climbed into the car that smelled of tobacco smoke and stale coffee. He came around the other side and got in, closing the driver's door and letting out a grunt as he fell into the seat. He looked at Sarah. She had a smallish build and her wet clothes looked too large for her. She was pretty in a very natural way, and because of that, the toll of what she witnessed tugged on her features, exposing her emotions in a manner that he knew was common for people in shock. Right then she was not thinking about police work or bodies or solving anything. In that moment she was concentrating on taking one breath after another and maintaining what composure she still had. He drew in his own air before speaking. "Like I said, we have folks on the way, coming in both directions. I imagine Sheriff Edwards will be here before too long." He paused. She was not looking at him. He backed off. "I have some coffee," he said, leaning over into the back seat and producing a Thermos. "Nothing special, but it's hot." He pulled off the top cap, which also served as a cup, smudged silver with green trim on the bottom, and then unscrewed the second cap. The Thermos had a bracketed handle on the side that clanked when you picked it up or put it down and it sounded loud in the car.

"Just had to pee," Sarah said absently.

"What's that?" Norton asked. Sarah laughed and looked through the windshield of the car.

"That's why I stopped. I had to pee. Normally I would have gone right by it." Norton poured the coffee into the Thermos lid and offered it to Sarah. She looked at it and shook her head. He tried again, but she turned away. The dog had stopped shivering and was sleeping in her lap. Norton set the hot coffee on the dash and screwed the lid back in. He took the coffee back in his hand and watched the deputy.

"I don't want to make you go through this more than necessary, but can you tell me what you think happened?"

Sarah said nothing for a moment, then looked at him. "No," she said. "Maybe..." and she looked back out the window. "Something escaped," she said. "Something got loose. I, I don't know. It was like something, someone, went mad inside of there but it knew what it wanted. It had a plan. It wasn't crazy. Not like you think of the word crazy. It wanted us to find what it had done. It goddamn—"

"Okay," he said. "Maybe now is not the time. Let's just sit here for a second."

"I'm getting rain on your seats. I slipped in blood, and..."

"Don't worry about that," He said. "You just take it easy. It's over for now."

"No," she said. "You're wrong about that."

CHAPTER 30

EDWARDS ON
AN ERRAND

The police cruiser was a disappointment to say the least, a relic that could have just as easily been rotting in a field somewhere like old farm equipment, covered in weeds and vines, sinking into the earth, season after season. The hulking old thing sat in a row of equally neglected automobiles and battered commercial trucks in the parking lot of the street department located across from the Taylor Branch municipal building. *More like a graveyard,* Sheriff Edwards thought, running his hands over a spot of chipped paint on the driver's-side door, his eyes moving over the spider web in the windshield. Parked near the entrance to the lot, his own vehicle sat, the engine idling. Inside, his wife Katherine was working a crossword puzzle from a large book of mind games her physician recommended. He could see her lips moving, talking through the clues out loud as she did more and more frequently. *Tarzan. Elevator. Dr. Jekyll. Easter Bunny. Galaxy.* Bill knew that when he got back in the car, Kat would have no recollection of why they were here or even where "here" was, despite having grown up on a large farm not five miles from the Taylor Branch city limits. He'd hoped that driving over from Winchester and into a place where she had spent most of her youth would trigger some recognition, but she simply looked out the window, a half-smile on her face that

213

he believed she kept in place to push away the more natural look of confusion and sometimes anger that came with whatever remaining awareness she had that her mind was slipping away from her like water running into a drain ditch.

"Well, it's not much to look at," said a maintenance worker with the name Roy on his shirt in raised blue cursive letters. The shirt was splotchy with oil and grass stains. He fished into his pant pocket and came out with a single key. "They said you was coming over from Winchester just this morning, so ain't had no time to see if it will even turn over. Last time it ran was from the parking lot where they picked it up to the maintenance lot right here."

Roy was a short, fat, balding man and Edwards surmised that he had worked for the street department for most of his adult life. He had an aura of indifference that most of the municipal and county employees had. Edwards could not say that he blamed them much. He felt it creeping into his daily routine now and again. It was part of the job. "Can't say if it will start now or not," Roy mused. He seemed to be enjoying the suspense. "Welcome to try."

Edwards looked at the key in the man's filthy outstretched hand, then looked back at the car.

"Probably could have saved myself a trip over," Edwards said with a slight irritation. "This is not exactly what was advertised over the phone."

Roy shrugged and dug at something under one of his grimy nails. "I just do what I'm told," he said. "I'll stick the key in the ignition and you can crank it up if you want." He walked around the Sheriff and pulled open the driver's side door. It yawned with an aggravated squawk, and he leaned into the car and put the key into the ignition and left the door standing open. The ignition switch made a harsh buzzing sound and Edwards put a hand to his chin and scratched at the stubble. Even if the engine did turn over, the vehicle looked like it would be lucky to make it another fifty miles before it decided to leave whomever was driving stranded on the roadside.

"Talk to the clerk if you want to buy it," Roy said. "I gotta get back to work." He left Edwards standing in front of the cruiser and walked back toward the maintenance building. Thunder rumbled overhead, and he stopped to examine the sky. He turned back to Edwards.

"Looks like we're in for rain," he said, then laughed to himself. "Hope she don't leak."

Edwards took one more look at the car, slammed the driver's door and turned to go back to his own vehicle. He opened his door and slid in next to his wife, who never looked up from her puzzle. He sat for a second, watching her. Then, as if he had been sitting there the whole time, or as if they were sitting in their simple den back in Winchester she said, "A jewel where nine gather to play."

Edwards looked through the windshield at the ruined cruiser and pulled the car into gear. "A diamond," he said and she smiled and wrote down the word, speaking aloud each letter as she scratched it into its individual block. He steered out of the parking lot and turned left onto Taylor Street.

He pulled his car along the curb in front of the diner where he told Kat they were going to eat. He cut the engine and she continued looking at the puzzle in her lap, rolling the dulled pencil between her thumb and finger. He had left a note scratched on a piece of torn paper at the office in case his lunch outing took a bad turn. He never knew if and when Kat might drift away to the point of needing to be taken home. On more than one occasion she had become so anxious that they had been forced to leave abruptly. He hoped that would not be the case today. He spoke encouragingly to her.

"You feel like eating a cheeseburger?"

"Okay," she said.

"You want to give that puzzle a rest and come inside with me so we can order one?"

"Okay," she said, but did not look up. He reached across the seat and gently took the book off of her lap. Only when it was out of her line of sight did she look at him. The recognition was slow at first, but then he saw something change in her expression and a flutter in her eyes and it was as if she had been woken from a nap, vision struggling to focus and adapt to the light.

"Bill," she said. She spoke his name in the same cadence that she used when identifying an answer in her puzzle.

"The one and only," he said. "Let's get some lunch, Kat." He opened his car door and walked around to let her out, and when he opened her door she looked up at him with a rare, genuine smile.

"Watson's," she said.

Bill smiled at her upturned face and nodded, taking her hand and helping her out of the seat and onto the sidewalk.

"Cheeseburger?" Edwards asked his wife. She was studying the menu, holding it up in front of her face so that he could not see her knitting her brow or biting her lip, although he knew that she probably was.

"How about a cheeseburger and a chocolate shake, Kat?"

"Is that what I get here? A cheeseburger and a chocolate shake?" She sounded like a child not old enough to discern what she did and did not like.

"Well," Edwards said. "It's a pretty good choice. That's what I'm planning on having." Kat continued to study the menu. Then she said, "Do you think Daddy's going to come to lunch today?" Edwards looked around for the waitress and then gently pulled the menu down from in front of his wife's face.

"No honey," he said. "Your daddy has passed. So has your mother." Kat looked hard at him and he thought maybe lunch was not going to work out after all if she processed this the way she sometimes did, merging the past and the present into an immediate shock that could send her mind and emotions reeling in every direction. *It's like drowning,* Bill thought. *It's like drowning and being resuscitated, and just when you get the water coughed up and spit out on the sand, and your lungs stop burning and the air starts to flow again, they heave you up by the arms and toss you back in where it's deepest.* He turned the direction quickly.

"They passed through already, remember? They have to go over the mountain to check on some things. We'll have to have lunch by ourselves today. That will be nice though, right?" The drowning was bad enough but coupling that with the innocent lying and cajoling hurt him even more. It was the right thing to do. There was no sense in forcing recognition where there was none. But it felt low and defeated, lazy even. The circle never ceased to be anything more than its own mocking self, time and again. The coaxing and faltering anticipation and the haggard patience that somehow, this time, just this once, she would see things with a clean and clear context. And of course when she did not, when she was once again unable, how he hated himself for the hot anger that possessed him, taunted him, and yes, almost begged him to throw something violently against the wall and leave the wreckage for another day, when it would begin all over again. Kat looked a second longer and then nodded with purpose. "Yes. Yes. Yes," she said and Edwards saw her mind trying to swim up to the surface, kicking hard for air. The couple looked at one another across the table, saying nothing and communicating just the same, eyes steady and intimately familiar with one another's face. Edwards smiled, raising his brows, offering assurance in a simple and relaxed gesture that had replaced words and even touch. *This is the new norm, Kat,* his expression explained without reservation. *This is how we work through each day, and this is how we will move through our lives, and this is how I will carry you forward through both sunlight and shadow. And you will not apologize for a deception that is not of your making. You need only to look back to me and I will find the way for both of us.*

"Are you folks ready to order some lunch?" Edwards looked and saw a middle-aged woman wearing a faded t-shirt with Taylor Branch High School's mascot on the front and blue jeans standing next to the booth. She was holding a ticket pad in her hand and was looking first at Edwards and then over to Kat, who was still looking passively at her husband.

"We are," said Edwards, glancing up at the waitress. "We're both gonna have a cheeseburger and a chocolate shake. And I think we'll split an order of fries."

"Okay," said the waitress. "I'll get you some waters. Be right back."

"Thanks," Edward said and turned back to Kat. "When we get home, how about we take that hike to the caves if the rain let's up? Get some exercise. You could use some fresh air and I could stand to lose about twenty pounds." He patted his stomach. Kat smiled. "That sound good to you?" She nodded and he was content to sit quietly until their food arrived. He looked out the window onto the street, which was dormant: ancient buildings in need of paint and repair standing no more than two stories tall, half the storefronts dark. An occasional car moved through, a kid on a bike three sizes too small for him. Kat was fiddling with her engagement ring.

"Excuse me." It was the waitress back at their booth. "Are you Sheriff Edwards?" He turned to face her and nodded. "I am," he said.

"You got a phone call earlier. Woman named—" she glanced at the slip of paper in her hand, "—named Rhonda. Says I'm supposed to interrupt you. Said she's been trying to reach you all over town. Phone's by the cash register." She set the slip of paper on the tabletop and walked toward a table with four older men drinking coffee, leaned into one another with expressions like they were awaiting a punchline after a long build-up. Edwards reached over and touched Kat's hand to get her attention. She startled and settled. "Be right back, honey," he said and climbed out of the booth and walked toward the register.

Katherine watched her husband cross through the diner, which was getting noisier as people were coming in for lunch. He weaved through the tables and over to where the cash register was located. He was holding the slip of paper the waitress had brought and she was confused because normally you did not pay until after you had eaten at Watson's. Then she saw him speak to a girl standing behind the counter and she handed him the phone and he looked down at the piece of paper, frowned, and crumpled it in his hand, then dialed. She turned her head and looked out the window and like a light switched on in a dark room, she saw Taylor Street alive as it had been when she was a little girl. She was riding into town with her father and mother and sister. Her sister was there in the back seat with Katherine and they were playing some kind of game where they clapped hands and sang a song. They were wearing the same dress and her mother and father were talking in the front seat and she had that unconditional feeling of safety that made things like sleeping so easy. From the diner, she watched her family's car coming up the street slowly. She pressed her head against the big window to see. Like waiting for the parade. As the car was passing her sister's face appeared in the window, but it was not her sister's face. The skin was stark white and the dress she had on was covered in dirt, like she had rolled around on the ground or had been covered in shovels full of soil. She had seen her mother's profile in the front seat, but her mother was not paying attention. The place where the small girl's eyes were supposed to be were only black and red holes. The car was coming exactly even with the diner window and her sister smiled at her and the holes pinched tighter. Katherine yanked her head away from the diner window and saw her sister frown and then smile again and wave, and then she opened her mouth and something red splattered against the window of the car. Katherine whimpered. The car was crawling out of sight. She watched and again she saw her sister waving at her from the back window before dropping down in the seat and out of view. Someone in the diner dropped a plate and it made her turn, the vision blinking out like someone had yanked the plug out of the wall. Temporary blackness. She looked and found her husband. The motions and the expressions on his face made something tighten painfully in her stomach and she felt very alone in the booth despite all of the people and conversations and she wanted him very much to come back and talk with her because what she was feeling was fear. Cold, tightening fear that she had experienced before, and like then, she could not find a place to hide from it and that felt colder still. Like being submerged in ice water. Knowing that when it finally showed its face, not in a dream or vision like the passing car, but when it came close enough to touch her, close enough to reach out and place its cold fingers on her skin, there would be no place to hide. Edwards came back to the table, his face taut as if he were in physical pain. He did not sit back down. Outside, the storm that had passed over the mountain was blowing into Taylor Branch.

CHAPTER 31

SARAH AND NORTON

State police and Marion County deputies moved around the rest area property in rain slickers. The EMTs had blocked the entrance off the interstate with yellow tape stretched between two trees, and now a state cruiser blocked the roadway as well. One officer took down tag numbers from the victim's automobiles, others moved between the parking lot and the building. Lee from the coroner's office came out of the front entrance then stepped off the sidewalk and lit a cigarette. He stood smoking, looking straight ahead, taking long pulls on the filter and jetting the smoke from his nostrils. The rain had passed, but gusts of wind shook the larger tree limbs and water fell from the leaves and landed on the saturated ground dotted with puddles. A fierce morning light streamed through punctures in the cloud cover, illuminating random patches of grass and sidewalk concrete and glinting off the chrome and the windshields of the vehicles. Sarah sat in Norton's car, holding the dog in her lap and looking out at the traffic building up on the interstate, drivers slowing and craning to see the cause for the emergency lights and flurry of law enforcement. In the rearview mirror, the bodies of the old couple had been covered with blankets, which somehow further emphasized their slight and defenseless frames. The dog lay still, Sarah's hand stroking its long body, the short fur a deep chestnut color that was slightly damp and warm to her touch.

"I'm guessing this is your first experience with homicide," Norton said. He too was looking at the interstate. He reached across her and opened the glove box and pulled out a pack of Winstons. He shook the pack and picked a cigarette out and started to put it between his lips and stopped short, looking at Sarah.

"You mind if I smoke?" he asked. Sarah turned and looked at the pack in his hand. Shook her head and he continued with the routine of lighting the cigarette. He rolled down the window a crack and exhaled through the side of his mouth, sending a jet stream of smoke outside the car.

"Think I could get one of those?" Sarah asked.

He looked at her and shook the pack again, flipping his wrist downward and until one of the filters stood taller than the others. He offered it over and Sarah accepted it and then he flicked the lighter wheel and she leaned in for it. She cracked her window and they sat without speaking, smoking and looking at the traffic.

"Any idea of what happened here?" he asked.

Sarah shook her head. She paused, about to speak and then closed her eyes. The smoke was horrible in her mouth but was having its desired calming effect.

"You know, I lived in Atlanta before I moved back here," he said. "Much bigger place, much worse crime. You start to expect, maybe even accept, horrible things in a place that size. Working in a morgue, anyway. I guess I got used to it on my own terms. Especially not the children. There's no amount of experience that will ever prepare you for the kids, but the adult homicides with the street gangs or a domestic violence case, drunk driving, that just all becomes part of the job. I had a boss while I was there that used to tell me that I had to shut out the reasons for the bodies showing up, said it would eventually eat me alive if I dwelled on the nature of the consequence. He was right, of course. Only makes sense. But this job—your job—these professions expose you to a side of humanity that others have the luxury of never seeing in the real world. Those people put murder in the same category as entertainment. You can't blame them. Why would you want to go too deep into that type of thing if you didn't have to?"

Sarah rolled her window down further, dropped the half-smoked cigarette out and rolled it back up. She was listening, but only partly hearing what he was saying. Processing anything seemed almost impossible, like she had been concussed or had just woken from a coma.

"I have to get inside," Norton said. "You sit here for a bit if you like." Earlier, Lee had come back to the car and rapped his knuckles on the window. His height made it necessary for him to lean way over to get even with Norton's face. He had started to speak, but when he saw Sarah, he held back. Norton appreciated Lee's sense of awareness. The entire response to the scene had been nothing shy of absurd. Even the state police and the locals from Marion County seemed lost, and Norton was not sure that he could blame them. After all that he had seen in his time in the Atlanta coroner's office, he had hoped that he was done with homicide of this severity and this magnitude of cruelty. What he had told Sarah about his time there was true, all of it, but the part that he had not shared was that he had come dangerously close to letting the job devour him and it was only a very thin luck that had enabled him to find his way out. Lee's discretion and competence made him feel a bit more in control. He had seen Sarah in the car and he had nodded knowingly at Norton and then stepped away from the car, straightening up and lighting another cigarette. It was a small instance of professionalism, but one that Norton found comforting as he prepared for the task at hand.

Norton opened his car door and stood. He looked at the scene behind him and saw the other Winchester deputy standing next to his cruiser. When Ethan saw Norton, he started walking across the parking lot, hands in his pockets and head bent down. Norton stood in place. Ethan looked up again and jogged the rest of the way over to the car and came to a stop behind the trunk.

"Is Sarah okay?" Ethan asked, and Norton saw for the first time how young the boy was. *It's like the two of them are playing dress-up,* Norton thought, pushing back on the cynicism and trying to replace it with empathy. *But Christ he looks like he was in the high school band and went straight from playing the trumpet to carrying a deputy's badge.*

"Well," Norton said, "it would be a stretch to say she's all right now, but she will be with some time. How about you, how are you holding up?"

Ethan shrugged. "Can't really say. Don't think I'll be sleeping too well for a while."

Norton smiled at the sincerity of the response.

"No. I don't guess you will, but that would be pretty normal." Ethan looked as if he didn't understand the meaning of Norton's last word.

"Can I talk with her?"

"Sure." The boy's innocence hurt to watch. He smiled sheepishly at Norton and went around the back of the car to the passenger window and gently knocked on the glass. Sarah opened the car door and Ethan squatted down to speak to her.

"Hey Sarah," he said.

"Hey," she said.

"Rhonda got the sheriff on the phone at the restaurant."

"Sarah?" She looked into Ethan's face and recognized the same bewilderment she imagined was framing her own.

"Okay," she said.

"He's on his way back. He has to drop his wife off at the house and then he's coming here."

"Coming here? How do you know?"

"I called Rhonda from one of the pay phones. She said sheriff asked about you and told her to tell me that I should stay put and help out where I could. But he wanted to make sure you were all right. That's what Rhonda told me a couple times. Sheriff said that the Marion County officers were in charge until he could get here." He paused. Sarah was no longer looking at him. He glanced at Norton, who was watching them, then turned back to the car. "Sarah, you okay?" He reached out slowly and touched her knee.

"Sarah I'm really sorry you were alone. I mean, I can't even believe it. It's just so awful. All that blood. All that blood. I mean, one of those state guys. The one who covers from White's Ridge over to here. He says he's been doing this job forever and has never seen anything like this before. He was in Vietnam too. Can you believe that?" He still had his hand on Sarah's knee and when he realized it, he pulled it away quickly. She looked at him appreciatively. "So much blood," he repeated. "And Herc. Sarah, don't you think Herc knew something when we were back by the fence? I think he saw something back there. I know he saw something back there. Sarah, I…" she stopped him by touching his hand.

"Maybe, Ethan," she said. "Maybe."

Norton took a step toward them.

"I have to join Lee and the other officers. Sarah, if you are up to it, I think you should go home and get some rest. You can talk with Sheriff Edwards later today. Ethan can cover for you here." Ethan was looking at Norton but spoke to Sarah.

"You want to go home?"

Sarah turned away and drew in a long breath.

"Yeah, I think so," she said. "What about this dog, Ethan?"

He leaned into the car and stroked the dog's head without replying.

Sarah thought about the question of leaving the scene and tried to imagine what emotional wave was coming next and where she wanted to experience it. Her mother would probably be at home, and maybe Jed unless he'd gone hunting or more likely drinking. She was not sure that was the best place to be, but she was afraid that they would ask her to go back inside the building and she did not think that she could bring herself to do that.

"I think I'll go home for a while, Ethan." She reached for the door handle. He backed away from the car and she climbed out with the dog and when she turned to shut the door, Norton was still standing there, looking at her with a neutrality she found hard to interpret.

"Thank you, Mr. Norton," she said. He smiled at her evenly, and Sarah decided that she liked him.

"Can I ask you something?"

"Yes," he said.

"When you were talking about your time away. You know, when you were working in Atlanta?"

"Yes."

"And you were talking about getting used to murder and people who did horrible things..." She had meant to pose this as a question, but it came out in a dejected, flat tone that implied she was answering her own train of thought.

"In a sense, but yes."

"Do you think you would have ever gotten used to seeing something like this?" She turned and looked back at the rest stop building. She felt her eyes beginning to sting and the burning was back in her throat. She looked at the ground and saw the cigarette lying there, no longer smoking from being on the wet pavement. She wanted to say more but knew it would catch in her throat and she did not want Ethan to try and console her and she did not want this man Norton to see her cry anymore. Something about him made her want to be strong. She looked back at the rest stop and one of the troopers had walked off to the side of the building where Lee had been smoking. He was standing with his back to them, looking into the woods. She could not see his face, but his rigid posture spoke. She saw the writing in blood on the mirror, and the bloodied knife with its teeth-like edge on the grimy toilet seat and she knew what the man was thinking as he stood quietly observing the far edge of the woods, dripping and electric green, the discordant sounds of the birds perched in the high limbs where they went unseen.

"I don't know, Sarah," he said. "Maybe. Maybe not. All I can say is that you can't accept responsibility for a consequence that you did not cause. It's nature, I mean. And that you will have a job to do once you rest."

Sarah looked at Norton as he said this, and then she nodded what she hoped would indicate her understanding despite the images that kept playing across her mind as if they were being projected from within, from behind her eyes and not in front of them. *Those were pearls,* she thought and felt faint. She steadied herself and began walking toward her car, Ethan following. Overhead, the clouds were moving away faster, and the sunlight was now washing over the top of the mountain; its clarity and unapologetic exposure of all things below seemed to Sarah an unwholesome thing, and she wanted to be rid of it and driving away from this despicable, careless, untethered event and the stains it left behind from its perpetrator who Sarah knew had been somewhere in the woods, watching them move up and down the fence line in their confusion and real fear, and there would have been a smile of pleasure for the acts that had been committed and the horror that had followed in their discovery. She opened the door of her vehicle, holding the dog under one arm. Ethan kept a respectful distance.

"I'll stay here," he said. "Wait on the sheriff." He was keyed-up to the point of snapping in two and Sarah thought about seeing if he wanted to come with her, but she did not think that she could take any more conversation and one of them needed to be here when the sheriff arrived. It should probably be her, but Sheriff Edwards would be by the house later and she was feeling very frail. Ethan must have read her thought because he looked like he was going to ask what she had almost offered. She put the dog into the seat before she climbed in and she turned to look at Ethan. The reality, she was beginning to realize as she looked at his youthful face, is that the murders would be a part of their waking and non-waking world for the rest of their lives. And whether she went back to work at the dollar store, or cleaning houses, or even if she joined the Navy and sailed halfway around the world, the faces of the dead would always be with her. But as she looked at the front of this building she had seen a thousand times before without incident, at Lee's lanky frame moving toward the glass doors, coming to meet Norton who was stepping over the bodies as he ascended the ramp, she realized that what would always overshadow the colorless faces was the fact that she and Ethan had missed an encounter with the killer by a matter of minutes and that the man whose motivation seemed both insane and riddled with malice and contempt had likely watched them from a distance and had done so because he wanted to know—wanted to see—how being that close to death would sit with them.

"Make sure you get Herc some water," she said. The shepherd was in the back of Ethan's vehicle, his nose pressed against the back windshield, obviously anxious to be outside, understanding his role was being delayed and his eyes, a marble black and brown, seemed never to blink.

"I will, Sarah." He patted the top of her car and the gesture in and of itself seemed so routine, so mundane, that Sarah allowed herself to once again pose the idea that all of this was a terrible dream, and when she awoke she would have to contend with embarrassingly wetting the bed and that alone would be the full extent of the horror, an accident that could be washed away and forgotten entirely.

"Ethan," she began and then realized she had nothing more to say and was stalling because she knew that she was very afraid of being alone. She looked at the Caprice and remembered its slipping transmission and thought of the miles of rural country road she would be traveling to get to her mother's house.

"Sarah?"

"Nothing," she said quickly and got into the car, gently pushing the dog into the other seat. The keys were in the ignition, she had left them there before going into the rest stop. Ethan watched her through the window. She waved at him and cranked the engine. The dog turned in several circles and lay down, watching Sarah as it did so. *You poor thing. What a fucking day you've had.* She backed out of the space and was heading east toward the on-ramp when the dog climbed into her lap and settled in. She thought of the two old people back on the handicap ramp, covered in ratty blankets like grotesque cocoons some venomous thing had left behind. She was on the interstate and heading down the eastern slope when she began to feel lightheaded. She pulled the Caprice over to a runaway truck entrance and as soon as she had the car stopped, her shoulders began to shake, and spasms racked her body. The dog sat up in her lap and began to whine and paw at her face and she stroked its fur and then held it to her chest until her composure returned and she felt clear enough to drive home.

CHAPTER 32

EDWARDS RETURNS HOME

Sheriff Edwards pulled to the curb in front of the modest one-story, two-bedroom house he shared with his wife. He put the car in park and got out, walked around to the passenger side, and opened her door. He took her hand and helped her out of the seat. When she was standing he reached back into the car and pulled out two white paper sacks that held their cheeseburgers, fries, and shakes. He stood and turned to Kat.

"Let's go in the house." He took her gently by the arm and guided her up the walk toward the front porch that held two green rocking chairs and several potted plants. The neat flower beds were edged cleanly, with tended shrubs and fresh mulch, but something about the look of the beds felt pitiful and disheartening, almost like they knew that the attention they were accustomed to receiving had dried up altogether and that their survival was in the hands of someone whose mind was elsewhere.

"Let's get you settled inside and then I have to go do some things for work." She shuffled, slightly ahead of him and looked from side to side as they made their way toward the door. The lawn was wet from the rain, and as they stepped onto the porch, Edwards looked to his left and could see the mountain in the distance, the sun above it, and as he turned back he found Kat facing him. She appeared small and delicate and an uncertainty twitched at the corner of her eyes. She wet her lips before she spoke.

"Bill," she said. "Bill, where are you going?" He looked at her with the same patient expression he had adopted since she had first started to forget things, but there was a sharp awareness in this question that stopped him. He stood thinking how to answer. The details from his phone call with Rhonda were fresh, and he had to concentrate to remain patient. He decided to put it to her plainly. The tone of the question seemed to warrant the truth.

"I've got to go up the mountain about some trouble that happened this morning. It's why I had to cut our lunch short. I'll probably be gone the rest of the day and maybe into tonight. I'll call and check on you though. I'll make sure you know where the phone is before I leave. That gonna be okay?"

She said nothing.

"Kat. You okay?"

She smiled, but there was something dismissive about it, something that felt like concession.

"That's okay," she said, but seemed to be looking past him. "You should be careful I think, Bill. Yes, be careful while you are away."

He looked at her, the formality of her speech unsettling, and now he could see that she was talking from someplace else, as if she were remembering a conversation he had never been a part of, or perhaps a memory that took place before he was a part of her life. The doctor had explained that it could and probably would happen. She would see something clearly in her mind and her thoughts would jump the time gap and speak of the past event in real time, as if reliving its details from then, but experiencing the significance now. It was the moments like this that made him think of his wife as a failing machine, and not the woman he had loved for all these years. He supposed that his objective observation was an older man's way of coping with something delicate, coaxing it along until it sputtered back into purpose.

"Kat, can we go inside?" She did not respond and the urgency of the call in the diner was tapping the inside of his skull like a slow steady knock. He took her by the arm, opened the door, and then guided her into the front room of their home. He walked her over to a chair in the den and helped her sit down. She made no effort to resist or assist. He stood back and was considering whether or not she might be suffering a stroke, when a recognition came back into her eyes and she was suddenly looking around the room, and he knew that she was trying to understand how they got there. He left her side and walked into the kitchen and took her cheeseburger out of the bag, unwrapped it and set it on a plate. He looked in the bag and found the fries and he emptied them onto the plate, the pile of potatoes limp with grease. He pulled out the shake from the other bag, grabbed a paper towel from the spool on the counter and took the meal in to his wife.

"Here's your burger and fries, my lady," he said. "And one chocolate shake. Just how you like it. A little warm so the ice cream melts." She smiled and took the plate into her lap. He put the shake on an end table on top of a coaster with a picture of their niece and nephew when they were just little kids, the faded image inset into the soft worn square of wood, protected by a scratched plastic cover.

"I'm gonna go back in the bedroom and get a couple of things and then I gotta go. You're gonna be okay if I leave you for a little while? I'll have Ethan come by and check on you around dinner. Maybe pick something up at the grocery for you to eat?" She was eating her burger and he slipped back to his bedroom for his gun belt and to change out of his shoes into some work boots. The phone call in the diner had been surreal, Rhonda talking a mile a minute until he had to finally yell into the phone for her to slow down and start from the beginning. Slipping his right foot into the boot and considering what he knew of Rhonda, he could not believe that she had possessed the presence of mind to track him down, even with the note he left behind to prompt her. Mutilated bodies at the rest area, Sarah finding the scene alone. *My God*, he thought. He had tried to process all of this at the checkout counter with the waitress smacking her gum and doing a poor job of pretending not to listen. Now sitting in his bedroom and the call juxtaposed with the realities of his life with Katherine, he was slightly amazed that he could remember how to lace up the boots. He stood and left the bedroom and hurried back down the hall where Kat was eating.

"You want to watch some TV?" She nodded, chewing. He found the remote and set it next to the shake and pushed the on button. The picture warmed up and her eyes focused intently on the screen. He reached down and took her chin in his hand and gently guided her face up to see his.

"I will be back tonight. The phone is right over there by the grandfather clock," he said, pointing in that direction. "I love you."

She smiled. "Love you," she said. He let go of her chin and went to the door, breaking into a trot as soon as it was closed behind him.

The highway between Winchester and the mountain was a flat grey four lane divided by a wide median choked with weeds and strewn with litter. There were also patches of wildflowers dotted here and there that had been planted by the Junior League as part of a highway beautification project. Edwards and his deputies had supervised the initiative and he recalled the small groups of women walking in the median and throwing handfuls of wildflower seeds out in front of them while the sheriff's cars sat parked on the shoulder with their lights spinning in an effort to slow down traffic. The flowers presented a sharp orange, pink, and red waist-high contrast to what would have otherwise been a dull strip of road cutting between large expanses of fields and farms on either side, ridgelines framing them in the distance. Travelers used the straight eleven mile stretch to make up time and the sheriff's department used it to collect revenue the last three days of every month. The mountain road naturally helped tick down speedometers, but as Sheriff Edwards came off the last flat mile and moved into the first turn of the mountain climb, he was doing well over seventy, passing a cattle truck that was laboring under its load. Out his passenger window, Edwards could see through the steel slats of the trailer and saw the soft noses and startled eyes of the cows huddled there, staring back at him with knowing expressions. His car continued to climb as he maneuvered it skillfully in and out of the lanes, cutting the tighter curves and moving around the other big semis creeping up the increasing grade. The inside of the car was silent save for the engine noise. The gun belt, which he rarely wore these days, pinched his hip, and the grip of the big handgun dug into his side every time he steered the cruiser to the right.

Less than a mile up the mountain, he ran into the traffic that had backed up. He yanked the car onto the shoulder and slowed his speed considerably. The high flat rock faces had been sheared clean when the interstate was built. They loomed above him, and periodically cascades of water poured over the side, coming from swollen creek beds that ended their circulatory courses in sharp drop-offs all over the cliff sides of the mountain, so much so that in the spring it was as though the mountain preserved a lake beneath its wooded and rocky skin. The gravel crunched under the tires as he came around the final turn and into view of the rest area exit. A state trooper vehicle and yellow tape blocked incoming traffic, and a trooper stood off to the side, closest to the interstate and was waving traffic to move along. Edwards pulled his vehicle to the side of the exit, careful not to put his wheel into the ditch, and got out of the car. A pickup he recognized was pulled off the side ten yards ahead of his vehicle. The trooper directing traffic did not notice him with his back turned and Edwards gave a sharp whistle. The trooper turned quickly. Edwards waved at him and yelled, "Sheriff." The trooper nodded and went back to directing traffic. Cars passing did not need direction. They slowed automatically, the passenger's faces pressed to the glass, their necks craned back to get a closer look at the spectacle unfolding. Edwards could see why, with the lights and the tape and all these cops, no wonder they were curious. He scanned what he could see of the parking lot. Besides the trooper's vehicles, he could only make out the tops of the other cars. He continued walking up the exit. He felt a slight burn in his thighs and he thought about the walk he and Kat might have taken to the caves if it weren't for this. Walking with her in the woods brought a neutrality to the dementia, as if it was willing to give them back an hour or two in an otherwise muddled and achingly long passage of daylight, walking among the very old trees, the shafts of sunlight spearing the canopy, the sound of running water, the chatter of birds and angry squirrels, the rare sighting of deer if they walked quietly. It was as if the disease, which normally was greedy beyond all comparison, felt that it would not lose any grip or ground by leaving her alone to walk through all those natural distractions, holding her husband's hand, who, plead and pray as he might, was never going to convince it to go away and let her have her mind back. It was no different than the monster who had killed these people on top of the mountain, and in many ways it was worse, because those people had encountered something, someone horrible, and their last moments had been terrifying and likely they had felt painfully alone. But this thing living inside his wife took its time. It had no sense of mercy or inclination to stop its ravaging. Enough was never enough until it had taken everything, and only when the body itself gave up would the slow deterioration cease, the corpse no longer a source of nourishment and the mind an abandoned shaft or drafty cavern.

Edwards crested the rise of the exit ramp and a tall, muscular man noticed him and came across the parking lot to meet him. He wore hunting attire and had spent the last couple of days outside in the woods from the look of his clothes, the ratty beard, and the greasy hair that dangled in strands from beneath the ball cap he had crammed on his head. Hair that Edwards had told him to cut more times than he cared to count.

"Sheriff," the man said, coming to a standstill, his hands jammed into his pockets, his frame slightly rocking as he pushed up on his toes and then back again, another part of the man's demeanor Edwards found less then professional, and distracting.

"Flip," the Sheriff said, and stopped so that the two men were facing one another. "I thought you were off today?"

"I was," Flip Thomas said, rotating his shoulders and thumbing a hand back toward the building. "Didn't have much luck. Was coming back over the mountain to the house and saw this mess. I turned around and came back up the east-bound side. I parked off the side of the ramp. Took me a while to convince the state boys down there that I was law enforcement." The sheriff nodded and regarded Flip again.

"You're lucky they didn't put you in cuffs the way you're looking."

"Well," Flip said, and toed the ground with his boot.

"You talked to anyone about what happened?"

"Nah," he said. "I tried to see if I could help, but they did not seem too interested." The sheriff nodded again.

"Will Tibbits from over in Marion County is up here, Sheriff," he said. "He's been asking about you. I think he's over by that entrance in the back of the building. Ethan's with him, or he was. Sarah went home. I didn't get the chance to talk with her. She was already gone when I came up. Ethan says she's in shock. I think Ethan's in shock too. He's not making a whole lot of sense. I have not been in the building, yet.

Ethan said it's something awful in there. Shit written on the walls and a deer head, and the carcass on a table in the back and good Lord knows what else." Edwards nodded.

"Let me find out what's what." He walked past his deputy and up through the parking lot, his head swiveling side to side. The coroner's vehicle was in one of the parking spaces and Edwards stepped onto the sidewalk in front of the building. The two bodies on the handicap ramp were covered and Edwards regarded them with an anxiety rising in his throat like a brush fire. Blood stains were on the concrete and the bodies themselves were unattended. He looked back at the parking lot and then back to the figures on the ground. *Are you ready for this, Bill? Are you ready to look it in the face?* He thought of Katherine at home in her chair, watching television, and he cringed at the idea of her seeing something like this. He scratched at the stubble on his cheeks and chin and went past the corpses on the ramp and around the side of the building. The sunlight was straining his eyes and he wished that he had his sunglasses that were in a case in his glovebox. He could hear voices on the back side of the building and he took a deep breath before emerging around the corner. The property at the rear of the rest area was more expansive than he remembered it being, and were it not for the police activity, he imagined it would be a very nice place to sit and rest. The voices were coming from a small group of officers gathered around one of the picnic tables located closest to the building's rear entrance. As Edwards came into view, one of the men said something to another whose back was to Edwards, and when the man turned, Edwards saw that it was Will Tibbits out of Marion County. Tibbits excused himself from the group and walked to meet Edwards.

"Will."

"Hey Bill. Good to see you."

"Likewise."

Tibbits shook his head. "Bill, this is a goddamn mess up here," he said. He pointed to the deer carcass on the table behind him. It sat like a macabre picnic decoration. "That right there don't even begin to prepare you for what's inside. Coroner in Winchester got us on the phone. He said they'd tried you every which way and couldn't get you. Your deputy said you were over in Taylor Branch with Kat. I hope you had a real nice lunch, Bill, because I'm about to ruin the rest of your day." Edwards pushed at the gun belt to position it further down on his hips and then looked back at Tibbits.

"Before we get started, let me introduce you to a couple people," Tibbits said. The two sheriffs walked back to the table where Edwards shook hands with the state police officers who were waiting there.

"Bill, this is officer Davis and this is officer Clemmons. Both with the state police and I want you to know how big a help they have been, considering how stretched they already are." Edwards thanked them both and their response was pleasant enough, but he could see that they were both anxious to leave. Something in their collective expression and posture bothered Edwards. *They're spooked,* he thought, watching their eyes darting back and forth to the carcass. He thanked them again and turned back to Tibbits.

"State police are glad to have helped, but this is local jurisdiction as you know. The interstate complicates things a bit, and might be that you have to involve the TBI. I'm not for sure," Tibbits explained.

Edwards looked to Davis and Clemmons. Neither seemed interested in speaking for themselves.

"I don't want you to take this wrong, Bill," Tibbits said and paused. "Not being able to reach you has got this all turned around. No offense to you or your deputies."

"None taken," Edwards said. "I think it's safe to say that we're not exactly equipped for something like this."

"That new coroner you got. He…"

"Norton," Edwards said.

"That's the one," Tibbits said. "Him. He took the lead on most of this. Contacted all the parties involved. Sharp fella. Took a lot on."

"Where is he? Norton."

"Inside, I think," Tibbits said, looking around as if the coroner might be hiding under one of the picnic tables. Davis and Clemmons shuffled, hands on their belts. Tibbits noticed and looked at both of them and then back to Edwards.

"Thank you both," he said. "I'll brief Sheriff Edwards from here."

CHAPTER 33

TIBBITS EXPLAINS

"Aside from the animal, you have four dead," Tibbits said. "Two in the men's room and the two you probably saw coming in on the handicap ramp. One of the men in the bathroom had his eyes removed and left in the women's bathroom, wrapped up and left in the sink. And all of them had their throats cut. I got our forensic guy here and your coroner out of Winchester looking at the bodies, but it looks like all of them were killed using a large hunting knife. We don't have to do much investigating on the dead, all of their wallets and IDs are still on their person. And we think he left the murder weapon sitting on one of the toilets in the women's."

"What?" Edwards said.

"Yep," Tibbits said, reading his friend's face, taking his hat off to run a hand atop his nearly-bald head. Edwards started to speak, but Tibbits replaced the hat and held up a hand to stop him. "Let me finish, if you would."

Edwards nodded.

"He wrote a bunch of stuff on the walls that seems like warnings or something, maybe trying to throw us in a different direction. That coroner fella thinks it's some kind of poetry but he can't place what it is. We'll find out soon enough, I guess. Not that it really matters when you consider how random this all feels. We ran the license plates and they all match up with the driver's licenses, and best we can tell there is no connection between any of the victims, save the two on the ramp. Our guess is that they were married. One is the attendant, one is from Illinois and the old couple at the front is from Toronto. They were all killed within minutes of one another, forensics thinks. Our guess is that he killed the attendant and the other guy in the bathroom and then caught that older couple coming in the front and killed them to make sure that he didn't leave anyone behind. The deer was killed sometime before and we think he brought that with him, however he got here, and for whatever deranged reason someone would be walking around the woods carrying a dead animal they had no intention of dressing and eating. Must be a strong son of a bitch cause that deer weighs every bit of one hundred twenty five pounds. Rain didn't help with blood trails so we can't be sure if he carried it in or not. Based on what your deputy told me they observed with your dog, the suspect probably came out of the woods in the back and ambushed the folks inside, not that there would have been any reason for them to expect anything like this to happen, rest in peace. My guys and your deputy cut a hole in the fence and poked around the woods to see if they could pick anything up, but we came up empty-handed." He sighed and looked at the fence line at the back of the property. "As you know, there's miles and miles of woods out there to cover and if he went back out that way, he's got a good head start on us. That rain didn't help our cause either." He paused and Edwards said nothing.

"Like I was saying earlier, the bureau is probably gonna get involved in this, Bill. I'm sure they'll welcome your help and of course I'll give you anything that I can, but this looks like it may be beyond our resources. This is psychotic behavior, and there is no telling whether whoever did this plans to stick around or if they've just picked out rural rest areas up and down the interstate to kill people. Jesus wept, Bill. Either way, bureau will get involved, although I can't say how quickly. I've spoken to our dispatch folks and my guys are going to watch the rest stops in our jurisdiction and the state boys said they've made everyone aware as well. Maybe we'll get lucky and catch him trying it again, but hell, I don't know Bill. I've never seen anything like this in all my years on the job."

"I'm real glad you are here, Will" Edwards said. "Thank you and..."

Tibbits waived him off. "Stop," he said. "Save it for somebody that don't know you any better." Edwards smiled

"This deputy of yours—Sarah Hicks, I think is her name—appears to have handled herself very well," Tibbits said. "I think she probably missed rolling up on this by a matter of minutes. She's damn lucky she isn't lying in the lobby dead. She briefed Norton. He briefed me and the state boys. We sent her home. She was about half a breath from dropping over. You'll need to circle back with her and make sure there is nothing that we missed or forgot to ask."

"Anything else?" Edwards said.

Tibbits looked at him with a half-smile as if the question struck him funny. "I think that will do it for now," Tibbits said. He removed his hat again and Edwards could see the perspiration. Tibbits had been the Sheriff of Marion County for as long as Edwards could recall. He was good at his job and a highly respected member of his community. He and Bill had worked together on several occasions, a couple of which had involved tracking down and arresting mountain people growing marijuana in remote areas far removed from the civilized world. The growers would use the interstate access to run the drugs off the mountain and this brought the attention of multiple jurisdictions. Tibbits had been shot in one of their joint raids and Edwards had helped carry the stretcher out of a deep ravine and through miles of woods with Tibbits making smart ass comments and declarations the entire time, a t-shirt tied around his thigh to staunch the bleeding from a bullet that had gone all the way through.

"You ready to go inside?" Tibbits asked.

"I guess so."

"Well come on," Tibbits said, and the two men turned together and walked toward the rear entrance of the building. Flies were buzzing around the deer carcass and Edwards recoiled at their angry biting and feeding.

The two men walked through the rear doors. The lobby was now well-lit and Edwards saw that the bathrooms were illuminated through the openings on the left-hand side of the room. He could hear people moving around inside one of the restrooms and the echoes of their activity. Tibbits was in front and he walked straight to the restroom entrance and then stopped, Edwards almost walking into him.

"Come here first, Bill." He turned to his right and went toward the front and stood in the doorway of the attendant's office.

"We think he came in through the back. And I keep saying 'him' because they," he pointed in the direction of the forensic team in the bathroom, "think it's a single suspect. We think he came in through the back and came straight to the attendant's office. We're guessing there was some kind of struggle in here. You can see where things got pulled off the desk. My guess is the attendant sees the guy coming in the door and goes out to meet him and ends up with his throat cut in a stall he probably cleaned an hour before." Tibbits was speaking factually, but his voice was strained. "We don't think he killed the attendant out here in the reception area. Not enough blood. They think he might have been forced into the men's and killed in there. The other guy in there was either on the toilet or came in after. It's hard to say, but either way, this sick son of a bitch placed them on the toilets like he was setting up a scene for someone to find. We're looking for prints but given the amount of people who come through here each day, identifying this guy will be next to impossible. We might get something off the knife, but then again, we might not and even if we do, chances are he's not in the system."

The day that Tibbits had been shot, they had been positioned behind a deadfall that was the result of the trees cleared for the rotting trailers where the dealers were squatting. They had used a bull horn to call them outside and Edwards remembered how loud and foreign it had sounded that far into the woods. It was a man and a woman who finally emerged from the trailer door. They were rail thin and filthy standing on the shabby little porch, seeming to lean against one another like refugees after a storm, their stares vacant and strained like the sunlight hurt their eyes. Tibbits had stood up from behind the deadfall and Edwards saw the gun in the woman's hand seconds before she raised it and got off a wild shot toward the officers. The bullet hit Tibbits and he went down immediately. Edwards went to him. Flip had been with them that day and he took advantage of the commotion to spin the woman backwards into the trailer wall with a rifle shot that hit her in the shoulder. She crumpled and sat stunned. The man screamed something at the officers and knelt beside her. Tibbits did a good job hiding the limp he took away from the raid, but Bill could see him favoring the leg while they stood in the reception area.

"Where's Ethan?" Edwards asked.

"Who?" Tibbits said.

"Ethan. My other deputy."

"The guy in the hunting outfit? Flip you call him?"

"No," said Edwards. "He would have been in uniform. He came in after Sarah."

"Oh," said Tibbits. "He's got your dog and is out with our K-9 unit, I think. He's a bit keyed-up. I thought he could use the activity. They aren't going to find anything out there, Bill. The rain and storm washed the trail. Still."

Edwards nodded.

"Let's go in here," Tibbits said.

The two men walked single file into the men's room where Norton, Lee, and the Marion County forensic tech were working. A camera flashed in the last stall, pulsing a sharp light that briefly illuminated the ceiling above. Norton came out of the middle stall and startled at the two sheriffs. He was wearing blue rubber gloves and he was chewing a piece of gum.

"Anything?" Tibbits asked. Norton looked at Edwards, offering a slim smile and tilt of his head.

"Nothing that's not already obvious," he said. "I don't think they struggled long. The cuts were clean and deep. And the business with the eyes, I think that was done postmortem. But he was precise there too. Guy knew how to use a knife is the short of it." Both sheriffs stood still, listening.

"They are not long dead. My guess is your deputy could have just as easily stumbled on this while it was occurring if she'd been fifteen minutes earlier getting here. But he may have known he had a short window given the location and the traffic that comes through here. We're thinking he'd done everything he planned on doing inside and saw the older couple coming toward the entrance as he was leaving. Took care of them as an insurance policy. If they had arrived five minutes later, they'd be on their way to wherever they were going." Tibbits smiled.

"Florida," he said.

"What's that," Norton said.

"My wife and I joke about rest stops on the way to the beach," Tibbits said. "I don't know. There's always some nice old couple on their way south when you pull into one of these places." Edwards looked at his friend who was looking at the floor of the restroom.

"Goddamn," Tibbits said. "What the hell kind of world have we made for ourselves when you can't stop off to take a piss…"

"Will," Edwards said softly. Tibbits looked up. "Maybe you've seen enough for today." Tibbits shook his head. "No. No, no. I'm okay. Sorry Bill. I just started thinking about…"

"I understand," Edwards said, and he did. The cruelty of what they were seeing was not lost on any of them. Norton glanced at Edwards for permission to proceed and Edwards nodded to move on.

"Well, some of that stuff written on the walls is from a poem called 'The Wasteland'," Norton said. "I read it in school when I had loftier intellectual aspirations. The poet's name was T.S. Eliot." Edwards and Tibbits passed a look. "I did not know what it meant then and I certainly don't know what it means now. I just recall some of the phrasing because it was so bleak I probably tuned out most of it, but there are parts that have stuck with me for whatever reason. I may try and look into it tonight if I can find a copy. Mostly it's about disenchantment with life."

"Well that fits," Tibbits said and grunted. "Whatever the hell that means."

"Anyway, we are about to wrap up here. We'll keep the bodies at the morgue until we hear from you, Sheriff. And I'll let you know if I come up with anything that makes sense of what he wrote on the walls and mirror."

"Good," Edwards said. He walked around the coroner and went to the back of the room where the Marion County forensic tech was taking pictures of the body. As he neared the stall entrance the man came out and Edwards could see in; the man's head was leaned back and touching the wall, the wound as startling as an electric shock. He stepped a couple of paces back and opened the second door. The deer's rounded black eyes glared back. He looked above it: THE THIRD WHO WALKS BESIDE YOU. He closed the door and moved to the last stall. The dead man was positioned in the same way as the first, but his eyes had been taken from their sockets. "O LORD THOU PLUCKEST," Edwards read aloud, his deep voice echoing off the tiled walls, in sharp contrast to the dead man's silent expression which was waxed and still above the lengthy incision, and the wash of blood that almost obscured his name tag.

Tibbits turned and walked out without speaking. Edwards followed and Norton was left alone in the room. The forensic guy popped another picture in the stall with the deer head, bursting white light onto the ceiling. Norton started to spit his gum into the trash can that was mounted on the wall beneath the paper towel dispenser and spit it into his hand instead, its flavor gone and its firmness making his jaw hurt from chewing. He walked out of the room and out the back entrance, glanced at the carcass on the picnic table, and went around the side of the building to find his pack of cigarettes.

He was crossing the parking lot when the memory came back to him. He had been in his office late. A metro cop had stuck his head inside his door to tell him that the wife was outside waiting to ID the bodies of the man and boy he had just addressed. The man had been teaching the boy how to ride his bike and the kid had gotten the hang of everything except the brakes. The neighbor had seen the whole thing. The boy was moving quickly down the sidewalk and he was yelling to his dad that he was "doing it." The father had been trailing behind, shouting back encouragement *and he must have forgotten that they were working on the sidewalk at the intersection, the neighbor had said, because the kid just went right through and the man, I mean Mr. Davis, went running after him and stopped the bike in the middle of the street, but the truck was already coming…*

Norton went out into the waiting area to meet the woman. Her composure was intact, but it was fragile and she followed Norton with her eyes as he entered the room and waited patiently for her to speak.

"I know that they are gone," she said. "I know that because I'm here in the morgue talking to you. But I don't know why they are gone," she said. The cop came in the room with a cup of coffee. He looked at Norton. He motioned for the cop to leave. The woman was slight and Norton thought that she would have a hard time physically recovering from the accident. Maybe it would be booze or pills or maybe it would be the sedentary life she would adopt, living in a house full of ghosts, watching daytime television and waiting around to catch up with them.

"I guess that's what we all want to know at a time like this," she said. Her jacket looked very big on her and she put her hand on a red plastic chair to steady herself.

"You. Me. Him," she waived at the cop who had left. "Why?" Norton thought for a second and then spoke honestly.

"I don't know, mam," he said.

"No," she said. "You don't. And never will."

CHAPTER 34

EDWARDS AND HIS DEPUTIES

Edwards came through the rear doors of the rest area and saw two men with shepherds in harnesses crossing the area between the back fence line and the building. The dogs were not straining their leads, and were obviously fatigued, and the two men were talking to one another casually as if they were neighbors sharing a suburban sidewalk. Edwards came up the rise and met them halfway. Ethan had Herc and everything in his demeanor screamed exhaustion, his expression one of disbelief as if he had seen color for the first time or possibly listened to his very first notes of music. He smiled when he saw Edwards and the sheriff felt an impulse to put a comforting arm around the deputy.

"Ethan, son, how are you?" Edwards said, realizing the absurdity of the question even as it was coming out of his mouth. Ethan stopped in front of Edwards and the dog instinctively sat down, gently panting. The other officer pulled on his harness leash and the two went past Edwards and the deputy, the unnamed shepherd looking back over its shoulder at Herc with empathy, his eyes soft and remorseful in a consensual admission of defeat. Then the officer pulled on the leash again and the dog trotted away obediently.

"Ah Sheriff, I don't even know," Ethan said. "We didn't find any-thing. Trail was cold and Herc ended up running around in circles, dragging me along with him. I guess I'm tired and pretty freaked out." Edwards reached down and scratched the German shepherd behind the ears. The big dog inclined his head to give Edwards a better angle and he gave a quiet groan of contentment. *If they could speak,* Edwards thought, looking at the dog's upturned face. *If he could articulate what he smells, sees, and hears, point to the things that we so clumsily miss. How frustrated with us they must be.*

"I'm proud of you, Ethan," the Sheriff said, extending his hand to shake the deputy's, which came up shyly and in slow motion. "You and Sarah both. Took real enough guts to do what you did this morning." Ethan reached down and scratched the dog's neck and Edwards could tell by the pinch in his face that he was trying very hard not to lose control.

"If you need to walk a bit, let's head over by that stand of trees in the back." Edwards reached out and took Herc's leash from Ethan's hand and touched the boy's shoulder, gently turning him away from the building and the other officers. The two of them walked back toward the fence line. There were longer shadows in the woods and it seemed to be getting colder. He had completely lost track of time. The sun, which had fought hard for its place all day, was starting to sink in a brilliance of hot orange and bleeding purple into the western horizon. Now Edwards did put his arm around the boy's shoulders and pre-pared to listen, as a father might. They walked a few paces, and Ethan stopped. His head drooped and his entire frame began to shake. The sheriff stepped away and removed his arm, letting it fall loosely to his side. His eyes were vacant and haunted and his jaw tightened. Tears were forming and Edwards felt a vacancy open in his head. Even hav-ing seen the violence for himself, heard the cobbled together theory behind the attack, the strength of the shock that it had produced in Ethan set him off balance. "*The World is too much with us,*" he thought. *Who had said that? Kat maybe? Probably. Kat and her educated obscurities that came in random snippets from time to time. But it fit, didn't it?* A wind moved through the tops of the trees hovering above them and Edwards looked up to watch the branches move, indifferent and reacting only to the whims of the wind and nothing more. Silent witnesses to what had occurred there that day.

"Ethan, son, I have to go to Sarah's. I know this is a lot to take, but I promise you, things will be a little easier tomorrow. I want you to take Herc back to the station and then I want you to go home. We'll meet together in the morning. You okay with that?" Ethan looked at the dog standing next to him, its nose sniffing the ground.

"Sheriff," he said. "You think maybe I could take Herc home with me tonight?"

Edwards looked at the dog, and then back to Ethan.

"I don't see why not. No junk food for him." He looked at the deputy and he smiled and Ethan tried to smile back. Edwards handed the leash back to him. The two men turned to go down the rise as Flip Thomas came up to meet them.

"Flip, I want you to follow Ethan home and make sure he's okay," Edwards said. "He's had a hell of a day and could probably use the company."

"Sheriff, I, uh, had plans tonight." Edwards looked at Flip, cocked an eyebrow.

"But I can cancel them," Flip said.

"That's good of you Flip," he said. "I'll see you boys tomorrow." He walked toward the rest stop building, where things seemed to be coming to a close. Lee and the Marion County forensic tech were moving back and forth between the parking lot and the rest area doors. The troopers had all departed except for one car still blocking the exit ramp. Edwards stopped and turned back to look at the two men. "Keep it to a 12-pack, boys," he said and turned the other way, pushing down on both sides of the gun belt where it was biting into him. He started back to his car and remembered what he had promised Kat and turned back to the deputies. He gave them a short grocery list and asked them to deliver her dinner and make sure that she did not need anything else. They were not aware of the full extent of her condition, and Edwards considered filling them in, but then thought better of it. Kat might come off as an older woman, but she could be conversant and Ethan's uniform would help her put the pieces together and not be scared by them coming to the door. She would eat, watch TV, and go to bed.

He might even be able to get home in time to kiss her goodnight. As he walked back to the car, he scanned the area around the building out of habit. They were missing something. He could feel it. There was obviously a big hole where the motive should have been: robbery, rape, mental illness…the way that the scene laid out now, he would not have been surprised if the suspect had been sitting on the front step with the murder weapon, whittling and waiting to show them how proud he was of what he had done. That would almost have made sense, but instead they were left with reeking empty rooms and jumbled clues that were neither coherent nor were they telling. The murder weapon was there, but he did not hold out much hope that it would lead them to the killer. Someone capable of that level of violence may be without his mental faculties but mistakenly leaving behind the knife he had used seems implausible. They were being taunted. *Or tempted,* he thought, without knowing why. *Tempted by what?* He worried that the mundane nature of the crimes he typically solved would diminish his thinking. They were so routine and for the most part putting things together was like placing the very last piece of a puzzle in its glaring empty space. This made him think of Kat and her word games and he picked up his pace as he got closer to the car.

CHAPTER 35

SARAH AT HOME

Sarah sat in an oversized, worn Naugahyde recliner in her mother's dark house. Her hands encircled a white coffee mug with faded dandelions, half-filled with Jack Daniels. She had carried the dog inside and given it a bowl of cat food and a small bowl of water, which she placed on a towel along the wall. The dog had ridden in her lap the entire drive home and now was gingerly investigating the house. It had not seen the cat yet. They would work things out themselves like animals do. *Some animals,* she thought and the dead deer's eyes looked into hers. She had taken a shower and was wearing a terrycloth bathrobe that belonged to her mother. Years of cigarette smoke lingered on the collar of the robe, along with whiffs of cheap Calvin Klein perfume her mother bought at the cosmetic counter at Lily's Beauty Products. The television set was on with no volume and Sarah sat rocking in the chair, looking out a bay window that framed the small acreage of the yard and beyond, where the valley floor stretched toward the base of the mountain like a mismatched green and brown throw rug thick with thistles and scrub. The sun was failing and stabs of soft light came through the window glass and touched objects here and there around the room: a remote control, a small giraffe figurine, a pair of fingernail clippers next to a red plastic lighter with a broken spark wheel. She sipped the whiskey, holding the mug with two hands and grimacing at the mash's after-bite. She felt its amber creek move down her throat and expand into her stomach in a small explosion of tingling warmth and she shivered and let out a slight cough.

Her eyes, painful from crying, were fixed on the distant mountain slope. Across the room, stretched atop the hearth of the fireplace was the cat, Stetson, cleaning its paws methodically with quick flashes from its rough tongue. She had no idea how long she had been staring out the window when the big feline jumped into her lap and forced its head against her arm, sloshing the whiskey in the mug. It sniffed aggressively, smelling the dog, who had gone to sleep under the table near its food and water. Stetson did not seem to care. The cat's indifference personified in its spineless posture and arrogant stare. She touched the animal's head and it lay across her legs, purring thickly and stretching its long form, showing its sagging belly thick with fur, kneading its claws as if working the cloth fiber like a lump of biscuit dough. Dark came and Sarah saw headlights far down the county road, growing larger as they moved closer. Then they were passing in front of the house and slowing to turn into the drive, and she could just make out that it was her mother's little Ford pick-up, in need of brakes and probably a quart of oil. Sarah took a deep breath and then a larger sip of the whiskey and waited for her mother to come through the kitchen door, her Food Mart name tag pinned to her pink uniform blouse and her hair piled on her head like a stack of unfolded laundry. She heard the rattling idle of the truck and then the engine knocking once it was turned off and then her mother Renee came inside with her hands clutching plastic grocery bags and her key ring held in her teeth. She dumped the load on the littered countertop, the canned goods clanging against the Formica. Her footfalls fell silent on the scuffed and torn linoleum flooring. She let out a long sigh, like she had a thousand times before. The end of a long and thankless workday. She turned on the light in the kitchen and then she pulled open the creaky cabinet that held the assortment of short glasses and mugs and the squat glass bottle of liquor whose height barely allowed it to sit between shelves. There was silence and then Renee stepped into the cased opening between the small kitchen and the living room where Sarah sat in the dark. Her slight frame cast in shadow, her left hand on her hip and her right shoulder leaning against the jam.

"Sarah?"

"Yes, Mamma."

"Did you take my Jack Daniels?"

"It's out on the counter, Mamma, and yes, I took some."

Renee walked back into the kitchen looking for the whiskey. Sarah heard her slide the glass bottle off the counter and she could not see, but knew she was examining the level inside, not to gauge the consumption, but to measure the bottle's longevity. The ritual was based on a necessity, and the necessity was based on supply and despite all of her mother's shortcomings, finding the bottle with a mere trickle of the brown liquor left was one thing that she guarded against with an almost religious fervor. Sarah heard her mother pulling an ice tray out of the freezer and cracking the cubes loose with a twisting motion of the plastic and then the expectant clink of the glass followed by the muffled sound of the air bubbles moving up through the body of the bottle and finally the bad plumbing rumble and a rush of water that would add the final splash to the evening's numbing process. Renee came into the room holding her drink like a cheap trophy and walked around the front of the chair where Sarah sat. The dog rose from where it was sleeping and regarded Renee and lay back down.

"Who is that?" she said, pointing in the direction of the dog.

"An orphaned dog," Sarah said. Renee eyed her daughter and decided to let the dog discussion go for the moment.

"Not like you to get into the hard stuff," Renee said, sipping the dark brown drink and making a face. Sarah did not respond, but looked up at her mother, who had always been pretty, and wore an expression of fatigue now.

"And in a coffee mug no less," her mother said. "Something wrong?"

Sarah sipped and looked out the window. "There were four people murdered at the rest stop on top of the mountain this morning. I was coming off my shift. I was the one who found them."

Renee was not certain that she had heard her daughter correctly. She stood looking down at her in the chair, the glass half-raised to her lips.

"What did you say?"

"I found them," Sarah said. "I was coming off shift and there they…"

"Baby," Renee said, dropping her glass by her side. "Baby, are you okay? Were your hurt? Are you hurt?" She knelt next to the recliner and set her glass on the carpet. She reached out and took Sarah's face in her hand and turned it toward her. Her child's eyes seemed to focus and retreat and Renee strengthened her grip, waiting for Sarah to continue, to explain.

"I'm okay, Mamma," Sarah said. "I'm just really shaken up. It was fucking awful."

"Tell me what happened," Renee said.

"Not now," Sarah said.

"What do you mean, 'not now'? Where is your uncle? Was he with you?" Her expression had turned from concern to anger. Turned quickly.

"Was he there with you, Sarah?"

"No," Sarah said with as much finality as she could muster. "He was with Aunt Katherine. He came as soon as he heard…"

"Goddammit," Renee hissed. "That sounds about like him."

"Oh stop, Mamma. Just stop. You're always going on about something you know nothing about. He came when he could. It's not like he knew what happened. Just, please. Stop." Renee looked at her daughter, weighing the gravity of the event and her instinct to do the exact opposite of stopping. Sarah, sensing the gathering storm, evened her tone.

"He's supposed to be here later," she said. "He didn't do anything wrong, Mamma. Just away. Nobody did anything wrong. I was just coming off my shift and they were just—" She paused. "They were just there. Dead. It was like a dream, but too real to be a dream. Too real to be anything other than real. Mamma," she turned away from the window. "It was awful. Like nothing else. Blood everywhere and their throats. Oh god, their throats and their faces." She sipped greedily at the whiskey in the coffee mug.

Renee stood and picked her own glass off the floor and studied her daughter. The cat still lay in Sarah's lap, no longer elongated, but now curled and content in the folds of the robe, its breathing rhythmic and controlled. Renee glared out the window, the familiar effect of the whiskey coursing through her bloodstream, turning on lights and alarms as it went, propelling a current to her brain where it would fan out into tangles of sparking, fraying wires that plugged into old outlets of self-doubt. Renee narrowed her eyes as she looked out the window, buzzing and snapping behind the sockets as she tried to process and formulate an appropriate response. Sarah stroked the cat's back and looked with her mother into the darkness.

"What happened?" Renee asked again. It came out flat and hard. Sarah sat still. The tone of her voice was cautionary and robotic, a mere inch from that dangerous ledge. She looked into her mug. Renee turned away from the recliner and observed the orphaned dog. It slept peacefully under the table, and for a fleeting second, she felt the irrational urge to kick it, to blame the animal as if it were complicit. Its innocence woke something malevolent in her that she had spent a lifetime trying to keep locked away, but somehow it always managed to push a hand between the frame and door and it would shove and bang and scream to be let out. She took in a breath and turned away from the dog under the table and was going to ask her daughter again what happened, but Sarah cut her off.

"Don't make me tell it twice, Mamma," she said. "Soon enough."

Renee finally backed down, unnerved and the tension just below the surface.

They sat in silence and then, as if directed from backstage, distant lights appeared on the road and both women looked intently out the window. Like floating orbs they gained ground toward the house and then redirected as the vehicle moved into a curve and then they were growing in strength as they came up the straightaway that ran in front of the house and then they saw the vehicle slow, overcompensate for the turn into the driveway, and then it was out of their sight.

"Goddamn him," Renee said and left Sarah, walking swiftly back to the kitchen. She listened to her mother slam the glass on the countertop and then she almost felt her yank open the door and could visualize her standing there in her work clothes, haggard and peering out beyond the cheap carport in the slanted light. Then she heard a car door close and her mother demanding, in that climbing whiskey-tinged voice, an explanation.

CHAPTER 36

JED

Jed Hicks got out of the car on wobbly legs. He'd been gone since just after lunch, driving forty-five minutes east to apply for a job at a scrap yard that was rumored to be hiring, but when he walked in the shabby 1960s-era lobby of the main office and saw five other men filling out paperwork on clipboards, he had walked back out again, climbing into his car and steering the clattering Toyota back west, stopping at a ratty beer joint that was on the edge of an enormous man-made lake the Corp of Engineers had built around the same time the scrap yard had opened. He'd sat with a couple other unemployed men, consuming beer after beer and discussing the inequities and frustrations of the job market and the seismic wave of immigrant labor. Now, standing in the dim light of the carport with his mother blocking the kitchen entrance to the house, all of his bravado and bar-top-pounding defiance dripped out of him like a leaking faucet, and he realized how drunk and tired he actually was. He steadied himself with the driver's side mirror, swaying and trying to piece together a story that would at least get him past his raving mother and into the sanctuary of his small room in the back of the house.

"Where the hell were you?" she screamed across the carport.

Jed made his way around the front of the Toyota and put his hands in his pocket and stood looking at her.

"Jed?"

"Yes, Mamma."

"Oh. It's you," she said, the disappointment undisguised. "Where you been?"

"I went to apply for a job," he said.

"A job," Renee said. "It's 7:30 at night, Jed. Where does someone apply for a job at 7:30 at night?" Jed shuffled his feet, looked at the ground searching for a response that might provide even the slightest shred of credibility. His drunkenness swarmed up to meet him, and despite his efforts, he stumbled.

"I see," Renee said, and closed the door.

His head was a bowl of lukewarm soup. He pulled off his cap and ran his hand through his hair, which was long and unwashed. His patchy beard itched and his tongue was swollen. He walked into the front yard at an angle and pulled a pack of cigarettes from his shirt pocket and lit one, looking up in the sky at the fat white moon. The smoke in his mouth tasted chemical and he wished he'd stopped for more beer on the ride home, but knew he was already pushing his luck driving in his current state. He considered the men he had seen in the office applying for the job and wondered if any of them had been able to secure it. Then he thought of the two men who had seemed so enlightened in the beer joint, their thin arms and skinny chests hovering over the cracked and weathered bar top, lost in their sudsy fog of denial and succumbing to the indecency of unemployment, their inability to elevate themselves above the rotting red plastic barstool cover as palpable as the smell of the men's urinal. The indifference and enabling movements of the bartender who was a right-place, right-time step ahead of his customers and could just as easily have been on their side of the bar, shadowing their consternation and drowning self-worth. Jed was neck-deep in self-pity when the realization occurred to him that his *condition* and his limited prospects should come as no surprise given his circumstances. Dirt poor family. Piss education. A father who hit women, a character flaw only outdone by his willingness to abandon them to live hand-to-mouth in a community populated by people in not much better or worse situations. Job or no job, the outcome for all of them was likely the same. They could struggle and persevere until their hands bled and they would never have much more than they had right now. He jetted smoke through his nose and rubbed the back of his neck. How many times had he seen evidence of it? Women scrambling frantically through their purses at the grocery, praying to locate a coupon or some loose change, the cashier bored, having seen it with one out of three customers in the last hour. The guy behind the woman and her kids with a case of cheap beer, just off work, filthy and on his way home to drink himself to sleep just so he could get up and do it again the next morning. And worst of all, the disheveled little kids who always seemed to be hanging around, like wet clothes on a makeshift wash line, watching their parents' behavior and outbursts. Or you would see them making the best out of some secondhand toy in the yard or a bicycle they might have received as a gift two or three Christmases prior, their imaginations already beginning to weaken and go brown like the patches of grass in the dirt yard where they were expected to entertain themselves. Then there was the male rage that always ran beneath the cultural surface, like a swollen creek, the currents corrosive in their reckless path, and eventually cresting the banks, resulting in bruised eyes, broken arms, and sometimes going into the house to find a gun. And the women. *Jesus Christ, the women.* They were victims like it or not. Tethered by food stamps and promises as empty as their pantry. And those who fought back used pills and booze to cobble together the courage to stand up and swing a malnourished wrist at the swaying figure in front of them. How they looked so old, their faces and bodies so routinely neglected. It was as if they had all walked onto the same conveyor belt that had been securely fastened to the crumbling front steps of the high school, each of them lined up to receive a crippling weight that was the equivalent of carrying a picnic table on their back for the next twenty-five years.

How many times had his father knocked his mother on the ground with the back of his hand, or caught her off guard with a belt after she'd shown him resistance or stood up for her kids? Jed had been young when his father left, but not so young that he could not feel the eerie calm before the first blow, be it physical or a spewing of profanity that left a different and more lasting kind of mark. The anticipation of the violence seemed even worse than the act. It was enough to wreck your morning and on into the late afternoon when the time seemed to stall out altogether and he and his sister and his mother, left waiting in the house, quietly offering their individual prayers that he would not come home that night, or any night thereafter. And while John Hicks had never touched him beyond the rough grabbing of his arm, Jed knew that it was simply a matter of time before his father required a more formidable opponent.

Lights appeared on the road. Jed dropped the cigarette into the grass and stepped on it and walked back toward the carport. His nerves jolted when the cruiser pulled in, its headlights on high beam. He shielded his eyes and waited, wondering how much of the afternoon he had actually lost track of.

Edwards killed the engine and got out of the car, closing the door behind him. He walked toward the carport. Jed stood looking at him and Edwards could tell by the way he kept shifting his weight that he had been drinking for a while. As he approached, Jed pulled his Braves ballcap down tighter on his head to hide his eyes.

"You coming or going, Jed?" Edwards said.

"I'm coming," Jed said.

"Glad to hear that," Edwards said, now standing in front of his nephew. "You drive home like this?"

"I guess so. Yes, sir."

"I need to tell you what your mother would do to you if you got picked up for DUI, never mind the judge over in Marion or Franklin County?" Edwards considered lecturing his nephew about the slope of getting picked up drunk behind the wheel. How he had seen men not much older than Jed go from one offense to four in a matter of weeks, their thought process going from *I can make it home* to *who cares if I do,* and once they reached the point of ceasing to care the rest of the collapse came on like a landslide. Edwards wanted to believe that an early intervention would make a difference, but his experience said otherwise. For now he told himself that he would have to be content that Jed had made it safely back one more time and that lectures and predictions would have to wait.

"No, sir," Jed said.

"Your mother and sister home?"

"Mamma's here," Jed began and as he did so, the kitchen door flew open and Renee came through it as if the house were on fire.

"Goddamn you, Bill Edwards," she yelled, coming across the carport quickly. "What in God's name are you thinking sending Sarah into that rest stop with a murderer in it?"

Edwards looked at Jed who was obviously confused.

"Renee, calm down," he said.

"Don't you tell me to calm down," she said. "I'll calm down as soon as you tell me why you weren't available while a blood bath was taking place up there." She flung her arm in the direction of the mountain. "Sarah could have been killed up there. My little girl…"

"Stop, Renee," Edwards said firmly. "I was over in Taylor Branch. I came back as soon as I knew what was going on. Things are under control now. I need to speak with Sarah. If you can keep from screaming at me while we talk, you are welcome to sit with us, but I don't have time to stand out in the driveway and argue with you."

"What are y'all talking about?" Jed asked, trying to get the words out without slurring them. Edwards and Renee looked at him and he shrank back.

"Can we go inside, Renee?" Edwards said. She looked again at her son with a mixture of pity and anger, then turned and walked back in the house. Edwards started to follow and then stopped, turning to Jed.

"I'd recommend that you make yourself scarce for a bit. Don't even think about getting in that car and going anywhere." Jed nodded and Edwards followed Renee inside. She was standing in the kitchen, making another drink when he entered.

"She's putting some clothes on," she said. "I came home from work and she was sitting in the dark with the cat in her lap. She made me wait till you got here to tell me what happened, so I did. Now here you are, so tell me what happened." Edwards looked at Renee and the drink she was holding in her hand.

"We'll wait for Sarah," he said. "How many of those have you had?" he asked, pointing at the bottle of whiskey on the counter.

"That's none of your goddamn business," she said.

"I may be her uncle, Renee, but this is police business we need to discuss. I'm as sorry as anyone that she had to go through that this morning, but we have a serious problem to deal with and I can't do this with you ranting and raving at me the whole time." Edwards had prepared himself for what he knew was going to be a rough fifteen minutes with Renee. She had always harbored a grudge against him, ever since she found herself raising two kids by herself, her absent husband a brutal contrast to her sister's happy marriage to a man who had done everything by the book and with full transparency.

"Uncle Bill." Sarah stood in the doorway to the kitchen. She wore a pair of jeans, a plain white t-shirt and white socks. Edwards looked at his niece and she came across the room toward him and he let her hug him. He held her firmly against his chest while looking at Renee over the top of Sarah's head, which smelled of shampoo.

CHAPTER 37

SARAH RECOUNTS

Renee went back to make another drink. She was now on her fourth and was no longer bothering with the splash of water. Edwards sat on a wooden chair that he had taken from the table in the kitchen and placed across from Sarah who was back in the recliner. He had taken off the gun belt and was sitting forward, elbows on his knees, looking at his niece and deputy. They could both hear the sound of music from behind the closed door to Jed's room, muffled. Sarah had gone through the whole morning at the rest area with him and she was visibly exhausted. Her mother had punctuated the recounting with gasps and exclamations of profanity, the Jack Daniels burnishing the edges of her speech like sanded wood.

"Sarah," Edwards said.

"Yes."

"Thank you. Not just for what you did today but going back through that again. I know that was hard." Sarah nodded and wiped at her eyes with her palms.

"You know, I only offered you this job as a way to help you get on your feet and maybe find a way out," he said. "God knows I never expected you to see or be a part of something like this." Renee came back in the room and offered a sharp laugh that made both of them look up.

"I know that," Sarah said. Edwards sat back in the chair. It creaked with his weight.

"I would not hold anything against you if you wanted to file this report and then move on to something else."

Sarah's head snapped up. "And what, Uncle Bill?" she said loudly, and without thinking she looked over at Renee, swaying in the faint light of the kitchen. Her mother registered the look and retreated. They heard her fumbling with the outside door handle. Sarah hissed and pointed after her. "Become that? Working a register, and getting shit-faced every night just to keep things from coming off the rails?"

Edwards followed to where Sarah had pointed.

"I suppose not," he said

"Goddamn right," she said. Edwards saw flashes of Renee's temper in his niece's face and thought back to the time when he had offered Sarah the job, recalling his honest intentions to help a girl who he knew possessed talent and potential. Law enforcement was a means of getting clear of a family history that threatened to hang around her neck for the rest of her life like a giant bell, alerting any prospect in her path to turn around and run the other way.

They sat together in the little room, having said all that was necessary. Edwards rose to retrieve his things, but first walked to where Sarah was sitting and leaned down and kissed her on the top of her head.

"Take tomorrow morning off," he told her. "Then come into the station and I'll fill you in on what our role is going to be in all of this this. I'm sure they are going to take over the investigation at the state level, but they'll need us in some capacity. I'm just not sure what that is just yet." Sarah nodded again. They heard Renee come back into the kitchen, drop something, and curse.

"Get some sleep," Edwards said.

"Hey, Uncle Bill," she said, getting up suddenly. "How's Aunt Kat doing?" Renee walked into the doorway to the living room and watched them.

"She's doing okay, Sarah. Nice of you to ask," he said, looking at Renee. "She's losing her memory. More and more each day, but we're getting along. You ought to come see her sometime. She would like that."

Renee huffed and waved her hand drunkenly at Edwards. He looked at her as he put on his gun belt, glanced once more at Sarah and walked out of the room, having to turn sideways to get past Renee. He was reaching for the door when she spoke.

"Nice that some of us can forget," she said, not looking at him. Edwards closed his eyes tightly and gripped the knob until his knuckles whitened. He pulled the door open and walked through it without bothering to close it behind him.

CHAPTER 38

AARON

Electric lights were not commonplace for him. There had been warnings against them and the current that they brought into your life. He recalled oil lanterns and patches of rooms that were always bathed in shadow, even during the day, because the tree canopy blocked out the light, and he had grown accustomed to darkness for both its power of concealment and the calming effect it had on his crowded and sometimes very loud mind. He stood ten paces from the glass door that opened onto the back patio. He listened carefully for the sound of a dog, or anything else that might be moving about in the dark. He breathed in a steady pattern. In through his nose and out through his mouth. He believed that he had the ability to slow his own heart and he believed that controlled breathing sharpened his eyes and ears. He looked through the glass patio door and saw the woman sitting in a chair watching the television. She was very still and he could tell that what she was watching was not of interest because the expression on her face never changed. It was blank and sad and he knew that feeling because he knew what being alone was like and that being alone felt like standing amid a forest where everything looked the same and then suddenly looked very different and confusing, and the pattern of the trees could play tricks on your eyes and the leaves rustling were like another type of language. Like the language from the books he had been given and memorized. He waited patiently, adjusting the pack on his shoulder, knowing that to rush would be a mistake. To rush would ruin everything that he had hoped to accomplish. And accomplishment was a process. You first did this, and when that was finished, you did what came next. Finish each task before you move to the next one. The woman sat very still, and then she stood up in a very gentle, fragile way, and she walked over and turned off the TV. Then she walked around the room and turned out the lights, except for a light from somewhere on the side of the house that he could not see, and that light would be fine, he thought. She walked back through the den and disappeared behind a wall and after a few moments, he saw that light go out and then he saw her shadow behind a curtain walk into the bedroom and take off her clothes and get into the bed and turn off the bedside lamp. And then the house was dark and he walked to the patio door and waited, his dim reflection looking back at him with an inner stillness. Then he removed his boots and set them on the concrete, followed by the pack that he set gently onto the ground. He unzipped it and removed a long knife with an antler handle that was a dull color and sturdy. Then he opened the door very slowly and just enough to let his body slip inside. The house was neat. Everything was in its correct space, and there were pictures in frames, and dishes in the drying rack next to the sink. The floor was soft and he made no sound. He stepped further into the room and he could smell the people who lived there. He waited again, and then he stepped around a dining room table and turned down the hallway. There was a window at the end of it and a door on the left. The light from the outside window was faint but he kept close to the interior wall so he would not create a shadow of himself. He paused outside the door and he could hear the breathing of readying for sleep. An older person sleeping, he thought. He stepped into the room and he could see the frame of her body beneath the covers. To his left there was a chair with what looked like pants thrown over the back. There were windows above the bed and the same weak light came through, but his eyes had adjusted to the dark. He walked over to the chair and sat down, facing the woman in the bed. He stared hard at her and as if willed, she sat up.

"Who is there?"

He held the knife across his lap, his posture very straight. A smile came across his lips. He thought of the dog earlier that day. Seeing him where the others could not. Knowing that he was out there and now she was like the dog but she was not behind a fence, and she would not come to bite him. She would be still and that was what he wanted. He wanted to be in the stillness for a long moment. He could hear now that she had started to whimper, softly, and he knew that she wanted to turn on the light, that she wanted to scream but knew that it would not be of use. Knew that she was alone in a way that he had been most of his life, taken into the darkness of that place and made to wonder what would happen next, his mind scrambling like crawling up the side of a very steep slope, strewn with loose rocks and crumbling dirt, feet struggling for purchase. His body hummed with an cold alacrity that sparked and buzzed, feeding and building off the panic that was rising off the woman with a recognizable scent. A cold familiarity was washing over his nerves, steadying his vision, his hands, the synapses in his brain. He understood the not knowing's power and importance. The significance and finality of waiting. The woman was now crying. She spoke and he knew that her face would be wet, and then the words gurgled into the room like something dislodged from a drain.

"Who is there? Please. Is it you? Please, who is there?"

His movements were precise and he felt no need to rush himself. He felt as if his hands were being guided, and where he normally would have resisted being controlled in this way, he was very much at ease.

"Please," she said again, and now the scent he was inhaling began to turn rancid, creeping like the smell of something only recently dead and beginning to decay and his face twitched against it, and the patience turned quickly into something harder and more determined. He stood with a confidence that seemed to take its strength both from the pleading sound of the woman's voice and the comfort of the room's darkness.

"Please," she said. "I never meant..."

"No," he whispered as he crossed over to the bed, the word catching strangely in his throat and the guided hand readying.

PART 4

THE VOICE
IN THE WOODS

CHAPTER 39

TERRELL

I never fully understood what Aaron had meant about the voices he heard in the dark woods and how they had disturbed or moved something inside of him that would cause him to attack Sophia the way that he had. The night after, when I had returned home and we were in the cramped room of the cabin, I realized that something was chasing him and had been for a long time and that his rage against the only mother he had ever known was born of something that would not be appeased by the solitude in which we lived. That *something* was its own kind of solitude, only overrun by whispers that constantly gurgled as a natural spring. It flourished of its own accord and was all he knew of consistency. I saw in the way that he looked at me as I selected a book from which to read aloud that the true fear was not of the voices and their taunts, but that they would one day cease to acknowledge him. He was still a boy, in his mind, and I know that is what saved her life. If he was the man that he would grow into, he would have choked the life out of her with no more thought then he carried a load of new pipe up to one of the still sites or chopped a cord of wood. He was unnaturally strong, and driving back from returning Sophia to town, to her freedom, I realized that at some point he could turn on me. There was more of John inside of him than I realized, and despite all of my efforts to distract him with other things, he was drawn to something more complicated and troublesome in our bloodline and the voices that plagued him were strengthened by the prospect of the son one day becoming the father.

His mother, a woman named Katherine that I never knew, may have found a small cave to inhabit inside of Aaron's head, but she never emerged, and in those periods when he went quiet for days at a time, I don't believe that it was her that he was communing with.

I have had many years to think back on the nature of motivations and the actions that result. Ever since the mill fire, I have been harsh with my self-judgement. I felt that I owed a debt on behalf of the suffering my father brought into the world. It was not a debt that I embraced willingly, but one that I could not ignore, nor abandon as my mother had. And I could not siphon from it the way that John had, letting the anger move through his veins, thick and oily like the run-off from an animal pen. Still, I removed myself from society because I realized that once a man has committed murder, he is that thing above all else and will never be recognized for traits or talents beyond that single act of killing, even if that man takes strides for the rest of his life to elevate his status to put the past behind him and cover it over with decent pursuits. The stills did not square with decency, but they were simply a means of remaining isolated and in control of my own life. The man who owned them had all but left me alone in the cabin. We spoke by phone now and again, and I dropped off the bottles with regularity even though it seemed what we were making was no longer as necessary as it had once been. That was not my concern as long as the money arrived, and even that had become less and less important. The land around the cabin had plenty of game to hunt, and there were the streams and the lake for water and the fish that moved beneath the mostly still surface. It was a simple life until Aaron.

Several weeks after Sophia was gone, I found the boy named Earnest in his camp one late afternoon while checking on the upper still. I had walked up alone to find out why the boxes had not been brought down to the cabin for the trip into town. Earnest was simple, but dependable, and no matter how many times I tried to convince him to build something more substantial than the shelter he was living beneath in the woods, he never made any effort to change his circumstances and for reasons I did not fully understand but certainly felt ashamed of later, I allowed him to exist as he wished. Amid that ramshackle camp is where I found him. I had come through the trees calling to him, angry at being made to walk all the way back into the trees. He was sitting with his back against one of the large oaks, his legs stuck out in front of him and his hand to his face. I came alongside him, but he did not turn to speak to me. The fire outside the cover of the tent structure was out, tendrils of smoke came up lightly from the piled ashes and embers. The air was turning colder and he was not wearing a jacket. His arms were thin as saplings and I could not see what he was concealing behind his palm. I spoke his name, thinking he may have been into the liquor, which he had done on more than one occasion, but he did not answer nor did he groan or shift. The few possessions that he had were stacked neatly, and the wooden crates that we used to haul the liquor were also stacked on the perimeter of the camp as if he had been readying to pack the bottles and bring them down the hill to the cabin. I stood in front of him and looked closer and saw that his dark shirt had been saturated and then dried through with cold. It was stiff against his body and as I came closer I saw the blood caked on his hands and wrist and when I pulled his hand free from his face his right eye was missing and whatever had taken it had been extremely rough and indifferent to the rest of the face. I let the hand drop and stepped away from the body and realized that it had been two mornings prior since I had last seen him. I went to the still and found a shovel and came back through the trees to the camp and began to dig a hole that would hold the boy and everything that belonged to him. I dug for many hours, late into the night, and I tried not to listen to the sounds that were beyond the fire I had lit so that I could see my work, but something was there and it watched me with patience and what I thought might be expectation. For what, I don't know.

When I was finished I went back down the hill to the cabin and went inside. Aaron was sitting in the room, looking at a book of poems I had shared with him. When I entered he did not look up and did not acknowledge me. This was not strange, but I knew he had been up to the Ernest's camp just as I knew he would have killed Sophia if he'd had the strength then. His posture was humped sitting at the small table, his shoulders large and powerful from chopping wood and carrying heavy crates back and forth, up and down the slope. But there was an unnatural strength emerging in his frame as well and I stood observing him, and when the urge to confront him over the killing seemed as if it might spill out, I went back through the door and walked the half-mile to the lake where I felt safe because I could see clearly what surrounded me. I waited there until I thought he may have gone to sleep and then I went back up the path to the cabin and approached the porch and was going to the door when he spoke.

"Are we sinful, Terrell?" he said, his voice very subdued. He had been waiting for me to return and I was afraid. Not afraid of his person, but of his mind, which did not seem to belong to him alone and was constantly being tested and tempted to overpower his reason and lash out like an animal that had been pinned to one place by a trap with rusted teeth and an unforgiving grip.

"Yes," I said. "We are tainted by it."

"And should we accept that and treat it as we do the water and the animals and the things that we eat?"

"We cannot exist without it. It is part of who we are and part of the world and we must live within it. Did you kill the boy at the still?"

"Yes," he said.

"Why?" He did not answer.

"Are you ashamed of it?" Again, he did not answer.

Then he blurted out. "Yes. But I was not free to choose it. It spoke and I went. It…"

"It?" I said. "There is no *It* to blame. There is only the sin and the shame, but no *It* that forces us. There is you and there is me. There is no third. And there was Sophia, but now she is gone because you made it that way." He was sitting on the boards of the porch and I thought he might be crying into his hands. There was no movement from where he sat and he had started the conversation in a bold tone, but he had reverted back to something childish as he often did.

"Are you mistaking the words and the books that I have shared with you with your thoughts. Are they confusing you?" He did not answer but I could feel that he was listening; wanted me to help him see beyond it.

"Did you think that killing the boy was a test?"

"Yes. A test. But also a bidding."

"I don't understand that," I said. "I don't read these things to you, I do not explain these things to you as a bidding. They are to help you be natural with yourself and this place where we live. Do you want to have to leave this place?" He wailed at this and I stepped closer to him on the porch and then I hurried and crouched beside him. "You came to me and I have raised you and I will take care of you, but you cannot interpret those things that have been shared with you with the voice that you say is inside of you. That voice does not live, does not breathe air. It has no say..."

"Not inside, Terrell. There," and he pointed beyond the dark yard of the cabin.

"Yes," I said. "There. But we must listen to the things that are here, between us and not outside of us. Those are voices that will deceive you. You must look to me to understand. Can you feel my hand on you now?" He nodded. "Good," I said. "It is there to steady you. Feel its weight." He reached up and touched my hand and his skin was cold and rough, calluses worn into place from labor. "There," I said. "I am here now. I am with you." He struggled to breathe and turned his head and pressed his face into my chest and for that moment it was like he had been as a small boy, full of raw intensity and confusion that often resulted in angry outbursts, but sometimes manifested in a collapse as if he had been holding a door shut with something large and determined pushing from the other side and finally it had shoved its way through. A force that was relentless and consuming. A force that wanted little more than to conjure and tempt.

The next morning I took him to where I had buried the boy and I made him help me collect his things and burn them. We stood in the clearing next to the old still and watched the black smoke make its way toward the sky and he observed this without expression or remorse nor regret, or else he would have expressed it through a question.

The man that I met the day I had arrived, the thin one working the lower still, had left soon after I took over. We had words and he cussed at me and wandered off into the woods, but every now and then he would come back. The fire was burning down and I looked across the open area and saw him watching us.

"Deakins," I said. "What do you want?" He came into the clearing. His frame was thin and his arms hung limply from his sides, a rolled cigarette in one hand. He was wearing a stained pair of overalls and no shirt and a worn felt hat that was greasy and out of shape, the band torn. It had turned cold but he did not seem to notice.

"You want a coat?" I said.

"Don't want nothing," he said. "What are you and the boy burning?"

"That doesn't concern you," I said and looked at Aaron but he was not paying attention.

"Something," Deakins said. "Burning something."

"The boy left," I said. "He left his things. No reason to leave them there in the woods."

"Yeah," Deakins said and dragged from the cigarette. "He's gone okay. Not far though, I suspect." He smiled at me, his front teeth black and rotting. "Might be your boy there knows where he got to. You reckon?" I looked at Aaron. He was standing still and watching the last of the fire dwindle out.

"Look here, Deakins," I said. "There's no cause for you to be coming around. You left and you got paid for your time. It's been years now. Go away and leave things alone. Leave us alone."

"Might be I leave," he said. "Might be I take what I seen with me. Might be it makes a good story to tell when I get back into town."

"And what would that be?" I said. "What have you seen?" He smiled again and crushed the cigarette between his fingers. "What is it you said? 'That don't concern you?' You come up here all that time ago, took my job. Made it so I had to go back to working in that pit in the stove factory. Could be that I found a way to send you along. Could be I've waited long enough."

"Are you talking about the sheriff?"

"Sheriff? Who said sheriff?"

"Sheriff," Aaron repeated.

"He ain't right in the head," Deakins said, turning his attention to Aaron. "Sheriff or no, I don't reckon I would close my eyes around him there." He pointed with a crooked finger at Aaron and shuffled his feet. "What I seen was enough to know that I would not do that."

"What you saw was nothing," I said. "And if you were to talk to someone about whatever it is that you think you saw, there's nobody going to believe you."

"Could be you're right," he said. "Could be that they might want to know more about that still and the one down yonder from us. Could be they might want to do some digging while they are up here."

"You go," I said. "Digging for what?" He smiled a final time and turned to leave, then he stopped at the edge of the clearing.

"I never cared much for little nigger boys up here. Never thought that was right. Don't care how they associate with outsiders like you and him. But that don't make things okay in the eyes of God. Not what I saw and not what he done." He pointed at Aaron again.

"Go," I said. "Don't come back here." He turned and went into the woods and I thought about the grave and how easy it would be to uncover it. I turned to Aaron. "Stamp out this fire, and let's go back to the cabin. We have things to do." He moved toward the burning pile and walked through it, kicking and stomping the dying coals. I looked in the direction that Deakins had gone. He was a pathetic, lazy man and had come around only when he was looking for a handout. He'd made threats about the stills before but I never thought much about that since he had been part of it all and would likely be too stupid to keep his own part out of the tale. But I knew what he had seen because I had seen it too, and even Deakins, with his sour mouth and weak constitution, could not incriminate himself in something he had only observed, likely hunkered down at a distance, holding his breath and trying to remain quiet for fear he would be next.

I turned and looked at Aaron stepping on the remnants of the fire. His pants were filthy and too short and they made the proportions between his legs and torso look off, like pictures I had seen of men who had grown into distorted giants, uncoordinated and sad in their countenance. I had a thought to let things pass as they might. Sheriff or no. Deakins was right in that something plagued Aaron's head. He would not suffer the memory of this in the way that the death of my father came to hover over me in the darkness of night, the smell of the wood smoke and burnt flesh in my nostrils. This deed would be banished to make way for other thoughts that would likely end in senseless brutality, blamed on a voice that he alone could hear, whispering to him from the quiet woods. Its foul attempts had flickered around me, but I had pushed it away and it had found no need to pursue me beyond the unsettling fear it left in its wake. I had told him there was no such thing and no such voice but that had been a lie. There are things in isolation that can't be explained away or simply dismissed. That ignorance was the reason people lived in towns and cities even though there was no real safety in a row of factory houses or the thick heat and sweat of a tavern. Souls would burn in ice if their keeper was only willing to listen close enough.

Several days later, I was hunting alone. I had been tracking a turkey through thick undergrowth when I heard the engine of the deputy's car. I stopped, holding the gun up, and peered through the dense brush and caught sight of the black and white vehicle climbing the rutted road that wound down to the lake. I wondered if Deakins was with them and decided that he was probably not. He had probably gotten drunk and wandered into the sheriff's office and run off at the mouth about the stills and that he had seen the Negro boy killed. They knew Deakins in town just as I did and I thought it was strange that they had even bothered to come out this far. I knew that they drank the same liquor that we made and had decided that the pleasure they got from the bottle was more important than the law that prohibited it. I followed the car from a distance, keeping low. They had the windows down. I could hear one of them cussing as the tire dropped in and out of the ruts. The lake was a long walk from the still, but if they had come that far they would get out and walk around and even if they did not climb the ridge, they would stumble on the cabin where Aaron was. I went a little further until I would be forced to come into view in the tree line that went around the water. They had stopped the car and were both outside, smoking and talking to each other. It was then that I could have turned and gone, leaving Aaron to fend for himself. But he would have not gone with them and it would end in his being shot. I knew that, and I knew that to abandon him would be a betrayal to John and to myself. Their backs were to me when I came into the clearing. It had grown cold and I could see their breath and the smoke from their cigarettes drifting over their shoulders and moving out into the thinning air. The sky had darkened and I knew that it would bring rain, maybe even sleet. I racked the shotgun and both of them turned at once. I did not recognize their faces and I was grateful for that. One of them started to put his hand on his gun and I pointed mine at him and shook my head.

"Howdy," the one who was looking at me but ignoring his sidearm said. I did not respond to him.

"Any reason you're pointing that at two deputies?"

"Must be you know," I said. "You come up all this way to find me."

"How do you know we're up here for you?"

"Who else?" I said. The man looked at the other deputy, who had put his hand behind his back. Both of them were still facing away from me.

"Turn around," I said. "Away from the lake."

"Hold on," the man who had started for his gun said. "We just came up here to talk."

"Talk to who?" I said. He smiled at me like we were sharing a joke.

"Well," he said, trying to relax his stance. "We're just. We're…"

"We're looking into the disappearance of a Negro boy," the other man said. "We got word that a boy was up here and might have gone missing."

"Ain't no one up here like that," I said.

"Well then maybe you can lower that gun and we can talk about what we were told. Might be that you could point us in the right direction. You Terrell Hicks?" I had not heard my last name spoken aloud in many years and it sounded funny coming out of a stranger's mouth in that familiar place. I nodded.

"Well, Mr. Hicks. We got word that there might be a boy up here working for you that could have come to some harm. Man we talked to…"

"Deakins," I interrupted. The deputy laughed.

"Yeah, that's right," he said. "You know him."

"Everybody knows Deakins," I said. "Knows him well enough not to come up in the woods looking for something he claimed to have seen."

"Fair enough," the deputy said. "Still, he mentioned that you might have another man up here with you. Maybe your son?" I did not respond. "Well," he made a long pause before speaking again. "He's who we'd like to talk to if you don't mind." The rain started as I suspected it would and I could see the other deputy who had been mostly quiet shiver against it. The clouds were low and had capped over the lake. There was daylight, but it was waning and muted. The men looked small against the landscape and I was above them on a slight slope that ran down to the water.

"Ain't no boy missing up here and it's just me in the cabin. Your mistake was listening to Deakins. The breath coming out of his mouth should have told you that what followed was gonna be a load of shit."

"I can't argue with you on that. I've known Deakins since he was a young man and he certainly has not improved with age. But he was specific about what he said he saw and I think we need to check it out. That's our job." He talked easily for a man with a gun pointed at him and I knew that under different circumstances I would have liked him, maybe even sought him out as a friend.

"You think that you could point that gun at the ground, Mr. Hicks? This is starting to feel very uncomfortable." When he said this, I almost lowered the gun. He was someone's father. Not the younger man standing next to him. There was a boy at home somewhere, younger and probably high strung. The easy way that he talked, the gentle rhythm and tone of the words as they carried and how he was demanding something of me by asking a question. He was patient and he was practicing that patience now, only the stakes were much higher.

"You have any rope in the trunk of that car there?" I said. Their faces eclipsed and the effort they were making went out of them, their eyes widening and their lips pressed tightly together.

"Mr. Hicks, there's no reason…"

"I did not ask about that," I said and motioned with the shotgun. "Open that trunk and pull out some rope if there is any."

"There's not," the quiet deputy said. I tilted my head at him.

"Okay," the other deputy said and I could see now that he was in charge because he was older and held his face in a patient way that indicated that he knew what was at stake and he would be best served not to show it. He carried himself with more patience and he looked more disappointed with himself than afraid of me. "Okay," he said again and touched the younger man on the shoulder as he went past him. He took keys out of his pocket and opened the trunk and then stood back from it. I moved closer and looked inside and saw the spare tire and the tools and a canvas bag. "Look in that bag," I said. He leaned into the trunk and I realized that I might have made a mistake and that there could have been a gun in there, but he dumped the contents out on the ground and there was a length of rope among some other things. A flashlight. A pair of pliers. Some discolored rags. I stepped back from them.

"Pick up that rope and go around the front of the car toward the lake," I said. The younger deputy was shaking now and I watched him and tried to think about my father and the time that he had beaten my mother half to death. The older deputy picked up the rope.

"Go," I said. They turned and walked away from me and I was glad that the lake was there so that they would not get the idea to run. They stopped in front of the car and stood looking out at the water, the rain falling steady.

"You, on the right. Tie his hands behind him," I said. The young man turned around and looked at me and I motioned with the shotgun. The older man swiveled his head and nodded and the deputy took the rope from him. "Get him on his knees," I said. The older man did this, and when his hands were tied I told the other deputy to get on his knees facing the same way. I went behind him and tied off his hands and with the one piece of rope they were bound together. I was grateful that I could not see their faces. My clothes were clinging to me and specks of ice were catching in my beard. I took the keys out of the trunk lock and put them in my coat pocket and then leaned in the car and used the stock of the shotgun to smash the front of the radio. Then I turned to walk back toward the woods without looking at the men tied on the ground. I could hear the young deputy trying not to cry and the other man comforting him just under his breath as I went under the tree limbs and up the path toward the cabin.

CHAPTER 40

AARON

The single room of the cabin has grown very cold. The fire in the stone hearth has reduced to embers, and outside sleet and rain are falling from the sky. It makes loud banging sounds on the roof, and when the wind blows, the tiny flecks of ice peck the thin window glass and pile on the outside sill. The room is lit by three oil lanterns, their flames licking the log walls with black shadowy tongues. There are mismatched animal skin rugs covering the planked floor. There is a simple table with two chairs where we take our meals. There are makeshift shelves on one wall and they are heavy with books. On the opposite wall, there are large nails hammered into the wood where knives and guns hang suspended. There are also traps for animals that show gnarled, jagged teeth. Bleached bones of animal heads are scattered on a small work bench, and there is a box on the left side of the fireplace, a large stone on its lid, and inside there is a rattlesnake. You can kick the box and hear the serpent shake its tail and when you close your eyes, you can envision it coiling in the dark space of the box, poised, scared, and angry.

The snake had been beneath an outcrop of rocks that jutted from the side of the hill, near the lake. It was curled there and I heard it as I came up the path from the water. It was large and partly hidden by shadow and I stood for a long time looking at it under the rocks. The surface of the rocks was damp and I thought that there might be a

278

spring beneath them and wondered why the snake had chosen that place. It rattled at me and its head was very still above its coiled body, and its eyes were small like the black buttons on a shirt. I walked back toward the lake and found a forked branch on the shore and then I came back up the path and approached the snake. It continued to rattle and then began to raise its coiled form and I jabbed the stick under the rock and swatted the snake free and was able to pin its head to the ground with the forked branch. Its body swung wildly behind it and I reached down and grabbed its head from behind. When I touched the snake, it ceased to make noise and it went limp. I carried it back to the cabin and found an old box under Terrell's bed and I opened the box and found some papers in it and I took them out and laid them on the bed and I put the snake in the box and closed the lid and then I carried it out to the porch and found one of the foundation stones half-covered in the leaves and I used the stone to keep the lid closed on the box. When Terrell came back to the cabin, I was sitting at the table reading the letter from the man who said he was my father.

Terrell came into the room and asked if I done the chores he'd asked and I told him about the snake and pointed to the box on the floor. He walked over and kicked the box and the snake made its angry rattle sound. He came over to where I sat at the table and took the letter I was reading and walked over to the bed and sat down on it. Then he told me about the man who was my father and that he had brought me to the woods to be with Terrell. He explained that my mother had not wanted me and that she was from a place called Taylor Branch and that hers was a family that looked down on our kind and would never accept me as their blood. He told me that my mother had married another man and that he believed the man's name was Edwards and he and my mother lived together in a place called Winchester which was west of where we were. He said he knew because my father had told him. When I asked about my father, he told me to leave it alone. When I asked my mother's name, he said Katherine and then he went out of the cabin.

Now I sit on the floor next to the fire and stab at the broken and charred logs hoping to coax out a flame. The wood pile is outside, lengths stacked between two large trees, but I am hesitant to go collect the logs now that it has started raining and sleeting, even though I know he will be angry with me that I have let the fire die out when night is coming and we will need it to keep warm as we sleep. The air in the cabin smells of smoke and damp. It always smells of smoke and damp, except in the warmer months when it smells more of cooking and we can open the door to let the air from the outside mix with the stale air of the inside and the wind comes through the trees and seems to cleanse the space in a natural way that he will accept and that I have come to accept as well. There is the acceptance, and the odors, but there are also the flies that come in, their green, greedy eyes pushing out of their heads, seeing unnaturally, aware of all that moves and all that settles around them. They seem ever-present.

I have come to understand many things under Terrell's guardianship, and I have learned many things by watching his hands and listening to his vast interpretation of the world in which we live and toil under the eyes of something larger and more powerful. His teaching and his musing seem to point to something very significant and purposeful. I have not been given any clear sense of what that will be. Still, I feel something growing inside of me. Not flesh or bone, but an enlightenment that I know will carry me away from here and onto a path that others cannot and will not understand. I have been taught many things. Some quite simple, such as how to catch a fish and how to skin a squirrel and prepare it for eating. Some things I have been taught take many tries, such as memorizing the passages that he reads to me from the books, and reciting them back to him and explaining what they mean and how they are of relevance to my life and to his life, and what their consequence may or may not be for the lives of others. Many times he speaks angrily about the words that he reads and his words are like the thick black flies that pace over the waxy skin of fruit, their bent thin legs tapping and feeling. Always feeling. When Terrell storms in the room I sense that he is afraid, but I do not fear what he fears. He is consumed, as I am consumed, with the many images that the words from the books create. But the images are not like the clustering flies that feast on things that no longer live, but are like patterns of birds leaving limbs at once, departing this place because above the trees there is openness and light, but below there is a darkness, even in the sun and words become trapped here in this clouded space, just as I am trapped here with Terrell and his fear. Sometimes he takes my head in his hands and pulls my face close to his, so close that the wiry bush of his beard touches my nose and chin, and the reek of his spoiled teeth fills my nostrils. And he will kiss my forehead and clap my back as if a piece of meat were lodged in my throat. He is kind in his way. He has taught me many things.

Before the men came, I had left the cabin under a full moon and walked quietly through the woods to the second still. The boy had been sitting beside his tiny fire and he had been singing a song to himself and I watched him from behind the cover of a dead tree whose trunk was larger around than my locked arms, and whose top was jagged from where it had broken. I could see his breath and he behaved like a man, pushing the logs of the fire around and positioning a pot on the coals that smelled of cooking meat. When he was not singing he spoke to himself and although I did not make a sound, he looked from the lighted area of his camp and into the woods where I was and leaned his head as if he heard what I was hearing. I was afraid for him and I whispered for him to leave before I came but he would turn his head away and go back to something else. There had been a woman who I did not know who had looked at me many years before when I was smaller than the boy and we had stared at one another while she held me, but her eyes were not kind and she wanted to be rid of me and gone from where she was. The boy had looked with intent but he was not wishing anything gone, he was simply aware of something that had always been there, beyond the light cast by his fire, untamed and fearful like wild animals are. He sat again by the ringed fire and pulled the pan from the flames and was using a knife to cut and eat the meat when I came into the lighted area. He did not look at me, but he made a strange noise and I told him why I had come and that I would not be present when the thing would happen, but removed and looking away as it occurred and he said that he knew and that he would not run but could not promise to be brave throughout. After that I did not speak again, only went to where he was and he stood before me, offering himself much like the serpent who gives thanks for the vermin I drop inside his box.

"Aaron," he yells from outside. "Aaron come out."

I stand up from the floor and walk to the door. I open it and he is standing in the rain and sleet, holding a shotgun pointed at the ground.

I stand and look at him, feeling the sleet and the rain touch my face, my neck, my hands.

"Come with me," he says. He turns and walks back into the woods and I follow. We walk the path that is heavily trodden, the dirt smooth and slick. We create no sound as we make our way down a small slope and then back up a steeper rise. We turn off the path and walk single file toward the lake. Now we make a great deal of noise as we cross over the leaves on the ground. The sky is slate and the trees without their leaves are menacing as they sway, well-engineered sentries with their spiny limbs and ever-reaching crowns. He is walking in front of me, but as he dips down a slope, I can see the lake over the top of his head, round and flat as a coin on a tabletop. We come through the trees and into a clearing and I see that there is white and black car parked along the edge of the lake. There is no one in the car and its windows are down. As we come closer, he veers to the left of the car and I can see that there are two men on their knees with their hands tied by a single rope. The younger man looks to Terrell and then to me and begins to sob. Both are soaked through with rain and they are shaking from the increasing cold. On the lake, I can see the small ripples made by the precipitation. The young man begins to sob harder when he sees us coming closer. He is not like the small boy. He is not brave and he is not prepared for what is to come. He has not been warned and even if he had been made aware, I do not think he would have listened because his eyes are large with disbelief.

"Terrell," the older man says. He is struggling to speak, but he is being strong for both of them. My uncle looks at the man and stares and he waits for the man to continue. Finally Terrell speaks. "You see another way out of this?" The man shakes his head then takes a deep breath. "No, I don't. Is that him?" He motions his head toward me and Terrell looks over. "Yeah," he said. "That's him."

"And he's your boy?" Terrell nods. "In a sense," Terrell says.

"I don't guess I'd give mine up either," the man says and when he does the other man stops crying and looks at us both. "You don't have…" he starts. "You don't have to kill us. We was just doing our job. We just came up here looking for stills. That don't warrant…" The other man looked out over the water and I could see that he was now preparing.

"Hush," Terrell says, "or I'll tie your mouth off."

"It will be a mess," the man looking at the water says.

"There's always a mess when things come to this."

"Yeah, but for the sake of my partner here, I'm willing to drive out and say we never found anything. You. The missing boy. Him." He motions with his head at me.

"And Deakins?"

"Deakins is a drunk," he says. They talked like I had heard men talk in town. "I can explain him away. This boy's young, Terrell. Hell, he's only been working for the department for six weeks if that. There's laws and then there's something higher. I've been at this a long time, and I know that the laws that govern and the laws that come before those. He's a boy, Terrell. He's just a boy."

"All the more reason," Terrell says quietly. He is calming himself.

"Reason for what?"

"He'll talk. This alone and he'll talk and then I've got more than Deakins to worry about."

"He won't talk. I'll make him understand that he can't, that he's obligated."

"You spoke of experience," Terrell says.

"Yes, I have that. I have seen…"

"As do I," Terrell said. "There are things that are certain. Things that must have a beginning and an end. This is one of those things and we are part of it together and each have our roles to play. Your higher laws decree it."

"Yes, but…"

"Stop," Terrell says and it was the tone he used when I was saying a verse wrong or I had left the axe out in the rain to rust or not dressed a deer properly and left edible meat behind. This was wasteful, the pleading and the talking.

"Come here," he says. I walk toward him looking at the men kneeling and freezing on the ground.

"Take this," he says and hands me the shotgun. I check to see if it is loaded the way that I have been taught. He turns back to the men kneeling on the ground and walks in front of them, squatting and placing himself between them and the lake. He speaks softly to them, looking into their faces. "'And fear not them which kill the body, but are not able to kill the soul: but rather fear him which is able to destroy both soul and body in hell.'"

"Terrell, please. Terrell." He looks at the man and scratches the beard on his neck. He sits in front of them like a crow high above the floor of the woods. His eyes are only slits against the freezing rain and he sets his mouth in a way that I know means he has nothing more to say. Nothing more to say to the two men. He stood and came back to where I was waiting. "Be quick with it," he says. I look over the tops of the men's heads, out over the lake, and the face of the boy is there in the dark clouds and his eyes are open wide. They are brown encircled in brilliant white and he is not looking in judgment, but with anticipation as he is somehow part of this as well. He has crossed over and for just this moment he can see back through the dimness from where he passed from the light of the fire into a place that is quiet and unmoved by the actions of men. I step closer to the two men and lower the gun and it roars twice before they are able to make any further sound. They fall forward and gore is spread in a large pattern on the back of their shirts and the soft wet ground. Terrell does not look away but is holding in his breath and I am further into an absolution. There is nothing but the falling sleet and rain and Terrell takes the gun from me and strides back to the edge of the woods and leans it against a tree.

"Help me roll this car into the lake, Aaron," he says. "Then we'll go back and get what we need to finish." He spits on the ground. He reaches into the car window and pulls the lever into neutral while I push. He turns the wheel toward the lake and the slope down to the water. I push hard, my ragged boots digging into the soft mud, and the car begins to roll more quickly and then its front tires are pointed downward and the car begins to roll on its own. Its front tires enter the lake and I push once more and the water comes beneath it and pulls it out further, submerging the body, and then it begins to sink down, water coming in the open windows and flooding the inside. In a short time it is gone from sight.

"There now," Terrell says, and he turns and walks up the bank. I stand a minute longer, looking at the place where the car went in and then I go and stand over the men. Their faces are pressed into the mud and their ruined forms are starting to collect the sleet, which is shiny against the red blossoms.

"Aaron," Terrell says. I continue standing over the men and then look to the lake to see if the boy's face is still there, but it has washed out and there is nothing but the storm's clouds sitting above the water, emptying themselves. "Aaron," Terrell says again and I walk away from the men and follow him back through the woods, thinking of the dead fire in the cabin and how we will be cold inside the room until the flames can be worked up again.

CHAPTER 41

AARON AND
THE SERPENT

We put the men in the ground on the far side of a hill that overlooked the lake. The sleet had stopped falling, but it had coated the ground and it winked on an off when shards of sunlight came though the black canopy above us. Terrell did not speak while we worked and the soft ground was easy beneath the blade of the shovels and the bite of the pick. When the hole was large enough Terrell told me to put the bodies inside and I pulled them by their wrists into the wet grave and looked up from where I was standing below Terrell and his eyes were watching me like they had watched the men kneeling in front of the water. "Come out," he said, and I climbed out of the hole, feeling the grit and silt on my skin and a coldness that felt as if it were coming from inside my own body. We pushed the dirt onto the men in the hole and when they were covered, Terrell told me to help put sticks and clumps of rotted leaves over the spot where we had been digging. This memory and the things that remain within it exist as if they still live; as if I was still inside the hole with the bodies, motionless and piled on one another, discarded but always present and somehow alert, as if able to listen and hear the voices of those around them. They wait but they are impatient. They want to be left alone, but I can't leave them.

"Do you understand why?" he says now. I do not respond and want to walk back up the rise to see the lake, but he speaks again and I nod.

"It's because of the boy. They would have taken you from me if they found him and you would be put in a cell and made to wait there until they strapped you to a chair and ran the electricity through you."

"A cell," I say.

"Yes, and more than that. There would be a trial and..."

"The woman," I say.

"The woman?"

"The one we called Sophia."

"She's gone," he says. The voice had spoken to me about the woman he called Sophia. It told me that she would take him away from me and that I should stop her from doing that. She did not understand this place and she wanted Terrell for herself. I listened to them when they were sharing the bed and my head would fill with the whispering and sometimes I would stand above them while they were sleeping and I would feel the heat come into my face and something would stir beneath my pants and I would feel ashamed and angry at them for making it so.

"She's gone because of what you did to her." I had been alone with her in the room of the cabin and she had been looking away from me when I closed my hands around her. She had fought me but I had covered her mouth to stop her screaming.

"What speaks to you that way?" he says. "About Sophia? About the boy at the still? What comes to you?" The things inside my mind move and shift without my understanding. I see them as they are, but they are whole unto themselves and they kick and scratch at one another. I think about the surface of the lake, and when I see it I am standing on the bank and there is someone in the water. Something white and billowy is floating around her and she is yelling for me to go. I shake my head at Terrell and he looks at the grave and spits on the ground.

"We will not be absolved of this," he says. "They will come looking and there will be a reckoning. You will not understand this, but it will come. We will need to leave here. Leave here in our own ways."

"Leave," I repeat.

"Yes," he says

"To my father."

"No," he says. "He will not have you. He cares nothing for you."

"Katherine," I say. "To the place called Winchester?"

"No," he says. "She has known enough of bad things."

"A reckoning," I say. "A third person. A new throne. Eyes that have been taken from sight. They have not understood all of what has been demanded." The voice would speak calmly to me and tell me to be patient, it would tell me to see my path. See the path that was mine to walk. See the verse that had been imparted and written in a new way. On walls smeared in lifeblood. Away from the lake and back far into the woods, we would work under the sun and the clouds for long hours and then we would sit and eat and drink water and in the daylight when the voice was quiet as if it were sleeping or had gone underground to stay away from the light. But at night it would come back to me when I slept in the cabin, and it was almost as if I could see it moving over the ground like a mist and then I would feel it come inside the room and it would wash over and it would speak inside my head as if it had come through the cracks in the logs of the plank floor and then into my ears and my nose. It spoke in a loud voice. A voice that seemed to hold within it the passage of time, shrunken and haunted. And sometimes it would ask that I rise and come into the woods and there would be myself, and the shadow of myself made by the moon, and then a third, walking behind me but it would not be someone or anything that I could touch but I could feel it standing there with me, and I knew that it would require something from me when it chose. But time had become an uncertain thing, its meaning disguised and shifting like the dirt settling over the men inside the hole. I was suspended above it, speaking the same verse over and over and over with the violent images swirling about me, shifting and tortured and trapped so that I felt the pressure in my skull, causing me to close my eyes and place my hands against the sides of my head to stop the pulsing sounds, and when it left me, I felt that I had been scattered into pieces over time's domain and I was a broken pattern of colors and thoughts that bled together.

"We should not fear it," Terrell says and picks the shovel off the ground and then stabs it down into the dirt where it stands alone. "Take the things and let's go back." I collect the shovels and the pick and we walk away from the grave and away from the lake and walk down the path that leads to the cabin. The woods surrounding us are silent and we do not speak again until we are inside and the fire is going. Terrell goes to the shelf with the books and takes one down and sits at the table and reads from it aloud and I sit near him on the floor, listening to the words that seem to merge with the warmth from the flames. This is how we spend the evening and there is no supper, but Terrell drinks from one of the bottles. He does not look at me or ask what I understand about the book. When there is only black in the window of the cabin, he undresses and goes to the bed and lays down.

The fire is the only light inside and it makes patterns on his body and the blanket that he has used to cover himself. I see the woman who was in the lake yelling for me to stop and she is quiet now, looking back to the shore, her feet floating above the water. They are small and disfigured. Then she is pulled beneath the water and I turn and see the deer drinking, its antlers are white as the bone from which they are made and its tongue is forked, lapping at the water delicately as if the taste were sour. I stand and go to the window of the cabin and look out and can see where the path leading into the wood begins and the shimmer of the ice clinging to the trunks of the tree and beyond the entrance to the path there is nothing but the saturation of night. The bodies in the hole are still but I can feel that their eyes are open and staring. Then the boy's face is on the other side of the glass and he cannot see, but he is smiling with teeth that are broken and sharp and his head and body are jerking and then his arm comes up and he points into the room of the cabin and I hear the rattle from the box. I turn from the window and go to the noise and remove the rock and lift the lid. The serpent is inside but is not coiled and I pick it up and feel it move over my arm in a slow tangle like a vine. I walk with it over to where Terrell sleeps on his back, his mouth open and his breathing heavy. I study the snake around my arm and look back at the window to see the boy, but it is only a black square in the side of the cabin wall. The head of the snake rises and I lower my arm and allow it to crawl from me onto the blanket where it begins to move slowly across the sleeping form.

CHAPTER 42

IN THE BEDROOM

Edwards got into his car and sat behind the wheel, staring at the house he had just exited in a state of growing rage. The remark Renee had made, *nice that some of us can forget*, played over and over in his head. He had been tempted to walk across the room and knock the drink out of her hand and shake the life out of her. Shake her until she apologized and begged his forgiveness. Her selfishness knew very little boundary, and her past decisions and treatment of her sister had made it all but impossible for Edwards to summon even the slimmest tone of civility when in her company. And here they were now, with people murdered at a rest stop and Sarah being the officer to discover it and all Renee could think about was herself and her own demons. He knew that he should not let it enrage him the way that it did; his wife had forgiven Renee and had asked that he do the same, or at least remain indifferent. But that was a tall order, and while he tried his best out of respect for Kat, there were times, like now, that his inherent sense of right and wrong welled up and threatened to breach the banks of his own tolerance. He drummed his fingers on the steering wheel and took in several deep breaths. Then he started the car, backed out of the driveway, and pulled away from the house.

The rural road was pitch black and Edwards drove slowly, keeping his eyes open for deer. The dash clock showed ten minutes after ten. He had been away longer than he had intended. He no longer felt comfortable leaving Kat at home by herself. She would probably have gone to bed already, but he knew that being in the house alone made her anxious. Even before the dementia set in, she would call him at the station after it got dark, earnestly inquiring when he was returning home. In the early years of their marriage, he had often worked late and when she called about being home for dinner or just being home when it got dark, it provoked an old irritation and resentment that they did not have children. Children, he thought, made a home feel less vulnerable. They provided a sense of purpose and a level of accountability that helped adults leave their own inhibitions behind, helped them become something larger than their own wants and needs. Edwards was a sensitive and caring husband, and when Katherine told him the story of the rape and the child and that summer on the mountain with her mother and LoLo, he had almost come unhinged with both anger and grief. He had fought her time and time again to a stalemate, trying to find out who had committed the act, but she refused to discuss it.

The fact that an unknown man attacked his wife and got away with it was almost unbearable. The fact that an unknown man denied him children with the woman he loved was almost blinding in its irreverence. In fact, denied him children through the birth and abandonment of an unwanted and reprehensibly conceived child. He pushed the accelerator of the car a bit harder. He was ascending the mountain now, hugging the curves tightly and pushing the car out of them with more speed to keep from drifting. Through the passenger window, he could make out the open expanse, but could not see any of the slope's definition nor the thick carpet of trees that ran from the bottom all the way to the top. Edwards had given up on the idea of children not long after their second year of marriage. He had pressed her very hard in their home one morning, harder than he had ever pressed. Hard to the point of overturning one of the chairs in the small eat-in kitchen, his violent kick flipping the chair onto its back and skidding it across the floor before it slammed into a pie safe that had been Katherine's mother's. She had looked at him with an expression he had never seen on her face before. It was not fear or even hurt, but a look of surprise that he knew would crease into sorrow. Not for herself and her reasons for being childless, but for him. For her husband who she was so obviously disappointed and hurting. It had been that look that had stopped his requests. He had gone to her and taken her in his arms and apologized, both of them in tears and holding one another. He had picked up the chair and placed it back where it belonged and then he had gone out to the garage to get the lawn mower and by the time he cranked it and made a first pass across the yard, the feelings of regret and frustration were replaced with a relief that was comforting and manageable. He would be lying to himself if he said that he had come around and no longer wanted children. That would never be true. But he would not confront her about it again and that decision transcended his parental desires because his love of Katherine and his need to protect her came above all else.

Edwards came down the other side of the mountain and guided the car through a sleeping Winchester. It seemed that somehow the town existed between two parallel universes and because it had feet in both, nothing ever changed. A few more people here and there, a small business or a new restaurant might spring up, but otherwise it passed through year after year with very little news to report. No one recognized this more than Edwards and the deputies in his office. Their patrols through the town and out into the county provided a front row seat to the stagnation of the whole region. Still, it offered small comforts here and there. Less crime, or at least less before the crack and speed epidemic had washed into the community like an overflowing sewer. But that was relegated to certain types and they knew how to contain that to some extent. *To some extent,* he thought. His mind went back to the rest area and the corpses left there, flesh and blood positioned like stone statues in reverence to something unthinkable, greedy, and eerily vague in origin; their inertia and soundless expressions were nonetheless expectant and demanding and Edwards knew that they would leave their claw mark on all who bore their witness. Not even the worst of the addicts that he knew of, or had arrested, would commit such atrocities. They might spook if surprised in the middle of a robbery, might even commit a minor assault if cornered, but mostly they were exposed rabbits in a moonlit field, vulnerable and sadly aware of their impending fate. And that made them relatively harmless because the fight had gone out of them and death began to look like a promising alternative to the addiction. He had seen solid people turned into echoes of their former selves, and the more of that poison that they smoked or pumped into their arms, the further and further away the sound of their rational voice went. And then the only murder that they would be capable of was their own.

He pulled onto his street and then into his driveway. The lights were off in the house and he felt all the more guilty coming in this late. He shut off the car and walked to the front door. He unlocked it and stepped into the dark entryway, closing the door behind him. When he turned back into the room he froze. The porch door was standing open. A light wind pushed the curtain. Edward's hand went to the weapon on his belt. He popped the snap and brought the gun out and he walked further into the house. It was quite possible that Kat had left the door open absent-mindedly, but he doubted that. Despite her failing memory, routine things like checking the doors was not something she had forgotten up to this point. They rarely locked the doors when he was home and she may not have checked to see that it was locked when she went to bed, but he did not think that she would have left the patio door standing open. The house was very still, and he swept his eyes over the dim room to see if anything was disturbed or out of place. There was the milk shake cup and a half-eaten cheeseburger on a plate next to it. But that was not unusual now. Her clean house was his responsibility now. He was tempted to call his wife's name or to turn on a light but wanted to be sure there was no one in there with them. His thoughts jumped back to the car and the addicts that he had been thinking about, break-ins and the rare occasions of unplanned violence. But in the dark house and with the patio door standing open, the corpses stacked in the morgue, he began to reconsider, seeing the gaunt and sunken eye sockets of the man left sitting on the rest area toilet. *They have plans too.*

They have

plans, Billy.

He laid his keys softly on a table beside the couch and made his way slowly down the hall after giving a quick glance into the kitchen. There was a grocery sack on counter and what looked like a gallon of something. Tea most likely. He could see that the doorway to his room was dark. The doors to the other rooms off the hall were closed as they typically were. *Kids rooms,* the voice sang softly.

No kids, just empty rooms.

No kids, just empty rooms.
No kids, Billy. No kids for Billy and Kat.
Kat and Bill went up the hill.
To fetch . . .
Bill fell down and broke his crown.
And Kat lay barren after.

He brought the gun down and placed it behind his back. He was sweating under his arms and the absurdity of the voice was pushing his heart rate, speeding up and scattering his thoughts. If this was just another slip of Kat's mind, he did not want to scare her coming into the room with the gun raised. He got to the door and eased his head into the opening to look in. The room was dark and he could smell something rank. He thought he could make out Kat in the bed, but she was sitting up. He spoke her name and it came out more like a hiss in the still room. He reached in and found the switch plate. He gripped the gun behind his back firmly and his thumb found the safety and he clicked it off at the same time he threw the light. Soft orange haze accompanied by a buzz came from the light fixture above their bed. His wife was sitting up. Her hands had been tied to opposite posts with what looked like torn pieces of the bedding. She was in her nightgown and her head was slumped on her chest. Edwards crossed the room in two long strides and tossed the gun on the bed and climbed onto the mattress with his knees. The smell was much stronger now and he realized that she had lost control of her functions. He reached out and took her chin in his hands and felt something sticky. He pulled his hand away and saw blood there. He reached out again, panic drumming in his ears, climbing up his constricting throat. He lifted her chin and went rigid. His wife's face as he had seen her in the car that morning after looking over the junked cruiser came into focus. Her head was bent down, looking into her lap at the crossword. He was back in the car with her again, about to ask her if she wanted a cheeseburger when she turned her head and brought her face up to meet his, a jagged opening in the soft white flesh of her throat, her eyes dark sockets, their rims a purple red.

Is that what I normally get, Bill. A cheeseburger and chocolate shake?

Sitting upright on his knees in the bed he had shared with Kat since their marriage began, Bill Edwards started to scream.

CHAPTER 43

KATHERINE

It was Renee that she had thought of when she realized someone had been in the room with her. The evening had passed like any other in recent months, her mind flat like the surface of still water, her memories circling beneath the surface, unable to break free, suffocating. She watched them move through the stagnant liquid, wondering if she could extend her hand and catch hold of one darting thought and drag it into the light and the air, but she never did. Never had the courage to reach, for fear that she would grasp only a handful of lukewarm pond water, and the realities of her failing mind would settle after the ripples had dispersed.

The man had been across from her in the dark room and she knew that she should be afraid; knew that he meant to hurt her in the worst kind of way, but she could not process that obvious fear. Instead she thought of the fight that she had had with her sister in her room, all those years ago. Renee's explosion and vivid elocution of gritty sexual desire and the damage that she hoped it would cause Katherine and their mother. Damage that required a denunciation of her mother's attempts at normalcy and their father's steadfast avoidance of the avalanche that was girls who were growing into women. She was almost able to put the man with the knife out of her head entirely. He would simply be an instrument in ending a life that she no longer controlled and wished over in her moments of lucidity. Moments that she was unable to share with Bill or with the friends who had drifted beyond her recognition. She knew it could be interpreted as weakness, that even Renee would expect her to fight back, but she knew she had accepted futility in a way that others had or could not and so she waited and pictured her sister and herself, playing with the doll house and speaking for the dolls as a family who had moved in, slipping between the well-appointed minia-ture rooms in a fantastical harmony that, while not real or obtainable, was innocent and good to consider. *Renee,* she thought when the figure stood and came for her. *I forgive you and will ask God to forgive you when I see him. Mercy is not mine to give, but forgiveness is.* The man's hands on her had been gentle like a child's. She did not offer herself to him as much as she succumbed, and when the pain began she tried desperately to hold in the sounds that her addled mind wished to exhale. These noises would be useless as the noises of the deep woods were useless without a witness to look into the canopy to identify an accusing crow or to see the wind moving the branches into a heavy serenade. *I'm sorry,* she thought, although she did not know to whom she was address-ing the apology. Then there was only blackness and the small reprieve before his final stroke made even the desire to protest impossible.

CHAPTER 44

FLIP AND ETHAN

Flip and Ethan left the mountain in separate cars. They had gone back to the sheriff's office and dropped off Ethan's vehicle and they had loaded Herc into Flip's truck and then driven over to the grocery store and picked up the items that the sheriff had told them to get for Mrs. Edwards' dinner. They had also picked up beer for afterward. They were quiet in the car, not even making their normal small talk that consisted of an endless string of petty insults, each one playing off of the last. Herc sat between them on the seat, looking intently out the window and giving low growls at people passing on the sidewalk. They pulled into the Edwards' driveway, Ethan carrying the brown grocery bag and Flip walking ahead of him and knocking on the door. It occurred to him that two deputies knocking on the door of their sheriff's house might really rattle his wife and so he put a large grin on his face and prepared to speak immediately once the door opened. They waited and no one came. He knocked again and this time the door opened and Mrs. Edwards looked at them with an inquisitive and confused expression.

"Hey Mrs. Edwards," Flip said. "Sheriff asked that we drop off some things for dinner. He's…"

"Tied up with work, mam," Ethan said. "We brought you some fried chicken and some potato salad from the Winn Dixie." She looked at the two men, not moving, keeping a hand on the doorknob. She studied them, trying to place their faces.

"Mrs. Edwards," Ethan said.

"Yes," she said. "I'm Mrs. Edwards."

"You okay, mam?" Ethan asked.

"Yes, fine," she said. "How can I help you boys?" They exchanged a quick look and then Flip stepped a little closer. He turned and took the bag from Ethan and turned back to Mrs. Edwards and tilted it toward her so she could see inside.

"We have some hot fried chicken and some of the best potato salad in Middle Tennessee," he said, putting on his most reassuring grin. "We also got a jug of tea. Think we could come inside and set this out on the counter for you, Mrs. Edwards?" She stepped back from the door and nodded and the two deputies went inside and placed the grocery sack onto the kitchen counter, setting the tea next to the bag of food. She watched them standing next to the patio door. When they had finished, they came into the living room and stood politely waiting to see if there was anything further that they could do. Both men knew that her mind was leaving her but had no idea that it had reached a point of unrecognition. Both of them had been to this house half a dozen times for cookouts on holidays or a random Friday evening when the Sheriff had asked everyone over to eat before the high school game. She had been at the center of all of those visits, mothering them and making good natured jokes about her husband and his propensity to burn anything that he put on a grill. Now she looked at them as if they had come in to sell her magazines or a Bible.

"Okay, Mrs. Edwards," Flip said. "Me and Ethan are going to go now. You need anything else?" She steadied herself on the back of a dining room chair and shook her head. They went out, closing the door behind them. They climbed back in the truck. Flip started to turn the ignition and stopped.

"Goddamn," he said.

"Yeah," Ethan said.

"Didn't know it had gotten that bad," Flip said.

"Me either," Ethan said. "How long you think she's been that bad off?"

"Hell if I know," Flip said and started the truck. Herc whined. "Shoot me if it happens though." He backed out of the driveway.

Flip took a can of beer from the cooler sitting next to the couch that he had purchased for twelve dollars from a salvage store in Winchester. Its cushions were almost entirely flat and there was a long tear in the fabric along one of the arms. The can of beer dripped cold ice water onto the front of his jeans and he held it up and brushed the cold aluminum against his forehead. Disobeying what Sheriff Edwards had instructed, Flip and Ethan had plowed through a twelve pack of beer in less than an hour and were halfway through their second. The beer was sitting heavy on his stomach, but not as heavy as it had been sitting on Ethan's, who he could hear in the back bathroom throwing up his dinner.

Flip put his feet up on a rickety coffee table, the varnish long since scratched and chipped away. There was a pattern of concentric milky-white ring stains from the bottoms of aluminum cans left unattended, often three-quarters empty and weighted down with cigarette butts floating in the soupy liquid. His living room was cramped with hunting gear, piles of laundry, and a mismatched collection of food and alcohol containers that piled up until Flip came through every other week, sweeping the trash into a garbage bag that he kept on the floor in the kitchen until its contents were spilling over and then moved to the cub next to the rusting mailbox. He had to move his socked feet carefully to keep from knocking that evening's can collection to the filthy carpet. Herc was asleep under the little table near the entrance to the kitchen and he lifted his head up to look at Flip when he heard the empty cans rattle against one another. Flip set the can of beer on his stomach and opened it, tilting it toward the dog before taking a long swallow. Behind him, he heard Ethan clear his throat and nose and then he heard the toilet flush, followed by a miserable groan. Ethan came up the short hallway on shaky legs. His face was pale and his eyes were watery and his hair was stuck to his forehead with sweat.

"Better?" Flip asked. Ethan looked down at him and nodded unconvincingly.

"Want another beer?"

Ethan shook his head and walked around the coffee table and made his way gingerly to the battered recliner where he'd been sitting before. Flip turned and reached over the side of the couch arm and fumbled with the cooler lid. Then he produced a can of beer and whistled at Ethan, who was staring into space. Ethan shook his head, but Flip tossed the can over and he caught it, fumbled it, then grasped it with two hands, Herc watching as if a ball had been tossed.

"Drink up," he said. "You just made a ton of room." Ethan looked reluctantly at the can and then opened it and took a small sip. Flip smiled at him and Ethan weakly smiled back.

"Thanks," he said. "I sure as hell don't need this."

"Ahhh," Flip said and took a swallow. "Day like you had, you should be pacing me three-to-one." Ethan sat back in the chair and exhaled from his nose, shaking his head, closing his eyes.

"Who's on the phone at the station?" Ethan asked absently.

"Rhonda, I guess," Flip said.

"Okay," Ethan said.

"Flip?"

"Yeah, Ethan." He put a hand to the side of his head and leaned his elbow on the couch, cupping his face in his palm.

"I don't know what to make of that today. How you supposed to get right with something like that, man. How you supposed to do that?"

"Well," Flip said.

"I've heard about things like that in other places," Ethan broke in. "Maybe out in California or some big city up north, or I don't know. Someplace else. Not in fucking Winchester." He trailed off and took a drink from his can. He grimaced and dismissively put the can down on the floor next to the recliner. "I don't know, maybe I'm just ignorant."

"That could be it," Flip said, grinning.

"I'm serious, man," Ethan said, but not angrily. "I'm serious, man."

"I know you are," Flip said. He sat up on the couch and Herc's ears pricked-up. He pointed his can at Ethan. "You did real good today. You and Sarah both. Real good. We're all proud of what you did. That was some mean shit up there, man. Real mean shit. But you handled it all right. You went in there like a man, handled that dog like a man. Don't know that I would have done any better." Ethan stared at a spot in the middle of the floor and Flip leaned back into the couch.

"Maybe," Ethan said from far away.

"Sure you did," Flip said. "Sure you did. Ain't nobody gonna hold it against you if you take your own time getting your shit together. Hell, anyone with any sense is gonna need some time getting through something like that." He finished the beer and put the can on the table with the other empties.

"That's the meanest shit this county has ever seen. That's the plain truth, Ethan. Probably some of the worst shit that the state boys have ever seen."

Ethan nodded, his face troubled and tight, then said "He's still out there. He's still out there, and..."

"Yeah," Flip said. "And he'll be out there tomorrow too. But tomorrow we'll be back to work and you'll feel better about..."

"I don't know that I want to feel better," Ethan interrupted, slurring a bit. "What's that say about you if you get used to something like this. Something fucking as crazy as this..."

"You're drunk, Ethan," Flip said.

"Yeah, I know," Ethan said. "I know I'm drunk, Flip." He stood up and walked into the room, pacing back and forth. The dog, unaccustomed to the house and the loud talking, came from beneath the kitchen table and stood, looking at the two men. Ethan dropped his hand and the dog came closer and licked it, then sat down, letting out a small concerned whine.

"I had an uncle that went to Vietnam," Ethan said, kneeling down to scratch Herc behind his upturned ears. "Uncle Tommy. I remember him from before he went. He was my mom's brother. Used to take me fishing and let me ride around with him in his truck. Really nice to me for being a small kid that probably drove him crazy, you know."

"Yeah," Flip said. "I remember Tommy."

"Yeah," Ethan said. "He went over there to Vietnam and when he came back home to Winchester, he was really quiet. All the time just would be really, really quiet. He lived with us for a while after. In this room at my mom's house. Same room my granddaddy died in. That's a whole other story; that old man in the back room. Gives me nightmares to think about him. I used to think that we trapped something in there after he died. I was afraid of it. Tommy lived back there by himself and really just kept to himself. He would eat with us sometimes and cause

I was still a kid I would ask about going fishing or maybe riding in his truck out in the county and he'd say maybe we could do that, but his voice was really broken when he'd talk and he'd hardly eat. Wouldn't eat much of anything. I remember my mother trying to talk with him sitting in the kitchen and he would answer her, but only to say yes or no and I could tell. My old man didn't want nothing to do with him. Said he was all fucked up from the war and didn't think he belonged in the house with us. Maybe he was afraid of that room too. I don't know. You know, I could tell that something was wrong with him." He paused and Flip could see that Ethan was picturing everything in his mind, the house and the uncle and the mother and what he imagined was a poorly-lit back room, maybe off of the laundry, in the rear of the house. Maybe a room with just a single window, situated behind a mismatched washer and dryer set that was twenty-five years old. Ethan stood for a second not saying anything, not focusing on anything. He was swaying a little, scratching behind the dog's ears with absent fingers.

"My mom and dad were working. My old man was coming home less and less so I never expected him much. I was in the front of the house watching TV or something like that. I heard my Uncle Tommy back in his room and it sounded like he was crying. I walked back there to see what was wrong with him and I came through the kitchen and then down the hall to where he stayed and I pushed open the door and he was sitting on the bed and he had a gun in his mouth and he was crying. I just stood in that door there, watching him. I was just a kid, but I knew that wasn't right." He paused again, still patting the dog, and Flip could see that Herc's muscles were tensing as Ethan became more emotional.

"He was holding the gun with both hands and the barrel was in his mouth and then he looked up and saw me standing there and I think he almost went ahead and pulled the trigger, but something stopped him from doing it. It was like we was both stuck in time or something. He pulled the gun out of his mouth and set it on the bed and then he used his hands to wipe the tears out of his eyes and then he stood up and came across the room to me and I remember how scared I was waiting for him to get all the way across the room and to the door. When he got there though, he just put his hand on my shoulder and turned me around and pushed me out of the room. Then he closed the door behind me and I remember standing on the other side of that closed door and not knowing what to do. Just standing there like a dumbass kid. I remember that I did not want to stay inside the house. I remember that. I think I went outside to wait on my mom and when she came home that night, Uncle Tommy came out of the back room with his things packed in a green duffle bag and he told my mom he was going to find someplace else to live. She tried to get him to stay but he wouldn't and I was standing off a ways listening to them. They weren't fighting. Mom was begging cause she knew too. Guess she knew. But Uncle Tommy wouldn't put down his things. He stood there holding that bag and had this look on his face that was somewhere else. And then he just went out the front door." Ethan eyes were red and watery and Flip stood up and walked over and steadied him. "That room," Ethan said. "That sad fucking haunted room. Seems like everyone who went in there brushed up against death. Granddaddy died in there, choking on blood and pieces of his own lungs and then fucking Tommy. You think a kid should be around something like that? I don't think a kid should be around something like that. I was around it though, Flip. I saw it every time I closed my eyes." The dog took several paces back and sat on its haunches. Flip guided Ethan through the room and walked him to the shabby guest bedroom. He pushed some things off the top of the single bed and helped Ethan lower himself down onto the untucked sheet covering the mattress. Flip found a blanket in the doorless closet and brought it back and spread it over the young deputy. As he was leaving the room, Ethan spoke as he tugged the blanket around him.

"What do you think Tommy did over there, Flip? Over there in Vietnam. What do you think that he saw or did to make him put a gun in his mouth?" Flip turned and looked down at Ethan. He snapped off the overhead light and stood in the dark.

"I don't know what he saw or what he didn't see," Flip said. "Every-one I know that came back from that war can't seem to get things out of their own heads. I guess maybe it's just part of it. Who the hell knows?"

"I do, Flip," Ethan murmured, passing out. "I know."

Flip left Ethan sleeping and walked back to the front of the house. The dog was standing as he came into the den. He sat on the couch and opened another beer. He thought about Ethan's uncle and grand-father and now, in the quiet of the house, a cheap clock ticking away somewhere in the kitchen, Flip could start to make out Tommy's face. It was clean-shaven and smiling, and while Flip could not place the time or place, he remembered that Tommy had seemed friendly and easy-going. The image bothered him and he took long drinks of the beer, looking absently around the room. Among the empty cans, unpaid bills, and random garbage his eyes fell on a piece of scratch paper with numbers scrawled on it. He picked it up and had to hold it away from his face to let his eyes adjust. He smiled then, remembering the girl who had written the number down. He sat up and was pushing some of the cans aside to call her when the handset rattled in its cradle, making him jerk.

CHAPTER 45

SARAH

Renee stood in the doorway to Sarah's room. The sun had just come up, and her tongue was thick and her head felt as if it were stuffed with foam. After Bill had left, Sarah had gone to bed and Renee had stayed in the front room drinking late into the morning hours. She was still dressed in her uniform and she had woken on the couch to the sound of the phone, knocking the heavy empty glass onto the carpet with a muffled bump as she rolled over to reach the receiver and stop the painful ringing. Now she stood braced in the door frame watching her daughter sleep, faint light coming through the cheap blinds. Her face was drawn and hollow and her eyes were a tangled weave of glowing red sidewalk cracks. How many times had she watched over her children in this state, wobbly legs and aching head? Peering into their rooms like an intruder, their tiny heads poking from beneath the covers as they slept, unknowing of their mother's pathetic deliberations and lost sense of worth. Unknowing of her transgressions against decency and the people who had offered her a life so unlike the one that she had chosen. *A man, not a life,* she thought. *I chose him over that life.* And standing there now, the knowledge of her sister's death washing over her as she struggled to steady herself in that ridiculous uniform that was a tangible representation of exactly how far she had dropped from grace.

Something turned in her stomach and the thick scent of the whis-key in her nostrils made her mouth flood with warm saliva, an old resentment bubbling up and looking for her attention with a reckless and frantic determination like a cur sniffing around trash cans in an alley. She had blame. She had blame and would accept that. But she had also protected them from him, had stood her ground when they were helpless and shown him the door. Had made the life unappealing and restricting to him. Had asked only that he walk away. Go to his brother. Go anywhere and let them try to piece things back together. She had done that and she had held down jobs and she had begged her way back in Katherine's life despite Bill Edwards and his Sheriff's indignant stare and smirk. Had even tried to introduce her parents to the children and failed but at least secured some of their money after they were gone. That was something at least.

Renee stepped into Sarah's room and crossed over to the bed and sat down. The weight stirred her daughter and she moaned softly and turned over, and then came awake abruptly, finding Renee sitting there. She shot a look at the clock beside the bed and rolled back over.

"I don't have to work today," Sarah said. Renee touched her daugh-ter's shoulder and pulled on it. Sarah turned back over and looked at her mother and then sat up in the bed.

"What is it?" she asked. Renee looked into her daughter's face and reached out again and brushed some hair from her forehead.

"What is it, Mamma?"

"Katherine," she whispered.

"What about Aunt Katherine?" Sarah said. Renee looked around her daughter's room and felt confused. The images on the wall, the pic-tures of people she did not know, the paint color— all this was wrong. And the furniture looked shabby and cheap. It was not the furniture that their mother had put in their bedrooms. This was someplace else.

"Mamma?"

No, that's not right, Renee was thinking. Mine was a four-poster bed and it was next to the window, overlooking the farmyard. Just like Katherine's room did. We could see down into the farmyard from our bedrooms. Mine was next to Katherine's.

"Mamma!"

Why was everything out of place? The smell of the room was wrong. The cheap blinds were in place of the handmade curtains. The old carpet on the floor was stained and was not the wide planks of hardwood that she remembered. There had been a doll house that her father had given them for Christmas. She had fought with Katherine about who got to keep the doll house in their room, argued to the point that two men had to be called in from the yard to move it between their rooms every other month. She and Katherine had sat together on the floor in front of the doll house playing and sometimes singing together before being called down for supper.

"Mamma!"

Renee's head snapped up and she looked at Sarah, who was now sitting upright in the bed. She looked expectant and panicked.

"Katherine?" she asked looking at Sarah. "Katherine?"

"Mamma, what's wrong with you?" Sarah said, getting to her knees, reaching out and taking Renee by the shoulders, shaking her gently. "What happened to Aunt Katherine?"

"Gone," Renee said.

"Gone where? Aunt Katherine is gone where?" Renee closed her eyes and then opened them again.

"Dead," she said. "Katherine. My sister Katherine is dead."

Sarah climbed out of the bed and left her mother sitting in her room. She went out and into the den and picked up the phone and dialed the sheriff's office. Later she would wonder what had made her make that call instead of calling her uncle at home.

"Winchester Sheriff's…"

"Ethan," Sarah yelled into the phone.

"No," the voice said. "This is Flip."

"Flip!"

"Yeah."

"Flip, it's Sarah."

"Oh, hey there Sarah. You get my message? We need you in today. I know you were supposed to be off, but we need you to come in and help." His tone was unusually calm and measured. She pressed.

"What's going on, Flip? What happened to the sheriff's wife? What happened to my aunt?" The line was silent.

"Sarah, why don't you come on in and I'll tell you what's happened."

"No, Goddammit," Sarah screamed into the phone. "Tell me what happened right now."

"Sarah?" It was Jed, standing in the entryway to the hall leading into the den. He was dressed in jeans and no shirt or shoes. She whirled to look at him and then went back to the phone.

"Flip."

"It looks like she was murdered, Sarah," he said. "It looks like whoever committed those murders at the rest area went after the sheriff's wife last night."

"Oh God, God, God, no," she said. "While he was here with me. She was alone while he was here with me. And someone came into their house..."

"Sarah," Flip said calmly. "You need to come in."

She told him that she would be in as soon as she could. She hung up the phone and turned to look at her brother. She felt like someone had thrown the breaker switch inside her head and everything was slowly powering down. The gravity of the conversation and the confused look on her brother's face, her near-catatonic mother sitting on the bed, the deer head in the men's stall and its mutilated carcass laying grotesquely across the outside table, the half-smoked cigarette on the ground outside the coroner's car, the rain falling outside the grimy restroom window and the bodies positioned so that they stared blankly at whomever opened the closed stall doors.

O Lord Thou Pluckest

"Sarah," Jed said again. "Sarah, what's happening?"

"Aunt Katherine," she said.

"What are you talking about, what about Aunt Katherine?"

"Dead. Aunt Katherine is dead."

"What are you talking about?"

He went on talking but Sarah no longer heard him. She only looked out the window. The sun was out and the air had been cleansed by the storm that had come through the day before. It was the kind of day that made getting up and going to work seem purposeful. It was the kind of day that made life in Winchester seem less oppressive and the people living there less tarnished by the strains of poverty and ignorance.

She looked at her brother who was visibly hungover and confused, and felt no urge to be comforting. Seeing him that way angered her. Angered her that he was allowed to ignore everything that happened around him, around all of them. He was careless and helpless and she had spent much of their shared life ensuring that he was safe and taken care of, and now the events of that morning, paired with Jed's chalky complexion, his thin arms and scrawny chest, made her want to hurl something against the wall. She went out of the room to change, brushing past where he stood meekly in the doorway. For a brief minute, the only sound in the house was Sarah moving deliberately around her small room, not bothering to shower, but pulling on her uniform from the previous day. Renee had risen quickly from Sarah's bed when she came back in the room. She stunk of liquor, her hair oily and clothes wrinkled from sleeping on the sofa. Sarah had to step aside to let Renee out of the room, and they did not look at one another, did not think to console one another or share in the disbelief. Sarah knew from years of quiet observation how her mother felt about Katherine. Their disdain for one another as resolute as their unwillingness to discuss its cause, and now, whatever had held them apart for all those many years was no longer symmetrical and Renee would be forced to either hold fast to her moorings or risk a tide of regret and remorse that would flow but never ebb. And as she dressed, Sarah thought how strange it was that a simple phone call could change the course of a life with such indifference and certitude.

When Sarah returned to the kitchen, Jed was sitting at the table, his hands around a cup of instant coffee. He looked up when Sarah entered.

"I have to go into the station, Jed." He nodded and put the mug down on the table, scarred from years of eating without place mats and Renee's late-night friends drinking and smoking into the morning hours while Sarah and Jed had slept in their shared bedroom. The drunken adults had been loud and had played country albums through a cheap stereo with blown speakers that hissed and muffled the music in a way that Sarah had never forgotten. She thought that those speakers might have been stuck in a closet somewhere in the house, quiet at last, except for the incessant hiss that persisted in her recollection of their being alive, and she wondered if Jed remembered those sounds coming down the hallway when they all should have been sleeping soundlessly.

"What did Flip say?" Sarah looked at her brother and considered sitting down with him and having a cup of coffee. She started to get a mug and saw that the handle of whiskey was still on the counter from the night before. She wondered if Jed had poured some in his mug. He was bent over the table, his bare skin white and his slight frame not much bigger than when he was a boy. His shoulder blades were pronounced and everything about his demeanor was vulnerable. Sarah felt a familiar pang of sympathy as he stood and took a rumpled pack of Winstons out of his jeans pocket and found a lighter loose on the table.

"Just what you heard," she said, and closed the cupboard door deciding against the coffee. "I'll find out more when I get over to Winchester." Jed lit the smoke and held in his breath and let the plume out into the kitchen where it hung in a reeking cloud. Sarah started for the door, then turned and looked at her brother as he sat down again. When Renee had been absentee parenting, Sarah had watched out for Jed. She helped him get a bowl of cereal in the morning, helped him dress and to remember a coat when they had to stand in the driveway on winter days, waiting for the school bus. His timidity and innocence had been both endearing and worrisome to the point of making her furious, but intuition had kept her from forcing him into a premature adulthood. Something had caught in her mind observing her combative parents, and she realized despite her youth that undue pressure would turn Jed in the wrong direction. But now a coldness akin to those winter mornings in the driveway—when the air had bitten their gloveless fingers like an icy jaw—crept over her and she considered with something like guilt that she may have been wrong not to push a little harder, that she may have in fact done Jed a disservice by allowing him to remain timid and unaware, because the world had progressed despite her best intentions and she feared that the thin frame and soft nerve she observed sitting at the kitchen table, smoking and drinking spiked instant coffee, was a casualty waiting to happen.

"I need you to stick around today and watch Mamma," she said. "She and Aunt Katherine weren't real close, but she's pretty shook-up." Jed nodded and stood up again and came toward her, holding the burning cigarette. He took a glass out of the sink and filled it half full of water and went back to the table, set it down, and flicked ash in it. She turned again to leave.

"Sarah," he said.

"Yeah."

"I'm sorry."

"For what?"

"I don't know," he said. "For this. For that trouble on the mountain. For being a fuck-up." Sarah stood with her hand on the doorknob. Apologies had a way of deafening her. So many of them had passed through parched lips over the years and always they came tearfully from her mother who had allowed something to take place or made a remark that was truly unforgivable. She had learned to listen to them patiently, but they never registered their intended, ill-formed purpose and she stacked them away in anticipation for the next disappointment and subsequent plea for exoneration. But the hollow apologies were always there, like the speakers' hiss despite being stowed away. Jed had been the opposite and had needed the promise of their mother doing better as much as Renee needed to believe that she could actually keep it. His weakness caused her to tighten her grip on the doorknob.

"None of that matters right now, Jed."

"I know that," he said. "I just thought I should say something." She held the knob in her hand. It felt small and loose, but she was hesitant to let it go.

"You remember the time that Aunt Katherine and Uncle Bill took us to the fair?" he asked.

"Yes," Sarah said.

"Me too," Jed said. "I remember that. And I remember when they came to get us cause Mamma and Daddy were fighting, and when they got here, Aunt Katherine came in the house and took us out and put us in the back of their car and we went to the fair."

"And you got sick on junk," Sarah said. "Yeah," Jed said and laughed, spewing smoke. "I got sick."

The sun was brilliant and the sky was a peaceful blue. Sarah stood next to her vehicle and allowed herself to appreciate the simple warmth. Her brother's reminiscence had confused her, though she thought it was probably the spiked coffee talking, and her head was so full of images that she felt she owed it to herself to simply exist in the moment. The events of the last twenty-four hours were both stark and eerily vague and everything was jammed in together like a maniacal collage that kept shifting and changing shape, making her dizzy and fatigued. She concentrated on the clear sky and the radiant sunlight, willing herself to be as still as possible and for the second time that morning, her reasoning redirected and a voice from inside her head spoke to her with condescending ease. *Isn't this what you really wanted, Sarah? Isn't this the excitement that you were craving and isn't this enough, or do you need more? Do you need more, Sarah? Because there is a third that walks. Because your shadow at morning. Because the Lord Pluckest, Sarah.* She reached out and steadied herself on the hood of her vehicle. She counted backwards from twenty, feeling the sun's light on her face as she methodically returned to present, setting things back in order. She waited until she was confident that she could move freely and then made her way to the driver's side door and got in behind the wheel of the Caprice.

As she drove, she took stock of her childhood. It seemed, in the midst of everything that was circling her life in the moment, that she was no more than a product of her tense and disturbed environment and worse, the dilapidated structure of her family. The realization was familiar but always managed to startle her, and she went back through her memory looking for moments, incidents, or dreams that had not been tied to the lives of those who had surrounded her. She had been introverted from a young age and had realized that to avoid the sucking mud that was her parents' marriage she would have to be self-reliant. And she had been, but had found very little satisfaction in her ability to cope. She was pretty, but not in the way that the boys immediately noticed, and those boys who might have taken an interest were trudging through the same maddening maze, looking for their own way out. There had been girlfriends, but no one with any substance, and by the time that she was in high school, she realized that popularity had its defined price. The loss of virginity in the dusty, sticky smell of a truck cab. Drunken revelry by the side of a still lake. The numbing and loose effect of the pills that were offered in a crumpled ball of tinfoil. The alternative was an isolated existence in the confines of a cramped bedroom with people embroiled in daily combat just beyond the thin walls.

She drove and looked out at the landscape she was passing and it felt as though it was peering back at her, its broad expanse accusatory and defensive. What had she expected of this place, this rural wasteland where time seemed oblivious of its own ticking hands? There were no fairy tales here. No breathtaking experiences that enlightened a young woman's perspective. These valleys were the soiled bed sheets of the mountain and the mountain knew only naked severity, paradoxically coaxing its inhabitants into a faithful reliance that pinned them on the land like mice with their necks in a spring-loaded trap. She, like everyone that she knew, had allowed this place to define her and even in her most private moments; she was unable to see past what was so obviously a dead end. And as she started up the side of the mountain road, she decided that solving these murders, finding her aunt's killer, would be her most significant contribution to her own well-being. This would be her opportunity to do away with vainly searching through an already picked-over, flea market memory. This would be her chance at making things new, and even if that chance was bridled with something sinister and hateful, it would serve a purpose and that alone was a small, good thing.

She was coming over the top of the mountain in the westbound lane, parallel to the rest stop on the eastern side of the interstate. The barrels and yellow tape were still in place and she started to look away when a blur of motion caught her eye. She glanced in the rearview mirror and slowed to a crawl and pulled into the grass median between the east and west-bound lanes. She sped up, moving through the median to avoid getting stuck in the mire caused by all the rain from the day before. She hit her lights, gave a quick glance to her right, saw the opening, and spun across onto the eastern lanes, then off the shoulder and into the grass lawn that was in front of the rest area building and picnic grounds. A man in what looked like a grey jumpsuit was walking through the parking lot and looked up at Sarah as she came toward him, lights on the top of the Caprice flashing and the engine heaving. The man stood still and Sarah pushed down hard on the brake and brought the vehicle to an abrupt stop. She threw open her door and drew her weapon and screamed at the man to put his hands in the air, which he did almost before he was ordered to do so. He was stocky and short, wearing the jumpsuit and work boots. He wore a red baseball cap on his head and he looked at Sarah with wide eyes and slightly parted lips.

"Who are you?" she yelled from behind the Caprice's door. The man moved his left hand slightly and pointed to his hat. Sarah squinted in the sunlight but could not read what was on the hat.

"Mercer Distribution. Coca-Cola delivery," the man said. "My truck," and he gestured with his head toward the entry ramp, "is down there. I stock the machines," and he gestured again with his head to indicate the vending machines behind him that were enclosed in a door-less kiosk. "Can I put my hands down?"

Sarah came around the door of the Caprice and approached the man slowly. He kept his hands up. When she was within a few feet she could see the logo on his hat and on a patch above his left breast. She looked down the parking lot and saw the delivery truck parked in front of the barricade. There was a dolly sitting next to the truck's side entry door. "You can put your hands down," Sarah said. "The crime scene tape and barrels didn't make it clear that this rest stop is closed?" The man toed the ground with his work boot and let out a nervous laugh.

"I have a lot of deliveries to make, officer," he said. "I didn't come through the barricade. I just walked in to see if the fella who works here would let me stock the machines. I wasn't trying to make any trouble."

"The man who worked here is dead," Sarah said. "We had multiple homicides up here yesterday." The Coca-Cola man looked up, his eyes startled.

"George?" he said. "George is dead?"

"Yes. Did you know him?" The man stood silently.

"No. Well yes, but not really. Just enough to talk every time I came to stock the machines. If the weather was nice, he'd come outside and stand there while I...why in God's name would anyone want to kill George?"

"That's a good question," Sarah said. He shook his head and looked toward the building.

"Jesus," he said. Sarah glanced down the parking lot at the delivery truck.

"Mind walking me down there so I can check out your identification and registration?"

"No," he said and started to move toward where the truck was parked, bulky and out of place, as if it had been abandoned in the empty lot. Sarah followed closely behind, holstering her weapon but leaving the leather strap unbuttoned. They were almost to the barricade when the man looked over his shoulder and spoke. "You might want to send someone out to hunt down that other fella." He continued to walk toward the truck, but Sarah stopped short, hand instinctively going to the gun.

"What other fella?"

"Fella I saw walking around in the woods. Seen him when I was starting up to the building. Another reason I thought it might be okay for me to go ahead and stock the machines today." He pointed at the woods beyond the fence line where she and Ethan had followed Herc the morning before. "There," he said. "Beyond that fence. I think I saw someone walking up there. Can't say..." Sarah raised a hand to stop him from speaking.

"How long have you been here?" she asked. The Coca-Cola man looked at his watch.

"Maybe fifteen minutes. Why?"

"How well did you see this man walking in the woods?"

"Not real well. Heard him more than I saw him, I guess," he said. "I just looked up and someone was there. I don't know if he saw me or not. He was on the other side of the fence. I thought he was after his dog or something like that." Then something changed in his face.

"Jesus, did you catch whoever killed those people?" Sarah was searching the woods, hand on her gun, her eyes carefully scanning the landscape looking for movement. Looking for anything that would indicate they were being watched.

"We are going to walk down to your truck together and secure it and then you are coming with me to the sheriff's department. You can call your boss from there." He looked at Sarah.

"Okay," he said and started toward the truck. Sarah followed, her gun drawn and pointed up. She moved forward, turning in slow circles, then walking backward, trying to monitor the woods, the building, and the picnic area. Traffic was picking up on the interstate and Sarah knew that she might be causing a spectacle walking through the parking lot with her gun drawn, and her instincts told her that it was unlikely that anyone would confront them in broad daylight, but she had also seen the violence that had descended upon this place just hours before and every sense in her body felt like stretched, protesting wire. The Coca-Cola man walked around the side of his truck and picked up the dolly and set it inside. Then he closed the side panel door and came back to the front of the truck and walked around to the driver-side door and climbed into the cab to get the keys. Sarah kept her eyes on the woods. Nothing was moving and that made her even more anxious. *Nothing*, she thought. No birds, or squirrels, or wind. Something had settled over the woods. The Coca-Cola man did not seem to feel it, but Sarah felt it as keenly as being pricked by a thorn.

"Ready," the Coca-Cola man said. Sarah motioned for him to walk back toward the Caprice and she followed behind him, looking to the woods and then to the building and then turning around to look back the way they had come.

The Coca-Cola man was getting nervous, but he was also cooperating, and watching him walk ahead of her back toward her car, she realized that none of them knew for certain that the homicides were in fact the work of a single person. She glanced back up into the woods and still saw nothing. The Coca-Cola man was maybe five feet ahead of her but was not looking over his shoulder, and Sarah now found that she was having difficulty paying attention to both the open expanse of the grounds behind the building that led up to the fence and the man she was escorting back to her vehicle. *It's nothing to do with him*, she thought. *You're alone*, her mind answered back. And then the man in front of her stopped abruptly and she felt her hand tighten on the grip of the gun.

"Officer," he said. She braced her feet.

"What is it?" she answered and waited for him to turn around. He was doing nothing with his hands, but the fact that he had stopped and not simply spoken over his shoulder was…

"I forgot my wallet," he said and now he did turn around and Sarah expected his eyes to be missing and his throat an accusing smile. He put his hands up, seeing that the gun was pointed at his chest.

"Whoa, whoa," he said, frantically. "I don't have to get my wallet. I just thought that I might need it." Sarah lowered the gun and tried not to look away to monitor the woods while he was facing her. She was certain from the expression he was wearing that attacking her was the last thing on his mind, but her nerves were fraying in real time.

"Go back for it," she said, and he walked past her then quickened his pace as he went down the parking lot to the truck. She watched him go, and then standing alone, gun drawn, the world around her seemed to fall away and she could see the old couple and the dog and someone charging out the front doors toward them, blood on his clothes, gaining speed. She shook her head and saw that the Coca-Cola man was climbing into the cab of the truck and then he came back up the rise waving the wallet so Sarah could see it.

"Got it," he said, coming even with her, a little out of breath. She nodded.

"Let's get to the car," she said and he took the lead again. Sarah opened the rear door of the Caprice when the sensation washed over her again.

Oh Sarah, he PLUCKEST! HE PLUCKEST! HE PLUCKEST!— and in that vacuum she was suddenly certain that someone was behind her. That someone had emerged after waiting for their opportunity to pounce, so taking her hand off the door of the Caprice, she spun around to look back at the building and the eerily quiet woods beyond and saw nothing but the squat structure, dull and empty in what should have been pleasant mountain sunlight. Instead the brightness highlighted the dull colors of the building and accentuated the stillness of everything that encroached and Sarah could feel herself back in the men's bathroom, looking out through the half-open window, smelling the stale piss and damp of the tiled surfaces. Alone with the bodies in the stall and the storm overhead.

"You okay?" the Coca-Cola man asked. Sarah, still holding the gun, turned to look at him.

"What?" she said.

"I said, are you okay?"

She put the gun in her holster and motioned for him to get in the back of the car. She glanced once more at the building and climbed behind the wheel.

CHAPTER 46

NORTON CONSIDERS

Brent Norton was listening to the Beatles on the aftermarket Alpine car stereo of his used Corolla.

The song was "Run for Your Life" which to Norton had always seemed wrong. The cheery, up-tempo rhythm, jaunty English voices, and then that sinister warning at the end that sounded more like murder than a pop song break-up. *Murder.* Norton knew plenty about that. He'd grown-up in a small South Georgia town outside of Atlanta, the son of a minister and a milquetoast mother who saw the world around her as the yawning mouth of Satan's deception, ready to swallow them all without a second thought. Norton had graduated high school and gone into the Marines and served time in combat as a medic. He saw enough to know that there were two kinds of people in the world: bad and worse. He wondered sometimes if his mother's cowering perspective might not have been the real truth behind humanity and the divine forces that oversaw its actions and fates. He'd taken his medic experience and gone to college in Atlanta and eventually down a path that took him into his profession. *Caring for the dead,* he often told people who asked. Norton had risen fast in Atlanta, caring for the city's urban deceased. Gun violence. Knives. Fires. Car wrecks and accidents that left bodies mangled to the point of being almost unrecognizable. He had seen and processed it all. And sitting in the gas station parking lot, sipping murky coffee and listening to The Beatles, he tried to recall anything that he had seen in Atlanta that rivaled the scene at Sheriff Edward's home.

He had been there since the woman's body was found the night before and he had just left the house in dire need of a cigarette and some distraction. Now, despite his years of experience and professionalism, he could not distance himself from the bedroom and the body of the woman whose eyes had been removed and throat cut. The killer had been meticulous in his work, not allowing anything onto the bed linens or the walls, the carpet, the bed posts. Nothing. They found soiled clothes and towels in the bathtub, the curtain pulled across in a meager attempt to hide the morbid items, or perhaps it had not been an attempt at all, but more of an admission of sorts. This *worse* person, this enraged person seemed to care very little for the conventional methods of concealing his crime. This person seemed motivated by a desire to send a message, and this motivation was exponentially more dangerous and was a stark departure from anything he had ever been a part of. It meant that whatever drove this person had an allegiance unto itself. Nothing more, nothing less, and despite what Norton knew to be an impossible coincidence—the murders at the rest area followed immediately by the murder of a sheriff's wife—finding the common thread was going to be almost impossible. Edwards had been removed from the scene soon after the crews had arrived. Two of his deputies had to hold him up through the front door, his big frame tottering between their shorter bodies. He had not put his arms around their shoulders and they had borne his weight by pushing their own shoulders against his sides like a vice. Norton had watched him carefully for any sign of a heart or panic attack. How the man had not lost his mind there and then was a miracle unto itself. *Shock*, Norton thought. Winchester had been a gift to him after his burn-out in Atlanta, and he was protective of his adopted home. He had hoped when he took the job that he would never again be tested in the way that the crime and mistreatment of people had tested him in the big city. But here he sat, listening to John and Paul harmonize, seeing in a neat but childish hand, across Edwards's bathroom mirror, its painted red letters flashing on and off: *And he who was seated on the throne said, Behold, I am making all things new.*

After the rest area, he had come home and poured a large Scotch and gone to the attic to rummage around in an old box of unpacked books until he found a poetry anthology with his last name written on the spine in smudged black marker. His pulse jumped when he found the Eliot poem in the table of contents and he had sat on the plywood floor of the attic, moving his lips as he read between sips of the scotch, using a finger to go line by line as he plodded his way through the dense and heavily metaphoric verse. None of it made much sense to him, but the words registered in their gravity and tone and he sensed the underlying themes of loss and impending remorse. The imagery, although benign on the surface, was heavy with menace and sorrow, and when he finally looked up from the book, his glass was empty and he had lost the better part of an hour. He stood and took the glass and the anthology back down the wobbly, pull-down attic stairs and into the small, unadorned kitchen where he poured another scotch that he knew would help him on his way to skipping dinner. He sat down at the kitchen table and read some more. The longer he studied the poem, the more the lines blurred between the killer and his need to leave behind the veiled messages scrawled in the victims' blood. There was no way to clearly piece it all together. The speaker in the poem seemed destitute, resigned to fate and forced to contend with the mundane elements of a predictably patterned life. But that seemed somehow out of character with the suspect he envisioned. He took a long drink from the glass and his head loosened. *Maybe it's not so literal as all that,* he thought. Like the Beatles song from earlier that day. Maybe the words sang well to him and so he landed on those phrases by... accident? No, not by accident. It was all too obscure to be accidental. It was intentional and he meant for whomever came after him to be both confused and threatened. Horrified. *And maybe,* he thought, *he was trying to tell us that he was not in control, that the murders were the result of something outside of his control and...*

He looked down at the table and the glass was again empty. He was getting up to pour another drink when they had called about Katherine Edwards. He left the house quickly, taking along the anthology in the car. He'd driven through the empty streets and down the quiet road that led to the Edwards home, and the scene he found there was incomparable to anything he had seen before, a controlled rage that in its still aftermath left all of them speechless.

Now, sitting in the Corolla, he sipped coffee from a Styrofoam cup and picked up a cigarette that was burning in the ashtray. The anthology was in his lap, but his mind was considering what had been left on Katherine Edwards' vanity mirror.

And he who is seated on the throne said, Behold, I am making all things new.

Norton did not have to research the origin of that. His mother had spoken to him about the book of Revelations throughout his childhood and he could spot its warnings and prophecies from a thousand yards away. This message made more sense, had more context to where they were and the people who lived and worked in the area. This was the Bible belt and nothing festered more efficiently in the minds of these people than the word of God. He sipped and grimaced at the cooling coffee. There was nothing distracted about the words on the Edwards' mirror: there would be more to come. Maybe not in Winchester and maybe not in the state, but you did not leave the promise of vengeful change smeared in an old woman's blood on her vanity mirror if you were calling it a day. That message said that you were just getting started . He pulled on the cigarette, not looking at the filter, and burned his lip with the red coal. He stubbed the butt out and opened the car door, dumping the remains of the coffee on the asphalt as he stood up. He looked around the lot and then went toward the building to the payphone. He dropped change in and dialed his office number. When his assistant answered, he asked her to find the number for Will Tibbits in Marion County. She asked if he wanted her to call him back somewhere with the number.

"No," Norton said. "I'll wait for it." She came back on the line a minute later and gave him the number. He hung up, repeating the number out loud until he could get more change into the phone and dial the number. The dispatcher in Marion County put him through to Tibbits, who picked up on the first ring.

"Tibbits."

"Will, this is Brent Norton in Winchester."

"Sweet Jesus, Norton. I just got word about Bill Edward's wife. What in God's name is going on over there? I'd be there already, but we had a tractor trailer go over on the highway and we've had to work the wreck all morning, plus we've got a department review every April and I'm behind, but the hell with that. How is Bill?"

"About like you'd expect," Norton said. "I had them take him over to the hospital."

"Awful," Tibbits said. "You need help up there?"

"I don't know," said Norton. "But the reason I called, Will, is that this poetry he left on the wall at the rest area, he left something on the wall at the Edwards home as well. This time it's from the Bible. Revelations. It was left on her mirror."

"Like the women's room," Tibbits said. "God almighty, did he…"

"Yes," Norton said. "He mutilated her." The line was quiet.

"Sheriff, you there?"

"Yes," Tibbits said. "Go ahead, Brent." Now Norton was quiet, then blurted out, "Sheriff, what did you say about your department review?"

"What?"

"A department review. You said that you have a department review every…"

"April," Tibbits finished.

"April," Norton said and then repeated it.

"Yeah, Brent, April. What of it? You're not making any sense."

"Give me a second," Norton said and left the phone, the receiver dangling from the silver cord, as he ran back to the car. He reached inside and took out the anthology and then went back to the phone and balanced the receiver between his cheek and his shoulder. He flipped to the Eliot poem and it suddenly clicked into place.

"April is the cruelest month," he said.

"Come again, Brent?"

"April," Norton said.

"Yes, April, as in this month. April as in the month before May."

"No," Norton shouted. "It's in the poem. The poem that was in the rest area. The poem begins with 'April is the cruelest month.' The month of the crucifixion and Jesus rising from the tomb. And then the words from Revelations. He's warning us, Will. He's warning us that…"

"There's more," Tibbits breathed. "Goddammit, Brent."

Norton looked at the anthology in his hands. *Was this right? Was that really right?* Tibbits was quiet on the other end and Norton wondered if any of this meant anything to the old sheriff. It was a stretch for anyone to believe that it all had a cohesive meaning. And more importantly, did it even matter or was it a distraction that they could not afford to chase?

"I don't know about any of this, Brent," Tibbits said "I'm not saying that you're wrong, as crazy as all of it sounds. I don't know enough about all of that kind of thing. I'm a county sheriff trying to keep an impoverished county in line. That's speeding tickets, stray livestock, and your occasional fight that escalates into an accidental manslaughter case. What I do know is that we don't have anyone in custody and more bodies to bury. And if it was a poem or some deranged interpretation of the Bible that set this guy off, I'm going to be honest and tell you that I really don't give a shit. But if there's evidence to be found in what you are pointing out, and it helps catch this son-of-a-bitch, then I need to point you in the direction of someone who knows more about mentally ill people than I do." Norton nodded as Tibbits spoke, grateful his novice detective work had not been dismissed altogether.

"Hold the line," Tibbits said.

Norton reached into his shirt pocket for his cigarettes and realized that he had left them in the car. He was about to go back for them when Tibbits returned to the line.

"There's a guy I went to high school with who's in the state feds office in Nashville," he began. "His name is Jordan Ellis and he works in a special crime division up there. He's up to speed on things like this and I think it would be worth it for you to give him a call and tell him everything that you just told me. Maybe it helps and maybe it don't, but I'm ready to explore every option if it leads to an arrest and a conviction for the man who killed Bill Edwards' wife. Not to mention those poor bastards that stopped to piss at a rest stop. You got a pen to write down this number?" Norton pulled a topless ball point from his pants pocket and took the number down on the palm of his hand. He read the number back. Tibbits gave a long sigh.

"Tell the receptionist up there that I told you to call Jordan. Otherwise you'll never get a call back. They're swamped and it usually takes a personal connection to get anything done. Way it goes I guess when you've got people like this guy running around loose."

"Got it," Norton said. "Thank you."

"Don't mention it," Tibbits said. "You tell Bill Edwards when you see him that my wife and I will be praying for him and that if he needs anything at all, he knows all he has to do is call me."

"All right," Norton said.

"Your man Lee got what he needs?"

"It happened so fast, but I think we have it under control. Least for now."

"Okay then," Tibbits said and the line went dead.

Norton stood holding the receiver, listening to the insect-like buzz, realizing that his role in all of this had grown in the course of a phone call. *My God, a coroner playing detective,* he thought. He went back to his Corolla and lit another cigarette, leaning against the driver's side door. He looked through the large window of the store and watched the clerk roll her mop and bucket across the entryway, down an aisle and out of sight. And for a reason he did not understand, her sudden disappearance made him feel cold and very much alone.

CHAPTER 47

EDWARDS RECOVERING

S heriff Bill Edwards sat with his long legs outstretched on a bank
of worn red vinyl chairs in the Winchester Memorial Hospital.
He was staring straight ahead at a wall where there was a framed
photograph of a farm field at dawn. The colors coming over the horizon were a burnt orange and there was a tree without leaves in the
foreground, backlit by the rising sun. The tree's limbs were skeletal and
the light was coming through the gaps in bursts of harsh, messy light
from the delayed aperture. The location could have been anywhere in
the county, but Edwards thought it looked like it was shot somewhere
on the mountain where the light was always different than it was in the
valley below. His face was composed in what might have seemed like
concentration to a passerby, but in reality was an expression of complete
solitude and incomprehension.

Flip and Ethan had taken him from the house to the hospital for
reasons that he understood at face value but seemed confusing with
further introspection. He was not sick. It was his wife. It was Kat that
had needed medical attention and he could not work things out in his
head and the images from the last twenty-four hours were playing over
and over in his mind like he was leafing through one of the scrapbooks
collecting dust in the living room, turning each page with a renewed
determination as if he were searching for a clue or clarification in the
background of each picture, stiff glue dried around some of the edges

of the printed pictures like dried snot. They had brought him into the hospital and the deputies had spoken to the registration nurse and she had guided them down one of the beige corridors and asked them to wait. Then a doctor he did not know had come down the same corridor and addressed the deputies and they had talked like he was not there and now he realized, sitting with his legs outstretched and a desire to smoke that had not been this strong in the eleven years since he quit, that he recalled nothing meaningful of their conversation and he had acted much in the way that accident victims behaved after a wreck, stunned and blinking rapidly to regain both a literal and mental focus. He could clearly recall the conversation with Tibbits. He could recall the conversation with Renee and Sarah, and the admonishment he had given Jed in the driveway. These things, despite their context, seemed both mundane and unimportant and he tried to dismiss them but they were part of the turning scrapbook. He could recall the drive back to Winchester and pushing the car through the turns and the expanse of the mountain swimming beside him over the guardrail and out into the emptiness that hung over the slope like a clear sea above a forest floor. He thought he remembered his lights reflecting in the front windows and then he found himself lost inside of his own home which smelled both familiar and vaguely strange. There had been the patio door open that had set off the nerves in his mind and limbs and then the slow creep down the hall, sticking his head into the room to see what was there, heat and an undefined apprehension moving through his chest in waves that caused his breath to be shallow and one hitch away from uncooperative and panic-stricken. Then everything suddenly sped up and the night's images burst in his mind as if he were pinching a deck of cards between his thumb and fingers, squeezing and sending them flying in all directions with a loud snapping sound. He lightly touched his forehead and looked away from the picture on the wall and a voice from somewhere far away, an echo from inside a cave, maybe, spoke:

52 pick-up Bill? Billy. Billy, old. 52...

He on the throne. He is anew

This card here. This card that you are forbidden to see. A suicide king. His throne burnished

Behold, Bill. Behold Sheriff.

See things

A third who seeks you
A shadow anew. I am the shadow who sits upon the throne. I am
The one who Pluckest
Those were. Hers were
Oh Lord, Oh Lord, Oh Lord, Oh Lord, Oh Lord, Oh Lord, Oh Lord,
Oh Lord, Oh Lord
How

He heard footsteps in the hallway and pulled his legs in and sat up straight in the chair. The doctor was moving briskly toward him. He had a clipboard in his hand and seemed very young to Edwards. Khakis. Soft-soled shoes. White coat and tie beneath. He studied whatever was on the clipboard before he reached the sheriff, and when he got closer he stopped and looked down at the large man sitting in the chair.

"Everything checks out, Sheriff Edwards," he said. "Blood pressure and heart rate are normal. You are responsive although that may have changed after taking the sedative."

"I don't remember taking any sedative," Edwards said, looking up at the doctor. He felt a need to be assertive despite his mind's argument to remain docile and redolent. The doctor was speaking but was also observing. From experience he knew they were going through a rehearsed protocol.

"No, you probably wouldn't," the doctor said. "When they brought you in you were pretty much in a state of shock. We administered the sedative in case you came out of that state and…"

"And what," Edwards said, looking away. "Realized that my wife was dead?"

"Yes sir," the doctor said. "No offense, but you are not a young man and we wanted to take some precautions, considering…"

"Considering," Edwards said. His tone was even but he found himself anticipating the questions and was trying not to appear dismissive, failing.

"The nature of the crime," the doctor said. "Age concern or no age concern, anyone coming out of that is going to need help." Edwards nodded. He glanced back at the picture on the wall. He could see the doctor in his peripheral vision, saw him anxious and shifting his feet, eager to be moving on.

"Where are the deputies that brought me here?" Edwards said.

"I don't know, Sheriff," the doctor said. "I can check for you at the nurse's station."

"No," Edwards said. "Am I free to go?"

"You are," the doctor said. "But I would not recommend going back to work."

"And where would you recommend that I go?" Edwards said.

"Oh," the doctor said, looking down at his clipboard. "I'm sorry Sheriff Edwards. I did not even think about…"

Edwards pushed himself out of the chair with a grunt and walked toward the doctor. He reached a hand out and touched the physician's shoulder and nodded at him in thanks.

"We have a social worker on staff," the doctor offered up quickly. "You are physically fine, but if you need something further. You know, after." Edwards looked at the young man and felt an old sensation picking around his mind like a bird darting its beak through the remnants of a roadside carcass. He could not be sure if it was driven by whatever they had given him or if it was the product of a taxed conscience or mounting temper that had sent a chair skidding across his kitchen floor all those years ago.

"I'll check with the nurse's station," he said. "Thank you." The doctor nodded and stiffly moved around the sheriff and went down the hallway, flipping pages on the clipboard as he walked, white coat trailing behind him. Edwards turned and went the other direction toward the nurse's station and the admission desk. His head felt as if it were beginning to clear and moving around the hospital where he had been many times before was reassuring in its familiarity. He stopped at the desk and recognized the nurse working there. She looked to be about Sarah's age and he thought he knew her name but could not be sure. She was pretty in her uniform, with blond hair and expressive brown eyes. She smiled at Edwards when he asked to use her phone to call the station. She dialed the number for him and handed the receiver over the countertop, the curled cord making a rubber scraping sound as the sheriff stretched it taut and turned his back on the nurse.

"Winchester sheriff's department."

"Ethan?"

"Yes, this is Ethan. Sheriff?"

"Yes, it's me."

"Sheriff, you okay? We wanted to stay with you at the hospital but Flip said that you would want us back at work. You okay? Sheriff—"

"Ethan," Edwards said, trying to keep his voice even. "Have they wrapped up the crime scene at my house?"

"Yes sir, I believe so."

"Okay," Edwards said. "I want everyone back at the office as soon as possible."

"Yes sir," Ethan said. "Sheriff?"

"Yes Ethan."

"Sarah brought some guy in. Works for Coca-Cola."

"What for?" Edwards asked.

"Says he thinks he saw someone in the woods near the rest area this morning."

"Send a car for me, Ethan," Edwards said and hung up. He thanked the nurse and went around the registration desk and down another short hall toward the hospital entrance. He walked through an automated door and onto the drop-off sidewalk. Despite the sun, he could feel something wet and cold in the air and he pushed his hands into his pockets to wait on the car. Across the parking lot and the adjacent field he could see the bulky, sprawling form of the mountain. It was just after noon and despite the hint of spring warmth earlier in the day, clouds were beginning to move in and pile up, blocking out the light in a rumpled grey canopy that would bring rain by late in the day. Edwards looked away toward the road coming into the hospital. The sheriff's station was very close and it was not long before he thought he saw the flashing lights of one of the cruisers coming fast with no siren sound. Edwards turned and looked back through the doors of the hospital. The waiting room was all but empty except for a group of nurses who were standing together and laughing about something one of them had said. Edwards felt an urge to smile but swallowed it.

Beyond the cluster of nurses, standing in the second hallway entrance, clothed in a nightgown that he had given her for Christmas, was Kat. Her body lacked any dimension, and her arms were extended out to both sides in the same manner that she had taken when she had asked him to help her undress during a particularly bad spell. *Just like you found me, Billy. Just the same.* Her head was cocked to one side, tipped sadly on her shoulder. Her face was hidden by her tangled hair and he thought he could see her breath puffing up stray strands in light pulses like a steady breeze moving the new, vulnerable growth of a sapling. Edwards closed his eyes against the vision. He wanted to turn and watch the patrol car pull into the pick-up lane and be away from there. He held his breath and finally did turn, eyes still tightly shut, muted patterns moving with blotting and stabbing waves beneath his lids. He shuffled slowly in a circle, feeling what he guessed was the sedative affecting his balance and creating a heavy feeling in his feet and legs, slight nausea. When he was certain that he had reversed away from the hospital, he let out his breath and opened his eyes and she was there, immediately in front of him, hair pulled away from her pale, eyeless face. Blood was smeared around the empty sockets like a reckless or drunken application of makeup. Her head was still resting on her shoulder in supplication. Then she raised it to center, looking squarely at him, offering a wide grin, teeth clean and bright in contrast to the pale skin and murderous make-up application.

Why did you leave me at home, Billy? it hissed.

Why did you leave me all alone?

Bill Edwards shook and stammered. The world around him was moving out of focus. The parking lot and the overhang from the hospital entrance, the dying shrubs along the side of the building, the mountain with its gathering storm.

Why did you leave me at home, Billy? Why did you leave me alone? It was singing the words, emphasizing the rhyme. *Home, Home, Alone, Alone...*

Ethan pulled the cruiser into the hospital entrance and saw his boss standing still and staring out at the field next to the parking lot. He pulled the car alongside Edwards and put the window down, looking up into the man's expressionless face. He had to call his name several times before Edwards shook his head and made eye contact with him.

"Ethan," he said, his vision and recognition dull and vague.

"Yes, sir?"

"Sheriff?"

"Yes," Edwards said, looking back to the field trying to regain focus.

"You want to get in? I've got everyone back at the station. Tibbits sent a cruiser over from Marion County to watch your house while we're meeting. He called this morning and said he'd given Brent Norton the number of the State FBI. Said that…"

"Ethan," Edwards said, still looking away, over the top of the cruiser. "Do you smoke?"

"Um. No sir, Sheriff."

"Who does?" Edwards asked and walked around to get into the passenger seat.

When Edwards walked into the front room of the sheriff's office he could smell brewing coffee and it gave him the slightest of comforts. No one was behind the front desk, and he could hear the deputies talking in the back room. What should have felt like a familiar space now felt oddly disorienting. The cheap faux leather chairs, the dingy wall color, the tattered mat inside the door, the smell of the trapped air and the stained drop ceiling tiles, all of this two days before had made no impression on him. Now it was as if he entered a place he had never seen and he paused just inside the door, wondering if he was making a mistake trying to lead a half-assed expedition that could easily be disastrous. *Not an expedition*, he thought. *A manhunt.* Ethan went ahead of him and into the back room. He was gone just a minute and then returned with a pack of cigarettes in his hand and he walked over to Edwards and extended the pack.

"They're Flip's," he said. "He told me to tell you to take all you want." Edwards looked down at the cigarettes and took them. He pulled one free and looked at Ethan who looked back at him with a confused expression on his face.

"Got a light?"

"Oh. Right." He turned and Edwards stopped him.

"Never mind for now," he said. "Let's head back there and get started." Ethan turned and left the room and Edwards followed him, straightening his posture and trying to put together how he wanted to start. He came through the door and they were waiting for him. Their heads came up as he stepped further into the cramped room and Edwards felt their tension as sharply as if he had placed an unsuspected hand under a stream of scalding tap water. He met each of their faces: Sarah, Flip, Ethan, and Rhonda. Rhonda in particular looked truly unsettled. He had half expected her to quit, considering her reluctant constitution, but she had managed to pull her weight and fill-in while they had all been scattered and scrambling over the last forty-eight hours. He offered her a smile of thanks, which she returned by glancing in another direction. Flip had been leaning against the wall and he pushed off and came across the room.

"Sheriff," he said. Sarah stood up and watched. Edwards looked at Flip and then over to Sarah, then back to Flip.

"Flip," Edwards said and squared to meet him.

"Sheriff," Flip began but Edwards stretched out a hand.

"I know what you are going to say, Flip, and I can tell you right now that I appreciate each and every one of you for your commitment under what is...what is—" He lost the thread.

Why did you leave me?

Oh Bill, why. Why when you knew that...

They were looking at him and he suddenly felt the urge to turn around and walk back out the door and keep walking until his legs snapped and he fell over in an exhausted heap, waiting for what came next. He had no idea what came next, but that was beside the point. Kat was dead. Kat was murdered. Kat was... He felt the cigarettes in his pants pocket and he could not recall how they got there, although he knew their shape by touch. He pulled them out and looked at the design and the lettering. Then he remembered that he had taken one out already and placed it in his breast pocket. He took a step toward Flip and handed him the pack. Then he pulled the cigarette from his breast pocket and looked again at Flip and gestured with the cigarette hand. Flip understood and reached into his own pocket and came out with a red plastic lighter. He spun the wheel and the flame came alive. Edwards tilted his head to one side and Flip extended the lighter. The sheriff took a long pull and let it out in a gust.

"Ethan," he said. "Would you mind pouring me a cup of that coffee and seeing if there is an ashtray in one of those cupboards?"

CHAPTER 48

THE BRIEFING

Herc was sitting on the floor next to Sarah, paws extended, his head up and alert. They brought him in from his kennel when they heard him whining. Rhonda read in a monotone voice and Edwards watched her out of the corner of his eye. The others sat in their own chairs, elbows on their knees, head bowed as if in prayer before a church supper.

"Victims report," she said and let out an audible breath. "Calvin and Annie Tremble. Ages seventy-six and seventy-three, respectively. From Toronto, Canada. On their way to Fort Myers, Florida. Their daughter is Melissa. She lives in Lakeland, Florida. Jose Martinez. Age thirty-four. Contractor. No family here in the US. Plates on the truck were registered to a farmer in Tracy City. Farmer's last name is Maddox. Martinez was heading into work and never showed up." Rhonda took another deep breath.

"You're doing great, Rhonda," Edwards said. She looked up from the papers and Edwards could tell that she was anxious, wanted to be anywhere but the small, tight room that was in dire need of a ceiling fan.

"George Cecil. Managed the rest area. Age 53. We're waiting on his background from the state park department. No next of kin around here. He had been at that location going on seven years." Edwards nodded and looked around the room to his deputies. He could see that Sarah was making every effort to maintain eye contact with him.

"Go ahead, Rhonda," Edwards said. "What else have you got?" Rhonda lifted the top page and placed it in the back of the stack.

"Found prints on the murder weapon," she said. "Nothing that we can match with our files, least not yet. Same prints were all over the restroom and the rear lobby doors. Says they had a hard time identifying those considering how many people come through there on any given day. Without the weapon we'd have nothing to go on at all."

"What about the bodies?" Sarah said. Rhonda looked up and glanced at Edwards before looking back at Sarah.

"Doesn't say anything about prints on the bodies, but I can call over to Marion County and see if they made a mistake."

"No," Edwards said and grimaced. He looked over at Flip who was staring into the room with a perplexed, and what the sheriff imagined was also a hungover, expression. Ethan stood and went to the coffee machine and looked around at the group to see if anyone needed anything. Edwards nodded at Rhonda, signaling her to continue.

"The eyes in the women's room belonged to Mr. Cecil," she said and Edwards could see that if she was going to break, now would be the time. She was a short woman, stocky and heavy set. He had hired her part-time several years before when they had needed help with the phones and other office duties. He thought that he remembered her telling him that she held another part-time job at the county library where she sometimes worked in the little alcove known as the "Kid's Korner." *Hadn't Kat volunteered for that,* he thought. He could see his wife perched on a small stool reading in an animated voice to a pack of kids and he wondered if that had ever given her pause about children of her own. *Their own.*

Oh Billy

If only you had not...

Edwards stood quickly and walked over and touched Rhonda's shoulder and she looked up at him with a declaration in her gaze that he knew was a silent notification that her days working in the sheriff's office were soon to be over.

"Thank you," Edwards said and took the papers from her hand, which she gave up without hesitation.

"I think it is safe to say that what happened on the mountain," he paused, ran a hand through his hair. "I think it is safe to say that what happened at the rest area and what happened last night here in Winchester with…" His throat tightened, the vision of his wife from the nurse's station floating in front of him. *It's not real,* he thought, inadvertently rolling the papers that accounted for the dead. *That's not my wife. That's not…*

"What happened in Winchester is probably the work of the same person." Pushing out the sentence drained the color in his face, but he shoved the grotesque vision and the rising panic down into a dark place.

"And we might have a witness," Sarah said, standing up and looking at her uncle.

"How's that?" Edwards asked.

"Coca-Cola delivery," Sarah said. "On my way here," she said. "I saw him in the parking lot of the rest stop. He was trying to fill the vending machines."

"Is he clean?" Edwards asked.

"Yeah, he checks out so far," Sarah said. "We let him go home about an hour before you and Ethan got here. He knows not to go anywhere. I'm not sure how useful he is going to be, but he saw someone in the woods this morning."

"You let him go?" Flip said without disguising his anger.

"He was clean, Flip," Sarah said although having said out loud that they let their sole witness go home sounded ridiculous to her now.

"Where," Edwards said, ignoring Flip although he too knew how poor the decision had been, but before Sarah could answer him a light knock interrupted the conversation and they all looked at once to see Brent Norton standing in the doorway. He looked as bad as they did, eyes vacant and fatigued, unshaven, clothes wrinkled. Sarah thought he might be wearing the same shirt that she had seen him in the day before when they were sitting in his car, she holding the dog and Norton offering her a cigarette. Edwards was standing with his back to Norton and he turned around. The two men were about the same height and they were exchanging a knowing look that under other circumstances might have appeared adversarial. Norton crossed the room and extended his hand.

"Sheriff Edwards," he said. "I won't even try to pretend to understand how you must feel right now." Edwards took his hand and shook it firmly.

"And I have not had time to thank you properly for everything that you have done in the last twenty-four hours. We were just going through the victim reports and trying to put some of the pieces together."

"I thought that's what you might be doing, although as a medical professional I'm not sure that I approve of you being here given everything that..."

"I understand," Edwards said. "I've had a lot of people expressing their concern recently. This is something that impacts all of us and I believe that we are better off together than apart right now."

"I would agree with that," Norton said, looking at Sarah. "I've got some information that I think might be of use if you have some time for me to sit in. Do you mind?"

"Seeing that we're all trying to figure out where to start, I'd be happy to hear anything that you have to say. Have a seat." Edwards turned back toward the room, and Norton found a chair.

"Rhonda, would you give this delivery guy a phone call and tell him that we'd like to see him back here as soon as possible?" Rhonda nodded and left the room. Norton started to speak again but Edwards held out a passive hand to cut him off. "Let's wait till she's back, if you would. I want to make sure she can get ahold of this fella..."

"Lucas," Sarah said. "Don Lucas."

"Right," Edwards said. "Mr. Lucas is just about our only witness at this point and I want to make sure that he doesn't take it into his head to get back out on the road making deliveries." They waited in silence and soon Rhonda returned.

"Said he'll be here in thirty minutes or less," she said. "Should I wait for him up front?"

"If you'd like," Edwards said. She nodded and went out. "Okay, assuming that a Coca-Cola delivery guy is our best lead, why don't you go ahead and share whatever it is that you have to share, Mr. Norton. And let me say again that I appreciate your initiative." Norton stood from where he had been seated. He looked tired and far removed from his official duties. After being recognized, he paused and looked at the group assembled as if he was having second thoughts about moving forward.

"Thank you, Sheriff," he said. "But for what I'm about to discuss with you, your appreciation should go to Sheriff Tibbits over in Marion

County. He's put me in touch with a gentleman named Jordan Ellis. Ellis works at the State TBI office in Nashville. Apparently Ellis and Sheriff Tibbits played football together in school and have remained friends. It's the reason that I was able to get through as quickly as I did."

"And what did this Ellis fella have to say?" This had come from Flip, and they all looked in his direction. Edwards watched his deputy's knee bouncing freely and he recognized the impatience that often governed Flip's character. He was a good deputy and there was no one Edwards would rather have covering his back in the field, but his impatience got him in trouble more often than not and Edwards caught his eye and motioned for him to slow down and listen.

"Quite a lot," Norton said, not seeming to mind the intrusion. "There are a lot of layers at the TBI, and within those layers, a lot of specialization and expertise. Ellis specializes in serial homicide."

"What kind of homicide?" Ethan said.

"Serial," Norton answered. "Multiple."

"You mean serial killers?"

"I do," Norton said. "And other related crimes. Rapists, arsonists, bank robbers, cult activity—offenders who have suffered psychological breaks. He works with the bureau's profiling division, assisting law enforcement with understanding the type of person they are actually trying to catch. That's an oversimplification of their work, but I'm sure that you are more interested in what he had to say about our situation."

"Are you saying he might know who we are after?" Sarah said.

"No," Norton said. "Not exactly. But he can help determine the type of person that we are after beyond the obvious things that we already know." Flip grunted and Edwards gave him a warning glance.

"Sorry, Sheriff," Flip said. "It's just that I don't see how waiting on someone a hundred miles from here to come up with a—what did you call it—a 'profile' is much good to us sitting here. We should be out hunting this guy right now."

"Jesus, Flip," Ethan said. "It ain't always about hunting."

"Oh yeah," Flip said. "And what would you call it?"

"Stop," Edwards said and looked at Ethan. "You're both right. But first we are going to hear Mr. Norton out and the two of you are going to keep your mouths shut while he's talking. That clear?" They both nodded their heads.

"Ellis believes that the behavioral pattern of the perpetrator indicates that this individual is not fully cognizant of the meaning or the reasons for his actions," Norton said. "Anecdotally, he compared it to owning and loving a dog and then one day, for no good reason, it bites you standing in the kitchen. You don't know why the dog bit until it's put down and the vet tells you the animal was rabid, the rabies not being the dog's fault but nonetheless, a driving factor in turning something controlled and predictable into something that is volatile and violent." Norton looked at his small audience and realized that he was sorting things out in his own head as much as he was informing them. "Most importantly, Ellis said that based on what we know now, there's a ninety-nine percent chance he will do it again." They were all quiet after this.

"Sheriff, you think I can get a drink of water?" Norton said. Ethan got up slowly from his chair and walked over to the coffee pot and pulled out a mug from a battered and squeaking cabinet, rinsed it absently, filled it with tap water, and brought it to Norton, who thanked him and drank most of it before placing the mug on the edge of a nearby desk.

"I have a tape of our conversation I want you to hear," Norton said. "It's better than me trying to fill in all of the gaps. The quality's not great. I typically use this for dictation and I'm the only one who listens to it play back. But I think it will do. Okay if I play it now?"

"Go ahead," Edwards said. Norton took a small cassette recorder from his jacket pocket and placed it on the desk next to the mug, then he depressed the play button. The tape rolled and made a low background buzz, but the conversation was clear enough for them all to follow once it started.

Agent Ellis, I'm taping our conversation if you don't mind?

Why would you need to do that?

Because I want to play this for Sheriff Edwards when he gets back to the station and I would prefer he heard everything directly from you rather than me trying to get it right.

No, I don't mind.

Okay, thank you. Go ahead please.

All right. Hello Sheriff. To begin with, we already know about the murders at the rest stop on the mountain down there, and Mr. Norton has also made me aware that this has become personal for you as indicated by the painful loss of your wife. My sincere condolences to you and your family. We plan on helping you any way that we can, as soon as we can. What you probably don't know is that we think this guy has killed at least four more people before he got to you, three of them cops, and another a civilian. The cop that we found was in his cruiser at the side of a west bound interstate ramp in Adan Village. The murder weapon was undoubtedly a knife and we think that the actual killing took place outside the car and that his body was then put back in the car to be found. Not certain why the killer would have gone to that trouble, but he did. Two of the stab wounds, one in each eye, appear to be post-mortem. The other two cops went missing several weeks before. They had gone up into the hills on a drug trafficking tip and no one ever saw them again. They had identified a person of interest living up there, but when they went to question him about the disappearance, he was nowhere to be found. We can't tie it all together definitively but based on the books and other things in that cabin, we think our guy may have been living there and probably killed whomever they were looking for and then walked out. Extended theory being that the cop by the interstate may have stopped to question him and lost his life as a result.

Truth is, we've been playing catch-up with this guy the whole time and the communication between law enforcement in rural communities is poor at best. And unfortunately, by the time something like this lands on my desk, a lot of terrible things have already occurred.

So how did you know about . . .

Tibbits. He called me after he left the rest area scene and we started putting things together. We had not had time to reach out to Winchester because we were mopping up connected murders further down the interstate. It's a fucking mess you've got down there. Tibbits says that he has his guys looking all over the highway in Marion and State Police is obviously aware, but I doubt seriously you are going to pick this guy up thumbing a ride. He's only coming out of hiding when the urge forces him. He's a predator. He'll stay out of sight until he strikes.

How do you know that?

Because he's not motivated by the things that typically lead to a homicide. Not money. Not sex. Not domestic violence. Something is driving him that he is not in control of.

So he's mentally ill?

Probably. Or traumatized by something that happened in his past. Most of the time there is something that begins the cycle. Abuse, broken home, molestation, etc. He's compensating and behaving in response to impulses that are stronger than his rationale and distinction between right and wrong. He's an extremely dangerous person mainly because his motivations are unclear and capricious.

So now?

We got the report on the weapon from Marion forensics but because the prints on that weapon are not in the system there's no way to tie the murders together aside from their nature so we're blind here. You'll pardon the expression. The victims are essentially unrelated, meaning their only commonality is where and how they were killed, not why they were chosen. And, you are talking about searching for someone among thousands and thousands of acres of unpopulated, wooded countryside. Hell some of the people living there probably didn't have indoor plumbing up until ten years ago. As I said earlier, the cabin they came across looking for those two detectives was full of books and journals and that likely accounts for the notes our guy at the other scenes left behind, unless it's one crazy coincidence, although as you and I both know, coincidence is not a word that usually applies in our line of work. But that cabin belonged to a man named Terrell Hicks, and if the suspect was living there with him, no one has any idea who he was or what he even looks like. This Terrell fella is missing too, and they are trying to dig up some background on him, but from what I understand he was some kind of recluse... and older. Never caused any trouble, least not that he was convicted for. If our guy was there, we have no real way of knowing for how long and in what capacity, or how or if he relates to Hicks.

So nothing. We've got nothing.

Well, from our perspective we have what we need to begin building a profile. But that's not a lot of comfort for your people and the other law enforcement agencies working this. At least we are all aware of it now and while it's not much, it's a start.

Okay, anything else while I have you?

Yes. If the Winchester Sheriff's Department decides to go looking for this guy within their jurisdiction, they need to understand that he is not someone who can be talked to. He's not doing this of his own volition and that makes for a very unsteady individual. He is not going to hesitate to use violence. He's not going to differentiate between cops and citizens. He's making some kind of statement that he believes in more than anything else and he's going to make that point until he is physically stopped. It should go without saying that any engagement with this person should be considered life threatening. If he has moved on, hopefully we can build a strong enough profile that we can catch him out in the open and unaware. Unfortunately, time is what we need and time is what we are shortest on.

Thank you, Jordan.

You bet. But Listen…

Go ahead

I know everyone down there wants to catch this guy. Can't blame them for that and seeing how personal this is, not sure I can even make an argument that would stick. But at the risk of sounding like a condescending asshole, none of you are equipped for this. You've got a sheriff's department with severely limited resources and even less experience with violent crimes like these. The fact that you as the County Coroner are leading what—and you'll forgive me once again here—is already a very sloppy investi—

Norton turned off the tape and looked at Edwards apologetically.

"Sheriff, you want a break?"

Edwards had listened to the recording with what he had hoped was an objective and professional demeanor, but now he could feel his composure cracking and despite not hearing how Jordan was going to finish that last sentence, he knew what the message would be and he knew that the man was right. Not only was he right from a logistical sense, but he was right that they were already in over their heads. And the tide was still rising. "I'm okay," he said to Norton. Then he looked at the one man in his department who came closest to being up to the task. "Can I have another cigarette, Flip?" Flip crossed to where Edwards sat, took out a cigarette, and handed it over.

"This means we can smoke inside?" he asked.

"No," Edwards said. "But you can today. Go ahead, Brent. I'm sorry to interrupt."

"I don't have a whole lot more to offer," Norton said. "The conversation was helpful and informative, but I'm not sure that it carries us that much farther down the road. Honestly, Sheriff, what happens next is really up to you."

Edwards drew on the cigarette and looked across the room at Sarah. He was searching her face for any indication of what she thought he ought to do next. Her opinion meant more to him than the others. Sarah met his eyes and then quickly looked away. He could tell that her mind was on Katherine and he had to force himself to turn away from her, had to force back the urge to turn away from all of it—being sheriff and all of the responsibilities that came with the position. What had Ellis said: *It should go without saying that any engagement with this person should be considered life threatening.* And the warning was not an empty or generic threat. It had teeth and Edwards knew it.

"We're a small-town department," he finally said. "We deal with small-town issues and we're pretty good at what we do. This is something else entirely."

"But," Flip began.

"Let me finish, Flip. And while this is probably beyond our means, we have an accountability to this community we serve and we have an accountability to the victims. All the victims. It would be easier to wait, hope that this son-of-a-bitch moves on, and let other people pick up the pieces. But you all heard what he said, and I'm not inclined to pass the buck on this so some other family has to deal with a butchered loved one. I don't think that any of you want that on your conscience either. I know that I don't." He looked around the little room at his deputies and Norton who was also smoking and looking at him with real consideration. The air was thick with all of their exhalations and he remembered why he had quit all those years back.

"So what are we going to do?" Flip said.

"We're going to try and find him," Sarah said and offered her uncle a thin smile that reminded him of when she was a little girl, and it occurred to him that it was rare for Sarah to smile, even then when things were somewhat stable. There was always a heavy reluctance in the way that she carried herself and smiling was not something that came to her naturally. *I'm sorry,* he thought. *We should have done more for you and your brother. We could have done more.*

"But where would we even start?" Ethan asked, his voice hesitant.

"At the rest area," Sarah said, and she could see the old couple on the ramp unfolding in her vision. The dark little building with the faint light from the overturned lamp pulling long shadows in the lobby. The small dog moving about in the grass, shivering and terrified, a current moving through Sarah's limbs as she approached with the cold shotgun pointing forward, her shallow breath and concentrating face and the weight of the looming fog, air moving through the open window inside the men's room, George's cleaning supplies leaning innocently, purposefully in the corner.

"There's something else," Norton said. "I don't know any of this to be fact, but I think that there is more purpose to these killings than we understand. I don't know much about the murders before he got to us. Those do seem arbitrary and circumstantial. But here, they seem to be more deliberate. And the fact that Mrs. Edwards was targeted in and of itself seems far too coincidental. It's almost as if he used the rest area to stage a distraction." He looked to Edwards, who was peering at him intently. "I don't know why I bring this up," he said. "It's not enlightening, I know. But I can't shake the thought and since we are all in this together, I felt like I needed to share it." Norton wanted to pace. Something like anger was pushing an arc in his thinking. Everything seemed to be moving way too fast. His conversation with Ellis that morning had left him with a sour churning in his stomach. As the man talked he kept seeing the faces and torn necks of the victims at the rest stop. The dead black marble eyes of the deer head. The outspread arms of Katherine Edwards lashed to the bedposts, her head drooping onto her chest. He had seen so many things over the course of his career, had learned early on to force impulses back down and out of site. Had controlled urges to retch by poking mint after mint into his mouth until he had sores on his tongue. This though, this was somehow different in a way that he could not, did not, want to understand. The deliberate nature of the messages, their veiled metaphoric meaning and foreboding menace. These people in the room with him now, woefully unequipped to deal with the ravenous nature of whatever was out there waiting. Planned or not planned, this person, this id controlling its human form, was the embodiment of a raw and anguished hatred that Norton somehow knew would only ratchet up its need for bloodier resolutions, perpetuating itself like a virus that knew only how to consume and consume until nothing was left.

"So you think there was a motive?" Edwards said.

"I don't know," Norton said and dropped his cigarette into the empty mug. "I'm not a cop. I'm a coroner, but I have been around enough homicide cases to learn that most people, after the fact, are horrified at what they have done. They temporarily lost control of themselves and when the moment has passed they instantly regret their actions and even feel the need to be punished It's not like television murder mysteries. Killing one another is largely an unnatural act for human beings. This though, what happened here, reflects determination and loyalty and probably an internal justification that indicates..."

"Making things new," Sarah said.

"Yes," Norton said. "At whatever cost."

Edwards stood. "Brent, thank you for your work. We all appreciate the fact that you are here and have been such a big help. I don't want to rush you out of here, but we need to get started. He turned to the rest of them. "I want you to do inventory on our outdoor gear. We'll probably need tents and lanterns, and make sure that you bring ponchos. Make sure that you bring supplies for Herc and flashlights and everything you'd need in the woods at night. And somebody go get Rhonda and see if that delivery guy is here and tell her to plan on sleeping here tonight because I'm going to want every one of you with me." He looked at them to see if there were any questions. "Good," he said. "Sarah, I want you in here with me when this delivery fella..."

"Lucas," she said.

"I want you in here with me and Mr. Lucas."

"Yes sir," she said. He turned around and looked at Norton.

"Thank you again, Brent," Edwards said. Norton nodded and started out of the room.

"Wait," Sarah said. "What he wrote on the walls and the mirror..." Norton stopped and turned around.

"They are messages, I think," he said. "He believes that he is delivering a message to all of us and I think what he is trying to say is that out of despair comes rebirth and the price is severe and necessary." He looked at each of them. "Be careful," he said. "Please be careful."

CHAPTER 49

THE WITNESS

Rhonda walked Don Lucas back to the sheriff's office. The first thing that Edwards noticed as the man entered was how young he looked, younger than his niece sitting across the desk from him, looking pale and vulnerable. The briefing had rattled her, Edwards thought. Had probably rattled all of them one way or another. Lucas was still in his work uniform and ball cap and was visibly nervous as he sat down in the chair next to Sarah. Edwards felt like a high school principal talking to teenagers who were being disciplined for smoking or feeling each other up in the parking lot after class. *They are children,* he thought. Lucas had been driving the distribution route for about a year and Edwards had the impression that this was not the first time that he had brushed shoulders with authority, but had dismissed almost immediately the idea that he had anything to do with the murders. At worst he had been hauled in for a petty drug charge, or maybe he was a simpleton thief who had managed to get his life back on track through an honest job. His story checked out, but as Edwards pushed him for details on the person that he said he saw in the woods, the boy became increasingly anxious, as though he had been exposed, not by his own guilt, but by a presence—an association—he did not fully understand. His responses became more and more concise the longer the interview went on, and he kept looking at Sarah as if seeking corroboration. But Sarah did not seem to notice. She looked as if lost in the same tunnel.

His timid *yes sirs* and *no sirs* seemed to be pulling her tighter into her own space. Edwards back-tracked on his questioning.

"Are you sure that you saw a man in the woods?"

"Yes, sir."

"Sure?"

"Yes, sir. I think so."

"You think so?"

"I mean…" Edwards sat back. If he leaned in too hard, any information that he could pry out of Lucas would be muddled and speculative. He was already crossing a line interrogating a witness with what happened to Katherine. It would be what an attorney would call a *conflict of interest* and he realized that squaring protocol with motivation was not something he would be able to do. And honestly, he didn't care. But if he rushed, his professional misstep would be compounded by a compromised and bullied witness and they were already neck deep in black water.

"Was it just the one man that you saw?" Lucas looked at him with expressive eyes, the new direction of the question obviously putting him on edge. It was not a look of shame as much as it was an expression of skepticism.

"Yes," he said. "Just the one."

"Okay," Edwards said, keeping his voice even. "Could you tell if he was doing anything? Had he been down around the rest area building—maybe leaving out the back doors before you walked up?" Lucas looked at Sarah and then around the room. His hands were in his lap and he appeared to be using the left one to keep the right one still. Just a thumb was twitching, rubbing at the first finger like a soundless snap.

"I don't know, Sheriff. He was up in the woods when I saw him. I don't know if he came out of the building or if he was anywhere near the building. He was just there. I mean he was just there and I…"

Edwards stuck out a hand. "Okay," he said. "Okay." Lucas sat back in the chair and breathed out.

"Did he say anything. Wave at you. Turn and run?" Lucas shook his head, then tilted his neck back and looked up at the ceiling.

"You been on this route for a year, you say?""

"Yes, about a year I guess." He was still looking at the ceiling.

"And is this the only highway rest area you go to. You fill machines anywhere else on the interstate?"

"On the highway? No. Just this one."

"Okay," Edwards said. "Just want to make sure that you aren't confusing this location with another."

"No, sir."

"Do you remember what he looked like?" Lucas scanned the room again. Sarah was staring past Edwards' shoulder. She was listening, but her mind was somewhere else.

"Big," Lucas said. "He was big. I could tell that, but I could not see his face. It was dark where he was standing up in the trees. I just saw his shape there."

"And he was a bigger man. Bigger than me?" Edwards said, raising his hand above his head. Lucas nodded.

"Okay," Edwards said. He was getting frustrated, growing impatient. The suspect had more than likely been back to the scene and all he could get out of Don Lucas was that they were looking for a big man.

"You'd gone up there to fill the Coke machines?"

"That's right," Lucas said.

"But the attendant was not there?"

"No. Well, I did not know that. I saw the tape and pulled the truck off to the side and went up to see what was going on and when I saw the tape around the building as well, I came back figuring I would call in on the radio and see if they wanted me to stock it or not. Then I thought I'd open one of the machines and see if they even needed it and that's when I saw the man up in the woods. He was back behind the picnic area and that patch of dog-walking grass they have that runs along that back fence line. He was behind the fence there not doing anything."

"And," Edwards said, looking at Sarah. Nothing there.

"Then that's it. He was just standing up in the woods in the trees and I guess we might have looked at each other for a minute or something and then he turned and walked away."

"And you didn't…"

"I didn't do nothing," Lucas said and this time he sounded angry. "I didn't do nothing because I didn't know nothing was wrong. I thought that they'd closed the rest area cause they might be getting ready to pave the parking lot of something like that. I thought that maybe that guy had been hunting or something and had wandered down toward the property. I sure as hell didn't think that there had been a murder. Jesus, Sheriff." Edwards said nothing. If Lucas knew anything about what had happened, it was going to reveal itself now.

"You think…I mean. You think that was him? That I saw whoever it was that killed those people. I didn't know nothing about that until I rode back here with your deputy. You think I had something to do with this?" He paused, looking at the sheriff with disbelief. "I guess you do cause I'm in here answering questions. I saw some man standing in the woods. That's it. I was up there to stock the goddamn Coke machines. I feel like I've done something wrong…"

"Stop," Sarah said. Both men turned to look at her.

"You didn't do anything, Don, but being in the wrong place at the wrong time. But if you don't shut up, you're gonna make Sheriff Edwards think differently. You saw who did this. We know that. We felt it standing there. I felt it and I never saw anyone. I felt it the day we went up toward that fence after the bodies. The dog knew he was out there. Ethan knew it. I knew it. There's not enough ill will in this entire town to do what that man did and there sure as hell isn't enough in you. But stop running your mouth, please. It's making me feel sick." Edwards watched Sarah scold Lucas, and despite how unorthodox it was, he appreciated her bringing it to a close for the time being.

"Don, is there anything that you can think to tell us? Anything at all? Something small might even help." Edwards knew it was useless, but whatever had passed between Lucas and Sarah; whatever they had shared out in that parking lot had visited them both in his office and he felt he needed to ask a final time.

"No. No sir."

The air was getting stale in the small room and Edwards could smell the lingering scent of cigarettes on his clothes and it was thick on his hands when he scratched his cheek. He felt stubble there and that was a rare thing for him. Kat had never liked him any other way than clean-shaven and he had shaved his face religiously for her. No one would care now whether he groomed himself or not, and sitting looking at the two young people across from him, he wondered if he would ever bother again with the old habits that he had upheld for Kat. Shaving, hanging up his towel, not placing his gun on the nightstand, putting dishes away and not leaving them dirty in the sink before bed—how would any of these things even matter with him at home by himself? Edwards swallowed and looked hard at one of Renee's only positive contributions to the world around her and this made him pause and reconsider what he was doing in that office. They were both conflicted in this, and the further that they waded in, the harder it was to come back out knowing they may have already gone too deep. Neither one had taken a beat to even begin to grieve. *And maybe that's what you're up to, at least for yourself,* he thought. *You're pushing back on the inevitable.* He would be fully alone now for the first time in many years. Not alone as he had been with Kat's failed mind, but truly alone in that house with those memories and ghosts. That kind of isolation made you eerily aware of the sounds that your house makes when no one is home and those noises in the dark that may or may not be normal, and the shadows that watched you from across the room, when you were vulnerable and trying to sleep away stretches of time.

You can stop now, he thought. *You can stop and bury your wife and sit on the back porch and wait for the phone to ring. Wait for someone you don't know to call in a flat voice and tell you that the man responsible is either dead or in a padded room somewhere in Nashville awaiting his arraignment or the electric chair. You could pile up cans of beer and smoke in the house and...*

"Wait," he said aloud.

"Sir?" Lucas said.

"Sheriff," Sarah said. "Wait for what?"

"Nothing," Edwards said and stood abruptly. "Mr. Lucas you are free to go. Thank you for coming in. We will call if we need to see you again." Lucas sat still but glanced at Sarah. "Go ahead," Edwards said. "Rhonda has your information and we will call you if need be." Lucas stood and left the office. He did not acknowledge Sarah or Edwards, just stood and went to the door. He stopped before going through and turned back around.

"You think I could use the restroom, Sheriff?"

"I guess you had better, Don," Edwards said. "It's down the hall on the left." Lucas went out and started right and then corrected himself, disappearing around the corner.

"Wait for what?" Sarah said again.

"Nothing," Edwards said. "I was just thinking about something. What do you make of him?"

"He's not involved," Sarah said.

"I agree," Edwards said, rubbing his eyes with the palm of his hand. He could see Katherine sitting up in bed, the tear in her throat. The pale skin. "Sarah," he said, "I need you to know that I don't expect you to come along on this. I'm fairly confident that I've already crossed lines talking with a witness, and all of this is just so…"

"Fucked up," she finished for him and he nodded.

"Yes, that," he said trying not to look prudish although he had made it known in the office on numerous occasions that he did not care for profanity, and under any other circumstances he would have said something in protest.

"Before you get started, let me make it clear to you that as scared as I am, I'm coming," she said. "I can't go home to my mother's house and I'm not going to hide in here." She waved her hand around the cramped office. "I don't want any special treatment and I don't want you hovering over me being all protective." She smiled and he could tell that she was putting on a show for both of them. He thought about arguing and decided against it.

"Fair enough," he said. "I won't bore you with all the reasons that I disagree and I won't pretend that I can't use the help and the head that you have on your shoulders, but out there," and now it was his turn to gesture, "what I say goes. If I say we are pulling the plug on everything then that's what we are going to do and I don't expect you, or Flip, or anyone else giving me a bunch of talk standing up on that mountain. Clear?" She nodded.

"I need to use the restroom." She stood and Edwards watched her walk out. He sat quietly and went through the conversation with Lucas in his head. There was nothing there to follow. Not a single thread or trail, and he knew that the lack of direction should give him pause; at least long enough to consult higher authorities or even Tibbits, for that matter. But then it would be removed from his control and he was not sure if he could live with that arrangement. Ultimately, catching and punishing whoever did these awful things was the objective and if he could even play a small part in that process then he should be happy.

Happy my ass, he thought. *Content is what they would all want. Content to fade into the background, and make room for whomever came next. I don't know that I can do that. I don't think that I can, even though that is what Kat would have wanted. Would have demanded if she were still alive.* He looked up from behind his desk and caught sight of Ethan standing in the hallway.

"Ethan, what in the hell are you waiting for?" The boy startled and quickly went toward the back of the building. Edwards looked at the empty room; the silence was the first he had heard since sitting in the hospital corridor in the chair in front of the picture with the leafless tree and the angered sun rising out of the otherwise empty field.

CHAPTER 50

JOURNEY WEST

Aaron watched the snake move up onto Terrell's chest and he came awake and began to flail as if his blankets had been set afire. The snake rose and sunk its fangs into one of the old man's hands and he screamed with a high whine and rattle in his throat, and then his eyes looked up at Aaron standing over him, wild and disbelieving and ultimately clearing into a saddened concession. His legs thrashed beneath the covers and his hands waved in jerky motions in front of his face, trying to fend off the snake, but the snake was enraged and struck him again and then again. Aaron watched this from beside the bed, motionless. He was not afraid of the snake, he was learning from it. He was watching it deliver its poison, and when the old man finally went still after a fourth bite, the snake uncoiled itself and then slid like rain down a gulley onto the floor and moved over Aaron's feet and toward the front of the cabin. He went to it and grasped it behind its head and brought it even with his face and its tongue darted in and out and then it spoke to him through the voice that came and went. It spoke and told him what he should do and he opened the cabin door and released the snake out onto the porch. It stayed there and then slithered off the front steps and then made its way under the house. He came back inside and put things into a bag that was hanging on a hook on the cabin wall. He took some of the clothes that the old man had brought to him, a lantern and some matches, some blankets and some cans of the food. He took several of the hunting knives that they had used for skinning animals and wrapped them in an old piece of cloth and then set them carefully in the bag. He went to the bed and knelt down and pulled out the box with the letters. He found the letter from his father and read it again and touched where he had written an address. Then he rummaged through the box and found a leather journal that Terrell had kept. He opened the journal and read through some of the early entries and found one that talked about his mother and the name Katherine came back to him and he closed the journal and took it and the letter to his pack.

The old man lay still on his bed, the poison having overcome his blood, stilling his heart. The places where the serpent bit him were turning black, the marks where the fangs had punctured the skin discolored like a fierce sunset over the lake, and he could see where the venom had moved up from his hand and would begin rotting him from the inside out. He set the bag on the floor and pulled the old man off the bed and dragged him out of the cabin and onto the ground, pulling him by his hands off to the side of the porch. He went behind the cabin and found one of the shovels and began digging into the earth, which smelled of dead leaves and wet soil. When he was through he dragged the old man into the hole. He stood looking down at him, and when he heard the old man give out a soft groan, Aaron climbed down in the hole and put his face close to the old man's mouth and could feel the slightest breath on his skin. Aaron squatted in the hole and looked at the old man for a moment. Then he climbed out and took up the shovel and pushed the nose of it into the pile of damp earth and began to fill in the hole. It made very little sound when it landed on the old man's body and when he made another soft groan, he quickened his pace until he could no longer see the eyes and face. Something about the eyes and the face pulled him in the wrong direction from where he was now going. It was not a clean sentiment, but cloudy and his mind was busy with images of he and Terrell when their existence had been neutral and task oriented. And he realized that looking down at his uncle was a reversal of his own perspective from the wet grave when they had buried the men, and he had looked up at Terrell above him and had seen the recognition in his face that a *reckoning* would be at hand and he had not realized at that time that he, Aaron, would be the instrument of that reckoning and he shied from it as a child would have cowered beneath the immensity and the weight of the not only the circumstance but of the dense earth itself.

He went back inside and then returned to the shallow grave with the holy book and read from it and then scraped back some of the dirt and dropped the book in the hole and covered it back completely and returned for the bag with the things that he would need. Soon it would be dark. He looked at the grave one final time and then went back to the front of the cabin and then onto the trail that led to the lake. He passed the place where they had shot the men in the black and white car and along the tree line until he came to a small clearing. He set down the bag and made a small camp, using one of the knives to open a can of beans. He built a small fire using some sticks and some dry brush he found sheltered beneath the base of the trees. He placed some rocks into the flames and set the can of beans on one of the flatter rocks and sat waiting for them to heat up. He used one of the shirts from the bag to remove the can from the fire and he ate the beans with his hands, listening to the sounds of the woods at night. When he finished eating, he threw the can into the fire and lay down on the ground, pulling one of the blankets on top of him. He lay very still thinking of the coiled snake and its alert eyes, waiting beneath the cabin floor, its poison and purpose replenished.

The next morning he walked out of the woods and onto the road that led into the small town. He knew very little of how things worked there and was not accustomed to speaking with anyone other than the old man and the woman who had been with them before she had been taken away. He thought about the old man while he walked and tried to remember the things that he had been taught about these places where people came and went. He thought of passages from the books and they brought him some comfort. He knew from the journal that he would go to a place called Winchester, but he did not know how he would get there. He was afraid that the voice would not be able to reach him this far from the cabin, but it reassured him as he walked. He saw a car like the car he had seen near the lake and it slowed down and a man looked at him as he walked along the road. Then the car passed and went up ahead and then turned around and came back and stopped. The man got out of the car and asked where he was going and Aaron stopped and told the man and he laughed and asked if he was planning on walking. When Aaron did not respond, the man stopped laughing and asked if he might like a ride to the bus station.

"Do you have any money?" the man asked. Aaron shook his head.

"You know how long it will take you to walk?" Aaron shook his head.

"You know how to get there?"

"West," Aaron said. The man nodded.

"Yeah. Couple hundred miles, I'd say." Aaron stood looking at him.

"How bout I give you a lift in the right direction," the man said. Not asking. He walked to the rear of the car and opened the door and motioned for Aaron to get in. He stood looking and the man took his hand off the door and came closer to Aaron.

"Where did you come from?" he asked. Aaron pointed back toward the woods.

"Uh huh," the man said. "And why are you headed west?" Aaron looked at the man who was now outstretching his arm and pointing at him, stopping short of touching him. Aaron looked at the man's hand. The fingers were short but strong looking. He hitched the bag on his shoulder.

"My family," he said.

"Okay," the man said. "Why don't you get in the back and I will steer you in the right direction. Only a few minutes from here and you can be on your way." The man turned his back and walked toward the car. Aaron followed and got into the back seat and the door closed behind him. The man looked through the glass at him and then he walked around the front of the car and opened his door and sat down, settling behind the wheel. The interior of the vehicle smelled strange and Aaron sat up straight in the back seat, the bag resting in his lap. The man turned the car around in the road and headed in the direction that Aaron had been walking.

"Who were you with up there in the woods?" he asked. Aaron sat quietly. The man in the front seat turned to look at him. "Who were you with up there?" he asked again.

"My uncle," he said quietly.

"Who's your uncle?" the man asked.

"Terrell," Aaron said.

"Terrell?" the man asked. An image of the old man's face laying in the grave rose up in front of Aaron's eyes. The bearded face was puffy and black and it was full of venom and rancid blood and his eyes were bulging and his mouth was slightly open with dirt around the corners and in his nostrils. Aaron held the image and waited. Then the mouth moved and Aaron could see it was trying to speak but it was clogged with the wet earth and leaves. He concentrated harder and then it stretched wider. *Yes,* it croaked.

"Yes," Aaron said. The car was passing the small town's cluster of downtown buildings. Aaron looked out the window and watched the people on the sidewalks and in the parking lots. *Years I spent in those shitty little places,* the old man had said, looking out at the lake, Aaron holding a fishing line on the bank. *Nothing for you or me there. Never was. Never will be. People there have lost their way. Lost sight of anything that's pure. Sacrifice anything for a dollar, or a whore, or some made-up law. Can't be bothered. I ran from it. Ran from all of them who couldn't see. Ran so I could be here with you. Live in peace. Watch that line, Aaron. There is something on it.* The memory washed out. He touched the top of the bag and felt the shape of the knives wrapped in the cloth, placed just below the canvas. The man was talking into something he held in his hand, but he was not talking to Aaron. The air inside the car was hot and Aaron felt like the small space was shrinking around him. He wanted out, but the man was still talking and the car was still moving. He shifted in his seat and heard the things inside his bag clunk into one another. Then the man stopped talking and the car began to slow and Aaron could see a large bridge above him, through the windshield, spanning above the road. The man pulled the car to a stop, the brakes creaking, and turned in his seat.

"Okay," he said, smiling. "Here's where you head west." Aaron looked out the window of his car door and saw a sign with a number on it and below that the word "West."

"You follow this all the way to Winchester." He got out and went around behind the car this time and opened the back door. Aaron climbed out quickly, which made the man back away. Aaron hefted the bag onto his shoulder and began walking away from the car.

"Hey," the man said. Aaron stopped and turned around.

"How is Terrell, anyway?" Aaron turned to walk up the on-ramp to the interstate. The man began to follow.

"Hey," he said. "I'm talking to you. Stop." Aaron stopped and the man came up behind him. He shifted the bag in front of his waist and let his hand find the zipper without looking down. The man was right behind him and he was asking him to turn around. Aaron pulled the zipper along its seam and then the man was telling him to stop what he was doing and put his hands in the air. Aaron slipped his hand in the bag and closed it around the hilt of the knife. In a single motion he brought the knife out of the bag and turned on the man standing behind him, who was trying to grab at something on his waist belt. Aaron used the slight incline of the on-ramp to leverage his weight and he ran and fell forward into the man with his full body forcing them both onto the ground. Aaron brought the knife up and down and up and down and the man was yelling loudly and furiously and then his voice quieted and all that was left of sound was the thud of Aaron's pounding and the muffled rush of the cars above him on the bridge. He stopped and looked down at the man. His face was young and drawn tight in a grimace. Aaron tossed his sack into the roadside ditch along with the hunting knife and then came around behind the man's head and took him under his shoulders and dragged him back down the ramp toward the car which was still running. He dropped the man when he reached the passenger door and he opened it and then turned around again and hoisted the body up and fell back into the car under the weight, and using his feet on the leather seat, he pushed back toward the driver-side door, dragging the man with him, until his back bumped against it. He freed himself from beneath the weight and climbed over the body and back the way he had entered. He turned and pushed the man's feet inside and stepped away and then closed the door. Then he turned and went back up the ramp and stepped into the weedy grass to find the knife, which was resting on the slope of the ditch, coated in fresh blood. He took the knife and went back down the ramp and entered the car to silence the man's eyes, which had burrowed into his mind and he wanted to be rid of their stare.

Do you understand why?

Because we must be clear in what we see and do.

Yes, but the other? Do you recall the other?

Aaron straddled the man's body and looked through all of the windows of the vehicles, turning his torso in a spasmatic rotation.

"The other," he said aloud. "Some are not to see after the breathing has gone. They must be made to wander until such time that he is ready to receive them. This is the other."

He climbed out of the deputy's car and closed the door. He held the knife at his side and returned to where his things sat in the ditch. He stepped off the road and knelt down, spreading out his hands and wiping them free of the new blood and gore in the stiff and sharp weeds that protruded from the bank. He took up the knife and plunged it into the earth and twisted the blade. He did this several times, and when the blade was mostly clean, he laid it flat in the grass and dragged it back and forth until it showed only traces of dirt and mud. He pulled the flat sides of the blade over his pant leg to clean it entirely, then he picked up the bag, pulling it toward him, and dropped the knife inside and ran the zipper back up its seam. He lifted the bag onto his shoulder and walked up the ramp.

Behind him, the police cruiser sat askew at the base of the ramp. It would be almost half an hour before a mother and her three small children, riding in a station wagon, would come across the car. She would sit behind the idling cop car wondering why it was there and eventually she would get out, leaving her own car running and her children sitting in the backseat looking at a book. And when she saw what was inside the car, her scream would jerk up the children's heads and they would see her turn and run back toward them, and when she yanked the gear shift on the column into drive and turned the car around with a loud screeching of tires, they did not ask what she had seen inside the car and as she drove away feeling her hands shaky on the wheel and the children loud in the back seat, excited to be driving so fast, she knew that she had narrowly escaped something that she would never be able to name.

PART 5

THE MOUNTAIN

CHAPTER 51

EDWARDS BACK HOME

Edwards waited for Lucas to return from the restroom. Nothing about the interview had changed his mind as it pertained to the boy's involvement with the murders, but he was certain about one thing: something had happened to each of them during the course of the questioning, something unnatural and both physically and mentally disconcerting. Something had...*interfered.* He took a minute to himself to consider everything that had occurred in such a short period of time, was still occurring, and he was pulled by a strong inclination to turn everything over to the state authorities and go about the grim business of grieving and burying his wife. That would be the rational thing to do, he knew that, knew that deep down. No one would blame him for stepping aside. He had already considered this when Norton had cut the recording short to spare them all the embarrassment of being called out on their ineptitude. But then the same inclination shifted and he realized that at least one person would blame him for shirking the job, and this change in thought was more compelling and he was embarrassed to have entertained the other. This change in thought all but screamed that the overwhelming reality of the situation was that he would never be able to control or make peace with the guilt. It would haunt him to a greater extent than the images of Kat tied helplessly to the bed posts or those poor slaughtered souls at the rest area. That haunting would be relentless and he understood that he would prefer a quick, unsuspecting death of almost any kind to a slow, drawn-out decay of his integrity and inability to chase down his wife's killer. He was using his thumbnail to scratch at a chip in the side of his desk when he looked up to see Sarah standing in the doorway of his office.

"Uncle Bill," she said. Her shoulders were slumped over and she looked worn to the bone. "I don't even know what to say, Uncle Bill. Aunt Kat. I just don't understand. I just don't. Who would hurt some-one like that? And those people at the rest area. Why would anyone..." Edwards stood and came around the desk. Again, that feeling of two things moving at once came over him. He knew, looking at his niece and feeling his pulse tick up, that the sheer weight of the emotion was enough to cripple all of them, understood it clearly and with a measured respect that he felt was keeping him from tipping over the side of their slight little boat that was now surrounded on all sides by a tempest. The urgency in Sarah's voice, the fearful pleading lilt of sorrow and fear that came achingly across the room expanse like something wounded trying to find shelter. He put his arms around his niece, his large frame enveloping her small and shrunken one. She sobbed into his chest and he rested his chin lightly on the top of her head and gritted his teeth, fighting back the bubble of pain rising in his own throat. They stood that way for a long minute and then he took her by the shoulders and stepped her back away from him.

"We're going to do the only thing that I can think to do and that is to find this person and bring him in before he kills someone else. I don't think that we have time to wait and besides, our officers know the woods better than anyone from the outside and I trust of each of you with my life."

"But we don't even know if this asshole," she was drying her tears, anger Edwards knew came from Renee's hot blood seeping up from a deep well, "is even in the woods. Or if the person that Lucas says he saw was even there. We don't know anything."

"We know that he killed those people at the rest stop. And we know that he killed my wife and your aunt. We know he's probably not walking around town or eating in a diner somewhere. We'll start in the woods and we'll go from there. If he is up there, then hopefully we can at least keep him from coming back into town until we get more help. Okay?" Sarah nodded in agreement and went out of the office. Edwards took a breath and forced himself to believe that everything that he had told his niece and his deputy was true. He checked a few things in his office and went out the back of the building. Flip was coming out of the second building holding two shotguns. Edwards turned and went to the parking lot and got into his car and turned out of the lot and drove home. As he made his way through Winchester he began to feel uneasy, like something was inside the car with him. He thought of the vision at the hospital and the disfigured image of Kat that had appeared before him in the office. He stared straight ahead.

You left me Billy. It was coming from the back seat. *You left me and that mad man found me and tied me up and carefully took out my eyes and I screamed and screamed and you did not come because you were with that rattle-trap bitch of a sister, Renee.*

"How could I have known…" he said aloud. Sweat was forming on his forehead and the tops of his arms.

Oh Billy. Sweet boy. You knew because I told you. I told you about that animal in the yard beneath the tree, rutting and bucking on top of me. And she left with him and when it came for me again, you were with her. You were with her and her children and how you wanted children, Billy and how I would not give them to you, but now you can…

"Stop," he said quietly. "Please stop now." He was staring straight ahead and he was forcing himself not to look in the rearview mirror and he was beginning to wonder if he was actually losing his mind. He felt like insects were moving freely inside his head and he concentrated on steering the car slowly through the streets that were alive with activity and people coming and going and he knew that they had all heard about the murders at the rest area and that they probably also knew about Kat and they looked at his car the full time that he passed them and he knew that they were wondering to themselves just what he planned to do about this hideous business and would he be there to protect and to serve them.

Bury me deep, Billy. Bury me deeeep so nothing will come and dig me up, dig me up, dig me up! It sang the words so that they stretched over the seat and came into his ear like a tendril of winter fog. *Maybe it's time we had a talk about children, Bill. Maybe I need to tell you more about children and me. Maybe we should talk before they put me in the ground, Billy. Before you put me in the ground. Before he comes and puts all of you in the ground. Wont that be nice,* it hissed. *Wont that be nice, all of us together again waiting for him to return us all to the earth.* He pushed harder on the accelerator, putting the small downtown buildings behind him, and then he slowed with a jerk to make the turn onto his street. He saw that there were cars in his driveway and for the first time that day, he was anxious to be with other people. He came up Mountain Crest Lane quickly, brought the car to a halt, shoved it into park, and killed the engine, exiting the driver's door as he did so. He slammed it behind him and fell back against the side panel, bringing his hand up to cover his face. He was suddenly very thirsty and his skin felt like it was stretched too tightly over his skull. He turned and looked at the darkened house. The yellow tape was stretched across the front porch area and Kat's body was beneath a thin sheet on a steel table in Norton's morgue. It was a poorly investigated crime scene, and Edwards felt helpless at how easily their inadequacies as a department had been exposed. There were simply not enough of them to handle things properly, and now he was going to parade them all into the woods like a makeshift Boy Scout excursion on a trip with dangers that were real beyond the scope of anything he could imagine. Something was tugging at him to look in the house, a vain attempt to possibly unsee what he knew he had clearly seen. He started up the lawn toward the front door and was about to remove the tape when he stopped, looking in the black front windows and making out the familiar shapes of the furniture in the den. *This would be my undoing,* he thought. *If I go in there now, I'll never come out intact.* He turned away from the porch and walked to the garage and around its side where there was a door that had been unlocked since the day that they bought the house. He opened it and was met with the welcoming smell of gasoline and sawdust from his work bench. He switched on an overhead light and walked to the rear of the garage, trying to avoid looking at Kat's car, which she had been unable to drive for a long time. That had been a bad day. She had been in town at the grocery store and the store had called the station to tell him that she was having some kind of episode in the parking lot. He knew that she had been slipping, but it was not until he pulled in and saw her pacing around and yelling at the bag boy that the car had been stolen, that he fully accepted the new reality. The fact that her Lincoln was parked in one of the spots closest to the store entrance was almost comical, and the bag boy, who knew Katherine and the Lincoln, was so perplexed he looked almost afraid. It took him fifteen minutes to calm her down and get into the patrol car. She had been furious with him the whole time. He had gotten her home, and within an hour she had lost track of the entire morning. He went back for the car later that afternoon, pulling it into the garage where it sat idle, random items of hers still inside. A hairbrush, a scarf, a pair of reading glasses. Edwards had never had the heart to clean out or sell the car.

He looked at the back shelves until he spotted his father's old black trunk. There was a padlock on the latch, and next to the trunk was an upright gun case, also locked. Neither lock had been tampered with and Edwards knew that it was because the man who had been in their home was not a thief. Aside from what had occurred in the bedroom and bathroom, you would never have known anyone out of the ordinary was there, save the open door, which Edwards thought was probably an oversight on the killer's part. But his intuition shifted for the second time that day and he considered that the open door was more like the knife that had been left behind in plain view. Maybe the open door had a meaning all its own, and the killer had wanted to be certain that everyone knew he was deliberate, wanted to communicate in a not-so-subtle manner. He had been so careful about everything else, or at least it appeared that way. His methods appeared well-orchestrated, and the more Edwards thought about it, the more convinced he was that both the open door and the knife were demented calling cards of some kind, symbolic of whatever was driving this man—an invitation to pursue.

Edwards pulled his keys from his pocket and found the one he needed for the trunk. He popped open the lock and rummaged through the items inside, tossing what he needed behind him on the concrete and oil-stained garage floor. Then he found another key on the ring and opened the gun safe, taking out two handguns, a deer rifle that had also belonged to his father, and several boxes of ammunition. He found an oversized duffle on a shelf he had installed long before Kat had started to lose her memory, and he paused, looking at the mundane items there: a half-empty bag of potting soil, a plastic-handled trowel, some weed killer, a pair of pruning clippers, a pair of gloves for small hands. All had been put to good use somewhere in a recessed corner of time, a forgotten closet where the air had been sucked out and replaced with a musty scent and thick Naphthalene, cobwebs and dusty wooden floors replete with hand-knitted sweaters, blankets and quilts in moth-proof storage bags, a box of books and random letters. He envisioned her on spring afternoons, her strong body bent over in the front flower beds planting bulbs, the two of them sharing a bottle of beer on the front steps, maybe two or three more depending on what was planned that night. Going back inside with dirt from head to toe and stripping off in the bathroom. Letting him see her with no clothes on and sometimes, maybe after two or three beers on the front steps, he would climb in with her and stand behind her with a warm stream of water splashing on her front and splattering into his face, his hands guiding a bar of soap and her soft purr of being caressed and content. Then she would push him back playfully and rinse out her hair and he would stand at the back of the tub, beginning to get cold, and watch her graceful motions and wait his turn. And after the shower he would go out on the back patio with another beer and light the grill and a cigarette and soak in the spring air with its familiar scents coming across the lawn, cut grass mixed with the cloud of the Marlboro, and she would join him and take drags from the smoke and sit in one of the wrought-iron chairs that were situated around a round patio table and they would talk about the day or his work and she would laugh in an easy way that seemed as much a part of the night as the crickets and the birds that would settle in the limbs of the maple that had stood more than one hundred years in the back yard. And it was easy and light and it had calmed him, made him sensitive to things that he otherwise would have ignored or treated with little to no thought. These gratuitous visions that were coming to him now, these images of Kat displayed in the most horrific of ways, were threatening the sanctity of memories in the same way that the encroaching dementia had torn at their marital fabric through incessant whispering and capricious theft. He was seized by a fierce compulsion to see things through. If nothing more he would combat this heedless and premature finality. He would restore their shared dignity whether that entailed ending things with the bullet from a deer rifle or...

Or what, Billy.

The *what* had no meaning, nor sustained consequence. There was absolution down either path and resurrection if indeed there was something waiting on the other side.

He pulled the duffle off the shelf and went out of the garage with the guns now in the large bag that also contained the other items he had taken from the trunk. He went down the driveway with long strides. He spared a quick glance at the house from the front seat of his car, and its muted, boxy shape looked far different to him than the home he had returned to on Mountain Crest Lane, night after night, for years and years. It looked as if it had been left to sink into the earth, dissolving beneath the patterns of everyday life and the inhabitants who carried out those patterns with no expectation that they could be suddenly cut short by something as fundamental and unpredictable as a failed mind or an intruder who moved within shadow and preyed on the most vulnerable among them.

CHAPTER 52

JED

Jed sat with his elbows propped on the kitchen table, smoking another Merit cigarette and looking at the ash floating in the glass, the conversation with Sarah replaying itself in his mind, and the hangover from drinking the day before playing an erratic bass drum in his head. He got up and went over to the kitchen counter and took the Jack Daniels and went back to the table and poured some of the whiskey into the mug that still held a little of the now cold instant coffee in the bottom. He sipped from it and pursed his lips. The house was alive with all kinds of still images and memories and they moved around his head like yellow jackets on the lip of an unattended Coke bottle left outside on a summer's day. It seemed to Jed that he spent as much time fumbling through the unlit hallways in his head as he did actually navigating the world around him. Not that one was more pleasant than the other, and he reasoned that he kept returning to his childhood hoping to uncover a remnant of positivity or happiness, happiness that was not manufactured or contrived, or swimming in a gutter-puddle of alcohol or the dry-mouth fog of pills. But turning over those stones looking for something of value was often a foolish pursuit, because if there were memories to be found, they had buried themselves deep beneath the riverbed, covering themselves with muddy scenes like the one he was recounting now.

His mother and father had been fighting, which was nothing new. He and Sarah had been in the back of the house and Jed thought that they may have been fighting about whether or not they should be allowed to go with Uncle Bill and Aunt Katherine to the county fair. His father hated Bill and Katherine for reasons he could not understand at such a young age and he wished sometimes that he could go live with them in Winchester instead of his own home which was always dirty and smelled like smoke. There had been a knock at the door and his father yelled to his mother not to answer it, but she did anyway and Aunt Katherine said something to both of them and had come into the back of the house and picked Jed up and taken Sarah by the hand and marched them up the hall and out the door, right past his parents. She did not stop to close the door and came down the yard and to the car where Uncle Bill was standing and he opened the door for her and she ushered the two of them into the backseat and told them to put on their seat belts and then she had closed the door and gotten into the passenger side and Uncle Bill had got behind the wheel and they backed out of the driveway and went over the mountain and into Winchester where one of the streets had been blocked off for the fair. There had been a petting zoo and some rides and his aunt and uncle had let them do whatever they wanted, which included eating large amounts of cotton candy and hot dogs and ice cream, and when it was over, he threw up next to the car and he was allowed to sit up front with Aunt Katherine, who stroked his hair while Sarah rode in silence in the back, holding a stuffed panda bear close to her chest.

When they got home, their father had come out to meet them and he yanked open Sarah's door and told her to get out and Katherine opened her door and his father pulled Jed off her lap before she had a chance to stand and carried Jed back to the house on his hip, the jostling making his nausea come back all over again. His uncle told him to hold on but his father ignored him and went into the house and dropped Jed on the floor. Sarah followed them inside and looked down at Jed and then she let out a small yelping sound and Jed followed her gaze to their mother who was standing next to the hall entry, leaning against the wall. Her right eye was swollen shut and her lower lip was split and fattening so that it looked like a pink and purple slug was sliding above her chin. Their father had left the room and somehow that added to the tension more than his being there, towering over all of them. He remembered looking from his mother back to Sarah who had already turned away and was staring out the door at their aunt and uncle's car backing out of the drive and pulling away from the house. When they were out of sight, Sarah came to him and helped him to his feet and they walked together past their mother and down the hallway to their room where they sat on the floor and played with the panda and some old blocks that Jed kept in a small wooden box. It was a long time after that before they saw their aunt and uncle again and there had been no more trips to the fair or anything like it.

Jed threw his half-smoked cigarette into the glass of water and stood up from the table to go find a shirt. He went down the hall and he could hear his mother in her room making some kind of moaning noise that might have been crying or might have been from her own hang-over. He went into his room, pulled the shirt from the day before off the floor and put it on. Then he went over to a small dresser and opened the bottom drawer and found the envelope. He pulled it out and went back down the hall. Sarah had told him to keep an eye on his mother while she was gone but he planned to ignore that direction. He went back to the table and grabbed his cigarettes and lighter and pushed them into his front pocket. He had to go back to his room for his shoes, which had been kicked off before he went to bed and were lying on opposite sides of the room. He pulled them on without untying the laces and started back down the hall when he heard his mother behind him.

"Jed, honey," she said in a weak voice. "Where you going?" She looked frail and her puffy face resembled the cheap plastic Halloween masks that they had bought from the dime store before Halloween when they were small.

"Out," he said, looking back in the direction of her voice.

"Where?"

"Just out," he said.

"What have you got there?" Jed looked down at the envelope he was holding in his hand.

"Nothing," he said. "I'm going." He walked away from her and into the kitchen and started to open the door and went back for the Jack

Daniels. Seeing that it was not enough, he cursed under his breath and opened the liquor cabinet in hopes that there would be another bottle inside. There was, tucked back in the corner, and he took it. She called to him again but he ignored her and went out and got in his Toyota. He backed out of the driveway and went about a mile down the road and pulled off to the shoulder and picked the envelope off the passenger seat and read the return address: *Pell Road, Tyre, Alabama* was scrawled in a childish hand. He took a deep breath and then pulled the car back onto the road and drove east. He drank from the bottle and tried not to think of anything at all. The whiskey slowed the drumming in his head and the cigarettes started to taste better. He tuned the radio back and forth between a rock and country station and turned the volume up, singing along with the songs that he knew and keeping a clumsy beat on the steering wheel. He almost missed the turn-off to go south and over-corrected, nearly sending the car into the far ditch before he got it back under control. He looked nervously in the mirror behind him, hoping that no troopers were around and took another slug of the whiskey to settle himself. He slowed his speed and concentrated on keeping it consistent.

He was starting to feel fairly drunk by the time he reached the Tyre city limits and he had to pull off at a gas station to piss and ask for directions to Pell Road. The attendant didn't know the place but told him to go through town and then start looking for road signs, that it was probably out that way somewhere if it was considered within the town limits. Jed thanked him and got back in the car and sat behind the wheel. The interior of the Toyota was strewn with trash, and thin layers of dust and cigarette ash. There was a rough tear in the passenger seat with the yellowish cushion poking through, and the air inside was rank with the pungent smells of tobacco smoke and sweat. There was a rusted out hole in the back floorboard and when it rained, splatter from the road got into the car and added mildew to the trapped smells. He looked through the windshield at the lifelessness of Tyre. It looked like everything he had ever known, waking an unwelcome sense of familiarity. He passed a house where two boys that looked to be about ten or eleven were throwing a football. He pulled to the curb, leaned over the seat, and rolled down his passenger window and yelled for them to come over. They stopped throwing the football and looked at him and he realized how it appeared and with a noticeable slur asked them directions. They ran into the house and seconds later, a man came out the open front door and crossed the yard, holding a baseball bat in front of his chest. Jed hopped out of the car, raising both his hands.

"Hold up," he said. The man continued toward him, the baseball bat rising and falling, smacking his palm.

"Look," Jed said. I'm just asking for directions. "I just thought those kids might know the street I'm looking for. I wasn't after them or nothing like that." The man stopped, looked back at the house. The boys were standing in the doorway, the smaller one clutching the football under one arm. The bat stopped moving.

"All right," the man said and let the bat fall alongside his leg. He ran a hand through his hair and rubbed his eyes. *I woke him up,* Jed thought.

"Where you looking for?"

"Pell Road," Jed said.

"Where?"

"Pell Road. Believe it's here in Tyre. Or maybe out to the county."

"Pell Road's out past the city buildings. What you want out there?"

Jed stood without answering.

"You got kin out there?" the man said.

Jed nodded.

"It ain't none of my business, but if you don't got kin out that way I don't reckon you ought to be wandering up Pell Road without a good reason."

"I got kin," Jed said.

The man nodded and looked back at his kids again.

"Follow this road through town and around the square and then head south away from it and look for the city buildings on your left and for the sign on your right. I think it's still nailed up there on a big oak that sits right up on the road. You can't miss it. Every drunk on this side of the state has run into it one time or another." Jed nodded and recited the directions back in his head.

"Thank you." The man looked like he wanted to say more but turned and went back toward the house and motioned with the bat to the kids that it was okay to come outside and play. One of them ran from the open door and the short one threw the ball to him in a lazy, arcing pass that seemed to hang in the air for an impossibly long time. Jed went back to his open car door.

"Careful," the man said

"What was that?" Jed said over the roof of the car, but the man had reached the house and the kids were already bickering over who was going to play quarterback.

He came out of the town limits and went past Pell Road in both directions before he got it right. He turned in and slowed the car to a crawl. The road was littered with large potholes and the rain had eroded sections of the dirt and gravel surface. There was a slight ridge to his left and he could see narrow rivulets where the water cut its way through the scraggly patch of woods, weed-choked with rotting leaves, strewn trash, and matted clumps of pine needles. It was late afternoon and Jed realized that he still had time to stop and turn around. Maybe find a quiet pull-off and get some sleep, sober up, and then head home to see about his mother. But something stopped him from doing that and he kept moving up the road until he came to a clearing and saw the house and he knew without giving it any thought that it was his father's. There was a presence there and Jed felt it inside the car. The junk strewn around the place was a collection of mechanical failures that had bled-out their lubricants and were coated in rust; knee-high weeds covered most of the landscape except for a path that had been cut back between the spot where a pick-up sat and the front porch of the house began. The porch was a pile of lopsided lumber to the point of keeling on its rotting bow into the earth below. The chimney was coming apart and chunks of brick were missing, and Jed could see a squirrel coming in and out of one of the openings, chattering at him from atop the roof that was spotted with missing shingles and damp and rotting exposed plywood.

Jed put the car in park and killed the engine. Sitting, hearing only the engine ticking, he waited to see if he had attracted the attention of anyone inside. The pick-up was used and beaten but was not a late model and Jed dismissed the idea that the house had been abandoned altogether. He sat a moment longer and looked through the bug-splattered windshield. *It's not too late,* he thought. *Even if he came outside now, he would never suspect that it was you.* He reached absently across the seat and pulled the bottle into his lap, unscrewing the fat black cap and hefting it to his lips. It was half-full and he warmed a bit knowing that the liquor was essential if any of this was to go right, go at all. Aside from the occasional bird and the cooling engine, the end of Pell Road was silent. A thin breeze wound its way through the weedy lawn and when he opened the car door, he could hear it moving in the tree canopy as well. He had a vision of sitting on the floor in the house that they had all shared together, looking around the room and wondering where his father had gone. That cold feeling of anxious anticipation was washing over him again. He had to piss and he desperately wanted another drink from the bottle, but he shoved the urge aside and climbed out and stood in the decrepit lot looking up at the skeletal house where somewhere inside, John Hicks was waiting. He took the bottle off of the driver's seat and slammed the door harder than necessary, hoping it would wake something inside the house. He came up the trodden path to the front doorsteps, carefully putting one foot on the first plank and testing to see that it would hold his weight. When it held, he ran up the remainder of the steps quickly. He stood in front of the door and con-sidered for the last time the option of turning around and doing what Sarah had asked him to do, but the warm liquor in his stomach helped him to raise his hand and knock. He brought his knuckles down three times on the flimsy wood and then stood back from the door. Nothing. He knocked again and this time he heard someone moving inside. He stepped further back and away from the center of the door. The sham-bling inside continued and then the door pushed open and his father was standing in front of him wearing a pair of torn jeans and unlaced work boots. He blinked at the light from outside and looked to his left and then back to his right where he finally realized that someone was standing there. He took a step out onto the porch and looked harder at Jed, who was about to speak when his father began to laugh. The laugh turned into a cough and he bent over and put his hands on his knees and shook with the spasm that came thickly from his wet lungs. When it passed, he stood up again and assessed Jed through squinting eyes.

"Must be fifteen years, I'd say."

"About that," Jed said.

"Well, you come at the right time, boy," his father said, turning his glance to the bottle in Jed's hand. "I'm just getting up from a lie-down." They stood looking at one another, and with a sudden and exaggerated gesture, his father bowed and waved his arm toward the open door.

"Come in, come in." The interior of the house was a contained and cramped version of the exterior yard. There was a main room with a bump-out in the back to accommodate the tiny kitchen and a short hallway that Jed presumed led to a back bedroom, dimly lit through a filthy square window leaking in washed outside light. The couch in the front room seemed like it served as the primary bed. Yellowed sheets and caseless pillows piled on one of the fabric cushions and the coffee table was so littered he was not able to determine what color the top of it was. The kitchen had a pea-colored range, some upper cabinets, a small, noisy refrigerator unit, and a shallow, two-compartment metal sink that was overflowing with trash and discarded glasses and plates. Above the sink, a sepia-tinted photograph of two men, taken years before, hung on the wall with a thumb tack. The two men were young and they had their arms around one another. There was a larger, third man off to the side of the frame, wearing a broad brimmed hat pulled down on his head, a patched coat. He was holding a piece of lumber and staring at the younger man, who seemed to be smiling, but it was difficult to tell. Jed stood in the middle of the room while his father moved clothes and other items off a small table. He tossed everything into a pile on the floor along the opposite wall and turned around to look at Jed, staring once more at the bottle he was holding.

"See you brought me a present. I see you done that," he said pointing at the bottle, and then he laughed in a pitched cackle that was thick with phlegm. He was bent and sick, but Jed could still see the definition of the muscles in his arms, shoulders, and neck, muscles that reacted swiftly and decisively when needed.

"Yes sir," he said and raised it up. "I had some on the drive over, sorry there's not more." His father did not respond but moistened his lips and swallowed.

"Want to sit down?" Jed said. His father's eyes had glassed over and Jed could not tell if he was still looking at the liquor or if he was suffering some kind of spell.

"Daddy," he said. "You want to sit down and have a drink?"

"Yeah," his father said absently, and then tilted his head and pounded the side of it like he had water in one of his ears. "Yeah, sure. Sit." And he pointed to one of the empty chairs, straightening up his body and giving a final shake of his head. "Let me get us some glasses. He made his way to the kitchen while Jed sat and watched him rummage through a cabinet and inspect two glasses. He rinsed them both, having to move things out of the way and push trash to the floor to access the faucet. He brought them back to the table, drying them on his pants leg and then setting them down. One of the glasses had a ragged chip in the rim.

"You pour," his father said, taking his seat. He pulled the glasses closer to him and unscrewed the cap on the bottle and poured the whiskey into each glass, trying to be sparing with it, not wanting it to run out too quickly. He pushed one of the glasses across the table to his father and then he picked up his own glass and, noticing that he held the chipped one, he turned the sharp edge away from his mouth

"What we drinking to?" his father said.

"I don't know," Jed said. His father hunched over the table, staring at him with his hands encircling his glass to keep from shaking. His eyes moved from Jed's to the glass in front of him and back again to his skinny son who sat fidgeting and nervous, sitting just like he had when he was a little boy and had pissed his pants or left his toys out on the floor to be stepped on.

"How about health," his father said and coughed violently. The sound came from deep within his lungs and erupted up toward the surface only to get caught in his throat, which was raw and torn and the pain made him wince and close his eyes and when he did that, his face contorted and looked very much like the man in the picture standing to the side of the frame, holding the lumber and staring at the two *brothers*, Jed thought. He smiled and Jed saw that there was blood on his teeth.

"How about family, Daddy?" Jed said and watched his father intently. He knew that he had voluntarily walked into a forbidden burial ground, but the liquor in his system was pushing.

"Okay," his father said. "To blood then." They clinked glasses and drank. Jed felt as if in a dream, a dream that was taking place under water. The room was so thick with the rancorous smell and stifled air that it was hard to swallow the intensity of the sour mash, his mouth salivating with the lingering taste. His eyes itched and his skin felt clammy. His father tilted his chair on its hind legs and then tipped his head back and made a satisfied sound. He stayed that way, his unshaven neck worked the lingering taste of the liquor, savoring it, and then the sticky sound of his lips parting to speak.

"That's nice," he said. "I'm not used to something as nice as that." He let the chair rock back to its four legs and regarded Jed with a thin smile.

"You're not here to collect child support are you?"

Jed looked puzzled and his father spit and coughed a laugh across the table at him. The blood lined the grooves of the yellow teeth and smeared his gums.

"No," Jed said. "I'm just…" but his father continued laughing, bringing his hand up and down on top of the table making a loud slap each time his palm connected with the cheap wood. *He'll snap it in two,* Jed thought and waited.

"Child support," his father croaked. "Ain't that a joke."

"No," Jed said again. "I don't know why I'm here really. Just felt like it."

"Well, his father said, pushing his glass toward his son with a scrape. "Anytime you want to show up with a bottle of Jack Daniels, you don't hesitate." Jed poured them both another shot and they swallowed it in silence. The years of separation sat between then like an oversized balloon, its thin rubbery skin stretched to the point of bursting, and they forced their eyes from one another in hopes of not upsetting the delicate chemical balance. They fidgeted in their chairs and examined their fingernails and breathed in the stale air and Jed wished he had heeded the warning he had given to himself in the car and on the porch to turn back. He was not wanted here and the goodwill of the liquor would only carry so far. Jed sat determined not to speak first, and seeing this, his father charged clumsily ahead, reaching for the bottle and pouring the liquor generously.

"How is that old bitch Renee, anyway?" he said sticking his nose into the glass and sniffing. "She still twisting people's balls in a knot? I bet she is, ain't she, twisting away and complaining when people try and yank them back. That old bitch," he murmured into the glass, and then he drank it down and pushed it back toward Jed. He looked at his son and Jed was startled to see the clarity of his own features in his father's beleaguered face. The bad complexion, the darting, red eyes with mounting pressure behind the sockets like walled-up sewer water. He was looking at his looming future, observing the indelible marks left by time spent dulling the mind and forsaking people, ultimately hurting them in a grating, lasting way. He was not upset about what his father had said about Renee. Most of that was true, although Jed did not think she was as intentional as the old man. She was just lost most of the time. But she had stayed. At least she had done that, and she had pretended to care. He knew that because he felt it in her rare bedtime back scratching and he had seen it when she cried for no distinguishable reason, smoking at the kitchen table or looking out across the yard toward the mountain and all its fog. But he was in his father's house and glancing across this meager table, he could see anger stirring the barely contained resentment, heating up the explosive blood that also coursed through his veins. He knew that he had exposed himself and this realization made the room tilt. He stood up, almost falling, and went toward the door.

"Where you going?"

"Outside to get some air."

"Air don't suit you in here, Jed?" His father was cocked back in the chair again, his mood testing its axis. This was how it began, loaded questions for which there were no real safe answers, his father like a mean cat with something pinned to a dark corner, its paws banging the thing it had trapped back into the dusty recess, each swat making it more and more evident that it was trapped and at the mercy of something losing control of its predatory instincts.

Why did you come

Why did you come

You knew, you knew you knew…

Because maybe he would soften. Maybe it would be a reason to see beyond all this disquiet — this way of living that left no room for anyone else. Not a wife, or a daughter, or a son. Not even a son that was unintentionally following his depressive need for emptiness one numbing swallow at a time.

Why did…

I don't fucking know why. Because maybe even at his most vile, he's better than being alone and perpetually lost. At least he feels something even if it's harsh. Even if the smell of this rotting house at least lets you know that you are living. And what about the card that he sent? There had to have been…

378

"It's fine in here," he said. "Just want to step out for a minute. You want to come with me?" His father waved an arm at him and he went out the door. *This was a mistake,* he thought, standing on the swaying porch where there was a swing at one end, its chains uneven, and beyond only the trees and a field he thought he could see further on. *I never should have come here. Never should have come.* He pulled the cigarette pack from his breast pocket and fished one out, lit it, and exhaled, looking at his car sitting below. *I could just leave,* he thought. *Could just leave him with the bottle and get home somehow. Could get home and maybe start over. Now that you've seen it. Now that you have...*

"Jed!" his father bellowed from inside the room. "Come back in here, boy. I'm sorry to talk about your mother. C'mon back inside." *Set it on fire,* a voice in his head said. *Block the door and set that piece of shit swing on fire and let him burn in there.* Jed looked at the rotting swing, its cushion fabric ripped and brittle as dead leaves. It would burn. It would combust. He tossed his cigarette in the yard and went back inside. His father was sitting upright in the chair and he was pouring more of the liquor into his glass. The bottle gurgled, air bubbles lifting up through the brown liquid like transparent underwater creatures rising from the deep. He walked over and sat down again, the chair scratching across the floor. His father reached over and filled Jed's glass. *Here it is,* he thought. *He's testing me, wants to see if there is anything of him inside me.* They drank the rest of the bottle, back and forth like two men playing a game of checkers. When it was gone, his father went out to his truck and came back with some cheap rotgut that tasted like cough medicine. It was late afternoon and Jed could barely keep his head up, and still his father kept on and he forced the liquid down both of them with loud taunts. Then the older man rose and stumbled across the small room and threw aside a pile of clothes and flipped on an old receiver that sat beneath a turntable. Jed forced his head up and watched his father regain his balance and begin thumbing through a collection of records that were standing in a battered bookshelf. John Hicks flipped through the album covers and would find one that caught his interest and would let the whole stack flop, saying "now this is an album, boy" or something similar, moving the cover in and out of his vision's focus. Jed had witnessed this scene before in their house with Sarah and Renee, his father's inebriation reaching a pivotal transition. Even as a child,

Jed knew that the train was on a greased track and it would take only one distraction or one comment for the music to be drowned out by shouting and fighting parents who could go from singing along with Dolly Parton or Merle Haggard to squaring off in front of each other, their bodies so close that their red and growling faces almost touched. And now he found himself back in this place, only this time he was a long way from the sober and innocent observation of a child.

"Now here. Here's a record that shits on all the rest." Jed could no longer keep his head up, but he could hear his father bend over and pull open the plastic lid casing of the turntable and place the scratched black disk on the platter and drop the needle that made a loud pop in the speakers.

Jed needed to vomit. He needed to purge himself and he could no longer concentrate on what his father was saying and could only think about that morning with Sarah. The music was loud and distorted and he could not have guessed who was singing to save his life. It was a man with a high, whining voice and his head began to spin like the warped record. He looked down the dark hallway to the back bedroom and he could see through the sparse light that the sun was beginning to set. His memory was working itself backwards, the static images of his childhood rushing up to confront the failing present. He saw himself vomiting at the fair. Saw his mother's purple eye, her split lip. Felt Sarah's small hand help him from the floor and lead him back to their room. He saw the dead, shiny plastic eyes of the panda, its pink nose and flat black yarn mouth offering no emotion at all, just a sad neutrality, lifeless and judgmental in its simplicity.

"Aunt Katherine's dead," he said. His father stopped moving to the music. The high, urgent voice and the steel guitar accompanied by the repetitive bass line and monotonous drum filled up the empty spaces in the house. John Hicks lurched forward, back to the table. He picked up the rot gut bottle and drank from it and then slammed it back down.

"What did you say?"

"Aunt Kat. She's dead. Last night. I think. Someone came in. Killed her with a knife. Cut her throat, Daddy. That's what Sarah told me this morning, and I came down here to see you. I don't know why I did. I just did. Thought that maybe we could…"

380

"I seen her," his father said, touching his hand to his mouth and looking wildly around, waving the bottle, making shadows that were shifting and growing on the walls like shapes rising up from beneath the floor.

"What are you…What are you saying'?"

"I seen that tempting whore," he said. "Here in this place. She come and looked at me like she did back…"

"Daddy, what the hell are you talking about?" His father whirled and drank from the bottle, a long, burning gulp and the brown liquid spurted from between his lips and ran down his chin. He was swaying badly and mumbling to himself. He stopped suddenly and looked at his son, his lips curled back over his stained teeth and the whites of his eyes shot through with red lines like forging iron. His skin was white, pasty, and slicked with stinking sweat. He stood over Jed and then, with a quickness his son would never have thought possible, he grabbed him by the shirt and jerked him forward, fully off the floor, and then pushed him backwards onto the rickety tabletop that protested beneath the dead weight of his body.

"Fuck you say, boy?" Jed rolled to the floor, unable to break his fall. He lay on his side feeling the bile rise in his throat. He got to his knees, turning his head to find the door to the outside. The first song on the record had changed to the next and now it was a western swing number that was absurd in its plucky rhythm, and Jed felt like he might laugh at his foolishness, his pathetic attempt to reconcile with a demon.

"FUCK YOU SAAAAY! I'll teach that prissy whore not to send a runt fucker like you." His father was bellowing. He kicked Jed in the ribs with the heavy work boots and then stepped back and kicked him again. The pain went through him in thudding jolts. He tried to crawl away but his father reached down and held his belt and then he was on top of him, punching him with his fists, blows coming down onto his back and shoulders and base of his neck. He vomited and he turned his head to the side to keep his face from it and his father landed a punch into his jaw and Jed felt something give way and then the taste of vomit was accompanied by the metallic wash of blood. Then came another blow. And another. He was losing consciousness. He was going to die in this house. His father was yelling, incoherent screams of rage as if being attacked in the dark.

"Goddamn you all," he yelled atop his son. His head was back and his screams were reverberating off the low ceiling and falling back to the floor, wholly unmelodic against the distorted sound of the music coming from the record player.

"Daddy," Jed managed. "Daddy, please." He raised a hand to shield his swelling face.

"Noooo," his father screamed. "Noooooo. I will not listen to this. Goddamn you." He raised his hands together and clasped them above his head. "Not this time. Not this time you cocksucker. You will not..."

"Daddy," Jed whispered. His father, hands raised above his head, torso wavering, legs astride the boy almost motionless beneath him, stopped. He stood shakily and walked away from his son. Jed rolled over and tried to breathe. His mouth was now full of blood and he spat out a tooth. He tried to sit up but he knew that some of his ribs had been broken. He lay on his back and used his legs to push himself toward the door. His father was standing in the tiny kitchen, talking to himself and wailing. He was pulling at his hair and then he took an arm and raked plates and glasses and pans to the floor where they bounced and scattered as if detonated. He was wheeling and yelling and beating the cabinet doors with both fists. Jed felt his back hit the door. He raised his hand behind his head and managed to turn the knob. He pushed the door open wide enough to get his body through and then he was out on the porch and managed to kick the door closed behind him. He could hear his father inside and the muffled sound of the music and then that stopped and was followed by the crash of the turntable against the wall. Outside there was barely enough light to see. He forced himself onto his stomach and then onto his knees. He slid off the porch steps and used his elbows to pull himself down to the path between the house and the truck. On either side the weeds and grass were taller than he was and he could hear things rustling and scurrying away from the loud breaths and groans that he was making. The short grass and stubs raked his palms and stabbed at his knees and stomach as he crawled away, but he forced himself to the car, panting and spitting blood and snot. He reached the driver's side door and he stretched up and got a hand hold on the edge of the window and was able to pull himself to his feet. The pain was now immense and he counted to ten over and over to keep from passing out. *Oh Jesus God, please. One, two, three, four, five, six, seven...*

He opened the car door and fell inside. *One, two, three, four, five, six...* The pain was now flat and dull and his head was swimming in its own juice. The nausea rose in his throat and he leaned over and spewed a thin stream of liquid into the passenger seat. He groaned and sat up and managed to close the door behind him. The keys were in the ignition and he cranked the engine and it rattled to life. He looked back to the house and saw that the sun was escaping some-where behind it and the colors fanned around the sides of the struc-ture and strangely it looked peaceful. He reached down and put the car into reverse and using all of his strength, turned the wheel. *One, two, three* . . . The car bumped into something and the plastic bumper caved in. He put his foot on the brake and put the car into drive and then reversed the wheel and pressed on the accelerator. The car slowly turned and then was on its way down the hill and back toward town. He crept away and made it back to the main road leading into Tyre and drove along at barely a crawl. He managed his way through the square and then back north. He was counting over and over and slumping into the wheel. The statue of the soldier was in his rearview mirror and he forced his head to the left and saw the house where the two boys had been playing football. He jerked the wheel hard and ran the car over the curve and into the yard and then he shoved on the brake, falling forward, the weight of his chest on the steering wheel causing the horn to blare in the gathering dusk.

CHAPTER 53

JOHN

I know you, the voice said.

The hell you do, Hicks said. He was sitting on the floor. Urine soaked the front of his jeans and the bottle of rotgut next to him, overturned and leaking out its contents.

Oh, but we do. We've been with you for a long time, John. A long...

No.

Yes, John. Since the mill. Since Bishop's Well. Since the ravage beneath the tree. Since your mother left in the night.

No.

Yes, John. Yes. And we will always be here with you. We are who you are. We are as we see ourselves. We have things to do.

I did not kill her. That was not me. I only meant to...

John, it said. Then a chorus. *John...*

Leave me be.

For now, they said. *For now if you wish.*

Forever, he said.

Forever, he said again.

He sat in his stupor on the floor. Outside was an unnatural silence. It was as if the voices had commanded an unconditioned audience and Hicks imagined the animals sitting in perfect stillness, on limbs and in holes, on the dampened earth beneath the house, ears alert and eyes full of pupil, darting and wild with the fear of an unseen predator. He tried to sit up and sat back down heavily, the thick smell of urine in his nostrils, the vicious scene with his son retelling itself in clouded images, followed by more clearly defined pictures of the Winslett farm, the unsuspecting child in the bar balancing the tray of glasses, the judge falling from his chair, clutching his chest while Hicks looked on, smiling.

CHAPTER 54

AARON

Cars and large trucks passed Aaron in a steady stream on the road. He walked along the shoulder and sometimes down into the ditch of the roadside where paper sacks were rotting in a stale stream of water along with the rusting bodies of cans and the discarded bottles that had broken into large emerald-green shards. The speed with which the vehicles passed and the gusts of whirling air caused by the large semis made him nervous. He was unaccustomed to everything but the sounds of the woods. The times that he had been in town with Terrell were faint in his memory, and even then, the town had been almost as quiet as the woods around the cabin and the lake. He shouldered his bag and looked up the road. The clouds were form-ing atop the mountain far in the distance. They were pale grey and he knew that he would be walking in the rain sooner than later. His boots were worn and the concrete hurt his feet. He was thankful that it was not cold. His mind moved in a carousel of images: the man at the exit ramp, the eyes of the viper, the face of Terrell standing outside the cabin holding the axe, the men on their knees beside the black and white car, the tongue of the snake, the blackness far back in the trees, the light glinting off the smooth water of the lake, Sophia as she came out onto the porch. He did not linger on any one image and he would not try and process the images in any particular way other than to recognize them as things that had occurred and that he had been a part of those occurrences with varying levels of physical involvement and detach-ment. This was neither a relief nor enlightenment as his cognition was devoid of any emotional context. His expression rarely changed. His eyes were small and tight. His lips were thin and they rarely parted except to speak in short sentences or to take in food or water. His hair was ratty and hung below his shoulders and his frame was slight, but muscular. He was deceptively strong, agile, and alert and he felt the state of others in a shared capacity that allowed him to recognize fear before it actually manifested. Among the images that circled in his head were audible scraps of verse and prose that Terrell had taught him. They overlapped one another in Terrell's thin, gravelly voice and they jumbled together. He had difficulty dissecting them from one another. He had not bothered with names of the people who had written them or even their titles, it was the words themselves that he clung to, seek-ing them out as a means of control. At night in the cabin when the fire died out, he would quietly recite them, lying on his back, looking up at the ceiling. He would recite each one and then he would place it aside and would recite the next and on and on until he was asleep. But in the morning, they would have all collided again and he would wait until he had time to be still to put them back in order. Now as he went up the road the noises in his head were growing louder and louder and he stopped and went down the slope and walked twenty yards under the tree canopy and put down his pack and stripped naked and walked further. The voices and images were blowing around like a storm cell coming over an open field and he closed his eyes and tilted his head up and took in gulps of the air, crossing his arms in front of his chest and gently rocking from side to side. The woods were calm around him. He waited. It would come and reveal itself. And then it was there, steady and pulsing evenly, not angry, but strong and firm nonetheless and the collective voices obeyed and stopped their repetition, retreating on all fours into protective shadow. It was fully in him now and it was gentle and understanding. *Be still*, it said. *Be still, Aaron.* He nodded, standing like the Doryphoros. He stopped rocking and allowed his arms to fall to his sides. *I am here*, the voice said. *I am here and we are together and will always be together, Aaron.* He nodded his head. *Yes*, he thought. *We are here in this place and we are together. We will always be together.* Then it was gone and he looked around him and was unclear how he had come to be in that place and he looked wildly for his clothes and the pack and he could feel his heart begin to pump faster. His eyes widened and he bared his teeth and then...*I am here, Aaron.* He stopped all motion and walked back toward the road and found his things and re-dressed and pulled the pack onto his shoulder and came up the rise and returned to walking. He went another mile, keeping his eyes fixed on the mountain in front of him. Clouds were darkening and bunching together. Lightning came out of the mass and then a roll of thunder seemed to come down the road toward him. There was a sign up ahead but it was too far for him to read. He shifted the pack to the other shoulder and then he felt something following behind him and he turned to see a van pulling to the side of the road, coming toward him slowly. He stepped off the shoulder and into the weedy grass. The van came along beside him and stopped. He looked in and saw a woman behind the steering wheel. She leaned across the seat and forced open the passenger door. A dog barked from somewhere in the back of the van.

"This probably isn't the smartest thing for me to do, but it's the Christian thing to do. It's about to rain cats and dogs. You want a lift into White's Ridge?" Aaron looked at the woman. She was small and heavy. She had on blue jeans and a t-shirt that had a picture of a bird wearing something on its head and holding a pointed stick. The dog barked again and she said something to it, poking her head between the seats.

"Oh," she said, turning around again to face him. "He's all right. He's just mouthy. All bark, no bite." She laughed. There was something in her face, her eyes, that made him want to retreat down the slope. Words that she had spoken had inexplicably made him feel without clothes again. She seemed aware of the empty black and vast space that he often encountered, but did not fully understand and he stood looking through the open door of the van trying to work these things out in his mind like a man puzzling over a piece of machinery whose simple parts no longer worked as they should.

"Well, you want a ride or not?"

Aaron regarded her, then climbed into the seat and closed the door. "Here we go," she said, speeding the van up and merging back onto the road. "I hope you're not crazy," she said, laughing again. "For some reason, I just got it in my head that you might need a lift. Funny how that happens." Another short laugh. Aaron sat facing forward, his hands in his lap and the pack on the floorboard. The conditioned air smelled strange and unpleasant.

"Where you from?" she asked. "My name is Debbie."

"My name is Aaron," he said.

"Nice to meet you, Aaron."

"Debbie," he said.

"Yep. Debbie's Groomers. That's me. Just been up past Adan Village to see one of my customers up there. Her dog's old and can't travel. She still wants him groomed though. Poor thing. Be dead in a month don't you know. Say, speaking of Adan Village, there's something God awful tying up the interstate back there at the exit. You come from that way?" He did not answer but shook his head.

"Well, I don't know what, but something's going on. Cops all over the place. Took me half an hour to go 500 feet!" She laughed again and he thought that he had never heard anyone laugh that way. "I thought Sterno," she gestured at the dog in the back, "was gonna have a come apart with all that commotion. He was sitting up here with me and I had to put him in his crate for all his whining and carrying on. My husband named him Sterno cause he liked to kill hisself when he was a puppy. He went and ate half a can of Sterno that idgit my husband left sitting out on his work bench. Damn near died in the garage! He's gone now. My husband. No count. Ha, can't believe it's been three years. We're good though, aren't we Sterno!" She paused and looked over at Aaron.

"I'm single if you're looking," she said, laughing loudly and banging her hand on the steering wheel. In the back of the van, the dog lay flat in the crate. His ears were pinned back against his head and the fur on his neck and back was standing up. His eyes looked at the arm of the man sitting in the passenger seat. His nostrils flared and he smelled something like the dead carcass of a raccoon rotting behind the kennels in the backyard where he lived. He did not like being in the crate, did not like being confined, and the man in the front seat made him very anxious. He would be trapped if the man tried to hurt them and he believed that the man was going to hurt them. He growled a low warning and his master told him to stop. He stood in the crate and barked, but his master turned around and told him to be quiet. The man did not move or turn around and this caused him to whine and turn circles in the crate.

"I don't know what's gotten into him," Debbie said, turning on the blinker to exit at White's Ridge. "He's normally pretty good with strangers. Isn't that right, Sterno," she said, slowing the van at the bottom of the ramp and then turning right onto the state road leading into town. They passed rundown buildings with empty parking lots. A body shop connected to a muffler repair garage, a nail salon, and a video store and then a long, white single-story warehouse building with a blinking pink sign that advertised adult toys and exotic Asian massage. Rain had started to drizzle and the van's bad wipers squeaked and jerked across the windshield, which had a large spidery crack starting near the top and zig-zagging its way toward the middle. They came into White's Ridge and passed a row of dirty houses with scalped front yards, discarded toys, plastic pools, and rusting swing sets with tattered industrial rubber seats hanging from thin chains like breezeless black flags. In one of the yards a large tree had fallen and lay across the small patch of lawn, its scrawny branches reaching over the cracked sidewalk. A man in overalls was surveying the trunk, his right foot raised and resting on it, and a chainsaw in his hand. Debbie honked her horn as they went past and the man raised his free hand to her, the chainsaw idling, hanging by his side and sputtering blue smoke in the wet air. Debbie pulled the van into a gas station and got out and turned to look at Aaron through the open door. The rain was coming down harder now and she had to raise her voice to be heard over the pounding on the metal leaning roof that hovered above the pumps.

"I need to get some gas," she yelled. "I can take you back to the interstate after the rain quits. You can just hang out in the kennel office unless you want to wait it out here. I can give you some lunch, maybe. Christian thing to do, you know." Aaron looked at her and nodded. She slammed the door of the van and went to fill the tank. Aaron sat still in his seat. Behind him, the dog was turning circles in the crate and growling. He did not turn to look at it. He knew what it was thinking. He watched the fat drops of rain crash and explode onto the ground and then the run-off from the shelter came over the edge in sheets. The storm increased again and now it sounded like small stones falling from the sky and the noise pressed against the sides and the windows of the van, forcing its way inside. Aaron sat motionless, listening to the dog become increasingly agitated. Thunder banged in the sky overhead and lightning tore through the clouds just like the crack in the glass. It reminded him of being in the cabin when a storm would come through and he and Terrell would sit and listen to the rain on the roof and the wind that came through the trees with such angry force that it would rip the limbs from their trunks and fling them to the ground. After they would walk outside and he and Terrell would collect the broken limbs and stack them near the wood pile and wait for them to dry out and then they would cut them into shorter lengths and store them for burning.

Debbie climbed back into the van. Her shirt was wet and Aaron could see a clear outline of her right breast where the nipple pushed. He looked away and she started the van and pulled it back onto the road.

"I got soup at home," she said, brushing water out of her hair and rubbing her hand on her jeans which were stretched over large thighs. "That sound good?" Aaron looked at her and nodded. "All right," she said, and pulled away from the gas station and into the storm. She went another quarter mile and signaled to turn. She had to wait on a green pick-up truck to pass, and then she swung the van off the main road into a driveway. They sat quietly in the cab, the wipers off and the rain obstructing the view through the windshield. "Home again, home again, jiggity jig," she said and looked over at Aaron with a smile. "C'mon. Might as well brave it."

They got out of the van at the same time and ran around the side of a small brick ranch house. The bushes in the front were dead and brittle and there was tape across one of the windowpanes in the front. The yard consisted of weeds and muddy pools; a saturated stack of cardboard boxes was piled up and a row of Hackberry trees, their bark gnarled and tar-like with aphids twisted out of a rocky patch of ground and formed a crippled-looking barrier along the property line. They went past the house and into the rear yard where there was another brick structure. As they approached, they could hear the dogs beginning to stir and rouse. Debbie found a key on the ring she held in her hand and opened the door to the kennel. Aaron, holding his pack, followed her inside. She put the keys on a cheap desk and turned around to face him.

"You can sit in here while I go make us some lunch," she said. "I'll turn the TV on for you." She walked past him and touched a black box sitting on a shelf. The box hummed beneath the drum of the rain and then a picture with people sitting around a table came onto the glass surface and Aaron watched it with curiosity. She went past him and bumped into the .pack and the contents rattled. "Whatcha got in there?" He did not look away from the screen and she shrugged and went out the door.

"Be back in a minute," she said and ran across the yard and around the side of the house again. The room smelled heavily of the dogs and another odor that was chemical. He stood watching the television. The man at the table was yelling at the other people and there was laughter behind him, but the man was not laughing. Aaron tilted his head and set his pack on the floor next to him. Outside the rain came down even harder and he could smell the damp from when the door had been open, and it mixed with the scent of the dogs and Aaron thought about he and Terrell hunting in the woods and the time that they had killed a large buck and were dressing it in a clearing when it had started to rain and the smell mixed with the deer's blood and entrails and the water beaded on the fur and Terrell cursed the weather and they dragged the carcass out of the clearing and under the trees and finished cleaning the animal. They waited until the rain broke to carry the deer back to the cabin.

He looked around the small office and went to a door in the center and opened it. He saw the dogs in the cages on either side of the concrete walkway that ran between the enclosures. In the back of the room stood a wash sink and shelves that held brightly colored containers. Now he could also smell their waste. They were all moving inside their enclosures, pacing back and forth, making sharp turns and the noise bounced off the hard surfaces like rifle shots in his ears, not barking, but high-pitched yowling that sounded almost like screams. He closed the door and it only slightly muffled the sound.

"My word." He turned and Debbie was standing behind him holding a tray with two bowls on it that were steaming. "How did you get them riled-up like that?"

Aaron looked at her and then his attention turned to the television. She set the tray on the table and disappeared out the door. She returned with two glasses and a container of milk. She put them next to the soup bowls and then made an exaggerated shake.

"Goodness, but it's coming down. Bet you're glad I came along. You'd be out on the highway in this." She smiled at him. She had drops of rain on her face. "You ready to eat?" She turned and used two hands to pick up one of the soup bowls and then swiveled around and handed it to him. "Have a seat anywhere," she said. Aaron picked up the spoon and tasted the soup. The broth burned his tongue and he jerked his head back. "Hot," Debbie said. "Here, drink some milk." She took up the container and poured one of the glasses half-full and offered it to him. He put the spoon back in the bowl and took the milk and drank it. "Better?" she asked and went around behind the desk and sat in a chair with a ratty-looking cushion.

"I love a bowl of soup on days like this," she said. "Makes everything cozy." They ate without talking. The dogs on the other side of the door had settled somewhat. They watched the television. The man and the people at the table were no longer in the box. Now it was a man dressed in a hat carrying a gun in his hand. He would talk with other people and then he was behind a rock and firing the rifle at people who were calling out and running toward him with small axes and painted faces. "*Gunsmoke*," Debbie said. "You ever watched Marshall Dillon? My Daddy loved him. More than John Wayne even. He said that Marshall Dillon was the real deal, and my daddy would know. He was the real deal too." She smiled innocently, recalling the memory and sharing it with a stranger.

They finished the meal and Debbie took the bowls and glasses back to the house. The rain was barely a drizzle and when she returned to the kennel she said that she had some things to do in White's Ridge and that she would take him back to the interstate and he could move on to wherever he was going. "I'll meet you at the van in a few minutes. I need to visit the little girls' room." She went out and Aaron went over to the television set and touched it before getting his bag off the floor. He started out the door and the dogs inside the kennel began barking again. He came out into the yard. Everything was dripping. He looked at the back of the house where she had gone and waited. Something moved at the corner of his vision and he turned and saw the dog that had been in the back of the van. It was crouched and showing its teeth.

A low rumble came from its throat. It began to move toward him, moving each leg carefully and precisely. He set the pack on the ground and unzipped it. His hand went into it as he kept his eye on the dog. He brought out the hunting knife and then he stood still as the dog began to trot toward him.

Debbie sat on the toilet and thought about how desperate she must be to pick up a man on the side of the road and bring him home to her house. The truth was, she missed her husband. The only *idgit* in that relationship had been her. Her and her Christian upbringing. Every time that he tried to put his hand down her pants or up her shirt, she'd thought of a way to bring up Jesus. And she had brought up Jesus one too many times for him and after six straight months of drinking beer by the drum load, he'd gone out the front door and never come back. That was three years ago and for all her faith in her savior, she was as lonely as she could be. *So lonely that you're bringing in strays,* she thought. She flushed and washed her hands and was coming up the hallway when she thought she heard Sterno bark in pain. She had let him into the house before putting the soup on the stove, but now it sounded like he was in the back yard. *Oh, heck,* she thought. *I bet he got out the front door. I have to remember to get that lock fixed. I hope he hasn't tried to bite Aaron.* She picked up her pace and came out of the hall and went to the back door. She opened it as Aaron was bringing the knife up through Sterno's broad chest. He had the dog by the neck and the animal's body was limp. He was a big dog and to hold him like that must have taken tremendous strength, she thought just before she screamed in protest. Aaron, arms slick with blood, his face a blank mask, turned and looked at her. She backed into the house and slammed the door and was just stepping away from the threshold when Aaron's full weight collided with the cheap wood. She screamed again. The door bucked in its frame, shaking the wall. Debbie was trying to put it all together. *How could he pick that dog up like that? That dog weighed ninety pounds.* The door bucked again and then it was caving inward and she could make out his shoulder through the emerging cracks that seemed to grow in size like a widening smile with each violent thrust. She backed up and was reeling out of shock and thinking about the yellow telephone in the den when the door gave way entirely and Aaron stepped into the room. Pieces of the splintered wood pasted to his chest and his legs where the blood was spread in thick patches. There was a smudge of blood on his neck and his hands were dark with it. "Aaron, why would you—" and then she stopped and centered all her thoughts on the light everlasting which had washed over her in a calming wave that, had she had the time, might have presented itself as a reward for devotion and untethered faith. It was soundless, yet full of confident purpose, and she closed her eyes. When she opened them again, he was standing above her and she thought that there may have been a hint of mercy in his expression and in the briefest of seconds she hoped that her kindness to him would save her and she attempted a smile, her round face now perspiring and sobs beginning to rise in her chest. He still held the knife that he had used on Sterno and he watched her carefully and again she was filled with a soft hope that she might be spared. Sterno had been all that remained between her and her former husband and now he was violently gone, ripped from her not unlike her marriage had been. Debbie realized in the moment before Aaron fell on her that what she had always lacked was the confidence to stand up and fight on her own behalf and that all of the trust and sacrifice that she had made for Jesus, all of the strength that she had asked him for, were the futile and sad requests of a lonesome girl who had chased her man away with a misplaced devotion, putting her trust instead in animals and their indifference to those things that humans held sacred. She made a feeble attempt to kick at Aaron's legs, pushing herself tighter against the wall, cutting off any chance at escape.

He sat cross-legged next to the body. The animal had been brave and he admired its courage and wished that it had not been part of the sacrifice.

The world is not of my making
It is for the one who walks beside, for the one who pluckest out
and allows them to see in a new way.
See in a new way.
Behold, they are new. These pearls were his eyes.
Were her eyes.

Awake and knowing.

He reached out and touched the woman's breast and then pulled his hand away.

Sophia.

No, not Sophia.

Look!

He tasted the soup in his mouth. If he listened carefully he could hear the dogs in the kennel. They were savage now. More savage than before and their teeth were gnashing and their whines sounded like weeping and he wanted them to be still but he did not go back. He looked at the woman.

The world is not of my making
It is not me or you but a third and he sits
upon the throne.
He makes things
New

He stood and went down the hall and into the bathroom. He stripped and turned a handle to run water in the tub like he had seen a man in town do when they had gone to a hardware store. The hot water came out and he stepped into and it scalded his feet but he did not step out. He turned the faucet off and sat in the burning water and washed the blood from his body. It ran down the contour of his arms and chest in streaks and into the stagnant tub water, the coppery smelling of filth blooming into rust-colored clouds that floated around his white, hairless legs. He sat in the water until it became cold and then he stood and went back down the hall and through the kitchen and then into a bedroom. He went inside the room and the bed was not made and there was a light on next to the bed. He looked to his left and there was an open closet and there were men's clothes hanging there. He found a pair of pants and a flannel checked shirt and a new pair of boots. He put these things on and went out of the room and back up the hall and, stepping over the woman, he went out the door and into the yard where he retrieved his pack. He pulled the strap over his shoulder and went around the side of the house and passed the van and turned on the street and made his way back to the main road. At the intersection he looked in both directions and saw the gas station where they had stopped. He walked that way and continued south until he came to the ramp. He went up the rise and saw the mountain and the clouds had moved away from the crest and the sun was coming through, shining on the trees that covered the slopes. He walked until it grew dark and then he stepped off the road and down into the woods. He heard water running and he picked his way over fallen logs and large rocks until he came to the creek, which was moving fast with the rain and the sloped run-off from the surrounding hills. He set his pack down and sat on a stone and watched the water weave between the narrow banks of the creek. Its motion and noise lulled him and he leaned back against a tree and fell asleep.

CHAPTER 55

—

CLIMBING
THE MOUNTAIN

He woke in darkness and sat up. He heard something moving in the leaves and he remained still and after a few minutes it went past him. He stayed awake until the first light started to spread into the sky and then he left the creek and went back to the road. By mid-morning he was walking up the slope of the mountain. By mid-afternoon he was at the top. He left the interstate and rested behind an abandoned truck stop. He walked around the side of a large, single-story building. The parking lot was discolored from oil and gas spills and someone had knocked over two of the pumps. There were signs of homeless encampments behind the building. He put the pack down and sat next to a circle of stones where there had been a fire. He pulled a can of the food from the pack and used a knife to pry the top off and once again used his fingers to eat, placing the cold beans into his mouth and chewing methodically. When he was through, he tossed the can into the ditch behind him and went a short distance along the road and turned back west, into the thick trees. The new boots were stiff and the soft earth felt better than the road. He would come down the mountain that way. It was getting dark as he went across a flat field and then back under the cover. He dropped down a slope and saw the fence running in both directions. He stopped and listened. He could hear someone calling out from beyond the fence. He went closer and through a break he could see a small building with tables surrounding it. People were moving back and forth and coming in and out of the building. A child was climbing on one of the benches, using it to reach the top of the table, then jumping off the side and laughing. He stayed out of sight. When it was dark the people stopped coming and going from the building. He sat with his back against a tree, the hunting knife in his hand, and listened.

He woke when something touched his face. He opened his eyes slowly to see a deer standing in front of him. His hand tightened on the knife and he snapped an arm up and grabbed the animal, and in one fluid motion brought the knife into its neck. It kicked madly, screaming deep from within its chest, trying to get away from him, but he pulled it close to stay clear of the hooves and forced the knife in further, blood jetting onto the leaves and his clothes. The wild smell of the animal was thick in his nostrils and the blood that soaked him was hot. Finally it fell forward and was still, the full weight of its body slumping onto his chest and legs. He sat with legs outstretched, his back against the solid tree trunk, and looked at the animal's shape in the darkness. It was impossible to discern its features and he put the knife aside and ran his hands over the thick rib cage and the rump. The head and neck lay motionless against his body. With his left hand, he stroked the face and the cold rough surface of the nose. He knew that the eyes were open and looking into his face, and while he sat, calmly touching the deer, its lifeblood leaked from the wound onto his clothes and the ground and there was something reassuring about being washed in it. He closed his eyes and waited, and before long a chorus of voices, not just the single authoritative voice, began to chant inside his head. At first he was concerned that they were angry with him for so willingly cutting the animal, but as he listened closer he realized that they were instructing him, and that he, like the deer, was merely a vessel, an instrument of body and not of mind, and this relieved him because his fear was not driven by what the voices had commanded him to do, but rather that they would leave him all together, alone and no longer of use. The chorus took many forms in his mind, that of animal and man, but also a woman that he felt he somehow knew but was unable to see or touch because she was standing beyond his vision. His eyes fought for sight, but were covered in a slick sheen that covered his face and body like running sweat, and sounds were muted so that he could not hear the woman speaking, although he knew her tone was pained and tortured and he somehow understood, realized, that her pain was also his own, but he was not the sole cause of either. Then the vision would shift again and return in high-pitched voice through the carcass of the deer: sharp, steady, unsettled, repetitious, and demanding. He waited in the emptiness. The stench of the deer was heavy and suffocating, but he did not push it away from him. Light began to move into the sky but it was distant and blurred with the settling fog and rain. He began to make out shapes around him and inside of his chest he began to feel an intense swelling. His hands tingled and his eyes began to burn and itch. The blood was now completely dry on his skin.

He took up the knife that he had used on the deer. It too was caked in blood and bits of fur and flesh. He found the pack in the leaves and took out another long-handled blade, then he stood and went along the fence line, looking for a way through. The images that he had seen on the highway were flipping through his head, and the woman named Debbie had joined them, along with the pictures in the glass box of the people laughing at the table and the man shooting the rifle. He came to the terminus of the fence line and went back for the deer, carrying the body over his shoulder as he had seen Terrell do. He stopped when he returned to the end of the fence line and set the deer's body onto the ground and then knelt and used one of the knife to sever the head, using his full weight to push through the bone. When he was through, he carried the pieces to the rear of the building, placing the carcass on one of the concrete tables and pushing through the clear doors with the lifeless head held against his chest. A man came from a small room and spoke to him, surprised and confused and Aaron dropped the head to the floor and charged him, the knives raised above his head. The man fought but was easily overcome and then a second man appeared from another opening that had no door and he screamed and began to run but Aaron caught him quickly. The second man fought from his back on the ground, reaching his hands into Aaron's face, gouging at his eyes and kicking his legs wildly trying to throw him off, but it was soon over and the man lay peacefully. Aaron took the bodies into the stalls and removed their shirts and wrote upon the walls using the words that had been spoken to him during the night. He removed one of the men's eyes and took them into the other room and placed them in a cloth that he found in the new pants that he had taken from the woman's home and wrote on the glass there with the blood that was slick on his hands. When he was finished, he went into an empty stall and stood looking at the filthy walls with their own, harmless graffiti. Something began to bubble up inside of him and he became short of breath. He gulped in air and sucked in the smells of the restroom and then tears began to pour out of his eyes and he wiped at them furiously with his stained hands, rubbing the blood and gore into his skin. He coughed and choked for air and he bellowed in the cramped space of the stall. He placed his hands on the walls and fought to get himself under control, and when he had composed himself, he banged the door open with a flat, echoing sound and went to retrieve the deer head, jerking it from the floor and into his arms and then carrying it back into the men's room, where he placed it precariously on the toilet lid. He stroked the animal's matted fur and gazed into its lifeless eyes, searching for a direction. He left the room and came back into the rest area reception and saw the old couple with their dog milling at the bottom of the ramp. He had left the knife in his uncontrolled fit and he ran for it now, almost slipping in the deer's blood on the hard floor. He emerged from the vestibule between the bathrooms and ran through the front doors and fell upon the old couple, choked sobs spilled from his throat as he fought with the frail man and woman. When he was through, he watched the small dog cower between the bodies and his shoulders heaved as he observed them in the rain.

He came back inside and returned the knife to the stall where he had left it the first time and did not waste time there, fearing that whatever had attacked him from within would return. The knife sat askew on the toilet lid, a testament in its simplicity to what had taken place there. He went out and through the rear doors and back to where he had left his pack. Shouldering it, he heard the laboring engine of the Caprice.

He looked in the direction of the engine noise and he could see a shape through the rear glass doors. He tilted his head and waited. When he saw the woman come into the building, he backed away from the fence and went deeper into the woods. He sat hunched behind a tree and was patient. The woman went inside one of the rooms and she was gone for a long time and then she came out. Then a man came into the building, following the big shepherd and he backed further into the woods to where he could no longer see inside. He felt the dog coming up the slope and he knew that it could smell him. He picked up his pack and went down the slope of the mountain, running toward Winchester. He found a stream and he lay in it to clean off the blood. It came away from his skin and loosened from his hair, but only partly rinsed out of the clothes. He stood up and shivered in the damp air, the rain was subsiding to the encroaching sun. He sat on the bank and pulled out Terrell's journal and found the entry about his mother and read the name there. *Katherine Edwards*. He descended further and came to flat ground. He walked along the road in the adjacent fields, staying out of sight. After several hours, he saw a sign above him with the word Winchester on it. He returned to the highway briefly and crossed over it and then back down the embankment and onto the main road leading into town. He walked down the sidewalk with his pack in front of his chest. He came alongside a building with pictures of food in the window and he went inside and to the front counter where a teenage girl was talking on the phone. She stopped when she saw him and asked if she could help. He asked her if she knew where he could find Katherine Edwards.

"No," she said and he turned to leave when she spoke again.

"Hold on. If she's here in Winchester I can look her up." She pulled a thin phone book from beneath the counter and opened it. She ran a finger down a page and stopped. "You mean the sheriff's wife. I thought that sounded familiar. They live on Mountain Crest Lane. That's not far from here. What you want with the sheriff's wife?" She was still looking at the phone book. When she picked her head up to address him, he had already turned to leave, and the girl frowned at the stains on his shirt and pant legs, walking swiftly out of the restaurant, the sounds of people eating and laughing all around them.

CHAPTER 56

RENEE

Renee sat at the kitchen table in her old bathrobe. Her mind was weaving through the past in a loping gait, settling first on one memory and then trudging on to the next. It settled in finally on the last night that she had seen her husband. Since he left, there had been an occasional card for the kids on their birthdays, but those were few and far between, usually a cartoon of something and a rumpled five-dollar bill inside. Nothing to indicate that it was from him other than the scrawled return address in Tyre. And there had been an occasional phone call. Maybe he needed money. Maybe he was drunk and wanted someone to blame. But he never came in person, and she supposed that she could be grateful for that at least.

The last night that he was in the house was nightmarishly vivid. There had been people over, everyone drinking heavily and using drugs. Cocaine and pot mostly. Everyone keyed-up and off-balance. The kids were little. Watching TV in the back room with the door closed. Responsible parenting for the Hicks. The stereo was up loud, playing John's records and pushing the speakers for all they were worth. She remembered that Sarah had come into the kitchen to complain that they could not hear their show and she had got to her before John noticed she was there and she found some snacks and walked her back to the bedroom. Jed was on the bed holding a Snoopy stuffed animal and sucking his thumb. She lifted Sarah up next to him and stroked her hair and sat watching the show, feeling sick from the booze and her heart pounding with the coke. She lay down and would have passed out but something crashed in the kitchen and she could hear her husband yelling at another man. She pushed off the bed, the kids looking at her startled, and she went up the hall and John had the other man by the shirt and had pushed him up against the wall in the kitchen. He had a dull kitchen knife in his free hand and was waving it front of the guy's face. She came into the room and screamed for John to put the knife away unless he wanted to end up back in jail, and he turned on her, eyes wild with the drugs and his chest heaving from the excursion and yelling. She backed up and the man who had been pinned against the wall came for John behind his back and then they were both on the floor, rolling and kicking things over, profanity hurling in every direction. Another man came in the room and he got them apart and they backed to separate corners, eyeing each other.

You wanna fuck my wife, Dale? That what you want? Well here she is, Dale. Here she is. Renee had no idea what they were talking about, had no idea who Dale even was. She went to John and looked at him pleadingly. *You're messed up, John,* she had said. *Honey, you're just messed up.* Then he had looked at her and everything went into a black hole. He brought his hand up and knocked her to the floor. She went sprawling across it, slamming her head and shoulders into the overturned kitchen table. He came for her and thank God there had been other men there to stop him or she knew he might have killed her that night. It was not just the drugs or the liquor, it was them. It was who they were. It was the impious thing that was their marriage, born out of the most miserable of scenarios, and part of her wished that he'd gone ahead and killed her were it not for the children, and his inevitable targeting of them.

Outside the rain had started to fall again. Everything was grey and she could sense the blinding fog atop the mountain that towered above everything else, looking down upon them with indifference to any and all patterns of human life. Up there where those murders had taken place. Up where her daughter had gone. She had no idea where Jed went, but Sarah. Sweet Sarah. Her angel. She lit a cigarette and watched the rain blow against the thin windowpanes. Katherine. Katherine who had been such a good big sister. Katherine who would have helped her if she had just asked. She could see and smell the farm in the times before she had wanted so badly to leave it. It had seemed the center of the universe then. Now the center of the universe was a dry bank account, alcohol, and two children who wanted out more than she had ever wanted out of Taylor Branch. They deserved that, although she would be damned if she knew in which direction to point them. She certainly could not show it to them from the grocery store check-out aisle. Not on her best day. She thought about calling Bill but decided against it. He would not want to hear from her. She thought he would allow her to attend the funeral out of respect for her kids, but after that, he'd have no reason to continue any sort of relationship, and as much as she disliked his judgmental stare and terse responses, she was saddened at the prospect of leaving the ramshackle Baptist Church in Winchester for the last time, seeing those people for the last time and driving away from her sister for the very last time even though she had put so much distance between them over the years.

The idea of apologizing came to her and then balked like a reflux in her throat, acrid and in need of a rinse. That line of thinking had long since passed and it would have been a hollow effort at best. She had always managed to perceive her situation without considering her sister, and later, Katherine's husband, because the choices that she had made were her own, and to acknowledge the need for forgiveness now would be a pathetic admission of guilt and she preferred to carry that alone. The irony of Katherine being killed when it was she who had left with a man so capable of violence was almost laughable and she imagined that this was yet another example of fate having its twisted way with her. The reality was that her suffering would cease if it had been her instead of Katherine, and she believed that suffering was not through with her. Not by a long mile. It was not done the same way that she could hear John that night as if he were just down the hall yelling at her about a finding a clean t-shirt. Only he would not be yelling about a t-shirt or anything else that married couples normally hollered back and forth about. He would have her pinned to the ground, yelling at her through a fog of booze about fucking a stranger.

John had climbed off of her that night and was looking around the room, spinning in circles as if he expected any one of them to come at him next. He had roared at her, from deep down inside himself where all of the hate and rage burned like a stack of tires. He swung the knife in front of him with such force that she thought he might stick himself with it. They had all backed away. Some of the men were trying to talk him down but he just kept going and going until it started to sound like he was speaking another language. The words poured out of his mouth like he was throwing them up. Then he burned out and drooped his shoulders. He had long hair then and it hung in front of his face in disguising strands and when he looked back up he was weeping. He dropped the knife and it clattered on the kitchen floor. He went out and she heard the scrape of his truck keys against the wood table by the door and then he was just gone. After that, everyone left and the house was as quiet as it had been since the day they moved in with mismatched suitcases, garbage bags with clothes, a basket of toys for the kids and the wrath that was John Hicks.

She got up from the kitchen table and went into the front room, carrying the pack of cigarettes and the blue lighter with her. She sat down in the chair and looked out across the field. Stetson the cat was on his perch and then she heard something that made her turn around. A small dog was in the house. Someone had poured some of the cat food in a shallow bowl and left it on top of a towel on the far side of the room. There was a bowl of water there as well. Sarah, she remembered. The orphaned dog. Sarah had brought the dog home with her, that night after the murders at the rest area. It was curled up asleep and must have been dreaming to make the noise. Renee got up and went across the room, cutting an eye at Stetson as she did so. The cat was watching her with indifference. She made a clicking sound with her mouth and the dog raised its head and looked at her with eyes that were wary. She talked in a soothing voice and eventually the dog came to her. She picked it up and it licked her face. She went back to the chair in front of the window. Just as she thought, the mountain was clouded over. The little dog stood in her lap, turned four circles, and then sat down neatly. She stroked its head and looked out at the rain and tried to keep her mind from racing. The dog was a comfort she felt she did not deserve, but she would take it and treat it well and offer what little left she had to give. A gust of wind swept across the yard and the dog burrowed deeper into her robe as if it had felt it. She scratched it behind the ears. *It needs a name.* She could sit and think about naming the dog and that would keep her mind off of everything else. She went through biblical names, common names, and finally on literary names from her childhood books. She thought and smoked and finally it came to her. It was obvious and she smiled sweetly at the dog's upturned face as she scratched under its chin. "We'll call you Oliver," she said and gave it a playful pinch on the nose. The dog nipped playfully back. "Oliver Twist," she said. "The orphan dog that found an unexpected home."

CHAPTER 57

THE SEARCH

Sarah heard someone calling from the front of the sheriff's office. She wondered why no one was answering and then she thought that maybe Rhonda had decided to leave after the coroner's assessment and the brutality and psychosis that they were all likely up against. There was a part of her that wanted the same thing. She had to keep kicking it back down. She went to the front and saw a teenage girl standing in the middle of the room, appearing lost. She was snapping gum in her mouth, nervously blowing small pink bubbles. When she noticed Sarah she absently took a few stray strands of her long brown hair and began curling them around one finger, twirling the strands until they covered the length of the finger and then letting it go and starting over again. A meticulous and distracting process that Sarah imagined irritated the girl's mother to no end.

"Can I help you?" Sarah asked. The girl looked at her as if she did not understand the question. "Are you okay?" Sarah asked.

"I need to see the sheriff," she said. Sarah came around the front desk. Through the front window she could see Rhonda out on the sidewalk, smoking. *Thinking about running,* Sarah thought.

"He's not here right now. He'll be back in a little while. Can I help you with something?" The girl tried to see past her into the interior of the building and then turned back and looked at Sarah.

"I think I saw him," she said.

"You think you saw who?" The girl's face was blank. She was not chewing the gum anymore.

"I think I saw the man that killed that woman in her house. Everyone in the diner is talking about it. That and those killings that happened on the mountain. I think the man who done it was in the diner before." Now she began crying and wrapping the strands of hair tighter and tighter around her finger. She stammered, "I think I might have given him her address. Oh God, I think I might have given him her address." Sarah stood, disbelieving. She did not know the girl in front of her, but she looked like any other middle or high school-age kid living in Winchester, appeared and carried herself as Sarah once had, in a perpetual state of indecision and vulnerability, uncomfortable with her body and the attention it was beginning to draw. The girl's eyes flitted around the small room, and the enlarged pupils made Sarah wonder if she was on something and Sarah felt herself getting angry at the idea that some hopped-up kids had put this girl up to a prank that was about as far from funny as you could get. She watched more intently, trying to decide how to proceed and now she realized that the girl was truly scared. Scared in a way that she had not yet encountered, and she could not keep her focus because the fear had a strangle hold on her nerves. She was like a small bird that's trapped in a house, trying in vain to punch through a window with its own body.

"What's your name, honey?"

The girl flashed a relieved smile. Here was a question she knew the answer to.

"Jennifer," she said.

"You mentioned the diner, Jennifer. Is that where you work?"

"Yes. So does my mom."

"Okay," Sarah said. "And that's where you think you saw the man who might be responsible for killing these people?"

"Yes," Jennifer said. Her face had gone blank and Sarah could see the freckles around her eyes and a few that dotted her nose and she could see what Jennifer had looked like when she was a little girl. Sarah crossed to where she stood. The two of them were about the same height.

"Where did you see this man?"

"In the diner."

"Did he come in to eat?"

"No," she said. "He come in around lunch and asked where Katherine Edwards lived. It was late lunch, but we were still busy so I told him that I didn't know, but then I thought about the phone book and I..."

"Looked it up for him," Sarah finished almost in a whisper.

"Yeah, but I didn't know. How could I have known?"

"I understand," Sarah said. "Go ahead. You're not in trouble."

"Okay," Jennifer said. "He left after I gave him the address."

"Did he say where he was going, where he'd come from, why he was asking for Katherine Edwards?" Sarah saw the anger and the frustration creeping into her voice by looking at Jennifer. "I'm sorry," she said. "I don't mean to sound mad. We're just all concerned, you know?" Jennifer nodded.

"He didn't say nothing else. Just asked about Mrs. Edwards," and then she thought. "I did ask him what he wanted with her," she said and smiled a little, but it was weak and short-lived. "After he left I went back to work and then this morning I heard about, you know, the murders and I remembered that..." she was losing composure.

"You remembered what, Jennifer? What did you remember?" She was dangerously close to losing her witness to a meltdown.

"He had blood on him," Jennifer shouted. "I didn't think nothing about it when he came in cause I figured he'd been hunting and a lot of guys come in after hunting, drunk and trying to sober up before they go home, and they all have blood on them and he looked like he'd come out of the woods and so I don't think about it. But now I know it was him because he was asking after where Mrs. Edwards lived and I gave him the fucking address." She was almost screaming and Sarah went to her and put an arm around the girl, guiding her to the chairs sitting empty along the far wall. She helped her into one and kept her arm around Jennifer's shoulders. The girl's psyche was teetering, shoulders shaking, breaths hitching.

She had been alone with the knowledge of what she had inadvertently done and had been punishing herself in that degrading voice that teenagers reserve only for themselves. Sarah called out to Ethan who came into the room, placing batteries in a flashlight handle. He looked at the two women sitting in the chairs and Sarah glanced up. "Can you get me a glass of water?" He went back without asking any questions and returned with the glass and came around to where they were sitting and held it until Sarah realized that he was standing in front of them and she looked back to the girl and whispered something and the girl sat up and tried to brush the tears out of her eyes with an absent stroke of her hand. She had cheap bracelets on her wrist that were bunched and those that were made of cloth were fraying like something an animal would use to make a nest or den. Sarah took the glass from Ethan and helped Jennifer drink. She sipped the water and it made her cough and Sarah pulled the glass away, afraid the girl might vomit from all the crying.

"There," she said. "Just take a deep breath." The girl was settling but still shaking. The soft blond hair on her arms was standing up and Sarah saw the goose flesh and she glanced up again at Ethan and mouthed the word *jacket*. He left and came back with a coat, and rather than wait on Sarah, he stepped in and placed the coat around the girl's shoulders, who pulled it around her.

"That help some?" Sarah said, softly. Jennifer nodded and looked at Ethan. "Thank you," she said.

"Okay, Jennifer." Sarah reached down and took one of the girl's hands. "We are going to sit here for a minute and let you calm down. You did the right thing coming in. Here." Sarah picked up the water glass from where she had placed it on the floor. "Drink this for me."

They waited until Jennifer had regained her composure and then Sarah and Ethan took her back to a small room with a single desk and had her walk them through what had happened in the diner. She had only seen the man once, but she was able to provide a general description. White, about six foot, she guessed. Carrying a pack of some kind. He had asked for Katherine by name. No, she did not know Mrs. Edwards personally, but did know that she was the sheriff's wife, and thought she was being helpful. Of course, they told her. How could she have known who the man was? Sarah asked the questions and Ethan took notes. When they were through, Sarah asked if Jennifer minded waiting for the sheriff to get back. She did not but asked if maybe she should call her mom at the diner and tell her what was going on. She had not informed her where she was going and they were going to worry with everything that was happening and the dinner shift was coming up at the diner. Sarah told her that it would be fine if she

called her mom. Edwards came in soon thereafter and Jennifer went
through everything again. She started to unravel when she realized she
was talking to the dead woman's husband, but Edwards was reassuring,
fatherly almost, and she made it through the details a second time. Her
mother arrived and they explained how Jennifer had approached them,
that she was not in any trouble, and her mother sat and listened with an
expression of horror. Sarah could see the similar mannerisms between
the two women, the way their eyes went tight when they were about to
cry and Jennifer's mother wound her hair around her finger in the same
way that her daughter did.

After Jennifer and her mother left, Edwards assembled them all
in the back building with the dog enclosure and the weapons locker.
Rhonda had waited on the sidewalk until Edwards returned and she
tried to quit, but Edwards told her that she needed to stay until he
figured out an alternative. She tried to protest, but he would not hear
it, telling her she would receive triple pay if she went back inside and
controlled the small switchboard. The phone was ringing nonstop and
each time she ended a conversation it would ring again. The town
had moved beyond nervous, they all knew. The pulse of the panic was
quickening, and Rhonda was beyond her capacity, but she listened and
took down names and numbers and told the men who called to stay at
home with their families and the women who called that the sheriff's
department was on top of it and that yes, the sheriff was there despite
what had happened. And yes, the FBI had been notified, and on and
on it went. Tibbits had called and was sending vehicles to patrol Winchester. Edwards spoke with him behind a closed door, but the deputies
could hear that they were arguing about going into the woods and then
they could tell that Tibbits was insisting to go along and Edwards was
explaining that he needed the Marion County officers in Winchester
more than he needed them on the mountain, and finally his old friend
backed down and agreed to go along with what Edwards had planned.
Tibbits had called Ellis prior to phoning Winchester and as soon as
Edwards hung up the phone, Rhonda sent a call through from Ellis.
The deputies listened to the same argument through the closed door
and when Edwards emerged, they did not know whether they were
going or not until Edwards asked Flip if he had the gear packed and if

the dog was taken care of, and when everything was confirmed he told them that it was time to leave.

They collected their things and went out to the vehicles, Sarah riding with Edwards, Ethan and Flip bringing the dog in Flip's pick-up. When they drove out of Winchester, the pale sun was dropping behind them, clouded over by the rain that had come back as if a final, subtle deterrent, but they pushed it away with the steady back and forth of the wiper blades. They crossed the distance between Winchester and the mountain in single file, and then went up the slope with the big engines laboring and steady. They pulled off at the rest stop, moving around the orange barriers. They parked parallel to one another and each of them got out of their vehicle at the same time. They pulled their gear onto the parking lot ground and Herc stood watching them with his head moving from one to the other and then finally settling his eyes on the wooded area behind the building, his posture erect and his ears perked. They checked their weapons and then again, in single file, they went around the side of the building and up the slope and down along the fence line and around it and then into the thick woods, breaking their single file line and fanning out like a hunting party. Nothing moved and nothing made a sound except the rain coming through the trees, splashing on the fallen leaves that coated the ground, and that was good because the wet muffled their steps and disguised their advance. The patches of fog made visibility poor. The damp air was cold and heavy and the rain cut through in bloated drops that made flat sounds when it hit their parkas. They moved through the underbrush slowly, picking up their feet in an almost exaggerated fashion that allowed them to keep their eyes forward while also avoiding fallen limbs and protruding roots. They were beyond the sight of the building and the terrain was sloping downward. The dog was ahead of them, moving in and out of their field of vision, trotting back and forth in front of their line, head swiveling side to side, low to the ground. When it stopped and pricked up its ears, Edwards held his hand up and they all stilled, looking in every direction and straining to hear. The futility of searching the vast woods for a single man was as pervasive as the fog's silent cover. This thought needled each of them, even Flip who was more at home in the woods than he was in his shabby house. It would not be long before they would need the flashlights and the lanterns, and Edwards looked at each of his deputies, whose faces were alert and taut, and despite their bravest efforts, his confidence began to fade. As it stood now, he was still in control. At least he was in control of what would happen next. But he took very little comfort from that because equally as strong was the image of Katherine, bound and sacrificed in a bed they had shared their entire married life, her integrity once again hatefully stripped from her by a corroded soul whose violations were enacted as if he knew that eternal condemnation was just around the corner and his judgement already levied. Edwards looked ahead, straining to see through the trees, and he awakened his own fear. Fear that they would not find this man, and fear that they would.

CHAPTER 58

——

AARON

H e sat in the cave and opened another can of the food, not tasting it as he pushed handfuls into his open mouth. He looked out of the yawning mouth and watched the rain fall and the fog closing in around the dripping entrance but not coming inside, where he crouched like something prehistoric, frightened, and tense in his surroundings. He had refrained from building a fire. The voice had warned him against that and so he ate the food cold, chewing without consideration, biting the side of his cheek at one point and spitting out a mouth full of the chewed mush, tasting the slight copper-tinge of the blood's trickle. The cave was deep and the walls were damp from the pools of water that had gathered in the low spots. The pools of water were slimy and he did not drink from them. He had filled a canteen with water from a runoff stream he encountered on his way back up the mountain, and as he was filling the mouth, he had seen the cave openings punched into a large outcropping of rock, the two entrances burrowed in the stone façade like tunneled black eyes that watched him from above. He had come up the rise and stood looking into the entrances, holding his pack on his shoulder and the canteen of water in his free hand. He knelt and set the water on the ground and picked up a large stone and threw it into the first opening and then he stood and waited to see if anything emerged. The stone clacked against the interior walls of the cave and then it was quiet again. When nothing came forward, he picked up another large stone and threw it into the second entrance and waited. A fox appeared and looked at him, then went back inside the cave and returned a second time with a rabbit in its jaws and turned the opposite direction from where he was standing and made its way up the slope carrying its food.

He picked up the canteen and went into the first entrance. The floor was sandy and strewn with fractured pieces of rock and clods of rotted leaves and sticks. He went to the back of the cave and could not see the slope rising to the entrance, just the strands of fog and sheets of rain. He sat hunched and eating, reciting the passages over and over again in his head, calming himself, content to once again be in the woods. The *acts* had been both satisfying and perplexing and now that it was mostly complete, he felt an immense fatigue beginning to wash over him. He tossed the can to the rear of the cave and lay down to sleep. In his chest, his heart beat in a slow cadence. He closed his eyes and he could see the spectral mother sitting up in the bed in the dark room and he could still smell her fear. He saw the dog coming around the side of the house and he opened his eyes suddenly, regretfully. Had that been what was expected of him? He did not know. He lay back down and went through all of the events since leaving the cabin. Then he stood and went to the pack and pulled out one of the knives and lay down again, holding the knife against his chest with its point just below his chin.

In his dream, the mother was standing in a clearing. She was naked and her arms were outstretched. He was being shown the vision from outside of his own body. He was also standing in the meadow and the mother was calling for him, turning in circles with her arms still outstretched. Her eyes were missing, but she was smiling and he came across the matted grass of the meadow floor and her back was to him when he came close to her and then she completed her circle and was there in front of him, but not seeing him. She smiled and brought her arms out in front of her and walked until her fingers touched his face. They moved over the contours, caressing his skin. He stood still and allowed her to touch him, and then she stepped closer and put her arms around his neck and he was watching this from somewhere high in the trees above the meadow. She turned her head to kiss him, pulling him into her body that smelled of rot and decay. He tried to pull away but her embrace tightened and her hands, the skin almost translucent, found his throat. They gripped the soft flesh in an impossible vice. Her mouth was open and the reek of her was overwhelming. He fought, but her hands were locked. *Aaron*, she hissed. He was trying to push away from her, trying to get free, trying... *Aaron my sweet boy. Let your mother kiss her child.* He came awake on the floor of the cave, sweat covering his body. He had dug the knife into the sand, perhaps a dozen gouges in the earth in a random stabbing pattern next to where he slept. He looked wildly around the cave. It was black behind him and he could hear the steady drip of water and nothing more.

CHAPTER 59

AT CAMP

"Sheriff," Flip said. "Herc's got something, I think." They had been walking for half an hour when the dog went rigid ahead of them. The rain was still coming down and Edwards had started to lose hope that the dog would be able to pick anything up with all this water cleansing the ground of scent. Flip was standing to his right and they all fell in around him. The dog was moving up and down a poorly-defined path where it looked as though someone had walked. The leaves had been matted and the line went straight down toward a rock shelf, and then it stopped.

"Could be anyone," Flip said.

"Could be our guy," Sarah said, shaking rain off the hood of her parka. "What do you think, Sheriff?" Ethan came up behind them, holding the shotgun on his shoulder. "Let me look," he said and moved around Sarah.

"If it's a deer, why would the trail come from those rocks? They can't climb."

"He's right," Flip said, smiling at Ethan. "It's not an animal, at least it's not a deer trail. They would have come this way at an angle from wherever they found their way around the rocks. This comes straight from the climb, like someone came up the face and walked to where we are."

"Or went down," Sarah said.

"Or both," Edwards said.

"Either way. Dog could make that climb if it had to. Bobcat sure could do it. But I'm guessing…" he turned around and looked back the way they had come, "Yep, see it there," he said. "We just missed it coming this way cause we didn't know what we were looking for. Someone came this way for sure."

Flip walked alongside the portion of the trail leading to the outcrop, the dog a few feet behind. He moved the piled leaves gently away from the center with the toe of his boot, kneeling down in the dim light.

"There are boot prints along here," he said, pointing with a stick he had picked up. "See." They came at once. "Careful," he said. They slowed and stood behind him and looked over his squatting frame. "See here," he hovered the stick above a track. "And here. I'm guessing heavy work boots. Justin's maybe. Something with a thick rubber sole and probably a steel toe considering how rounded the front of the track is. Treads are really clean so may be new. You're not going to get a clear trail cause the rain has washed down toward that rock, but I bet you find ten or eleven more between here and there, and probably more than that if we tracked him back up the hill." He walked to where Herc sat and lowered himself down again and scratched the dog behind his ears, offering praise, his rifle resting across his knees, the barrel pointed away from where they were all standing.

"Any tracks like that at either of the scenes?" Flip asked over his shoulder. No one responded. "It's a good find, Flip," Edwards said sensing the discouragement. "A good start. Unfortunately, anyone could have been hiking back here in these woods…"

"Nah," Flip said standing up quickly. "Someone came through here recently, Sheriff. They were heading down the mountain and I know for a fact that there is not a house within ten miles in any direction, unless you want to count the rest area. Anyone hunting up here in the last couple days would have been ignorant or looking to get themselves on a suspect list. It may not be our boy, but with all this rain I'm betting it's not somebody out here watching birds."

"The rest area," Sarah said.

"What's that?" Edwards said.

"Nothing," she said quietly, but her mind was frantic. Until then she had kept the murders in their respective scenes, and now the mobility of the killer gave him a human form, free to move from one place to another, to observe from any vantage point he selected. This was not their manhunt. It never had been. and the clarity of this forced her to steady herself against a tree trunk, hoping that no one would notice.

"How far does the rock shelf go, Flip?" Edwards said.

"Don't know. I've only been back this way a couple times myself. Maybe a quarter mile. Maybe half."

The rain had eased and Edwards sat looking down the slope. They had less than forty-five minutes before they were in full dark. "Okay," he said. "We stay here tonight. We'll get separated wandering out here, and if you're right about the trail, I want to wait until morning to follow it." Flip began to protest but Edwards cut him off. "All right?" he said, looking at Flip directly. Flip nodded.

"Get these tents set-up and let's get the guns out of the rain and cleaned up. Spread that tarp between these trees and make a shelter we can all get under. Flip." He motioned for Flip to join him further down the slope.

They came even with one another.

"I want you to take the dog and search below that rock shelf. You think Herc can follow you down?"

"Yeah," Flip said, "unless it drops too far and then we'll both have to go around."

"Okay," Edwards said. "I don't want you to go far, but I want you to make sure that there's no one below us." Flip nodded and clapped his thigh and he and Herc went down. Edwards watched them, the dog in the lead and carefully picking its way down the rock face, Flip behind with his rifle pointed up, using his free hand to steady his descent. Edwards thought about sending Ethan as well but backed off the idea, watching Flip descend out of sight. *We're right here*, he thought and turned away.

The three of them made camp. Edwards helped Ethan tie off the tarp between the trees, cinching the ropes up high enough so they could build a fire. Sarah set up the two octagonal tents. When they were through with that, they took inventory of the gear, and it was not until they were setting out and testing the radios that Edwards realized that Flip was still not back. He stood suddenly and took his rifle and went quickly down the slope and looked over the edge of the outcrop. He saw no movement and he called back to Sarah and Ethan to be alert. He started down a wash between two of the rocks that had beards of green moss on their surface. He sat and put his legs forward and began inching his way down, the rifle strapped over his back. Small pieces of rock scattered and rolled down ahead of him and he was careful that each foot hold was firm before allowing his full weight to follow. He paused and tried to lean over and could not see past the stone face. He inched further down and stopped when he heard a loud yelp. He waited and could hear the muffled voices of Sarah and Ethan. Then he heard Flip yell at the dog to get back. Herc was barking fiercely. Edwards cursed his decision to send Flip alone and quickened his pace, descending faster and making less cautious placements with his feet. "Get back, goddammit," Flip yelled and Edwards was finally down and taking his rifle off his shoulder. He could not see Flip or the dog. He called but did not receive a response. His heart banged. He could not see around the side of the rock, but he could hear the dog growling low in its chest.

Why did you leave me, Billy?

Why did you leave me alone with him? Images of her standing in the parking lot at the hospital. Her torn eyes. Oh Jesus wept. *Oh Katherine, I am so sorry.*

"Get back, goddammit, I said. Move clear, Herc!" From atop the rock Sarah was yelling for him. "Sheriff," she screamed. "Uncle Bill."

He took in a deep breath and stepped clear of the rock, rifle raised and tight to his shoulder.

"Whoa, Sheriff," Flip said and raised his hand. His rifle was pointed in the air and the dog was staring at something still out of his site. "Rattlesnake," Flip said. "Herc," he yelled. "Get back, goddammit!" The dog barked once more and obeyed, stepping back away from the snake, but never taking his eyes off of it. Edwards came away from the rock and stepped back to where Flip was standing. He saw the snake near the base.

"Is he bit?"

"No, but damn near. Scared the shit out of him. Jumped like a toad. I never even heard it." The dog backed further away and sat looking at the two men. Flip reached to his side and pulled his pistol from his holster and sighted the snake. It was buzzing and tightly coiled, dark colors almost impossible to distinguish in the wet leaves, still as the stone above it save for the shaking rattle.

"Damn lucky," Flip said and shot it. The snake jerked and came off the ground and then dropped, elongated on the sandy floor beneath the rock. It twitched and Flip approached it and shot it again and it went still. Edwards stepped back and could see Sarah at the top of the rock. "We're fine, Sarah," he called up. "We're fine." She walked back from the edge without speaking. Edwards looked to Flip.

"Nothing down here, Sheriff, 'cept for that," he said and gestured with the pistol at the thick serpent that lay with a twist in its body, the head upside down and the hole that had gone through it, oozing blood that looked black. He put the pistol back in his holster and took a cigarette from beneath his parka. He offered the pack to Edwards and he took one and they stood smoking. "There's a clean break in the rock face couple-hundred yards that way," Flip pointed. "We should be able to make it up before the sun drops. It's too slick to go back the way you came down." They walked in the direction of the break, and when they had finished smoking, they went up, following the dog like a string of goats seeking a higher shelf. They came to the top of the outcrop and walked back toward the others until they saw Ethan and Sarah standing beneath the tarp. They were both holding their guns and Edwards called out. "Nothing," he said trying to sound reassuring. "How's that fire coming?" They lowered their weapons.

"We didn't start it," said Ethan. "Wanted to be sure."

"Right," Edwards said and then realized that the two rounds that Flip had fired would have been audible to anyone even remotely close to where they were. He let the thought pass. If they had not thought of this, then best to let it be. "That's smart thinking." They came under the tarp and removed their wet parkas.

"Sarah?" Edwards said. She looked at him and then down at Ethan who had knelt to start the fire. He had piled some sticks in a Boy Scout's teepee and he pulled a flare from one of the packs and broke it and jabbed the flame into the sticks. Moisture hissed from the wet wood and smoke funneled up in thick white tendrils. "Sarah," Edwards said again. She looked up. "You okay?" She nodded and walked away from the fire.

"We're gonna have to split up," Flip said to no one in particular. "There's no way we can cover these woods in a group. Too much of it. And besides, if he is out here, he'll hear us coming a mile away. No way to avoid it."

"Shit, Flip," Ethan said. "He's already heard us with you shooting like that." Edwards smiled at the boy. Flip looked irritated and embarrassed and was about to defend himself when Edwards raised his hand like he was pulling apart two brothers, prone to bickering and fighting.

"No," Edwards said. "I'm not sending any of you out alone. I won't have that on my conscience." Flip toed the ground, watching Ethan reposition the flare. A small flame had started to kindle.

"Sheriff," Flip began.

"No, Flip," Edwards snapped, looking at him, the growing flames now creating the slightest bit of warmth. Beyond the tarp, it was full dark. Flip was quiet and Sarah stopped unpacking one of the packs. She looked back toward the fire and saw Ethan's troubled, boyish face in the flickering light and it reminded her of Jed, sitting at their mother's table, full of remorse and misdirection and she wanted badly to put her arms around him and comfort him as she had done so many times when they were young and at the mercy of adults who acted as if they themselves were children in desperate need of guidance, compassion, and discipline.

"Flip," Edwards said.

"He's just one man, Sheriff."

Edwards bit his lower lip. "He's one man that has killed a lot of people, Flip. This isn't some addict squatting in a trailer."

"Don't you think I know that, Sheriff?" Flip said angrily.

"Yes," Edwards said. "I do. And for that reason I expect you to respect what I'm telling you. We've had too much taken from us to make a reckless decision now. I need you with me on this, Flip. I won't put any of you in harm's way if it's not necessary. Do we understand each other?"

Flip nodded but did not answer.

"Do we understand each other?" Edwards repeated.

"We understand each other," Flip said and skulked beneath the tarp and bent over his pack.

"Got it," Ethan said standing up and dropping the flare into the fire. "Got it, Sheriff." He was smiling and the regret that Edwards had for bringing the boy up here, for bringing Sarah up here, was enough to knock him over. What had he been thinking? The two of them knew nothing more about police work than writing tickets and the occasional tense discussion with a drunk. Neither one of them had any experience with murder, and neither did he for that matter. The last one that he worked had been more than five years ago and that had been pretty cut and dry. Wes Ransome had shot and killed his wife in their bedroom, and when the neighbors called, Wes was standing out in the yard in front of his collapsing modular home, waving a gun around that looked like it might have been used in the Civil War. Edwards had tried to talk him down, standing behind the open door of his car, his hand on his own pistol, asking again and again for Wes to drop the revolver and calm down, tell him what was wrong. Wes had not dropped the revolver and had instead turned it on himself. Edwards could still see him lying in the yard, blood pooling atop the slick mud. Now, standing on top of this mountain under a makeshift shelter, the fire light playing off their faces, Edwards felt more helpless than ever.

This must have been how Kat felt when things started slipping, he thought. *Knowing that your mind was coming apart as easily as crumpling dry leaves in your hand, the rough little pieces flittering to the ground when you turned your palm over, some of them sticking to the skin, the others cast off and blown in various directions. Helpless. This was a mistake.*

They were looking at him. *Mistake or not,* he thought, *you have to lead them off of this mountain alive. Not tonight. We'll need to make it through the night.*

"We'll take shifts standing watch," Edwards said. "Two at a time, I think, considering we are exposed on all sides. Ethan and Flip will take first." Edwards wanted either himself or Flip to be with Sarah or Ethan at all times if he could help it. Flip knew the woods, knew guns, and had enough redneck in him to be fearless. At least to a point. That was the good and the bad of it. Edwards had maturity on all of them, but what he gained in years, he lost in endurance, and there were physical limitations as well. He looked at the outcrop he had gone done earlier and knew that if Flip had been in real trouble, he would likely have been too late to help. Already he could feel the damp seeping into his bones and the slow ache that would ensue the longer he was out there.

"Everybody okay with that?" he asked.

They nodded.

"Good," he said. "What did you pack to eat?" He clapped his hands, realizing again that he was trying to lighten things, trying to make it more like a true camp-out rather than setting them up to be ambushed, and God knew what else. They had brought jerky and packs of crackers and there were several canteens with water. Edwards opened one of the packs and reached in and his hand touched glass. He moved aside a rolled-up shirt and saw the whiskey. He pulled it out and examined it, then looked across the fire where Flip was squatting.

"What's this, Flip?"

The deputy gave Edwards a sheepish look. Then he smiled broadly as if to charm it away.

"Case we get cold," he said, shrugging his shoulders. Edwards stood and walked out from beneath the tarp, unscrewed the cap on the bottle and let the brown liquor flow out onto the ground, looking at Flip while he did it. Finding the liquor ratcheted his nerves up another notch. Flip knew to look away and pretend to be busy with something else. Edwards came back to the fire and sat down next to Sarah, tossing the empty bottle aside. They ate in silence, listening to the sound of the fire. Ethan made a couple attempts at conversation, but they went nowhere, each of them turning the same thoughts over and over in their head and coming to the same crossroads that held no answers for miles in either direction—Flip energized by arrogance, Ethan struggling with his youth and effusive good nature, and Sarah... Edwards could not tell how Sarah was managing it. Her eyes were fixed on a point somewhere in the fire and the warm glow from the flames moved over her face in a way that brought out the natural beauty of the Winslett women.

She deserves so much better than this, Edwards thought, picturing Renee with a glass in her hand. *I should have raised her. WE should have raised her. Should have taken them away from those sick people and taken them to Winchester. What kind of protest would Renee and John have made? And if they had made one, couldn't I have used my influence to make them see differently? Shown them the inside of a cell for drugs and neglect. Oh, you could have done so much more by them, Bill. She could be working in an office somewhere or out having a good time with some well-to-do boyfriend or husband, living in a big city, far from all of this mediocrity and desolation and overall disparaging life. She could have been anything that she wanted. She was smart and capable and beyond this place, and instead she was being forced to work through one terrible situation after another, over and over, because there was little else to think about here. She might even have kids of her own by now, raising them away from the haunting of her own childhood and the familial weights and stagnant culture that kept her from something more significant than all of this. And Jed, well on his way to being a drunk like his daddy. Maybe not mean like that but lost just the same. And every time he climbed on a barstool, every time he stumbled out in the parking lot fumbling with his keys and swerving his way home on those twisted country roads, was one more step down an inevitable path that ended in a jumpsuit or a cheap coffin.*

"Sheriff?"

"Yeah, Ethan," Edwards said.

"You think we're gonna find him?" Sarah turned and looked at Edwards and then over at Ethan.

"I don't know, Ethan. Maybe."

"Could be that he finds us," Flip said, tossing a stick into the fire.

"Could be, Flip," Sarah said, giving him a look that warned him to back off if he was planning on winding Ethan up. She knew how that started, and like Edwards, she was having a hard time understanding why anyone thought having Ethan with them was a good idea. She knew that her uncle probably thought the same about her, but Edwards also knew that she was stronger than Ethan on his best day.

"Cause, see," Ethan began. "I never got a chance to call my mom before we left. And well, I just was thinking that if we did run into him…"

"That's enough of that Ethan," Sarah said. "You can talk to your folks when we get back down. You're gonna be fine. We're all gonna be fine. Right, Sheriff? Sheriff?"

Edwards was looking across the fire at Herc. The dog had been lying down and looking out in the woods. Possibly sleeping, but probably sleeping with one eye open. Now he was sitting up and looking

426

intently into the dark. Ethan had his head down. Flip was looking at Edwards and he turned to follow what he was observing. When Flip saw the dog, he reached beside him and brought the rifle into his lap and then repositioned his body, pulling his knees beneath him so he would not be sitting down if he had to shoot. Sarah caught the movement and it took her a second to register what was happening. Edwards pulled his sidearm from its holster, the leather creaking as he did so. He moved from a sitting position to his knees. Sarah waved her hand to get Ethan's attention and reached behind her and felt for her shotgun. Ethan looked around the circle, confused, and Sarah waved for him to come around the fire and get beside her. Herc did not pay any attention to their movements. The fire hissed, the heat reaching a sodden patch in one of the logs. "Flip," Edwards whispered. "Can you see?"

Flip did not turn but shook his head. They waited, watching the dog and the cavernous blackness that encircled them. The snap of a branch and Herc's lurch forward were almost simultaneous. Flip yelled at the animal and was up and running after it with Edwards yelling behind him to stop. The dog growled and barked and gave chase.

"Stay here," Edwards shouted at Sarah, picking up the deer rifle as he ran beneath the tarp. "Stay!" and then he was running away from the fire and following Flip and Herc, beyond the reach of the fire.

CHAPTER 60

———

OUTSIDE THE CAVE

After the dream he stood in the mouth of the cave for a long time, looking out into the trees, whose limbs swayed with a determined wind that had ushered in the cloud cover. On his left, the grade declined down, and to his right, it sloped upward toward the rock face he had traversed when he was making his way into the town after the rest area, slinking among the stone crevices and then weaving in and out of giant trunks like some hibernating animal awakened and hungry. Cold air moved around him as if the cave itself were exhaling damp soggy breaths that clung to his exposed skin like a spectral film. He thought of Terrell and the times they had spent together quietly watching the animals and the revolting weather patterns that changed the landscape in patient turns of color and temperature. In the winter, great swarms of starlings would arrive, flying overhead, a cacophony visualized in twisting and rapidly rising and falling swarms of wings that would stop and disperse as suddenly as it had formed. And then his uncle would loudly clap his hands together and the birds would lift from the limbs of the trees in all directions before coming back together effortlessly and miraculously without incident. He had watched the Starlings with a fascination so intent that Terrell often had to touch his shoulder to pull him out of the trance. He thought that they were the embodiment of the voice and he studied their movements for signs, messages that would validate his thinking.

Now standing alone, he felt the need to speak with Terrell or to sit on the floor of the cabin and listen to him reading from the books that he most admired, the old man spinning himself into great bursts of animated gyration as the words tumbled out of his mouth, and he would begin reading them faster and faster, and often he would throw the book aside and move about the cabin reciting from memory and he, as a boy, would look on and feel the energy rising within his own body, nourishing his thoughts and curiosity. Images that he did not know to be foreshadow flashed with winter star-like clarity and he smiled and received them as if each was a divine gift. Where remorse and nostalgia should have been, he thought instead only of razor-sharp severity that emerged from a deep, rock-lined well of resentment drawn up from the cold vitriolic spring with hand over sweating hand rapacity, the rough motion and rusted and squeaking pulley jostling and jerking the bucket, slopping out the unctuous liquid that slimed the wooden slats. This thing within him had a voracious appetite and it devoured and consumed in greedy slurping gulps, devoid of moderation, single and constant in nature, until its consumption clogged its own gorging appetite and then bent over, racked with cough, it spent its gluttony on the ground in a puddle of filth.

He went back into the cave and collected his things. He reemerged holding the pack and let his eyes adjust to the dark and then he turned up the slope and began walking. He knew the outcropping was directly ahead of him and he did not wish to climb it without the benefit of light. He turned and walked parallel with the towering rock, and when he thought he had reached the pass, he turned again and started climbing. The grade steepened and he could feel stone beneath his feet but it was not steep and soon his feet were back on soft ground. He walked further along the slope and found the pass and made his way up the ledge, carefully feeling for foot and handholds as he advanced. The thick mist was all around him and he climbed by touch alone, the contents of the pack rattling now and then as it bumped against his back and buttocks. He reached the top and pulled himself over the lip and rested on his hands and knees briefly before getting to his feet. He began to walk away from the ledge when he heard the voices to his left. He waited and listened, slowly retrieving one of the knives. He felt that something was aware of his presence and he dropped into a slight crouch, adjusting his footing and snapping a branch beneath his boot. He looked toward where the voices were and he heard the dog bark and knew that it had discovered him and was coming through the underbrush. He saw a fire flicker and then men were yelling and they too were running, chasing the dog. He dropped the pack to the ground and sunk lower. The oncoming sounds of the dog grew louder and he dropped one foot back to brace himself when the animal threw itself at him. It would tear at his throat and arms. He tightened his grip on the knife, making a right angle with his arm and pointing the blade in the direction of the noise, guttural and primal growls mixed with the crashing undergrowth. It knew him. It had been searching.

The man yelled something as the dog came through the mist just feet from where he stood, its jaws open, running full speed. It leapt at him and he brought the knife up to meet the weight of it, sinking the blade to its hilt into the soft underbelly of the shepherd and he rolled onto his right shoulder, redirecting the momentum of the animal's weight as he fell. He jerked the knife up and in. Hot blood jetted from the wound and he felt it on his face as he rolled on top of the animal. The point of the knife had punctured the heart and the dog was dead almost instantly. He tensed. The man who had called to the dog had stopped and he turned around and scrambled on his knees away from the body and down the slope. The man began shooting in the direction the dog had come and then there was another voice calling from further away, telling the first man to stop. He tried to slow his breathing, quiet himself. There was no movement. Then another shot and he saw the shape of the man come into view, spinning and calling out and the other man screaming to come back. The man in view continued to spin in circles, pointing the gun in all directions, and then he began to move, walking backwards to where he crouched with the dripping knife. He was moving away from the pleading voice of the second man, and then he was very close, tall but shapeless, calling softly for the dog. He sprang up and buried the knife in the man's neck. The gun went off again, loud in his ears like a clap of high thunder, and he pulled the blade free and brought it back down and now the man dropped the gun and flailed with his hands at the knife, but the fight was already draining out of him and he slipped to his knees and then onto his side, weeping and begging for it to stop and he pulled the blade free and brought it down a final time. The dead man's face was damp and shiny in the hinting light of the emerging moon. There was no noise from the second voice and he stepped backwards. The pack was somewhere near the slope, but he did not know where and he turned and ran.

Edwards stood still. He had chased after Flip and left his flashlight at the camp in his pack. He knew that both the dog and Flip were dead or dying. *Christ, Jesus,* he thought. He backed away, looking over his shoulder and trying to find the fire. He wanted to call to Sarah but thought better of it. *He doesn't know how many are out here. Or maybe he does and he's circling behind me. Coming at them from the other side.* The thought made him turn and run, the deer rifle held in front of his chest, his sidearm back in its holster. He picked up the fire through the trees and he came up close and stood behind a large trunk and spoke between pants of breath.

"It's me," Sarah said. "Ethan and Sarah, it's me. You here?"

"Yes," Sarah said. "Yes." He stepped around the tree and walked toward the fire. They looked at him as if alien. Their faces pale white, lips slightly parted.

"Where's Flip," Ethan said, voice quivering. "Where's Flip, Sheriff?"

Edwards put a finger to his lips and looked at Sarah, who looked back with no expression.

"Ethan," Edwards said as calmly as possible. "Ethan, is the safety on that gun?" The boy looked absently at him and then looked down at the shotgun and then back to Edwards.

"Yes," he said.

"Good. Sarah, you?" She did not have to look. Nodded yes and he came under the tarp.

"Ethan," he said. "Build up that fire." Ethan took some of the limbs that they had gathered and dropped them on the fire. Sarah looked at Edwards.

"Why would you want him to do that?"

"Because he doesn't have a gun," Edwards said. "At least I don't think he has a gun. And I want to be able to see around the perimeter as best we can." He went across to his pack and found his flashlight and came back to where they were both standing.

"Listen to me," he said. "I've got to go back out and see about Flip. I want you both to sit close to this fire, back to back and watch in all directions."

"But," Ethan began.

"Ethan," Sarah said. "Listen."

"I will be back as soon as I can," Edwards said and before they could ask him anything else he went under the tarp and away from the light, leaving the rifle behind this time. He clicked the switch on the flashlight and looked for where the leaves had been disturbed. He found the path that they had taken following the dog, and he went up it with his pistol in one hand and the beam from the flashlight fanning out in a sweeping pattern before him. The distance before he found the bodies seemed endless. Everything had happened so quickly and not more than fifty yards from where they had been sitting. He came to Flip first. He was on his side and it was evident that he was gone. He knelt beside the deputy and touched his shoulder. The entry wound was on the side of his neck facing down, but the killer had pushed the blade to the point of exiting the other side. Edwards recoiled and bit his hand to keep the bile down. He swung the light back around searching for Herc. He found the shepherd several yards away, also on his side, not breathing. Edwards felt gravity in a dizzying wave that forced him to place a hand on a nearby tree to steady himself. He turned to go back to the camp and stumbled, almost losing his balance all together. He righted himself and started back, but the dizziness washed through him again, powerful this time to the point of blurring his vision, and he wondered if he might be having a heart attack and if this would all soon be over, by his doing or not. He managed to ease himself to the ground. Sweat was coming out heavily on his forehead and he could feel it soaking his chest and underarms. Another wave and he had to fight to maintain his balance. His eyes were coming in and out of focus and he thought he saw something moving in the trees. Swaths of clear visibility were mingling with the dense mist. *There was something moving in the trees*, he thought. He looked up and could see the thumbprint of the moon briefly and then it was gone. He turned back to where he believed he had seen movement and Katherine was standing in a small clearing. She was not the hideous, poison thing he had encountered before, but youthful and desirable as when they had met on the Winslett farm decades before. She wore the plain white dress that had beautifully sculpted her figure and she beckoned him to join her. He ached with the vision. "No," he said out loud. "I can't leave those children. I won't leave Sarah."

She smiled warmly and waved for him to come again and he wanted badly to cry for her. She watched him from a short distance and he shook his head violently back and forth. *No, no, no, no! I have to finish this. I have to make this right, Katherine. I have to make this right and then I will come. Then I will come and be with you. Please let me make this right!* He wiped at the tears on his face and looked to the ground and then back to where his wife had been standing. Nothing. He looked around and saw his handgun was sitting next to him, the flashlight askew in front, casting a beam back toward the camp.

"Sheriff?" A light came up the path behind him.

"Sarah," he said. "I'm here." Her light found him and she ran to where he was sitting.

"What happened?"

"I'm not sure," Edwards said. "Flip is gone. So is Herc. We need to get back to camp. We'll deal with the bodies when it's light. Help me up." She did, and they made their way back toward the simple shelter, Edwards stepping carefully. They came under the tarp together, calling to Ethan before they emerged. When they came under the shelter, Edwards could see that the boy was on his last nerve. *More of a liability than an asset*, he thought. Edwards looked at Sarah and then back to Ethan.

"Son, I want you to get your pack and I want you to hike back to the rest area." Silence from both of them. "I know," he said. "I know. But we need to let someone know where we are." They waited for him to continue. "We never should have come here," he said, dropping his eyes, the emotion tight in his voice, the stiff feel of Flip's dead body flashing in his mind, the snake's head upside down, shot through and leaking black blood. "But we're here and I need you to do this. Marion County sent deputies over. You get back to the station and find one and tell them where we are and that we've lost Flip. Tell them to get up here as fast as possible. You understand?" Ethan swallowed.

"Yes, Sheriff. I think so, but…"

"I think he's gone the other direction," Edwards said. "Back down the slope toward the caves. I'm guessing that's where we'll find him if he hasn't headed all the way down. Don't ask me how I know. You have a big head start on him and you have the benefit of knowing where you're going." He smiled at the boy.

"What about Sarah?" Ethan said.

"She's gonna stay here with me," Edwards said. "We're going to see if we can pin him down until you get back with help." Sarah looked at Edwards, not with skepticism, but as if she understood that it was to be this way all along. She tightened her grip on the shotgun and looked in the direction that they would be going.

"Ethan, do you have your sidearm?" Edwards was speaking to him in a calm tone, like he was instructing a young boy on his first hunting trip. Ethan nodded and touched the gun on his holster.

"I want you to leave the shotgun here. You will need your flashlight to find your way and I want your other hand on that sidearm in case you need it."

"But I won't need to because I have a head start," Ethan said, looking nervously at Sarah who was thinking back to the early morning when she had radioed the station from the rest area parking lot, looking at the two dead bodies motionless on the handicap ramp, the small dog moving one of their heads in suspended time.

"No, I don't think you will need it but that does not mean that we need to take that for granted. I wouldn't send you if I thought there was any real chance of you running into him. Just keep a straight course in that direction." Edwards pointed the rifle back up the slope. The visibility was already bad and Edwards worried that it would get worse before it got better.

"You following me, Ethan?" Ethan nodded and went around Edwards and found his pack and slipped his arms through the shoulder straps. When he had it on and the front strap cinched, Sarah walked over and stood next to him. She considered hugging him and whispering something encouraging but was afraid he would backslide and not want to make the trip alone. She knew why Edwards was sending him back. She knew that her uncle had made the wrong, impulsive decision bringing them up here and now he was taking precautions

434

out of fear and a need to minimize casualties. Flip and the dog, dead not fifty yards away, had driven that home. She waited until Ethan's eyes were fixed on hers and she nodded at him. He nodded back. "Sure wish Herc was going with me," he said and the tremor in his voice and the innocence of the comment seemed to make the dark surrounding them press in tighter. He pulled the sidearm from his holster and held it against his leg. To Sarah he looked very small, like one of the trailer kids playing army in their front yard, running around in clothes too big for them, carrying sticks and making firing noises as they screamed *I got you. I got you!* Ethan walked toward Edwards and thumbed the switch on the flashlight. Moisture hung in the yellow light of the beam, floating and drifting in slow downward spirals like dandelion pappus. Edwards grabbed Ethan's shoulder and gave it a shake. "You'll be fine and you'll be there before you know it. Just stay in one direction. If you're not there in less than an hour, you have missed it. The grounds are not more than a mile or so back and you'll be going at a trot instead of walking and tracking. Just keep as straight a course as possible. You'll get there. No problem."

Sarah watched Ethan's face.

Edwards said no more and Sarah knew he was thinking the same thing that she had. Too much information and Ethan would freeze up. They watched him turn and go out of the camp and soon he was out of sight. They could see the beam of the light longer than they could see his body, but soon that too was shrouded over. Sarah was turning away when it occurred to her that Flip had been driving his truck and that his keys were probably still in his pocket and that Ethan was making his way back to vehicles he could not start.

"Sheriff," she said, running past him into the woods, calling over her shoulder "The keys! Flip had the other set of keys. Ethan won't be able to start the car." She charged up the hill. She could not hear Ethan and could not see his flashlight beam. She was running blindly with her hands out in front of her. "Ethan," she hissed. "Ethaaaan!" Branches tore at her parka and one scratched her painfully just below her eye. Edwards was calling behind her to come back and she ignored him, knew she could catch Ethan if she could keep from knocking herself out cold. She came to a steep rise and had to push herself to maintain her speed. She came back to level ground and was getting her legs beneath her when her foot caught on something and she spilled onto her knees and then chest, pushing the wind out of her lungs in a violent burst. She lay still. Something was standing to her right. She could feel eyes on her. Edwards had stopped yelling and she knew he was probably coming up behind her with a light, but it would take all he had to catch up. She was preparing to get to her knees when a light hit her full in the face and she shielded her eyes.

"Jesus Christ, Sarah!" Ethan said. "I almost goddamn shot you. What the hell?" He turned the beam away from her face and pointed it on the ground so she could see to stand.

"Keys," she said through strained breathing. "You don't have any keys." Ethan looked blankly at her.

"What?"

"To the truck. When you get back to the rest area. You won't be able to start the truck. Flip drove. He had the keys. Still has the keys." Adrenaline was moving throughout her body. It was stinging and pumping with a slow burn. She felt the knee that she had banged and thought it was all right. Ethan seemed to follow what she was saying.

"Oh Jesus, Sarah," he said. "I almost shot you." A light came through the trees below them, faint but getting brighter. They could hear Edwards laboring up the grade.

"Sheriff, he's here," Sarah said. Edwards came into view a seconds later, his face damp with sweat. He said nothing to them, but leaned over to catch his breath, putting a hand inside the parka and coming out with his keys, extending them to Sarah who took them and handed them to Ethan.

"Take the sheriff's car," she said. "Get going." Ethan took the keys and continued on without speaking. Sarah looked at Edwards, who was still out of breath. *How ridiculous we are*, she thought and placed a hand on Edwards' back. "Can you make it down?" His head went up and down. "Don't," he sputtered. "Don't do that again," he said and turned his head to look at her, offering a smile that looked more like a grimace. He stood erect and they went down the hill together, following his light as they went.

CHAPTER 61

RECKONING

He was running full speed down the slope. One of the boots touched the rock where the outcrop started and then his next step was into thin air and he was falling, managing just before impact to tuck his head, locking his hands behind his neck. He landed his full weight on his right shoulder, igniting a jolt of pain that made him cry out in a shrill, almost childlike scream. Then he was rolling, picking up speed down the slope, bouncing over limbs and roots and sharp rocks that tore his clothes and stabbed into his face and hands. He came over onto his backside and shoved his legs out in front of him, remembering to unlock his knees. The boots skidded and scrambled on the wet earth and at last he was able to stop himself.

He lay back, panting. Sharp and dull pain fanned out all over his body and he had to fight the urge to yell up into the sky. A clear patch in the clouds had appeared and he could see a cluster of stars. Blood from the man and the dog's body caked his face, hands, and clothes. He swayed and the pain in his head bucked and danced, kicking behind his eyes. His fury was clearing inside his head, and it was not long before its residue came welling up, screaming at him, cursing him. *Fucking child*, it said through gritted teeth. *Slinking little useless stain of a boy. Oh, how I hate you. Oh how we hate you all.* He shook his head and then brought his fists up against it, pounding at the voices inside. Pounding until he was sobbing. *That's it. Hit away you rancid orphan. Oh how we will pluck away at you. Pluck you clean motherless bastard. Pluck you…*

We are the one true
We wait at the base of the mountain
We make others to see
Pearls were their eyes, now they look
Now they
SEE!
We are the third. We are the third. We are the third and
No, he said
Yes, Yes, Yes. Yes! And we sit upon the throne and we are the shadow at morning and we will pluck, pluck, pluck.

Stop! Oh please make it…

He brought his hands hard and fast into his face, burrowing the palms into his eyes and pushing until the blotches of color swarmed in front of him.

Stop!

It was silent save a wind he could hear snaking through the tops of the trees. He stood in his ripped clothes, slimed with wet earth and the blood. The knife. He had lost the knife in the fall. And the pack. The pack was next to the dog. He felt the stampede of the voices coming back and he squeezed his eyes shut and held them at bay. He started back toward the cave and stopped again, teetering at the entrance like a drunk. He would be trapped if he went inside the cave. They would hold him there with the guns and he would not be able to finish what it had wanted him to do. He turned slowly and began to climb back to the top of the mountain. He could make his way through the woods and move around them, wait for them in the dark if he had to. He could use his hands if it came to that.

Before leaving the camp, Edwards collected the shotguns and the rifles and walked away from the dying fire and stashed them beneath the base of a tree, concealing them beneath leaves and brush he piled on top. "We've got plenty of shots between us with the sidearms," he said coming back under the tarp. "If we get separated out there, I don't want to increase the chances of us hitting each other with shotguns in a crossfire." Edwards stood in front of her, looking at her earnest face in the soft orange light.

"I must have lost my mind keeping you here," he said. "Why don't you get your pack and go after Ethan? I'll see if I can locate him and hold him there, maybe even shoot the son-of-a-bitch."

"No," she said. She had prepared for this, knew he would come around to this way of thinking after he had sent Ethan back to the rest area. "No. I'm going with you," she said, feeling the anger over Flip and the dog, the terror that had contorted Ethan's face, the dead eyes of the deer and the ruined bodies in the rest area, the assessment and warning that Norton had relayed from the state lawmen, the merciless and senseless death of her Aunt Katherine—these things came together with an impassioned reverence for seizing absolution. For making things whole again.

They left the camp and began the hike down toward the caves, their lights crisscrossing one another as they walked. They put fifteen paces between them and purposefully swung the beams back and forth in an attempt to confuse anyone who may be coming up the slope to meet them. They did their best to dampen the sound of their footsteps but she knew that they were announcing themselves. *So be it,* she thought. *Let us bring this to him.* They came to the place where the outcrop began and along the ledge the trees did not grow there. The cloud cover had drifted west and the overhead sky was relatively clear, a stretched sheet of blackness punctured with the pinhole light of ancient stars, and an impassive moon. They stood apart from one another, looking over the side of the rock, and could see no one moving below. Edwards looked at her and motioned her down. He came behind her and whistled quietly for her to stop. With one foot on the descent she looked up at him standing overhead.

"We can wait," he said and his voice was soft and neutral. "We can wait and protect ourselves if he comes back."

"No," she said. "I don't think that either of us want that. If we wait. if we hide, he will disappear and then all of this will be more senseless than it already is. We have to go. For what he did to Aunt Katherine. For what he's done to the rest of our lives." Edwards listened to this and nodded. He had not needed convincing; he just wanted to offer Sarah a way out.

"Go part way down to that ledge there and wait for me," he said quietly. "Then I can cover you as you go down the rest of the way and you can do the same for me. Careful. It's slick and loose from the rain."

She nodded and began to pick her way down, using one hand for balance and the other to hold the flashlight in front of her. She got to the ledge and she waited for Edwards to join her, keeping her light pointed to the base of the rock, hearing him softly curse as he descended after her. Then he was beside her and telling her to go the rest of the way down. She was almost to the bottom when her boot caught in a crevice, her center of gravity already falling forward in preparation for the impact. The wedged boot caused her leg and ankle to twist violently and then the sole came loose and dropped her heavily and without brace to the ground. She felt something crack inside when she hit and she groaned between clenched teeth. Edwards was scrambling down behind her, calling her name in a hiss. She had dropped the flashlight and it was rolling from side to side somewhere to her left, the beam picking up the base of the trees. It rolled to a stop and illuminated the hard surface of the moss-covered stone. Edwards knelt next to his niece and set his gun down. He shown the flashlight so that it would not be directly in her eyes but illuminating her face, which was tight with pain. She gritted her teeth, trying to remain quiet.

"Where?" he asked, gently touching her arm.

"Ankle," she managed. "May be broke. Might have broken some ribs. Goddamn it hurts." He reached out and touched her face, smoothing the hair out of her eyes. There was an owl, somewhere deeper in the woods, calling to its mate, hunting. Edwards sat trying to think of what to do. She was in real pain and there was no chance of her walking out, and he did not think that he could carry her. He passed the light around their perimeter. Silent and still in both directions. If they waited here they could at least have their back to the rocks and would only have to cover three directions, but judging by the height of the moon, that could make for a very long night and Sarah would have to push through with as little noise as possible, which he was not sure she would be able to do. He looked back at her and shook the light to get her attention. Then he pressed the flashlight to his chest and shown it up into his own face.

"Sarah," he said. "I am going to pull you into a sitting position and put your back to the rock. It's going to hurt, but I will try and be fast." She nodded and he stood quickly, getting his arms under hers and gently turning her torso in the other direction. He felt her deep inhalation and there was another groan. *I am so sorry,* he thought. *So sorry.* He managed to get her situated and then turned around to find her gun. It was not far from her flashlight and he picked both of them up and brought them back to where she sat, clicking off her light and setting it in her lap, then finding her hand and putting the grip of the pistol in it. "I'm just going to see about your leg," he said. He gently touched her upper thigh and moved his hand down until he was close to her ankle. It was already beginning to swell and she tensed when his fingers worked around it. He was sure that it was broken, and she would feel it for many years to come.

"Sarah, I'm going to leave you here and go on to the caves. I don't think it's a good idea to let him work his way up to us. It may be that he ran the other way, but I don't think so. He was coming back this way for a reason." She nodded both in agreement and understanding.

"Go," she whispered. "I'll be okay till you...till you get back." He reached again and found the gun in her hand and checked the safety. It was on and he clicked it into the firing position.

"It's ready to go," he said. "Keep your light off. Even if he gets past me, he won't know you're here if he can't see the light. I know it hurts like hell but try and stay quiet if you can. If he gets through he'll make noise and if he gets close you'll be able to get the jump on him. But if he's coming up, I'll find him before he gets here." She nodded.

"Uncle Bill." She was tense and now shivering a little bit. "Be careful. Please." He gave her as reassuring look as he could muster and stood, taking off his parka and the jacket underneath. He helped her lean forward and he put the jacket around her shoulders, careful that it would not restrict her hands if she had to move them. He touched her cheek and left her.

CHAPTER 62

MERCY

He was crawling on all fours. He was very thirsty and the blood on his skin had dried and a cold, anxious feeling was moving through his body. He was thinking about Terrell and could no longer remember why he had done what he had done, but he was being careful about how he thought because it was angry with him and he needed it to get out of these woods. He stood and quickened his pace. He would make it happy again. Make it love him again. He crisscrossed up the slope and then stopped. A light was coming toward him, bouncing slightly and disappearing as the beam fell behind trees. He squatted and tried to make out a figure, but could see nothing but the light, coming closer, and then he heard the breathing of a man and he lay himself flat on the ground, pressing himself as closely as he could to the earth and barely lifting his head to watch the light. Overhead the owl left its perch and flew through a gap in the trees and out into the empty sky, its black shape banking away from the mountain side and then out of sight. The light stopped moving forward and then resumed. Very close now, the beam swinging back and forth and he could see the outline of the man. His muscles tensed. The light would find him. The man's steps were loud and very close.

He pushed himself up and ran at the light, a raspy gurgling growl escaping from his throat. The light swung and caught him in the face and he ran harder toward it as the man backed away and began to raise his arm and then the shot exploded next to his ear and the world went completely silent around him. His body slammed full force into the man and they went over together and he felt the breath go out of him as his own weight crushed down. The man was raking his hand back and forth over the ground trying to find the gun and he closed both of his hands around the man's neck. The man stopped trying to find the gun and pushed his hands into his face and was trying to shove his thumbs into his eyes. He lifted off the man's chest and forced himself down on top of him again and the man's hands left his face and were trying to get free of the choking, but he squeezed harder and then shook his grip up and down, bouncing the head off the ground. He could hear nothing in his left ear, and it was like the struggle was taking place underwater. The man's legs were kicking and scrabbling behind him and he surged forward, bringing his face in close to the rasping and wheezing sounds of the air cutting off. *Pearls that were his.* He was drooling, thin strands hanging from his mouth and dropping onto the man's face and neck. His jaw tightened until it felt like his teeth would crack, currents of fresh rage surging though his shoulders, arms and hands. It was working through him. It was building in glorious strength. The man was strong, but he was weakening. His legs were only loosely kicking now and his hands were batting at his face with no more force than you would fan away a fly. He tightened his grip again and soon the man was still. He sat back, straddling him and he leaned his head back and laughed and sobbed at the sky. He climbed off and went looking for the gun. He found it and went back to the body and picked up the flashlight. Then he continued climbing.

Edwards had known before the gun went off that he had found his fate. Or that his fate had found him. What had rushed at him—the speed and unnatural agility of it—had no awareness of its purpose, only that it had one and would follow through with it no matter the deterrent. And through that, Edwards had realized in a flashing second that his role in everything until that moment had been predestined. It was like looking into the slowly evaporating pools of memory in Kat's mind. Only now the hateful resentment he had suffered for so long was giving way to a calm and clarity and he realized that survival only meant a prolonged state of loneliness that he was not prepared to endure. He had fought out of instinct and stubbornness, but as the hands around his neck tightened with their strength in that singular purpose, he heard her speak to him, smooth-faced, young in her white dress from near the creek where he had found and kissed her the first time. Let go, she said. Just let go.

Sarah pinched the webbed skin between her thumb and forefinger with her nails, trying to stay alert. She heard the shot and had raised her own weapon instinctively, but after the echo of the discharge died out, there was no other sound. She waited in the darkness, praying silently that Edwards would come up the hill and tell her it was over. Then she saw the light rising up the slope and she tried to straighten herself. It was advancing toward the outcrop quickly and with too much speed. *Too much to be Uncle Bill,* she thought. *Too much. But how can you be sure. How can you be.*

"Uncle Bill," she called out. "Sheriff?" No answer and she knew that she was only hoping that it would not be who they had come up the mountain to find, and the reality that Bill had encountered him further down the slope and was certainly dead—had to be dead—set in, and her inability to move, to run or fight was paralyzing. He had offered her a chance to stay behind and she had not taken it for fear that she would always regret the decision, and now her courage, the same courage that had guided her into the rest area, had vanished and she felt helpless and more alone than she had ever felt before.

The light went out and she could hear panting, and that sound brought her back into the moment, temporarily alert. She raised the gun and aimed in the direction that she had seen the glow. Then she raised her own flashlight and brought it up even with the gun and took in a deep breath and held it. The gun felt very heavy and it shook in her hand, but she steadied it, determined. She clicked the button on the flashlight and the beam fell on the mask of a face that was twisted and bloodied. She fired. Once, twice. The sound of the gun was a brief roar in her ears and then there was ringing and the darkness around her took on a deeper disillusionment, all of her senses buzzing and keenly aware, but confused about his presence, close and patient. Then as if he was plucking thoughts from her head, he moved in front of her and to her right. She swiveled the best that she could in that direction but did not fire the gun again. She swung it back and forth, trying to control her panic. A sound, much closer now, closed in, and the tension went out of her muscles and was replaced by an indecision that washed over her like warm water. Something was pulling away, receding back down the slope or maybe up through the thickness of the tree canopy, dispersing of its own accord. *My soul,* she thought. *It has abandoned me.*

"Let me pass," a voice said with no inflection. A full moment and then she spoke in a weakened voice.

"No. I can't do that. Where is the Sheriff? Where is Bill?" No answer. "Where is Bill?" she screamed. "Goddamn you where is he, you sick—"

"With the others," the voice said. It was tranquil and certain.

"What does that mean?" she said, crying now, feeling the desperation wash through her. "What does that mean?" she said again. The voice, mechanical, did not respond. "Please," she said, and she hated the pleading in her voice. Hated her ineffectiveness and the lack of outrage; the lapsed control and smallness of her sitting figure pinned against the unyielding stone face. She could not even stand against it, but was forced to stare up into the expanse of the night and be subject to a judgment in the pressing dark. A voice whose origin cared nothing for circumstance or emotion, but rather seemed to strengthen with the very essence of her fear.

"It means that all things seen have been unseen."

"Oh God," she said, aware of herself like she had never been before, her mind illuminated in a hot white, piercing glow that she was inclined to shrink away from, but could not. Then he emerged next to where she was sitting and he turned on Edwards' flashlight, shining it into her upturned, wet face. He knelt beside her and she tried to push away but the rock kept her in place and the pain in her ankle and ribs made her cry out. His face bore the rigid lines of his violence and was painted with dried blood and gore. He looked at her in the harsh light with curiosity and detachment. He reached to touch her face and she felt the adrenaline and anger come in a slow trickle. He was touching her face as if he were blind, but the touch of his fingers had no warmth or expression in them, they simply probed and traced. The gun was still in her lap, but he paid no attention to it. Then as suddenly as he had appeared, he was gone, moving up the side of the rock with agile and precise movements as if propelled.

Sarah sat feeling the cold oppression of the hushed woods. The encounter had been brief, but its gravity and consequence were overwhelming. She remained with her back to the rock, almost catatonic, waiting with a patience that she would not have thought possible; feeling the deadness of his fingers on her skin as if they were still there.

CHAPTER 63

NORTON

Brent Norton rode in grim silence back down the mountain. The sun was brilliant in the late afternoon sky and he could see a long way from this height, although it would be dark soon enough. They had been in the woods since the early morning hours. They had found Sarah passed out, on her side, her breathing shallow. Her face was streaked with dirt and traces of blood and the state men had talked about tracing prints and tracking the killer further, but he had been doubtful of ever finding him. They had not told her about Edwards' body being further down the slope, although she had asked repeatedly, and likely already knew. Now all the bodies were coming back to Winchester and he felt a pit widening in his stomach thinking about the unpleasant work that lay ahead. The questions and the intensified investigations and the hours and hours of forms that would have to be filled out, family members that were all searching for answers and the sickening, insane horror that would overshadow it all, would overshadow everything from here on out. And that was what seemed to bother him the most. The senseless deaths and the idea that a human being could be capable of such ferocious acts was disconcerting to no end. But the knowledge that nothing would ever return to normal, that savagery could wander into a life with no warning and send one's sense of security scattering into the coldest recess of shadow meant something else entirely. It was the stuff of nightmares, but these nightmares were not images or feelings that you could shake loose in the light of the day. They were creatures unto themselves that fed on fear, feasted on the unknown and their surrogates were called forth with a recklessness that roamed the woods and towns with a determination that crippled one's faith in the humane. It would return, he knew. This heedless pattern of bloodshed and ruin. It would arise to seek out more souls that would otherwise have been at peace. For the time being, he would do what he could to bring comfort to those left behind. He could at least do that.

CHAPTER 64

FLOWERS

Ethan walked down the patient corridor at Winchester Memorial. He had a bouquet of flowers he had purchased at the grocery store and he was dressed in civilian clothes. He stopped in front of a closed door and went to turn the knob but stopped and knocked instead.

"Come in," he heard a voice respond and he pushed open the door and looked inside to see Sarah sitting up in the bed. Sunlight came through the window and fell on the bed sheets. Her ankle was in a cast and they had wrapped her ribs. A television was playing on the far wall, but the sound was turned almost all the way down.

"Hey Sarah," he said. She smiled. "How you feeling?" She shrugged.

"Okay, I guess. You?"

"Oh, I'm fine," he said. He looked at the flowers in his hand. "Thought you might like these. Maybe cheer the room up a little. Seeing how..." He broke off and looked away.

"It's okay, Ethan," she said. "You don't have to explain. It's hard enough having to think about it all."

He looked at her gratefully. "I'll just set these over here." He put the flowers down on a built-in dresser and put his hands in his pockets. They looked at one another again, neither knowing what to say.

"Norton came by," she offered. "He said that they could wait until I got out to have the funeral. Funerals, I guess."

Ethan nodded.

"We buried Flip," he said and Sarah looked surprised. "His mom and dad didn't want to wait, I guess."

"You go?"

"Yeah," Ethan said. "They had him cremated and the service was up on the mountain near Sinclair Gap. You know, where he liked to hunt. It was nice. Lot of people came."

"Lot of pretty girls?" Sarah said and grinned.

Ethan blushed. "Yeah, I suppose," he said. "I don't really remember. Can't say that I was too excited to be back up there." Sarah looked out the window.

"You remember much of what happened?" Ethan said.

She waited to answer.

"Enough," she said and her expression softened. "They don't have any idea where he is, do they Ethan?" He realized then that she probably did not know about Hicks and he thought about telling her, but decided it was not his place. He probably would not be seeing much of her after this anyway. The Winchester mayor had come by the station and asked if he would fill in until they could find a new sheriff, but he had declined and turned in his resignation then and there. He planned to go to work with his father and save up some money and maybe go back to school and learn his own trade. It was the news from Tyre that had floated west to Winchester that had made his mind up for him. He had been on the fence up until that point, the anger and regret he held onto for Flip and the Sheriff and even Herc had kept the balance tilted in the direction of staying, but when he found out that the killer was still out there, he decided that he'd had enough. It was not necessarily fear that forced the decision, but the need to live an existence where things like murder were not part of the bargain. He was not cut out for this work and he knew it and once he made the choice, he felt part of his old self returning and that felt genuinely satisfying. Saying goodbye to Sarah was the last thing he knew that he needed to do before setting out to reclaim the life he had known before.

"No," he said flatly. "They don't and I don't think that they will." She looked at her hands in her lap and nodded like she had already come to that conclusion.

"They keep kind of quiet about the whole thing in here," she said absently. "Guess they think I'm better off not knowing. But really, it's the not knowing that is hardest, I think. Not because I'm scared anymore, but because not understanding makes it all the more unreal. If that makes any sense. It's like a dream that you can't come out of. I sit here and try to think about everything that happened and it's like watching my mind fighting itself."

"Maybe that's your way of trying to recover from it," Ethan said and she smiled at him once again, appreciating his innocent insights and approach to the world around him.

"You have a nice way of looking at things, Ethan," she said.

"I try," he said and without warning his face fell.

"Ethan," she said, and he turned away from her.

"Ethan, look at me." He did and there were tears in his eyes.

"Oh God, Sarah. I'm so sorry for all of us. I miss them so much. Maybe I should have stayed. Maybe I could have helped and Sheriff Edwards would still be alive…"

"Stop that, Ethan. You did what you were asked to do and if you had not gone I might still be up there." He sniffed and composed himself. "I quit," he said and she looked at him curiously. "The sheriff's department, I mean. I turned in my resignation."

"Oh," she said. "That's all right. I don't blame you for that. How could anyone blame you for that after what we went through? You deserve better."

He nodded and brushed the tears off his cheeks. "What are you going to do?"

Sarah looked again out the window. "I don't know," she said and he could tell that she was tired and that he probably needed to leave before he confused himself even more than he already was. He crossed to the bed and gave her a hug, which she returned warmly. "You take care, Ethan." He nodded in his gentle way, starting to tear up again. "You too," he said and went out before there was anything else to say. When the door had closed behind him, Sarah sat very still in the bed, thinking about Ethan's question. *What are you going to do now, Sarah?* She pictured Renee and Jed and their lives together in the small house in the valley below the mountain. One of the nurses said that they would be coming by later that afternoon. Jed had apparently been in some kind of accident and had just gotten out of the hospital himself. Renee was picking him up and then they were coming to get Sarah and take her home. The prospect of being back in that house made her sigh, the cramped, trapped feeling weighing her down in the uncomfortable hospital bed. *Maybe I could,* and then, mid-thought, she noticed the flowers on the table. She smiled at their easy grace. They would need water if they were going to survive.

CHAPTER 65

VOICES RECEDING

The Tyre City police car turned onto Pell Road and came up slowly. It was not their first visit to the dilapidated house sitting at the top of the hill. Cyril Parker had brought the Hicks kid in a few days before and they had taken him straight to the hospital. When he had woken up, they got enough out of him to know where to look. The cruiser pulled into the clearing below the house and the two officers got out of the car and came up on the sinking porch. They knocked and announced themselves and the cheap door came open. They looked inside. The entire place was thrown upside down and from the looks of it, the kid had put up a good fight. They called into the house and got no response but could smell something wrong.

"Could just be this shithole he's living in," one of the officers said.

"Maybe," the other one said.

"Let's look around back," the first officer said and they came off the porch and went around the side of the house. The grass and weeds were tall and they had to pick their way around rotting pieces of equipment and unidentifiable junk. They came to the back and found the body lying face-up in the sunshine. They stared at it. The eyes had been removed and the face was set in a frozen mask, the skin void of color and the teeth clenched as if he may have been alive while being attacked. A screwdriver was next to the corpse and it was this simple tool covered in the victim's blood that was most upsetting. The officers turned away, incredulous, and the second one tapped the other one on the shoulder and pointed to the side of the house. In darkening blood, the word *ANEW* was scrawled.

"Sweet Jesus," the first officer said. "This is some sick shit, right?" The other shrugged.

"I guess we'll find out soon enough," and he told him to stay put while he called the station. He went back around the side of the house to the car. He stopped before opening his door. He couldn't be certain, but he felt like something was watching.

He watched them from the cover of the woods that encircled the small lot of John Hicks's home. They were dressed like the man who had taken him to the place where he had started his journey west and he knew that they meant him harm. A quiet had befallen him that he could not recall ever feeling and he turned from the scene and walked back beneath the thick canopy. The voices had left him entirely and he could not decide what the emptiness meant. There was something hollow in both his mind and his gut and he struggled to find a valid and satisfactory interpretation. He stayed out of sight that entire day, watching the people come and go, moving around the property like ants building a coned hill where they came back and forth in deliberate patterns that were complex and frenzied. When it grew dark, he moved down to the house and waited for the voices to return. He heard nothing but the steady hum of the crickets and the occasional wind gust in the pine trees overhead. The fading white paint of the house reflected the stark light of the moon and he studied it with something that felt like longing. He considered Terrell and the measures he had taken to educate and enlighten him, and though he did not grasp this in its entirety, he valued it and experienced the first signs of disguised remorse that would walk with him for many years to come, overshadowing his footsteps and dulling his mind with a keen regularity. He sat in front of the house through the night and when the thinnest rays of light came, he stood and walked up Pell Road, stumbling occasionally on the rutted and washed surface. He was hungry, tired, and lost. This was not his time or place, but the blood that stained his skin belonged to him and he took some small comfort in its itch as he walked into the rising fire of the eastern sun.

EPILOGUE

*D*eath is the awareness I embrace. Its voices are many and divisive. I watched the boy, my son, come for my husband, enraged and coveting a peace that he did not know he even sought. The deaths and the reckonings were abrupt as they often are. This, in some ways, offers a peculiar mercy that contradicts my own disappearance from a mortal life. But it is nonetheless deeply and resolutely sad. Bill makes his way to me now, and though I am unable to see him, I can feel his blossoming presence and he, mine. The children are safe. The scarred children that I failed to protect. And the child, the child that was not mine, but also fully mine, has been cast out and set free. These voices that taunt and deliberately confuse have used him for their limited and selfish purpose. With good fortune he will fade beyond them. His bravery was stronger than my own, and his sacrifice has made things once again whole. I will rejoin my lapsed and paralyzed memory now, and see as I have not seen, since first this all began.

Made in the USA
Columbia, SC
16 July 2021